DARKNESS FALLS

BRUSHSTROKES TRILOGY, BOOK 2

GINA DALE

Gina Dale Publishing
United Kingdom

Printed by Amazon KDP

Disclaimer
This novel is entirely a work of fiction. The names, characters and
incidents portrayed in it, while at times are based on historical
figures, are the work of the author's imagination.

A CIP catalogue record for this book is available
from the British Library
ISBN 978-1-9996103-2-6

Also available as an eBook
ISBN 978-1-9996103-3-3

ACKNOWLEDGEMENTS

I would like to thank the following for their help, expertise and encouragement in producing my second indie novel 'Darkness Falls':
Editor Rachel Gregory, pedanticpolly@gmail.com
Cover designer Jenny Quinlan, USA historicaleditorial.com.
Typesetter Catherine Cousins, 2QT Limited.
Website design Joey Williams, ginadalepublishing. com

Images from Wikimedia Commons

Napoleon III at the Battle of Sedan 1871 by Wilhelm Camphausen official German war artist used on book cover.

Manet and his Easel drawing by Jean-Frederic Bazille 1868 used on back cover.

Other titles in this trilogy

Brushstrokes (Book 1)

The author has her own website
www.ginadalepublishing.com
where pictures relating to Books 1 & 2 can be seen

1

He contemplated finishing the painting he was working on, but it was 5 p.m. on Friday and most of his students had already left; only Antonio was still at his easel. Marie had not come in that day as she was overseeing the workmen at home, who were decorating the entrance hall. She said they worked harder if she was in the house, supervising. Knowing her, she would be a hard taskmaster, but he thought the men would be more distracted with Marie around; *he* certainly would have been. She also tutored Jacques in languages and music on a Friday morning and she was proving an admirable teacher. She had insisted that they speak English at home for the last month in an attempt to help Jacques. He had struggled a fair bit as he had never been to the country and his knowledge was from textbooks.

Marie was now approaching her ninth month of pregnancy and was absolutely blooming. Her skin and complexion were radiant, her blue eyes sparkled with life and her waistline had expanded to accommodate her bump, but unless seen in profile it was sometimes hard to tell she was pregnant. He had enjoyed every moment of her pregnancy, particularly the developing breasts (even the thought of them made him feel desperate to get home).

He packed up his palette as most of the colours had been used. He told Antonio he was going but he was welcome to stay as he had his own key. However, Antonio advised he was going to meet a young lady in the Café Rouge at 6 p.m. anyway. Charles laughed and told him Paris did not need any more Italians in it, so he could refrain from reproducing with all the French women. He knew how attractive Antonio was to the local women. He could charm the birds out of the trees with his Italian good looks, flirtatious manner and his accent, which seemed to have an extraordinary effect on women. It wasn't just the young women either; Antonio could have women in their sixties drooling over him. He never had to find his own breakfast; he only had to walk through the marketplace and women would appear from all directions offering him free fresh fruit, ham, bread and cakes. His nickname, given to him by the locals, was "Italian stallion". Antonio loved the attention, but he was very clever about avoiding the sexual attention of those women he did not wish to pursue. He did it with such charm and grace that none of them were offended. It didn't help that Antonio was now firm friends with Manet and his crowd, who were not the best examples for him to follow. Manet was a born practical joker, inveterate drinker and a skilled womaniser and he could not resist telling women that Antonio fancied them when he hadn't even laid eyes on them.

There was a time when all the female sitters used to fall for Charles but now, Antonio was proving to be the new stag. Still, that let him off the hook as he would not dream of being unfaithful to Marie and if any of them, including his wealthy clients, indicated their willingness for sexual attention, he was quick to rebuff them.

He set off home through the busy streets, which were teeming with life and people. He crossed the Seine and was home within ten minutes. When he came into the house, Marie was not in the hall, kitchen or lounge. He shouted up the stairs and Jeanette appeared.

'Where is Marie?'

'Madame is in her room, sir. She has started in labour and I have sent a groom to fetch the local midwife.'

He bounded up the steps shouting, 'And why did you not send for me?'

As he got level with her she replied, 'Sir, it is only the early stages yet and we knew you would be back soon.'

He pushed past her into his bedroom and found Marie sitting at her dressing table. He rushed over and knelt behind her, holding her tightly in his arms.

'Darling, how are you? Where does it hurt? Can I get you anything?'

Marie smiled at him in the mirror. 'Oh Charles, I am not even sure I am in labour. I have only been getting a slight twinge in my back. It was only when I noticed it was happening every five minutes or so that I even thought it may be the onset of labour.'

'Every five minutes,' he repeated in horror, 'but it's too soon; we are not ready. Do you think the baby is in distress?'

Marie replied, 'No, not at all. There has been plenty of movement and probably, the baby has been repositioning for the birth.'

He was overcome with fear and panic and he needed to get these emotions under control so as not to frighten Marie.

'Do you think you should be in bed, darling?'

'No, I am perfectly fine as I am. I find I cope better being upright.'

He saw her face change and she gripped the top of the dressing table and caught her breath. Oh dear, if this was only the start then he knew he was going to be a gibbering wreck by the time of the birth. Maybe that was why men kept away during childbirth. They couldn't bear to see their wives in pain... and he was sure he could feel some discomfort himself. It was probably nerves or fear that was turning his stomach. He must calm down. He thought of his father's utter calmness and authority when the mare was foaling... but he had years of experience under his belt. Charles had no experience of childbirth.

He pulled himself together and asked Marie, 'Have you had anything to eat, dearest? You need to keep your strength up.'

Marie snapped back, 'I couldn't eat a thing. I have been sick once already. Why don't you and Jacques get your dinner and I will see you later?'

Shocked by her flash of anger and instant dismissal he said, 'What, and leave you on your own?'

She rounded on him again. 'I am not dying, just in the early stages of labour and when and if I need you, rest assured I will call.'

He was dumbstruck as she would never have spoken to him like that normally; she must be in far more pain than she was revealing. He had no option but to do as she asked. He had promised her he would abide by her rules during labour and if she didn't want him with her then he would have to comply. He put his arms round her and kissed the top of her head. He felt her stiffen and she pushed him away and put both hands on the dressing table while the pain washed over her. He turned and left her in peace, but he was devastated.

He went downstairs to find Jacques who was in the lounge, reading a book. He leapt up and asked, 'Is Marie all right? She was in some pain this morning.'

'She has started in labour and she seems to want to be alone.'

Jacques replied, 'Well that doesn't surprise me; my mother once hit my father over the head with a cooking pot when she was in labour and thereafter he took himself out into the fields when she was in labour.'

'Well, I am glad it may have been a response to pain rather than being directed at me personally. I had better have something to eat; it could be a long night and I do so want to be with her.'

'Really? You're a brave man then, Charles. Most men can't get out of the way fast enough at this crucial time.'

Jeanette came in and said, 'Sir, do you wish me to stay tonight as Madame is in labour?'

'Oh, Jeanette you will have to ask her yourself. I have already been told to leave her in peace and I don't want to be accused of making a wrong decision.' *What on earth was he going to do with himself all night if Marie didn't want him with her?* He wanted so much to be a part of this experience and to share the pain with her.

The doorbell rang and Jeanette ran down to answer it. It was the midwife. He caught them halfway up the stairs and told her that he wanted a report on Marie's progress immediately after the midwife had examined her. He contemplated sending for Marie's mother. It would only take Jacques, an hour to ride over there and he knew his way. He daren't leave her himself in case she needed him. He dismissed this idea as Marie had never mentioned wanting her mother at the birth. He thought that if she needed a woman it would be quicker to get Suzanne, Manet's wife. He decided he had better wait until she got a bit further into the labour, but at least he had thought of an option.

The midwife came back downstairs. She didn't look unduly concerned. 'Your wife is progressing well, but this is her first baby and it is difficult to estimate how long she will be, and she is rather small down below. It could be any time between five and fifteen hours before the baby is born.'

Oh God, one or both of them could be dead in fifteen hours; she with the pain and him with the stress of not being with her. He rounded on the midwife, 'Then go back to her and don't leave her for a moment but tell her I am here for her and if she utters my name you will shout me immediately, do you understand?'

'Yes sir!' She bobbed and practically ran back up the stairs.

Aware that Jacques was eyeing him with some concern, he poured himself a brandy and left the dining room. He went to the lounge as this was directly under their bedroom and he wanted to hear exactly what was going on.

Jacques followed him sheepishly and asked him, 'Would you prefer to be alone?'

'No, Jacques. If you wouldn't mind staying here, perhaps reading, as I may need you to ride over to Marie's parents to get her mother or run over to Manet's to get his wife.'

'Certainly, Charles – just tell me what I can do to help.'

He tried hard to calm down and made sure he only had one glass of brandy. He could hear her stifle a cry, probably into a pillow, at the peak of each contraction and he became obsessive about timing them. They were certainly coming at shorter intervals – around every four minutes – but they weren't giving her much respite in between. This went on for the next hour and by then he was so fraught with stress, he felt like he could murder someone. Finally, Marie let out a piercing scream and he could wait no longer. He took the steps two at a time, flung open the door and saw Marie on her back on the bed, in her chemise, with sweat pouring down her face. She had been using a rolled-up towel to stifle her screams. The midwife was sitting on a chair, totally ignoring his wife. He stormed over, grabbed her arm and marched her out of the room.

'Get out and don't come back. I will deliver this baby!' He slammed the door and returned to the bed, scooped Marie into a sitting position and knelt beside her now sobbing body. 'Sweetheart, I am here now and together we will get through this!'

As her sobs eased she cried, 'Charles I am so frightened, and it hurts so much; please help me!'

In tears himself, he carefully lifted her chemise above her waist. Before he could go further, she started another contraction. He ran his hands over her swollen and tight stomach and could physically see a ripple of pain running through her belly. She grabbed his hand and screamed in pain.

'Sweetheart, just scream and let the pain out; don't try and stifle it. When it eases a little, can you raise your knees up? I need to see what's going on.'

'Only if you promise not to touch me internally. I feel like I am being ripped apart as it is.'

'I promise I will only look this time Marie, but I

need to know where the baby's head is.'

She did as he asked, and he saw that the baby was not in view. He carefully inserted three fingers inside her but before he could go any further another contraction started. He lifted her up on to the pillow and said, 'I think you need to stand up and let gravity help you get the baby further down the birth canal.'

Just at this moment, he was aware of the doorbell ringing. Could this be someone who could help? He told her to stay there; he would be back to help her stand up in a minute. He ran out of the room, back down the stairs and got there as Jacques opened the door. To his complete amazement, Henri was on the doorstep. They looked at each other and Henri said, 'God, Charles, whatever is the matter? You look dreadful.'

Just at that point, Marie let out another piercing scream and Charles said, 'Marie's in labour and I need your help.' Henri turned and went back to his horse and unfastened a saddlebag. Charles and Jacques followed him out.

Charles turned to Jacques, 'Do you know how to deal with his horse? Give him a small amount of aired water, untack him, find some sacking and put straw underneath it until he has stopped sweating, then rug him up.'

'Of course, Charles. I used to deal with changing carriage horses in Lille all the time. I know what to do; I won't leave him till he has dried off and then I will give him some hay and a short feed.'

'Good lad', replied Charles. He and Henri ran up the steps into the hall.

'How far gone is she, Charles?'

'She has been in labour lightly since midday today and now she's having contractions every three to four minutes. The baby's head is not visible yet.'

'Ok, it's a good job that I have attended four births, but I have only delivered one baby myself. Have Marie's waters broken?'

'No.'

They were soon in the bedroom and Marie could not understand how her brother had suddenly appeared; she thought she was dreaming.

Henri leant over her and kissed her cheek. 'Marie, it's Henri but just forget I am your brother. I have delivered four babies recently and I will do my utmost to deliver you safely. Now, I need you to lay back and open your legs and let me examine you.'

Marie groaned but did as she was told. He motioned to Charles to help her get her chemise over her head. He went to his bag and selected his baby stethoscope and a small crochet hook. He could feel Charles watching him. He put his finger to his mouth to warn him to keep quiet. He put the stethoscope to her stomach and moved it round until he found the baby's heartbeat. He beamed with delight.

'Marie, the baby's got a strong heartbeat and is coming the right way but I need to feel how far down it is, so can you be brave? If you feel a contraction coming, tell me and I will stop. Charles, can you hold her hand and comfort her. Marie, I need to turn you, so your legs are over the edge of the bed.'

Charles watched in horror as Henri put his hand inside her with the crochet hook between his fingers and the flat of his palm. Marie yelled, and he held her hand and kissed it. He realised he had stopped breathing and took a sharp intake of breath. Marie writhed to twist away from Henri, but he forced her shoulders back onto the bed. Marie's scream was silenced by the flood of fluid that ran like a river down her legs and onto the floor.

She gasped and cried, 'Bastard brother and a bastard husband!'

Henri replied, 'I know. I'm sorry, but I had to break your waters. We need to get this baby out.'

She shouted, 'Well bloody well get on with it then, even if you have to use your sword. Just get this baby out.'

Henri calmly replied, 'Right, now stand up and face Charles and put your arms around his neck and use him for support.

'Stand up? I can't even feel my knees, never mind my feet.'

Henri pulled her up. 'That's because they have gone numb with lying down. Put some weight on them and try walking around with our assistance. I promise you the pain will lessen if you stand up and lean forward when the contractions start.'

Charles had hold of her arm on one side and Henri supported her on the other. After a slow start the feeling came back in her knees and she could stand unaided. Henri fetched her chemise and brought her a glass of water. He helped her put it on and she drank the full glass of water. The next contraction started, and she put her arms round Charles's neck and he supported her as the wave ran through her body.

Henri instructed, 'Marie, don't hold your breath. You need to breathe through it or you will feel faint.'

She snapped back, 'Oh Mr Bloody know all; I'd like to see you giving birth!'

Henri retorted, 'That's better, you sound more like my little sister now. Take your pain and anger out on me. I can stand it.'

Marie shouted venomously in Russian and gave Henri a severe telling off.

Charles said, 'What did she say?'

'Nothing you need to worry about, Charles. Some of those swear words I had forgotten but the gist of it was, she was very angry and threatening to kill me slowly and tortuously. You must remember she is in so much pain, she has no idea what she is saying or doing. We are getting nearer to the birth every minute.

Henri took two pillows off the bed, and a sheet, and laid them out around the bottom of the bed. 'When the head is crowned, I need you to sit on the edge and get Marie to kneel in front of you. Put a pillow over your knees for her head and I will deliver the baby. Do be careful, she could easily bite or scratch you because she is in pain. If I have to cut her, I will need her on her back on the bed again and you will have to hold her down.' He went to his bag and produced a large pair of scissors. Charles's face must have said it all – Henri smiled, 'Don't worry, we won't need them if she listens to me. I can assure you my needlework was far superior to hers when we were children.'

Marie suddenly had another contraction and she screamed, 'Oh my God, I want to push.'

Charles manoeuvred her to the bottom of the bed and whispered to her, 'It's nearly over now; just let your body take over and don't fight it and listen to Henri's instructions.' He kissed her wet cheek, put the pillow on his knee and told her to bite into that if she needed to. Henri lifted the back of her chemise and tucked it into the top. He could see the head was there but had not crowned yet. He leant over Marie and spoke to her.

'When the next contraction comes I want you to start pushing really hard but into your bottom this time. If I tell you to stop you must obey me instantly. Have you heard me, Marie?' She nodded her head in consent. The next contraction tore into her and she started to push. Tears were pouring down his cheeks and sweat was pouring down hers. He was terrified of what was happening, but he couldn't leave her now. Henri shouted encouragement and she took another deep breath and pushed but let out a scream so loud, he was deafened. Suddenly, Henri shouted at her to stop pushing and start panting, and he touched her face to see if she had understood. She did his bidding but her whole body was shaking. Henri told her to push if she could and within seconds, the head was born. Two more pushes and the shoulders were out, and Charles saw his baby in Henri's arms. He covered Marie's head in kisses and his whole body was heaving as he sobbed.

Henri said to him, 'Can you carefully pick her up and turn her round so that she's leaning with her back to the bed and sitting down so I can cut the cord.' He lifted her off her knees, twisted her round and gently leant her back against the bed. Her eyes were half closed, and she didn't speak, but then her eyes flickered open and she looked down and saw the baby. Tears poured down her cheeks. Henri tied the cord off and deftly cut it with the large scissors.

Charles said, 'Did you have to cut her?'

'No Charles, I didn't, but I need to check she is not torn internally.'

Henri had a towel and was wiping the baby, which made it cry. He wrapped it in a second clean towel and handed it to Marie.

'Congratulations on the birth of your beautiful little girl, born at 1:30 a.m. on 25th June 1869.'

2

Charles dropped to his knees beside Marie, and he kissed his daughter for the very first time; her crying subsided.

Henri said, 'Charles, can you keep Marie still there until the afterbirth comes? Just watch she doesn't pass out as she will be very weak. I will prepare the bed ready for her after the afterbirth has come and I have washed her. I will leave you both to get acquainted with your daughter. Do you think you are up to bathing her, Charles, when I see to Marie?'

Charles nodded, still unable to speak due to the enormous lump in his throat. Marie stirred and unwrapped the towel to examine her baby in minute detail. Her facial features consisted of blue eyes, a button nose, and a shock of dark hair. She had long, slender fingers and beautiful pink toes. She was small and probably weighed around five pounds. Henri left the room in search of hot water.

Charles turned Marie's chin towards him and said, 'Ma cherie, I am so proud of you. You have delivered our first child with such bravery and fortitude, I thank you from the bottom of my heart.

I only wish I could have borne the pain to make it easier for you. But we both owe your brother a huge debt of gratitude. I doubt I would have been able to perform like he did; he was just sensational. He went into action and I panicked. Please forgive me.'

Marie sighed, 'He does always seem to turn up at the right moment, whenever I am in trouble. Did you send for him?'

'No, I thought of sending for your mother or Suzanne and Manet, but Henri just turned up on the doorstep at 10 p.m. Never have I been so relieved to see him in my life.'

Marie suddenly grimaced and said, 'Take the baby, Charles. I want to push again.' Charles grabbed her and stood up and at exactly the right moment, Henri appeared with two pitchers of steaming hot water. Charles took the baby over to the dresser to wash her. Henri put the pitchers down and was back on his knees by the bed with Marie.

'Perfect timing now just relax – this won't hurt – but only push very slowly; we don't want the afterbirth to tear. I'm sorry but I need to check you internally again for any retained afterbirth or any tears.'

Marie smiled weakly at him, 'Well, considering I feel like I have been ridden over by an entire cavalry troop, one more intrusion will hopefully put an end to it. No, don't tell me, Trooper Croizette. I know the drill by now.'

'I'm pleased to see your sense of humour is

returning, dear sister. By the way, I have been promoted to lieutenant. However, a little word about your foul-mouthed language and your threats to my body. Do you remember them?'

'I vaguely recall swearing at you in Russian and threatening to cut your balls off, yes.'

'Well, that I can forgive due to the pain that you were experiencing. But I must take exception to your threats towards Charles. You said you would not allow him near you and there would be no more babies. May I remind you that he is your husband and he has every right to his conjugal rights and to have as many children as he considers necessary. You are perfectly healthy and capable of producing several more children. If I hear you have been misbehaving I will drag you to the barracks and horsewhip you in front of my entire troop. You don't appreciate what a wonderful husband you have, Marie. He loves every bone in your body.' Henri had been skillfully washing her from head to toe as he spoke to her and then dried her off with a fluffy white towel.

'Stop it, Henri. I didn't mean it; I was just in so much pain and he was the one who got me pregnant and as usual, I hit out at the wrong man. Did you tell him what I said?'

'No, I didn't. He's been to hell and back today as it is, and I was sure you didn't mean it.'

'Thank God for that. I do love him, you know. I have since I first set eyes on him.'

Henri hugged her. 'I know that, but just try to

keep your temper under control. I appreciate you were under a lot of stress. I am going to pick you up now and put you in your nice warm bed, so you can feed your baby and then have a well-deserved sleep.' He swept her up into his arms, sat her on the bed while he slipped a clean nightgown over her and then propped her up in bed.

Charles was toweling off the baby, so he went over to him. He realised that Charles was still sobbing, and he said quietly, 'Whatever is the matter?'

'Henri tell me the truth. Is there something wrong with her head?'

'Oh, forgive me Charles, I should have told you. She is absolutely fine; it's just that babies' skull bones are not fused together until about twelve months after the birth, that's why it's not a good idea to drop them. They come out with their heads pointed like that because they have to pass through a very narrow birth canal and I promise you within twenty-four hours, her head will have filled out. You poor man, you must have gone through hell worrying about her. Look, she is perfect – ten fingers and toes and everything that's necessary in the nether regions.'

Charles heaved a huge sigh of relief. Henri bent over and said, 'Babies are born with two natural reflexes. Watch.' He put his finger near the baby's hand and she reached out and grasped his finger with all of hers. 'That's the grasping reflex and it can be very strong. Open your shirt.' Charles obeyed, slightly stunned. Henri wrapped the baby in the towel and put her in his arms, close to Charles's chest. She immediately started rooting with her mouth, towards his nipple. 'That's the suckling reflex and you had better give her to her mum before she realises you have nothing to satisfy her.'

He was elated now that Henri had banished all his fears; he could have danced for joy. He waltzed her over to the bed, where a contented Marie was watching him closely.

'You can't feed the baby, Charles, that is my job. Now give her to me so I can have a go at this breastfeeding lark that you are so keen for me to do.'

She undid her nightgown and took the baby from him and put her to her left breast. The baby rooted for her nipple and latched on very quickly. Marie took one look at Charles's besotted face and laughed, 'What am I going to do with you? Your face is a picture; you look like you have died and gone to heaven.'

'I have, and I have waited nine months to see you feeding our baby.'

Marie suddenly gasped and Charles said, 'What's the matter?'

Henri came over and said, 'Sorry Marie, I should have warned you about that. That is your womb contracting after the birth and it occurs for a few days, particularly when you are breastfeeding. It shouldn't be too painful, but you may find you bleed slightly when it occurs. It is perfectly normal.'

Marie shouted, 'Enough Henri, do not tell me

another thing unless you two want to raise this baby between you. I do not wish to know what other horrendous things I have to look forward to over the next few months. Henri, when I was teaching you to conjugate Latin verbs as a boy, if I had only known you would be lecturing me on the art of breastfeeding, twenty years later. I would have drowned you.'

Both Henri and Charles laughed at her, delighted to see the colour back in her face and a contented baby suckling at her breast.

'Oh God, Jacques must still be out in the stable with your horse!'

'We will leave you to practice and go and rescue Jacques… and I think we both deserve a drink.'

They went downstairs, Henri bringing the pitchers with him. They found Jacques asleep in the kitchen; he stirred as they came in. Startled, he jumped up and asked, 'Is Marie all right? Has she had the baby?'

'Yes, a beautiful girl. I am a father at last.'

'Congratulations, Charles. You must be delighted.'

Charles asked Jacques if he could rustle up some black coffee for them before he retired to bed, and he readily agreed. When Henri returned from checking his horse, and thanked Jacques for doing a great job, they went into the lounge. Charles poured them a large cognac but before he gave it to Henri, he put his arms round him and gave him a bear hug.

'Henri, I can't thank you enough for what you

have done today. You keep turning up like a guardian angel and saving me. Last time it was your help and advice that got me through the duel and now you have just saved my wife and daughter's lives.'

'Rubbish, Charles, you would have managed today without me; you have seen enough foals born. It might have taken a bit longer, but nature would have taken its course and you would have got there in the end.'

'But what if I hadn't been able to get the baby out? I would have been too terrified to cut her. And you were the one who guided her through the birth. I was a gibbering wreck. Explain to me how you have delivered four babies when you are a soldier stationed in barracks in the outskirts of Paris, and how you came to be here tonight?' They both sat down with their drinks and Jacques brought them two steaming mugs of black coffee.

'As you know, I volunteered to train as a medic as it interested me. I am not a doctor. I have no surgical skills as such, but I am trained to deal with battle wounds and would be on call to deal with the injured after a battle, should I be lucky enough to still be alive. I am a soldier first and foremost and I could be court-martialed if I stopped fighting to help the wounded, without the permission of my commanding officer. I have been promoted to lieutenant recently on the recommendation of my commanding officer, as he likes to have me watching his back. You may not know but there are women both in the barracks and out on the road with us as part of the supply team. I believe the Russians do the same. Men need the comfort of women before they go into battle and it stops them getting sexually frustrated and bad tempered if there are women available to relieve their tension. There are about fifteen or so women based at the barracks who you could describe as prostitutes, but they also work – doing cooking, cleaning and grooming the horses. So obviously, they are going to get pregnant frequently and that's where my introduction to childbirth began. I have delivered three babies from the camp followers, and that of an officer's wife who was visiting and went into labour while she was there… much to my horror. Thankfully, it was her second baby and it was quick and trouble-free.'

'But why were you coming here tonight?'

'We have all been given forty-eight hours' leave to go back to our families. We pull out on Monday for the German front; we will be at war with Prussia within the next few weeks. I had hoped I could spend the night with you and then go to my parents tomorrow.'

Charles groaned, 'Oh Henri, I am so sorry. I will pray for your safety every single day. Marie will be heartbroken at this news.'

'Don't tell her then, Charles. She is too emotional now, after the birth.'

'Henri, will you do me the honour of becoming godfather to the baby?'

'But I may not be here for her; I may be killed in the first battle. I wouldn't be much use to her dead.'

'But you brought her into the world and somehow I just feel that she could act as your guardian angel and keep you safe in return.'

'That's a wonderful idea and I would be honoured, but you would need to baptise her quickly as I have to be back at the barracks by 2 p.m. on Monday.'

'We could all go back to your parents. I am sure the priest would do it on Sunday under the circumstances and we always intended to baptise her in the church where we were married. Do you think Marie will be up to the journey?'

'Yes, but better by carriage than astride. I don't think she would be too keen on riding the day after giving birth. However, she is fit and strong. Don't allow any of this rubbish about lying in for two weeks after the birth. You get her up and out; the women recover so much quicker if they are back at work with their babies by their side. There are far fewer complications after the birth with these women than those who stay in bed for two weeks after delivery.'

He showed Henri up to a bedroom next to theirs, to get some much-needed rest. Henri promised to be on call should he be needed during the night.

Charles went into his own bedroom. Marie had clothed the baby in a little white nightie and wrapped her in a light woollen shawl and she was fast asleep in the crib next to their bed. He bent down and gently kissed his daughter's cheek and he felt so protective of this wonderful new life he had created, he could have wept. He undressed quickly and slid into bed next to his beautiful sleeping wife. She had made him so happy and content on the birth of their daughter. He snuggled up to her and fell into a deep sleep.

3

He woke to the sound of snuffling and a little cry, which he thought was a puppy in the room. As he came around in the bright sunlight, he realised his baby moving in the crib had woken him. He looked at his watch and it was 7 a.m. Marie was still fast asleep, but he leant over and unwrapped his daughter and picking her up gently, cradled her in his arms and leant back on the pillows for support. He just gazed in wonder at her tiny nose and bright blue eyes. She responded to the smell of him and started rooting for his nipple. He brought his knees up to his chest and lay her on them, so they were face to face. She put out her hand and touched his nose and gurgled contentedly. He still couldn't believe that he had been responsible for creating this perfect little girl who seemed to be an exact replica of her mother.

Marie stirred and moved over to him, leaning back against the pillow. She stared intently, transfixed by the baby. 'Did I really give birth to her last night? It feels like I am in a dream.' She unbuttoned her nightie and lifted the baby to her breast. Within seconds she was suckling, and he felt tears of happiness coursing down his cheeks at the sight before him. He leant over her and tenderly kissed her lips.

'Marie, you are wonderful. I couldn't live without you by my side.'

She pushed him out of the way and said, 'Move over, I need to see what I'm doing. It's too early for me to do this instinctively yet. I am terrified of squashing or choking her.'

'What does it feel like?'

'Charles, you do ask some difficult questions. Well it feels… just… natural. It doesn't't hurt, but then she has no teeth yet and my milk hasn't really come through yet. I guess this is all colostrum and just as vital to protect her as it is with a new born foal.'

'I love you, darling, you were so brave last night, and I was just hopeless. It's very hard seeing the woman you love in such pain, but I wouldn't have missed it for the world.'

'Well, may I suggest you bear the next one and give me a break?'

'I would if I could sweetheart, but I will be here for you every step of the way. What do you want to call her? I know we discussed Marie-Ann before the birth, for a girl.'

'Charles, tell me truthfully – are you disappointed I didn't have a boy?'

'Oh no, not at all; there's plenty of time to have a boy.' He leant over and kissed her and helped her switch sides with the baby.

'Can we call her Marie-Ann Henrietta Carolus-

Duran?'

'Oh, Charles that sounds perfect and Henri will be so pleased. She might not have survived without his intervention. He was a hero for me last night. What was he doing here, anyway?'

Charles paused to think, carefully. 'He has got forty-eight hours' leave from the barracks and he called here to see us last night and he is going home today.'

'Why only forty-eight hours? Where is he going when he gets back?'

'He didn't say he was going anywhere.'

'Charles, you should know by now you can never lie to me. I can see it in your eyes. He's going to war, isn't he? My little brother is going to risk his life for bloody Napoleon against the Germans.' She broke down and sobbed heart wrenchingly.

He took his daughter out of her arms and held them both close to his chest.

'You knew Henri would go to war one day and these are turbulent times. It was his choice to join the cavalry and you wouldn't deny him that. We will pray for his safety every day. I have asked him to be the baby's godfather, but we need to baptise her tomorrow, so I thought we could all go back to your parents today. You know we briefly discussed possible godparents before and, strictly speaking, a girl should have two females and one male godparent. Would it matter if we had Henri, Manet and his wife Suzanne? I think we can get them all to the chateau tomorrow if I act quickly.'

Marie sobbed, 'Yes that would be fine but are you expecting me to ride there? I am supposed to be lying in for two weeks.'

'No, of course not. We will take the carriage and Henri will drive, Jacques will ride Henri's horse and Manet and Suzanne can join us on Sunday. I will go and get Jacques up and send him round to Manet's. Your brother does not agree with lying in, Marie, so you had better get up soon. Are you in any pain?'

'No, just dying of a broken heart at the prospect of losing my brother to a pointless, stupid war. Now he's a medic, will he be able to stay away from the front line more?'

'No, sweetheart. Henri has already said that he is a soldier first and foremost and he won't be spared any of the action. You change Marie-Ann and I will bring you a coffee and some toast and then you had better have a bath. I will look after her while you get ready.'

oOo

Charles quickly got dressed and went downstairs to the kitchen. He popped across to the stables to feed Henri's horse. He took his rug off and admired his shining black coat and his fit condition. He patted his sleek neck and said, 'Good lad, please bring your master safely back from the battlefield; we all love him so much.' He gave him a good feed and filled his hay net. He felt powerless to do anything to prevent the loss of his brother-in-law. He knew his biggest danger was the cannon. Why they persisted in the cavalry charging against cannons, he could not comprehend. To him, it was suicide as the majority would be blown apart long before they reached enemy lines.

He went back into the house. Henri was up and making himself some breakfast.

'How are the girls?' he said.

'Fine – they had a good night. Marie fed her at 7 a.m. and I have told her our plans for the baptism and she is in total agreement. She would love you to be a godparent and we have decided to name her Marie-Ann Henrietta in honour of you.'

Henri took a deep breath and fought back his emotion. 'I really appreciate that, Charles. I just hope I can see her grow up and have her own child.'

'Why don't you take Marie this tray and talk to her while I despatch Jacques to Manet's? I have seen to your horse; he's fine and superbly fit. In fact, the pair of you are looking well. Do you think Jacques can cope with your horse on the ride home?'

'He can be a bit of a fool when he's fresh and he has had some of the grooms off several times. It depends how competent Jacques is at riding.'

'I believe he had plenty of riding experience as a lad and he has had no problems with my horses but they're not in the same league as yours. Shall we put him in the field and see, or perhaps you could take the sting out of your horse before we set off. What do you call him, by the way?'

'He became "Jester" by default as he can untie knots and undo stable doors as and when he wants. He got me into so much trouble because, not content with letting himself out, he has been known to let other horses out as well. He has an extra bolt low down on his stable door now. When we line tie them up outside I have to muzzle him, or he can get loose. Imagine if he did that in battle and we lost an entire troop of horses.'

'Oh dear, sounds like he's a handful.'

'It has its advantages too. I have taught him some tricks, which I hope will improve our chances of survival. In close combat fighting he is phenomenal; he knows instinctively how to weave so that I can use my right hand with the sword to best effect against an opponent. He will rear to move me away from an opponent and he will deliberately push the opponent's horse away and use both his teeth and legs to do it. If I am ejected from the saddle for any reason he will come and get me on a whistle command, as well as automatically, as I might be unconscious on the ground. I have taught him to lie down so that if I can't walk he will let me get on from the ground. I don't use the reins in a charge; I knot them on his neck and steer him with my legs and control his speed with my voice. That allows me to have a pistol in my left hand and my sword in my right so if I make it to the enemy lines, I have two weapons. I have had to learn to shoot a pistol from my left hand, but it will only be of use over short distances. Our rifles are anchored on the saddle but there will be no time to use them in a charge. However, I am a crack shot at rifle shooting from any distance. I learnt those skills in Russia, out hunting. I can bring a bear down from 100 yards with a rifle but unfortunately, I can't bring a cannon down. I do get picked for advance surveillance because of my rifle skills so maybe I might avoid some direct charges because of it, and my sword skills are well honed. I could take you on now, Charles, and win.'

'That's amazing, Henri. Do you have any other weapons on you?'

'Yes, of course – a short dagger down each boot and a longer one sewn into a pocket on the inside of my jacket. Unfortunately, though, they depend on me seeing my opponents coming. I would have no chance if I was in someone's rifle sights from any distance. We could do with some armour on the chest but unfortunately, armour and shields are no longer issued.'

'Let's pray to God that you keep safe out there.'

Charles gave Henri a tray with enough toast for two. He went in search of Jacques, to send him to Manet. Henri took the tray upstairs, knocked on Marie's door and went in. He was pleased to see her looking fresh and well after last night's ordeal. Her face lit up when she saw him.

'Ah, my hero brother bearing gifts of food. I am starving.'

Henri sat down beside her on the bed and inspected his niece in her cradle, sleeping soundly. Her head was already filling out and he winced as he remembered Charles's fear last night of her being brain damaged. He should have told him straight after she was born why the head looked misshapen. The sight of the baby reminded him of an area of life he may never have the joy of experiencing due to his chosen profession. He would have found it a great deal harder to leave a wife and new baby to fight for his country. At least if he never came back he wouldn't have shattered anyone else's lives, just his own. He had been wise to keep his relationships with women on a very temporary footing. However, he had never explored the possibility of finding a wife. Maybe if he survived this battle he would have to pursue that on his return. He was only twenty-two, so he had plenty of time – God willing.

Marie interrupted his thoughts, 'Henri, how have you become experienced in delivering babies? You are supposed to be a soldier.'

He told her about his four deliveries and she was surprised to hear that women were allowed to be stationed in the barracks. She had to ask him, 'Have you been responsible for any of the babies you have delivered?'

He hesitated. 'No, not exactly… although one of the women, I did have a brief dalliance with, but she was already pregnant. I delivered her little boy. She is one of the grooms who looks after Jester.'

Marie was quick to respond, 'Oh do be careful, Henri, don't lose your heart to her. Papa would be furious if you married someone like her; he has high hopes of you finding a more aristocratic wife.'

'But how? God knows how long I will be away, even if I survive… and would you be happy for Charles to leave you with your new baby and set off to war? How many of your aristocratic women would want to cope with that?'

'Of course, there are many families of dukes and counts that still have their titles, but maybe not their land. Leave it with me and while you're away I will do some investigating.'

'Marie, I don't want just a meek and mild lady of the court, I want someone like you; educated, spirited, highly strung, loyal, courageous and totally unaware of the meaning of danger. I want a marriage like yours in body and soul… so where on earth can you find me someone like that in France?'

They were interrupted by Marie-Ann waking up. Henri lifted her into his arms and cuddled her and then passed her to her mother.

'I am honoured that you named her after me and I hope she can be my guardian angel while on the battlefield. Now, back to being your doctor. Is everything settling down below?'

'Henri, you have seen and felt far more of my intimate areas than any man should ever see, but I think apart from some soreness, everything is returning to normal. At least I didn't tear, and I have no stitches thanks to your expert delivery skills, so I think I will be fine. I will feed her now. Then, if you would take her down to Charles while I have a bath.'

'Just remember it will be Monday before your milk comes through and it will make you feel very emotional. I know that you respond by being evil and cutting with your tongue, but don't take it out on poor Charles. You can admit that you are vulnerable without losing face, you know. You should take a leaf out of Charles's book and talk about your feelings more. I have brought you some salt from the kitchen to put in your bath to speed the healing.'

Marie groaned, 'Salt in my bath, you really do have sadistic tendencies, brother. I think you are paying me back for all the times you got me out of trouble in Russia.'

'Yes, I do recall your first bear hunt, madam, when you made a near fatal error by getting too close when the bear went down. It was only temporarily winded by being brought down by the hounds, but you forgot that it had to be shot and it came around and lunged at your horse and tore its flesh with one paw from the wither to the elbow; you were within inches of death. How I shot it cleanly through the heart from 100 yards away I will never know. One wrong move and I could have killed you.'

Marie said, 'Perhaps you are my guardian angel, which explains why you turned up in the nick of time last night? Oh dear, the baby is so small, I have trouble holding her in the right position.'

Henri pulled a pillow off the bed and put it under the baby, so that Marie only needed to use one hand to support her. He said, 'You know that if you want to delay any subsequent pregnancy then you need to fully feed her for as long as you can. Even when you start weaning her onto solid food you need to continue to breastfeed or you will fail to suppress your reproductive cycle.'

'I am not even thinking of going through this again for quite some time and I know Charles will not allow a wet nurse in the house. Please don't mention this to Mother as she will be horrified.'

Henri laughed, 'Marie, it is perfectly normal. How do you think the rest of civilisation exists? And it gives you such a close bond as well as having countless health benefits. You may find you enjoy it once you have mastered the art.'

She promptly handed him the baby and said, 'Here, godfather – get started on your duties and change her while I have my bath.'

'Marie, my skills cease after delivering babies. I haven't a clue how to change a nappy or rear a baby.'

Marie responded vehemently, 'Do you think that just because I am a woman I should instinctively know how to rear a baby? I can rear foals and puppies from experience, but this is in a different league and is extremely daunting.'

'Marie, I have every faith in you. Once you know what you are doing, you will be fine.'

Henri picked up the baby's clothes and nappy

and took them downstairs with the baby in the hope that Charles might have a better idea of how to dress her. Charles was in the kitchen and could hear Henri approaching as Marie-Ann had realised her breakfast was over. He took her from Henri and she instantly stopped crying, recognising both the voice and smell of her father.

Just at that moment, Jacques returned with an excited Manet at his side.

'Charles, congratulations on the birth of your daughter. I had to come and see you all straight away as this was the completion of my project – I pushed you into asking for Marie's hand in marriage. Both Suzanne and I would be delighted to be her godparents.' He had a peek at her in Charles's arms but refrained from picking her up as babies were not his forté. 'Jacques says the labour was a bit of a trauma until you arrived Henri and saved the day.'

'Rubbish. Charles would have coped admirably without me.' replied Henri.

Charles was fussing with the baby's nightie and Jacques took pity on him. 'Would you like me to show you how to change her, Charles?'

The look of relief on Charles's face was paramount. 'If you know what to do I would be more than grateful. I can't even undo the buttons on her nightie with my clumsy fingers.'

Jacques picked up a cushion and laid the baby on the kitchen table and deftly whipped the nightdress over her head and she lay, wriggling her arms and legs, in just her nappy. Jacques went for a jug of water and a bowl while Charles stayed with her.

Manet asked, 'What are you calling her?'

Charles replied, 'Marie-Ann Henrietta Carolus-Duran – after the uncle who delivered her.'

Manet said, 'How very apt, but why the immediate rush to baptise her? She's not in any danger, is she?'

Charles replied, 'No, not at all; it's just that Henri only has forty-eight hours' leave and we need to get it done before he goes.'

'Does that mean that Henri's being posted?'

'Yes, we are moving off to the German border, but war has not been declared yet. Napoleon is just moving us into position.'

Marie appeared in the kitchen doorway and said, 'Heavens, a kitchen full of men in thrall to one little girl. I think I will be the one who returns to the studio next week and will leave Charles and Jacques here to tend to the baby. You are doing a very good job, Jacques. Did you used to care for your siblings at home?'

'Yes, all the time, Marie. I am an expert on changing babies, rocking and singing them to sleep.' replied Jacques.

Marie said to Charles, 'I hope you were paying attention? Don't think for one moment you will be avoiding changing nappies.'

Manet stepped forward. 'Marie, what a beautiful little girl you have. I can see Charles is quite besotted with her already and Suzanne and I would be delighted to be godparents. I had to come around and meet her straight away, but we will ride over early tomorrow for the christening at your parents' house.'

Marie asked Jacques to make them some coffee and bring it through to the lounge. Marie let Charles have charge of Marie-Ann, so they could get to know each other.

When they were all settled in the lounge, Marie turned to Henri and said, 'Henri, we can't tell Mother that you delivered my baby. She would be horrified... unless you want to tell her?'

Henri replied, 'No, I think it's best we say I just turned up and you had called out a doctor to deliver you. It's going to be hard enough explaining that I am going away, without adding that to the equation.'

Marie said, 'She's going to be mad enough with me for not being in bed for two weeks as it is, and she will expect me to have a nursemaid with me to attend to the baby.'

Charles laughed, 'Well you've got me or Jacques for that role; choose whoever you think is the most capable.'

After a brief chat they all dispersed; Marie with the baby to pack a bag, and Henri, Jacques and Charles went to put Jacques on Jester to see whether he would cope, and to tack the carriage horses up for their journey. Manet was going home.

Henri tacked Jester up and took him into one of the small paddocks and schooled him for a while, to get the freshness out of him. Then he went into the orchard and gave him a canter round. He brought him back to the smaller paddock and Jacques got on and did some schooling with him. He behaved impeccably. Henri thought he would be fine as he was used to being in "troop mode," so he should just switch off while following the carriage. They tied Jester up outside the stables while they tacked up the carriage horses. It had been a while since Charles had harnessed carriage horses, so he was glad of their expertise. The five servants they employed (including one groom) did not work at weekends as Charles preferred to have the weekends to themselves.

Charles went back to see if Marie was ready and she had packed them an overnight bag but was fussing over what she could christen the baby in as she was convinced the family christening gowns would be too big for Marie-Ann as they had not been baptised until around three to six months after birth. She was also panicking about what she was going to wear as she wasn't expecting to get back into her pre-maternity clothes quite so soon. She did not relish wearing a corset whilst she was breastfeeding as she would be far too restricted. She realised her mother would notice, and she knew she was going to get some grief off her mother for her inappropriate behaviour. She must try and keep quiet about Charles being with her at the birth as she had raised the issue the last time she saw her – under no circumstances was she to let Charles be present at the birth as it would put him off her for life. Obviously, there had been no point in telling her mother that Charles knew every inch of her body intimately and had taken great pleasure in watching her body change from that of a girl into that of a woman.

4

They assembled on the drive at 1 p.m. to depart for the chateau. The drive was expected to take just over an hour and a half at a leisurely place. Henri was delighted to be driving the carriage as it was a long time since he had driven four in hand. He had, however, ridden the gun horses when he had first started in the cavalry. He had proved himself to be as good at firing cannons as he was at rifle shooting. Since his promotion to lieutenant however, those days were over.

Charles took charge of Marie-Ann on the journey. She loved his attention, gurgling contently in his arms and trying to put his finger in her mouth. He had already decided he would spend the first week at home with them both as he wanted to support Marie as much as possible as he was aware of her slight feelings of inadequacy. Antonio could cope in the studio and he would just have to delay one portrait session, which was booked in at his studio for Wednesday. He would send Antonio out into Paris to take his students on an architecture course, which he would be more than capable of teaching.

At 2 p.m. Charles called Jacques over and told

him to ride to the chateau and inform Marie's family that they were on their way, so that they could prepare. He also told him not to gallop Jester as the prospect of him being unsound would have ruined Henri's plans.

They arrived after a pleasant journey at 2:40 p.m. and Marie's parents were outside, by the front door. Three grooms had been summoned to take the horses and Pierre was admiring Jester and chatting to Jacques. Her mother ran down the steps and didn't even give the groom a chance to open the carriage door before she flung it open herself and instructed him to pass the baby to her, so she could see her first granddaughter. He passed Marie-Ann to her and then helped Marie from the carriage. Pierre hugged and kissed her and then Henri joined them, having handed over the care of the horses to a groom. When Louise saw Henri, she could not help the tears running down her cheeks at the realisation of Henri's departure to war. He hugged her in turn, taking care not to smother Marie-Ann.

They went into the house where a bevy of servants was rushing around, laying out afternoon tea in the drawing room. Louise was fussing over Marie and telling her to sit down and rest as she should not have been out of bed. She didn't ask about a nursemaid but had commandeered one of her lady's maids to see to the baby; Marie-Ann was handed over to her with instructions to bring her back when she needed feeding.

Louise said to Marie, 'You will only need to deal with the feeding for about a week and then the baby should be handed over to the wet nurse.'

Marie responded quickly, 'Mama, there will be no wet nurse. I am feeding her myself for as long as I can.'

Louise interrupted in horror, 'Don't be so ridiculous, Marie, you can't do that. You will never get your sylph-like figure back after feeding a baby.'

Charles was anxious to jump to his wife's support, but Marie continued, 'Mother, I am the wife of an artist not a king and as my husband has already informed me, God gave me two perfect vessels with which to feed my own child – and that's exactly what I intend to do!'

Louise took a sharp intake of breath and gasped in shock. Pierre raised an eyebrow and looked at Charles and Henri in amusement. Jacques did not know where to look as he was having trouble controlling a desire to laugh. He knew she wasn't telling her mother a lie as that was exactly what Charles would have said. Charles wished the floor would open and swallow him up. He didn't know whether Marie had done this deliberately to put him in the firing line or whether she was openly declaring her support for him.

Pierre came to the rescue and said, 'Charles, perhaps you could write a note for the priest about the arrangements you want for the christening tomorrow. I have a servant waiting to take it to him.'

He led him over to the bureau and pulled a piece of paper and a pen out.

Charles sat down and took the paper and Pierre leant forward and whispered, 'Did you really say that, Charles? How very astute of you... and what was my daughter's response, may I ask?'

Charles replied quietly, 'The subject came up on honeymoon and Marie assumed she would have the services of a wet nurse on hand after the birth of a child and that was my rather angry response. I am sorry sir, if you are offended at my proposal, but I do feel very strongly that a baby should be fed by its own mother – both for bonding purposes and health reasons.'

Pierre interrupted, 'Charles, I am not in any way criticising your intention. Marie is under your jurisdiction now and as her husband you have the right to insist she obeys you. I am just curious to understand how well she has taken your advice and to congratulate you on taming my wild daughter into an obedient wife and mother. You have done more in twelve months to tame her than I managed in eighteen years.' He then left him to write the note.

Charles looked over at Henri, who gave him an amused look. He concentrated on asking the priest, politely, if he would mind baptising Marie-Ann after the normal Sunday service tomorrow and apologised for the lack of notice but explained that this was due to one of the godparents only being available on Sunday to take the vows. He sealed the note in an envelope and passed it to Pierre to address.

Charles helped himself to some tea and cake, watching with concern the tension between mother and daughter. Louise finally switched her attentions to Henri, so he moved over to the sofa and sat next to his wife. He was concerned that Marie needed some rest as it was only a mere twelve hours since she had given birth.

However, the maid returned with an angry and hungry baby who had now realised both her parents were out of sight. Marie was about to undo the bodice of her dress and feed her baby when her mother loudly intervened saying, 'Marie, take your baby to your room or to the nursery, the salon is not an acceptable place to feed a child.'

Charles was furious and instantly removed the baby from the servant and bent down to Marie and said, 'Come along sweetheart, you could do with a sleep anyway, after your journey.' He saw tears running down her face, so he helped her up and then led her out of the salon and upstairs to their room.

When they were inside, Marie ran to the bed and threw herself face down and sobbed, 'Why is my mother being so difficult about my breastfeeding? Surely we have a perfect right to decide how to rear our own child?'

He carefully placed Marie-Ann at the top of the bed and scooped Marie up into his arms. 'Darling, your mother is just trying to impose her ideals of how she thinks a French child should be raised and she has no right whatsoever to question our wishes. I shall have cause to intervene if she does it again. Now let me help you take your dress off and then you snuggle up in bed with Marie-Ann and have a sleep, you must be exhausted.'

She undid her dress and Charles helped her out of it and she got into bed in her chemise. She picked Marie-Ann up and took an extra pillow, put it under the baby and then started to feed her. His heart was overcome with emotion as he looked at them and he perched on the bed next to her and took her free hand and kissed it gently, saying, 'I love you so much, ma cherie. Nobody will hurt you or the baby while I am by your side.'

Charles wandered to the nursery to see if he could find a crib for them to use in their bedroom. One of the lady's maids was putting fresh sheets into a tiny crib; she agreed to bring it to their room with some extra nappies and baby clothes. He went back to Marie, who had finished feeding Marie-Ann. Marie demonstrated how to change their daughter's nappy, then he had a go and did a reasonable job.

'Why don't you sleep now, darling? You can stay in bed for the rest of today. There's no point in going down to dinner this evening; you need to recover for tomorrow.'

'I am going down to dinner because that's what mother expects me to do. Did you not see the look she gave me when she saw I had no corset on? She thinks I have turned into a peasant already and I will not give her any further cause.'

'You cannot possibly wear a corset; you will be unable to breathe, and you certainly won't be able to keep your blooming breasts inside some of your low-cut gowns. Your mother will have even more cause to complain if you expose yourself at the dining table.'

They both laughed at the image he portrayed, and he hugged her.

'Marie, you go to sleep. When the maid brings the crib, I will put Marie-Ann in here next to the bed. I will check on you at about 7 p.m. and if you are both fast asleep I won't wake you but will ensure there is some food brought to the room for you later. If you are awake and feel up to going down to dinner, then we can all three go to dinner.'

'Charles, babies are not allowed in the dining room, especially during dinner.'

Charles retorted, 'Our baby goes where we go, Marie. If your mother has someone to care for her during dinner then fine, but if not, she will stay with us. Between you, me, Jacques and Henri, we can pass her around, so we all get chance to eat.'

Marie roared with laughter. 'Oh, you are such a wonderful husband. Can you imagine what mother would have to say at that scene, especially if Henri was dangling her on his knee?'

There was a knock at the door and the maid appeared with the crib. She set everything up next to the bed and told Marie she just had to call if she needed anything and she would care for the baby during dinner. He left Marie chatting to the girl and went back downstairs. He heard piano music coming from the library and so he went in and found Pierre sitting next to Jacques at the piano, watching him play a complicated Mozart piece. Pierre had set up piano lessons for Jacques in Paris and he attended a private tutor twice a week. Marie helped him with his practice and composition twice a week. He could think of nothing more relaxing than sipping a strong brandy and listening to Jacques play Mozart, so he poured himself a drink and settled himself in a comfy chair. The boy was good; there was no doubting that. In fact, Jacques was good at all his studies and it would be difficult for him to select which profession he wanted to pursue. He felt that Jacques' father's hope of him following his career as a doctor was the least likely option as he was such a sensitive boy; he didn't think he would take too well to the cut and thrust of surgery.

Charles woke about an hour later to find Jacques still playing but Henri had come into the room. As it was approaching 6:45 p.m. they all departed from the library to get changed for dinner. He entered their room quietly. Marie was asleep, and he tiptoed over to the cradle to check his daughter. She was still not twenty-four hours old and he was besotted with this tiny being. What a huge shift in his lifestyle now he was a father. He felt so protective of her, he would find it difficult to leave her to go to his studio. Then he contemplated the prospect of having to leave her to go to war like Henri was, and that terrified him even more.

Marie started to stir in bed, so he waited until her eyes had opened and then he whispered, 'Go back to sleep precious, you look so comfortable tucked in there. I might even be tempted to miss dinner and jump in there with you.'

Marie propped herself up on the pillows and said, 'Oh really, you have already broken all the rules of French husbandry as it is. 'I will make it for dinner if I have to crawl there.'

He sighed and said, 'You had better tell me about all these unwritten rules I am supposed to have flouted.'

'Where would you like me to start? First of all, once my pregnancy was confirmed you should have restricted your activities to no more than once a month and after five months, removed yourself completely from the marital bed. You should have been drinking yourself under the bar whilst I was in labour and on no account should you have seen your child until she was at least a day old. I should be confined to the marital bed for two weeks, lying in after the birth and confined to the house for a further four weeks before it is appropriate to be seen in public. On no account would you be allowed to return to the marital bed until the six weeks was over. I should only feed the baby for a week and my figure should have returned to its sylph-like self within the six weeks.'

'Now I know why so many aristocratic Frenchmen have mistresses if they are expected to go for six months without sex. So why did you not tell me all this when you became pregnant? Could it be, madame, that you didn't want me to follow this code as considering pregnancy made you even keener for sex than you were before, you did not want to risk losing me from your bed?'

Marie laughed, 'Precisely, I could not have coped for six days without you in my bed, never mind six months!'

'But as your husband I make the rules of the house and if I wish to dispense with all this nonsense then surely that's within my rights?'

Marie-Ann stirred and as he had just removed his shirt he picked her up, sat on the bed and cuddled her close to his chest. He was tempted to undress her, so they could have skin to skin contact but he realised that they would have to get a move on if they were going to make dinner.

Marie said, 'Hand her over. I'd better feed her now because if the maid has to interrupt dinner to fetch me I will be in trouble again with Mother for causing a scene.' She fed her and then rushed to get washed and dressed while he changed her and amused her. Marie got dressed and banished all thoughts of putting a corset on when she looked in the mirror and saw the increase in the size of her breasts. She was going to struggle to find a dress with a high enough neckline as it was. She asked Charles to put her hair up in a chignon as, now she was a mother, etiquette dictated that her hair should be up at all times and never allowed to flow loosely down her back. He was getting extremely irate about all the protocol and threatened to consider moving back to Spain or Italy. He rang for the maid to come and look after the baby while they were at dinner. They practically ran down the two flights of stairs to make the 7:30 p.m. deadline.

Marie's mother gave her daughter a disparaging look when she spotted that she was not wearing a corset, but had she commented, Charles would have intervened. He had already decided he was going to excuse himself from the mens' after dinner drinks as he was anxious to return to his daughter. This would also give Henri a chance to talk to his father alone as both were going to find it hard to say goodbye under such daunting circumstances. He knew it had been Henri's choice to join the cavalry; he had not been put under any pressure by his father to join up. If only Henri's talents in the medical area had been discovered earlier, he could now have been training to be a doctor rather than facing call-up to war.

Released from dinner, they left the room holding hands, which was immediately spotted by his mother-in-law. Charles smiled triumphantly as he thought she was probably worried he was going to ravish Marie. Marie-Ann was fast asleep and although the maid offered to take the baby to the nursery and see to her all night, he declined as he was having nobody else look after their child.

5

Charles turned to Marie, 'Do you remember our wedding night when you undressed at your dressing table and I watched you in the mirror from the bed?'

'How could I ever forget that night, Charles? It was only nine months ago.'

'Do it again for me now please, darling.'

'Of course, your every wish is my command.'

She undid the rich red silk dress and let it slide gracefully to the floor. She sat down at the dressing table and slowly unpinned her hair and brushed it through. She paused when she saw him get up and remove his clothes and then lie propped up on the pillows again. She stood up and removed her tights and drawers, making sure he had the perfect view of her buttocks, but left her chemise on. Then, she sat down and unlaced her chemise, watching him closely in the mirror. She pulled it down over her shoulders, exposing her breasts. She was delighted by the look on his face and she stood up and turned slowly round, allowing the chemise to slip down her naked body.

'Tell me what you see now, Charles?'

'You have transformed from the beautiful virgin to having the rounded figure of a wife and mother… and you know I find your breasts irresistible.' He moved towards her and kissed both breasts gently. He then picked her up carried her to the bed, pulled back the covers, laid her down on her back and got in beside her. He leant over and kissed her lips then ran his tongue down her neck and chest, straying to her right nipple for a few moments and then to her left. She pushed him over onto his back and said, 'It's me that's given birth and is indisposed but looking at that ardour, you are not going to want to wait six weeks to relieve it.' She ran her tongue downwards from his navel and he let her take him to heaven and back.

Afterwards, he cuddled her from behind and played with her beautiful long hair and said, 'You do know I love you so much my heart physically hurts?'

'I think your reaction to my relieving your ardour may just have given me a slight impression that you could be fond of me.'

Just at this point, Marie-Ann started waking up and Charles said, 'My other beautiful girl wants some attention.' He reached over and lifted her from the crib and laid her across his chest and held her tiny little hand. She nuzzled against his chest and he gazed down at her. 'Do you think as she has all your features she may have my quiet temperament rather than your fiery temper?'

'Wherever did you get the idea that you are not

bad tempered? When you don't get your own way, you can get as angry as I do, and you are far more stubborn than me.'

'Hush madame and feed my little girl.'

'You are going to spoil her, aren't you? If you were an aristocrat rather than an artist, you wouldn't see the baby again until she was walking.'

'No king could feel as happy as I am on the birth of my daughter. I intend to have just as close a relationship with her as I do with you, and no stupid rules on etiquette are going to put a stop to that.'

oOo

He woke the next morning and was careful not to wake Marie as he recalled the baby waking at about 2 a.m. for a feed and he wanted her to sleep for as long as possible as this was going to be a long day for all of them. Carefully, he slid out of bed, put his robe on and went around to the cradle to check his baby. She was filling out – both in her cheeks and her head – and she was sleeping contentedly. He went and checked out of the window and it looked like it would be a perfect, warm June day. He pulled a chair up to the cradle and sat down, taking in the scene of his sleeping wife and baby. No man could feel happier than he did and today he was going to church to thank God for his gift of a beautiful daughter and for the safe delivery of his precious wife. In the scheme of things, if there was a God, he was doing well with his favours. He had been granted Marie's hand in marriage, survived a duel within twenty-four hours of marriage, fathered a child within the first month of marriage and now he had Marie-Ann – all within eighteen months. He hoped God would grant him a son over the next few years.

He knew he must also remember to pray for Henri's safety in battle as he was very fond of his brother-in-law and Marie was extremely close to her brother. He dreaded to think how she would cope if he died. Their time together in Russia had cemented a bond between them and still, he could not quite believe that Henri had shown up on his doorstep just when they both needed him most.

Marie-Ann started to stir, and he watched her come around from her sleep. Her eyes finally opened, and she moved her arms. She was not too amused when she couldn't move her legs as the blankets restricted her movement. Just before she protested he picked her up and held her close to his chest, hoping he could amuse her and give Marie a bit more sleep. When she became fretful he walked around, hoping to keep her quiet a bit longer. However, he noticed Marie stirring in the bed and her hand went out searching for him and when she didn't find him she opened her eyes. He went back to the bed, pulled the covers back and lay next to her.

She sat up and he could tell she was uncomfortable due to the speed she put the baby to her breast and winced when she started feeding.

'Oh, Charles I am feeling tight and sore now

my milk is coming through. Am I going to regret breastfeeding?'

'No, not at all. It is four hours since you last fed her, and you will be fine when she has had her fill. Henri said you had to feed her on demand, not by the clock, and that you hadn't to leave her too long between feeds.'

'I am beginning to think this was a conspiracy between the two of you to deprive me of my freedom. I might as well be one of the brood mares in your father's paddock in Lille.'

'Be patient, little firebrand. Just because you won't be coming to the studio doesn't mean your work will cease. You will still have my students to organise, all my accounts to do, Jacques to tutor, the house to oversee and a new baby to raise so I think you will be busier than before. When we get home, I need to paint you and the baby before I go back to work.'

'Oh no, you are not painting me nude looking like this. I absolutely forbid it. I know you are delighted at the increase in the size of my breasts but what about the flabby stomach and stretch marks?'

'Darling, calm down. It would be for my eyes only, not for public exhibition. You don't think I would paint it to exhibit in the salon for a medal, do you?'

'You said that about the honeymoon pictures and yet I know you have shown them to Manet because he said something that he could only have known had he seen the waterfall painting.'

'Manet is an artist as well as a friend to both of us Marie, and I do value his opinion of my work and he mine. Now feed the baby and calm down; we have a big day to get through and you are stressed out already.'

He retired to the bathroom to get washed and changed. He realised that Marie was just feeling vulnerable, but he hoped she would be able to control her temper today. He feared that if her mother slighted her, there could be an almighty row. He thought he would have a word with Henri before breakfast about trying to keep them apart.

When he had finished and went back out into the bedroom, she had fed and changed Marie-Ann and was playing with her on the bed. He heard horses on the drive and looked out of the window to see Manet and Suzanne arriving.

'Manet has just arrived. I should go and greet him. Do you want me to send the maid up to you to look after the baby while we have breakfast?'

She nodded in agreement. Concerned about her, he went to Henri's room and tapped on the door. Henri appeared fully dressed in the doorway, slightly surprised to see him as he had assumed it was one of the servants.

'Charles, what can I do for you? Do come in.'

'I'm just a bit concerned as Marie has bitten my head off this morning and seems really stressed and it doesn't bode well for the rest of the day.'

'Oh dear, I only told her yesterday that she would feel like this when her milk comes through. It is purely a hormonal reaction and I told her she would be evil as she always uses her tongue when she is under stress. Don't worry, I will go and have a word with her. I think we need to keep her and Mother at a distance today as with Marie so emotional, she will be spoiling for a fight.'

Charles went downstairs to greet Manet and summon the maid.

Henri finished dressing and went to his sister's room. He knocked, she answered, and he went in. Marie was still in bed with Marie-Ann on the bed next to her.

'I just came to see how my patients are before their big day?'

'Dreadful, I woke up tight and sore and it hurt when she fed. Charles had the temerity to suggest he wanted to paint me nude, but how can he when I look so awful and feel like a brood mare?'

He laughed, 'What did I tell you only yesterday about you being evil when your hormones are unbalanced?'

There was another knock on the door and the maid entered and came to take Marie-Ann to the nursery. He turned to her after she had gone.

'Marie, you are just experiencing a massive surge of hormones and it will make you feel vulnerable and lacking in confidence, which for you will be a total shock as you are normally just the opposite.

You have coped extremely well with the birth and feeding her so far; you are doing so well. Don't be put off, it will settle down in the next couple of days. If you stop you will be at risk of mastitis and believe me, you don't want to experience that. You are a mother now and you must put your baby's welfare above your own. You are so lucky you have such a wonderful husband as Charles who wants to be at your side and help you. Most of the women I deal with have to raise their babies alone with no support from a loving husband or any financial support so just try to recognise how very lucky you are.'

Suddenly, Marie threw her arms around him, sobbing like a baby and he just held her tightly and he could feel his tears running into her hair. Would this be the last time he hugged his wayward sister? He held her while her sobs subsided, and he managed to control his own emotions. He left her to get ready for breakfast and he went back to his room to gather his emotions together as he had a stressful day to face too.

oOo

After breakfast, the two carriages arrived to transport them the short distance to the church. Marie had gone back upstairs to dress the baby and she appeared, descending the stairs with Marie-Ann in an ivory full-length silk and lace christening gown last worn by her as a baby. Marie was wearing a royal blue fitted silk dress with no corset in sight, but she was wearing a chemise underneath with an embroidered lace bodice, which gave her extra coverage over her breasts. She wore her sapphire necklace and earrings and he marvelled at how well she looked so soon after the birth.

He went to take her from Marie as he was to hold her in the carriage containing the godparents and Jacques, all except for Henri who was in the carriage containing his parents. She was awake and aware that she was in her father's arms and she lay still while he checked over her dress and found that she was wearing another short dress underneath the christening gown – probably to make it fit around her tiny neck and shoulders. He hoped she wouldn't be too hot in the church. They arrived in good time for the normal matins service; the christening was to take place at the end of the service. The priest who had married them was officiating at the christening and he gave them a brief outline of the service.

Louise came over to look at her granddaughter and he could feel the vibes she was emitting, probably because he was holding the baby. Henri rescued him and dragged her away on the pretext of admiring a stained-glass window.

The service began. Charles loved the warm feeling the sheer ritual of the familiar words and the sound of the organ music gave him. The last time he had been in this church was the day after his wedding, after the duel, when he felt he should thank God for keeping him alive – and absolve himself from killing

Beauchamp. He knew the service well as when he had been in Italy he had spent every Sunday attending a different church. His favourite had been the Sistine Chapel because he loved the Michelangelo ceiling. When they were seated, he balanced Marie-Ann against his knees, so she faced him, and they could have eye contact. She never cried once, and she listened intently to the music. Towards the end of the service was the offertory, where the congregation could go up to the altar steps for the bread and wine. He told Marie and the godparents to go first and that he would go after them once he had left her in Henri's care. Marie had been worried that if she held her during the service she may want feeding again and could then cause a disturbance if she wasn't fed immediately.

He knelt at the altar and said his silent prayer of thanks for his daughter's safe delivery, and for his wife. He also prayed for Henri's life and for him to be spared the ravages of war. When he returned to the pew, Marie-Ann was getting a little anxious in Henri's arms and Charles saw his mother-in-law watching her son intently. He took her from Henri and cuddled her close; she instantly relaxed now her father was holding her again.

oOo

The service was over, and people were filing out of the church. Many in the congregation stopped and offered their congratulations to him and Marie on the birth of the baby. They moved over to the font for the baptism service and again, he held Marie-Ann until it was time for each of the godparents to take their vows with the baby in their arms. Both he and Marie cried silent tears when Henri took the vow, both fearing that he might not be able to carry out his duties if he didn't return from battle. Henri himself was doing a sterling job of keeping his composure but when he handed Marie-Ann back, Charles gave him a pat on the back to comfort him. During the signing of the cross on Marie-Ann's head with the holy water, she remained totally composed. She was wide awake but quiet and serene and made a triumphant first public appearance.

He committed the scene to memory; he intended to paint it later, as the rays of sunshine coming through the stained-glass window left shards of colour across the christening gown. He must ask Marie if he could borrow the dress as the intricate detail of the gown combined with the reflected, coloured shadows made Marie-Ann a surreal image. He would paint it with Henri holding her at the font, just in case this was their last family gathering together.

The service over, they filed out of church. There were still people milling around and some of the off-duty family servants were waiting to greet them. The old stud groom came over to them and offered his congratulations and said Marie-Ann was as pretty as a picture. Well, of course he knew that, and he would make sure he painted many pictures of her throughout her life.

The carriages drew up at the church; they retraced the short journey back to the chateau. He held Marie-Ann in the carriage as she was getting a little restless and rooting for some food. When they got back to the chateau, Marie ushered them into the small salon, so that she could feed the baby and be with the godparents and Jacques before lunch was served. Marie started to feed a hungry baby on the sofa, next to Suzanne.

Charles went over to Manet, who was having difficulty keeping his eyes off Marie. He turned to Charles, 'I thought as a girl she was beautiful but as a mother, she is stunning.'

'Well believe it or not, she doesn't feel beautiful – she is having a crisis of confidence – her hormones are all over the place. She is panicking about her stomach and stretch marks. She has forbidden me to paint her.'

Manet laughed, 'Oh come on, she's an artist herself, she knows how the changes in her body from girlhood to motherhood have driven you into a frenzy and she won't have the heart to deny you the pleasure. Once she has settled into motherhood she will let you paint her. You don't think she would let me paint her instead?' Charles studied him closely, desperately trying to work out if he was joking or serious. Manet broke down laughing. 'I was joking, honestly, Charles. I could not guarantee I could resist touching those enviable breasts. I bet you are going to be frequently absent from your studio now you have something so delectable to go home to. It would seem Jacques finds Marie irresistible too.'

Charles followed Jacques' gaze, and he could see the hunger in his eyes as he watched Marie breastfeed.

'I knew he was falling for her in a "hero worship" way because of the sudden improvement in his music abilities and languages... but I didn't realise he was doing it in a sexual way too. However, he is only fourteen and he is intelligent enough to know that if he stepped over the line with my wife, he would be back in Lille within hours. He may have fallen for Marie, but he respects me too.'

'Then you are going to have to divert his sexual attention elsewhere. Let him out with Antonio; he knows plenty of young girls who would be delighted to introduce a virgin boy to the delights of sex.'

'May I remind you I am responsible for his education and I need him to concentrate on his real studies, not sex. If he tries anything on with Marie, she will be more than capable of letting him down gently without destroying his confidence. He is a very spiritual boy and he may never behave inappropriately towards her, he may just be satisfied to worship her from afar. He's not the first student I have had that fancies her, even Antonio has overstepped the mark on a few occasions (usually when he has had one too many drinks), but Marie has skillfully kept him in his place. I am just thankful it is a woman he favours as more than one of my pupils has been the other way inclined.'

'Charles, you need to channel him in the right direction or he could go off the rails.'

'Don't worry, I intend to keep him so busy he will have no time or energy left for anything else. I have been looking at sending him to Rome so if he proves a problem I will despatch him sooner rather than later.'

Henri joined them with a suggestion that after lunch, they have a fencing competition, so he could show Charles how much his skills had improved. They both thought that was a wonderful idea as Manet said he had not fought any duels recently and he was a bit rusty. It would also give Charles an opportunity to introduce Jacques to the fencing arena.

oOo

After a wonderful lunch and an hour's relaxation, Manet and his wife, Henri, Charles and Jacques walked down to the stables to the gaming room for fencing practice. Marie went to feed Marie-Ann and said she would wander down later.

They arrived at the games room and laid the mats on the wooden floor, which would act as the fencing arena. They agreed to warm up in turn with each other and then have a competition. All the equipment was available in the games room, so they tossed a coin for the first draw. This was Manet versus Henri. Henri was concerned that as most of his training was with the heavier sabre, he would be at a disadvantage with the lighter foil.

Charles watched with delight as Henri had improved so much since he last saw him fence. He was at the peak of physical fitness and extremely sharp in his movements. He soon had Manet out of breath and he teased him about spending too much time in the bars, which Manet admitted was his downfall.

To give them a break, Charles showed Jacques the basic positions and how to control his foil and explained the rules of the game. Jacques had a quick mind and soon worked out the strategy. Charles knew that with tuition, he would become a competent fencer. After showing him the groundwork, he pitched him against Henri, warning him to take it easy on the boy. In one bout, Henri could not resist disarming him as he had lured him into his trap, but it was good experience for Jacques and the boy was enjoying it. He could do with enrolling him in some classes as he needed some physical exercise to keep him fit.

Charles then took on Manet and soon had the overall advantage, even though Manet came up with some moves that were technically against the rules. He warned him that if he got called in a duel he would have to sharpen up his physique as well as his technique. He then switched to a sabre and challenged Henri to a sabre fight.

Charles concentrated very hard as he knew

Henri's physical fitness was above his own and the only way he was going to win would be by forcing him to make errors. Manet oversaw the scoring but was slightly lenient in interpreting the rules. They had three five-minute rounds and although Henri beat him by one point, he was pleased with his performance. He was also overjoyed at Henri's improvement and he recognised he would prove a formidable close contact sword fighter in battle, where no rules applied. The problem would be if he was targeted by a rifle at the same time from a much greater distance. He hoped his speed and skill would make him less of a target. If he was able to use a dagger in his left hand at the same time he would be unbeatable against a single opponent, but who knew who else may have him in their sights.

6

Marie finished feeding Marie-Ann, left her in the charge of the nursemaid and wandered down to the stables. Henri's horse Jester was in the stable across from Favorit. She went in to see him and one of the grooms led him out for her to inspect in detail. She wanted to ride him, desperately, so she instructed the groom to tack him up. She kept a watchful eye on the door of the games room and prayed that none of them would come out whilst she was riding him. Her dress was loose enough to give her the freedom to ride astride. Jester looked slightly surprised when she mounted in her blue silk dress. Charles had told her about the work Henri had put into Jester, and she wanted to see it for herself.

She took him into the schooling paddock to get to know him a bit better. He had a very light mouth and was naturally balanced. Cavalry horses do not do a lot of trot work as on patrol, they are generally kept in canter and during a charge, they are in gallop. Jester had a fantastic, rounded, balanced canter and obeyed the leg aids instantly. Henri had done a brilliant job of teaching him to respond to any signal from the seat, knee or thigh. She dropped the reins completely and did three laps of the paddock, alternating between trot and canter, just using her legs. Henri would have taught him to respond to the shift of the rider's weight to change direction, as in a close contact battle Henri would be standing up in the stirrups to attack his opponent. She warmed to his obedience and submission. She did want to try him at a faster pace, so she left the paddock and hoped she could slip away and take him down to the beach for a canter on the water's edge.

They trotted through the wood and out to the beach where Charles had painted her on Favorit. Jester was enjoying the sand under his feet and so she moved him up into a canter. She switched to voice commands and he responded very quickly. She couldn't resist a gallop back up the beach and he was certainly fast enough, but he had never faced live ammunition before and he would have so many distractions to cope with. She wondered whether he would be able to concentrate on Henri's commands in the heat of battle. She knew that cannon fire blew huge craters of earth out and he would have to be so careful in the terrain he was galloping over, as one slip could bring them down. She stopped and stroked him, telling him what a good boy he was and that he must bring Henri back from the war. She also knew that if Henri was unhorsed, his chances of survival were limited. Would Jester really go back for him when all his natural instincts would be telling him to get away from the noise and turmoil and keep running with the other horses?

She was walking him back through the woods and she could hear raised voices at the stables. *Oh dear, had somebody discovered that Jester was missing?* As she rode back up the stable drive, she saw Henri talking to the groom. He relaxed when he saw them both returning.

'Marie, why are you riding my extremely fit horse only two days after giving birth? Charles told me he banned you from riding after the fifth month of your pregnancy.'

'Well I agreed to those conditions, but only whilst I was pregnant. I just wanted to sit on him and reassure myself what a wonderful job you have done at training him for battle. He is an absolute credit to you Henri, and he must put you streets ahead of your troop.'

Henri said, 'I came out for some fresh air having thrashed Charles in a sabre fight, saw his door open and thought he had let himself out as he is more than capable of doing that.'

The games room door opened, and Manet and Charles came out for some air. She saw Charles grimace when he saw her astride Jester. They both came over to them.

'What, may I ask, are you doing on Henri's horse?'

'I just wanted to sit on him, that's all.'

'Marie, you haven't just been for a gentle school in the paddock on Jester, you have been riding him on the beach, as he has sand on his legs and he is wet through up to his belly… and he has obviously been cantering as he is sweating on his neck. I recall we agreed to no riding after the fifth month of pregnancy.'

'Well I did as you asked but expected to return to riding after the baby was born.'

'The fact that you have a newborn baby to rear, never crossed your mind I suppose?'

'Charles, I was perfectly safe on Henri's beautifully-schooled cavalry charger. I would not have ridden an unknown or unbroken horse yet. I wanted to know for myself just how good he is, and I am pleased to report he is a credit to his master's training.'

Henri laughed, 'Well, that's certainly praise coming from you, madame. Now get down before Charles loses his temper at your irresponsibility.'

The groom came over and she dismounted. He led the horse away.

7

The day dawned, sunny and bright. Charles hastily made a coffee and had a stale bread roll with jam for his breakfast. Gone were the days of having fresh croissants. Wheat wasn't getting through to Paris and bakers were struggling to obtain stocks to bake bread at all. He set off from his studio to the Louvre at 8 a.m., which he knew should give him plenty of time to prepare for painting the Velázquez portrait of *Philip IV on Horseback.* Manet would be joining him at 9 a.m. to copy Velázquez's *Rokeby Venus.* He had deliberately waited until Manet was free from his military duties and back in Paris, so that they could work together to copy their favourite master's paintings.

He had set up both paintings in a small gallery that had plenty of natural daylight and meant they could work uninterrupted by the other artists who were copying paintings held in the Louvre. This would be the first time he had painted a complete copy of one painting. In his role as an art tutor it had fallen to him to decide who copied which painting. This often meant that several different artists painted parts of each picture, which they were skilled at producing. For instance, he had painted horses in several different copies as he was skilled at painting horses.

Jeannie, who was one of the American pupils, had allocated herself as his personal production assistant and she was already setting up in the gallery. Antonio came in to see him as he was supervising the Italian Renaissance copying and his speciality was architecture. They chatted about the artworks until they heard footsteps approaching and Manet swept into the gallery. His eyes went straight to the *Rokeby Venus* and he stopped about ten feet from the canvas and surveyed the scene before him.

He turned to Charles, 'Do you really think I can do this painting justice? I have been tossing and turning all night, terrified of messing it up. Seeing it in real life frightens the hell out of me!'

Charles was surprised as Manet was usually so confident about his work.

'I do know what you mean as it is a huge responsibility – one slip of a brush and you could give the game away. Both these paintings are well known, and we must fool the best art critics as well as the public. But you Manet painted *Olympia* after studying Velázquez's technique, so you are halfway there already.'

Manet replied, 'I don't know whether that makes it harder rather than easier. I think I will have more problems drawing Cupid than Venus as the head is at such an acute angle.'

Charles said, 'Jeannie will set up your palette if you wish, or you may prefer do it yourself.'

'I think a black coffee would be welcome first and then I will get down to work after last night's over-indulgence.' He then took his jacket off and paced a twelve-foot semi-circle from the painting and examined it in minute detail from all angles.

Charles was thankful he had remembered that Manet rarely stood still while he painted. He always paced around, visualising the subject to be painted before doing each section. He had set up his canvas a good twenty feet away from Manet as his pacing would disturb him; he liked to stay focused and work non-stop.

When Manet's coffee arrived, he walked over to the *Philip IV* canvas and scrutinised it minutely.

'Well, you certainly will do justice to the horse Charles, better than I could.'

Charles laughed, 'You could say both paintings reflect our interest in the subjects. You love the form of the female body and I love the intricacies of drawing horses.'

They settled down to their work in companionable silence. Occasionally, Manet would approach him and ask his opinion on a colour or technique. After four hours they broke for lunch and Jeannie brought the food in and set up a table.

They chatted about how many of the master's paintings had been copied at the Louvre as Manet was involved in transporting them to their safe haven.

Charles admitted he had deliberately held them back from the paintings chosen to go to London as part of an exhibition, because he could not bear to be parted from them. In much the same way, he had been rash in keeping his wife and child in France. However, that was proving to be a very sore point as now, Marie was in even greater danger being near Lille than she would have been in London.

They resumed their work; Charles was working on the landscape background of his equestrian portrait while Manet was working on Cupid and the mirror image of Venus. At around 3:30 p.m. several other copyists working in the Louvre came to observe their work. Charles checked whether Manet had any objections as it didn't bother him – he was used to having students watching. Manet agreed to let them observe but in silence, and they were not to ask questions. Charles noted that many of the female artists were interested in Manet… and not just from a work point of view. Manet had a reputation as a renegade and a womaniser and several of them had never seen him in the flesh before.

They finished at 7 p.m. and went to one of the only cafés still open, to have a meal. The menu was extremely limited as there was no meat available so most of the dishes consisted of vegetables or eggs. However, the bottle of cognac Manet splashed out on, made up for the lack of food. They returned to his studio and Manet decided to stay and sleep on the sofa as it seemed pointless him returning home as there was nobody else there. They chatted about their families, both revealing frank details of their past, their tongues loosened by the cognac and now by the bottle of wine they were consuming.

Charles was totally unprepared for the bombshell that Manet was about to drop on him. He admitted that Suzanne became his father's mistress after taking up her post as piano teacher to Manet and his brother Eugene. Manet started a relationship with Suzanne in his late teens and her "brother" Leon was in fact her son. Charles sat bolt upright as realisation dawned.

'So, who was Leon's father, you or your father?'

Manet smiled. 'We have no idea but as Suzanne had been in a relationship with my father for two years without conceiving before we became lovers, it is more likely that he was my son. Why do you think I did not marry her until after my father died in 1862?'

Charles was stuttering, 'Did your father know about you and Suzanne and did he confront you?'

'Of course, he knew, but he never confronted me with the knowledge. Just as my mother knew what was going on but never confronted either of us on the subject.'

Charles exclaimed in disbelief, 'You never discussed it at all! How in God's name did you all live with such a secret all these years? Does Leon know who his father is?'

'No, of course he doesn't. His birth certificate has

Suzanne as his mother and his father is declared as "koella". Suzanne reared him from birth and told him his father died before he was born.'

'God forbid, Manet. What a dangerous web of deceit and lies have been spun around this deed. Don't you think Leon deserves to know who his real father is?'

'Yes, but at the time of his birth there was no point in tearing all our lives apart. Nobody could be sure which one of us was his father anyway and Suzanne was adamant he was not to be told. Of course, we will tell Leon at some point as both my parents are now dead. I have been financially responsible for him since my father's death anyway. It is Suzanne who is afraid of the repercussions of telling him the truth. I would do it tomorrow but as I am legally not his father, I have no jurisdiction over his life.'

'Édouard, you have shocked me to the core with this revelation, but I promise I will keep what you have told me a secret. I hope you will tell the boy the truth eventually.'

'What difference would it make to Leon? Suzanne is Dutch, and she and her family do not want Leon to think badly of her, so she would rather he thought of her as his sister rather than his mother.'

'I am sorry Manet, but I can't believe you would deny the boy the right to know that you and Suzanne are his biological parents, however bad the circumstances. We are living through a war and you could die without acknowledging him as your son.'

Manet turned on him. 'Charles, I can do nothing without his mother's consent and no amount of regretting my actions now is going to change the situation. I have had plenty of time to reflect on this over the last few months but all I can do is ensure their safety and welfare. It has been difficult accepting that we have had no more children and I believe that fact may be as punishment from running away from the situation in the first place.'

Charles went over to Manet, put his arms round him and gave him a hug. 'Édouard, I do grieve for you on that count but now I maybe understand you a bit more.'

'You mean you understand there's a reason why I am such a cowardly, selfish, weak bastard where women are concerned. Don't worry, I know in my heart there is no excuse for my behaviour, but it doesn't stop me repeating it time after time.'

Charles remained silent as he knew Manet was deeply affected by the issues surrounding Leon's birth. It would be foolish to discuss it as he did not want to lose his friendship. He went to his room and Manet settled down on his sofa, but he found it difficult to sleep with the revelations churning around in his head.

oOo

The next morning, they arrived at the Louvre, determined to finish their paintings. Charles was thankful that his landscape background had dried so he could start on the outline of Philip IV and his rearing horse.

Around lunchtime, they heard heavy footsteps briskly heading towards the gallery and Courbet appeared.

Charles groaned, 'Oh God, Courbet. I was hoping we would get these portraits finished before you got back. Promise me you are not going to pull our work to pieces?'

Courbet laughed, 'As you two well know, it is all about your interpretation of the Master. You have to convince me that your work mirrors Velázquez and as I consider myself an expert, you have a difficult job to do. However, you both appear to be doing a reasonable job.'

Manet exclaimed, 'Don't think you are staying here to watch me paint this for the rest of the day. I do not need the pressure of you behind me watching and maybe criticising my work. Charles may be used to it, but I certainly am not!'

Courbet laughed, 'Don't worry Manet, I totally understand as I would not want it either. I will leave you both in peace and come back around 7 p.m. Perhaps we could have a drink later?'

Charles said, 'We have to finish today so there can be no breaking off until the portraits are complete. Manet has to leave tomorrow to return to Le Havre and his troop.'

They had a brief break for lunch and then continued in total silence. Manet finished first at around 6 p.m. and several of the copyists were watching the final stage. He prowled round his painting, viewing it from every angle, and eventually asked Charles to take a look. He surveyed both portraits from six feet away and was delighted with the result. Manet had crafted his work to mirror Velázquez's longer brushstrokes, and the definition of the Venus figure was perfect.

'I think you will be able to fool the majority of people with this painting and that's all that matters. Our aim is to produce copies should the Germans decide to purloin them and remove them from Paris. Hopefully, they won't have the expertise to know whether they are originals or copies. As long as we have the originals in a safe place then that is the most important thing.'

He returned to his easel to make the final touches to Philip IV's horse and by 7 p.m. he had finished. Courbet returned and confirmed his approval of both canvasses and they left to go to a local bar for dinner.

After the meal, Courbet had to leave so Manet and Charles lingered with a bottle of wine.

Manet said, 'Have you had any news of Marie recently?'

'No, my last letter was six weeks ago and now all post has ceased, and the only way is via balloon. I pray for their safety every day and if I get them both back alive and well I will never be parted from them again.'

'Come back to Le Havre with me; you will be safer there.'

'I can't, Manet. I have too much to do to protect the paintings in the Louvre. Only two-thirds of them have been copied and people are relying on me to organise the work. Maybe once they are finished I will consider getting out of Paris, but it won't be easy.'

'I will be bringing in food from England in two weeks' time; promise you will consider it again when I get back.'

'I intend to see it through Manet and will join the National Guard and protect the Louvre for as long as I can.'

'Charles, you are no warmonger and once the Germans invade Paris you will be extremely vulnerable.'

'Perhaps I am fighting for a lost cause rather than to defend my country, but I would rather die than live without Marie and my daughter anyway.' He hugged Manet and said, 'You keep yourself alive Manet, the art world needs to see more of your work, so don't go getting yourself killed.'

They both left the bar together, returning to their own studios, both acutely aware that this could have been their last meeting.

8

Marie crept into the stable-yard under the cover of darkness and made her way to the sixth stable in the first block, which belonged to the horse she had selected to steal when she had observed them from a distance last week. He was a dark bay gelding with no white markings, standing sixteen hands and although there were better bred horses, she could not risk taking one that gave anybody cause for suspicion. She unbolted the door and shut it quietly behind her. The horse was lying down, but he jumped up at her intrusion. She went straight to his head to stroke and calm him as she did not want him to make a sound. He nuzzled her cloak and immediately found Marie-Ann tied in a sling across her body, fast asleep. She moved his nose away from the baby for fear of waking her up. She had taken a saddle and bridle from the tack room in the yard and she put the bridle on first, leading him to the door to put it on. She adjusted the fit as best she could in the dark. She threw the saddle and cloth over his back and girthed it up. She pulled the four pieces of cloth she had made, from the bag on her back and slipped them over each hoof of the horse, tying them up to deaden any sound of his metal shoes.

It was now around 1 a.m. and she was grateful there was no moon visible at present, just a cloudy, dark sky. She led him out of the stable and closed his door furtively. She led him away from the stables and thankfully, none of the other horses whinnied. She found the mounting block, jumped on and then tightened the girth again. She walked him over towards the field where they were turned out during the day. Her safest way out would be jumping the stone wall at the far side of the field, but she had no idea whether he would be willing to jump it, especially if he could not see the landing side.

As if prompted by her plight, the clouds parted, and a sliver of moonlight filtered through. She cantered him down to the wall and let him walk up to it and she selected the safest landing she could find as the ground was lower on the other side. She then trotted and cantered him in a small circle to test his responses to her aids. He obeyed her every movement and she took a deep breath and cantered him towards the wall. The moonlight had increased, and she steered him to her selected take-off point. They were precisely three strides from the wall and she talked to him quietly and urged him forward. To her great relief, he took off and they cleared the wall perfectly and landed safely on the other side. She cantered down the hill on the route she had walked several times and headed for the river below. When she reached the river, she jumped down, took the covers off his hooves and put them back in her bag. Marie-Ann stirred but was still asleep. She remounted and took him along the river pathway, which ran parallel with the road, and started her long journey from Lille to Paris.

She walked along the path as it was too narrow to go any faster, especially as it was dark under the trees. After about twenty minutes she left the river and came out onto a grassy track. She knew this led into a village that was not held by the Prussian army. She had selected a suitable farm where there was an empty barn and she led her horse into the barn and gave him some hay and water and then she fed Marie-Ann and managed to sleep fitfully for a few hours.

At 6 a.m. she woke Marie-Ann and gave her small pieces of an apple to eat and some strawberries she had brought with her. Marie-Ann toddled round the barn while she tacked up her horse. She had a look at his teeth and reckoned he was about six years old. His breeding was a combination of a saddle horse crossed with a Hanoverian and he had retained more of the lighter frame. He had big eyes and ears and a gentle nature. He showed obvious interest in Marie-Ann as she toddled towards him and he lowered his head to nuzzle her hair as she came within range. Marie checked the area to ensure nothing was in sight and then pulled on her young man's cap and fastened the cloak around her, concealing Marie-Ann from view completely.

She steered around the village perimeter and just as she turned the corner, she heard approaching horses. She pulled into the churchyard and hoped she could conceal herself and the horse from view by the hedge. Three German soldiers appeared. The first was an officer with two troopers riding behind as guards, all well-armed with rifles and swords. She put her hand on her horse's nose, fearing he would whinny. To her horror, the commander halted at the gate into the churchyard and ordered one of the guards to dismount and as she pressed herself into the hedge, the guard opened the gate and proceeded to knock on the door of the house that was attached to the church. She could see no escape for them as the churchyard had a high wall on two sides and a big hedge on the other. Her only way out was through the gate. The guard had not seen her as he walked up the path and banged on the door, but the other two were on the other side of the gate. The door was answered by a woman who obviously did not speak German. The guard shouted for his commander and he dismounted and came up the path towards the house. She assumed they were asking for a drink or some food, so she waited until the officer and guard were invited inside and she walked slowly towards the gate. She could hear the guard on the other side holding the two horses; she had no alternative but to try and break out before the other men returned.

As she dug her heels into the horse, the house door opened again, and the commander appeared with a basket of food. He saw her immediately and shouted 'Stop!' in French. She kicked her horse through the gate and turned right, away from the guard. He had difficulty controlling the three horses, which gave her a few seconds' head start but she knew the commander would be after her in a flash. She galloped back in the direction she had come, hoping she could make it to the farm she had sheltered in. The officer had recognised the tack on the horse and knew it was German. As he galloped after her, gaining ground on every stride, he raised his pistol… but just as he was about to fire, his horse tripped, and the gun discharged. The bullet went whistling past her cap by her left ear, but it had enough force to knock her sideways as it discharged. She felt her left shoulder hit the ground, and then oblivion.

The commander reached her first and as he dismounted, he heard the cry of a child. He had a pistol in his hand and went over to her and he could see she was unconscious. He grabbed her cloak, which revealed the child, fastened by a sling to her chest. At this point he assumed she was a boy until he noticed the pins in her hair. He bent down and gently released the child, picked her up and handed her to one of the guards. The other guard had retrieved her horse. He knelt over her body and saw that the bullet had gone through her cap and grazed her left ear but had not penetrated the skull. It had exploded after it missed her, and the force had made her fall to the ground. Instinctively, he knew she wasn't Belgian; her outstanding beauty could only have been French. Suddenly, he saw her hand move as she started to come around. He lifted her into a sitting position and supported her against his body with an arm around her neck and his pistol in his left hand. He saw she was struggling to focus her eyes and he spoke to her quietly, in French.

'Madame you are safe, but you have fallen into the hands of Major General Herman Reissman. I control the French prisoner of war camp at Lille, to which I am taking you.'

Marie was still struggling to come around and then she realised that Marie-Ann was not there. She could only groan her name. Her captor said, 'Your child is safe and unharmed.'

He issued instructions to his guards and began undoing the bag on her back, which he tossed to one of them for inspection. The other guard was dandling Marie-Ann on his knee and jabbering away to her in German. The first guard alerted him to two knives in her bag, one of which was a six-inch-long dagger.

'Apologies for the intrusion madame, but I must check you for concealed weapons.'

He pulled her shirt out of her breeches and ran his hand over her breasts then down her breeches and over both thighs on top of her drawers. This had an explosive effect on Marie as she tried to twist out of his grip and threw a punch, which landed him squarely on the left cheekbone. He grabbed her tightly in his arms and levelled the gun at her head.

'Madame, you are now a prisoner of the German Reich and a horse thief, do not force me into shooting you here. I do not intend to rape you or harm your child. I need to know your name, age and where you have been and where you intended to go with my horse.'

He kept the gun at her head and she replied, 'My name is Marie Carolus-Duran, and this is my daughter Marie-Ann. I am nineteen years old and have been living in Belgium since the war began. I was trying to return to Paris to find my husband who is in the National Guard, now that you have captured Paris.'

'Did you not consider how dangerous your journey would be with a child? You could have been shot by your own troops or mine.'

'Well I wasn't going to leave her behind, was I?'

He could not help smiling at her anger and the flash of hate he saw in her beautiful blue eyes.

'Ah madame, you are no ordinary woman. Do you think you can stand with my support?'

He helped her to her feet and finally replaced the gun in its holster. Marie was dizzy and had to grab his jacket. He issued instructions to his men in German.

'Madame, you will ride in front of me on my horse and Kurt will carry the child.'

'I'm perfectly capable of riding my own horse.'

'I am sure you are madame, but you are not to be

trusted and you will ride with me.' She was about to respond angrily when he shouted at her, 'You will do as you are told, or I will have you bound and gagged and roped over the saddle of your horse, which will be far more unpleasant than riding in front of me.' He immediately jumped back on his horse and trotted over to her and in one swoop, picked her up and deposited her in front of him on the saddle saying, 'Do not make me have to tie your hands; you need them for balance.'

He cantered off and she saw Marie-Ann was safely in the arms of Kurt as he rode one-handed. She could feel a strong grip around her waist and knew she would not be able to get away from him, and she had Marie-Ann's safety to consider. This German intrigued her as he was not what she had expected of a German officer. He was over six feet tall, blonde, muscular, handsome and about forty-five years old. She remembered his hand touching her breast and the moment of fear when she thought he might rape her, but she did not think he would have done that to her. She remembered Charles' last words when he left her, when he had said that no man would ever want to shoot her, but many would want to possess her – and to choose life over death if she had to. She was glad he hadn't found the dagger hidden in her boot, as she knew she may well need it.

9

Reissman reflected on this beautiful woman whom he had nearly killed and was now his prisoner, with a child in tow. When he got her back to camp in Lille she was going to be impossible to keep safe. He could only keep a handful of women prisoners to serve in the kitchens, stables or laundry. His orders were to kill any children as they would be too much trouble to rear within the confines of a prison camp. He could not allow her to serve in any of those capacities as all the men were sex-starved, even his own troops, as well as the French prisoners. He could not put her with them as they would fight each other and eventually kill her. He could not keep her locked up as he knew she would become demented. Perhaps he could keep her as a servant for himself, but she had given him enough trouble already and she was far more nobility than peasant girl. She was painfully thin and probably weighed under seven stone. Her hip bones and shoulder blades were very prominent, and she had virtually no milk to feed a one-year-old child. She was close to starvation and it would take months to restore her to full health.

She was so beautiful, he could tell he was falling

under the spell of those hypnotic blue eyes. Although he was married with two girls of his own he knew he could not harm her child, but a prison was no place to bring up a child. He doubted she would consent to have the child reared elsewhere and yet the child would be as vulnerable as her in the camp. He knew he would never harm a child but there were many men in camp who might be capable.

They stopped at lunchtime in a small village and he sent one of the guards to buy food. Marie took Marie-Ann and fed her under her cloak and he was overcome by the tenderness she showed when holding the child. It must have been very difficult for this young woman to cope during the last year. When the guard came back with the food he took her over some bread and cheese and a glass of wine and her eyes lit up. Even though she was starving, she offered the child food first and ate the remainder of the bread and cheese, quickly.

They approached the Lille camp. Reissman could tell that Marie was struggling to stay awake and he was concerned that she could be suffering from concussion. As they rode in, they soon became the centre of attention for his soldiers and the prisoners in the pens. As he lifted Marie down, she took one step and then fainted; he just caught her before she hit the ground. He picked her up and took her straight to the medical ward in search of Dr Kohl. Kurt followed behind with the child in his arms. Dr Armand Kohl came hurrying over and ushered them into a small room. Reissman said, 'I think she may have concussion from a stray bullet and she is very thin and weak. She is also still feeding the child and has very little milk. You must do something to get her back on her feet quickly.'

Kohl answered, 'I am just a doctor, Herman, not God. Her condition has been deteriorating for the last six months at least. Leave her with me to check both her and the child over. What's her name?'

'Marie, and the daughter is called Marie-Ann. She doesn't speak German – only French. I will call back later. Make sure she eats something.'

Kohl examined her head and ear where the bullet had skimmed her and then started to undress her so that he could check her over fully. The little girl was toddling around the room. He took her clothes off and was shocked at how thin she was. He got a fresh cotton nightgown and pulled it over her head. Just as he finished, she started to come around. She panicked when she saw him, and he spoke to her calmly in French. She sat up, looking for the child and he picked Marie-Ann up and placed her in the bed with her.

'Madame, you need to eat and rest to recover your strength. I will get you some food and hot coffee. If you like, I will take the child for a bath and put her in a nightgown and bring a crib for her to sleep in next to your bed. No harm will come to either of you in my care.' He held out his arms for the child and Marie handed her over reluctantly, bestowing a kiss on her forehead, clearly terrified he would take her child away.

He took the child to the kitchen to seek out one of the cooks, whom he knew he could trust to feed and bath the baby. He selected some fresh warm bread and covered it in butter, took her a bowl of rice pudding and put fresh raspberries on top. He made her a sweet, milky coffee and took the tray back to her room. She noted her child wasn't with him and he placed the tray on her lap and sat down next to her.

'Madame, your child is being fed and bathed by one of the cooks; she is perfectly safe. Please try and eat as much as you can.' He saw her eyes widen as she saw the raspberries and he picked one up and she let him pop it in her mouth. He put the hot coffee on the bedside table next to her in case she spilled it. He could see she had been crying as the pillow was damp.

Marie tucked into the hot bread and butter and then started on the rice pudding, unable to contain her joy at the fresh bread.

'I need to ask you some questions Marie, to assess the health of you and your child. Please bear with me over the language.'

She looked up at him and smiled, 'I speak Italian, Russian and English if that makes it any easier for you. I can understand some German but have never spoken it, but I have sung in it. I was born and raised in Russia for fifteen years.'

He was quite amazed that this young woman was so well educated. He could tell by her looks and her confident attitude that she was no peasant.

'How old are you and the baby? When did you last eat any meat or fish?'

She replied, 'I am nineteen now and Marie-Anne is fourteen months old. I have not eaten meat for over a year and have only eaten what fish I have been able to catch myself, which has been very limited.'

He took her hand and inspected her fingernails. 'Your body is lacking in many essential nutrients. Is there any chance you may be pregnant again?'

She snatched her hand away and snapped at him, 'I am a married woman and have been parted from my husband for over twelve months. I was attempting to return to Paris now that you have finally seized it. My husband was in the National Guard and I have no idea whether he is alive or dead.'

At this point she burst into tears and he scooped her into his arms and stroked her hair. 'Hush little one, you are safe here now. You would never have made it back to Paris; there are hundreds of our troops between Lille and Paris. Drink your coffee before it goes cold.'

'Do you know what happened in Metz? My brother was there with Napoleon.'

He held her hand and said, 'Napoleon was defeated at Metz and lost many of his troops'.

There was a knock on the door and the cook

appeared with Marie-Ann freshly bathed and wearing a cotton nightgown. Marie held out her arms and the doctor removed the tray from the bed.

Kohl asked the cook, 'Is there anybody you know who may have some clothes suitable for the child and her mother?'

'Certainly, I will make some enquiries, Dr Kohl.' She left the room.

Marie unlaced her nightgown and fed Marie-Ann.

'I will leave you in peace, madame. Please try to get some sleep. I have asked for a crib to be located but if you can manage with the baby in your bed for the moment.'

Marie gave him a flash of a smile. 'Thank you, doctor; you have been very good to both of us. I am afraid I will find it difficult to be a model prisoner. I do not relish confinement.'

Dr Kohl replied, 'Do you have any nursing skills, Marie?'

'I'm afraid not with people, but I am good with animals and in Russia I learnt how to treat horse lameness, including making poultices using herbs and honey to treat wounds.'

'Very good Marie, those skills are very transferable to humans. Do you think you could work for me here as a nurse, treating mainly French troops? I'm afraid the nature of the work can be very harrowing, but you have a natural empathy, which would be a gift to your injured countrymen. Your beauty would work better than any drug to keep them alive.'

'I would do anything rather than be locked up but only if Marie-Ann could be cared for safely in my absence, well away from any infections.'

'I will speak to Reissman and see if we can sort something out, but rest now. I will check you and the child frequently, but you need sleep now.' He left the room and closed the door, but she heard no key being turned.

Dr Kohl went to find Reissman, who was in his office alone. He stood up as he entered and said, 'What's the matter? Is there a problem with Marie?'

Kohl new instinctively that Reissman was falling for Marie and he felt a slight twinge of jealousy.

'No, they are both fine and have been fed and are sleeping now. What do you propose to do with them? They are both in danger here; even if they don't contract any of the diseases that are raging through the prisoners, they are at risk of being raped or murdered, even by their own side.'

'I'm well aware of that. I shall confine them both in my quarters and she will have to be locked up most of the time. Even working in the kitchens would be too dangerous.'

'You can't lock her up Herman, she is already severely mentally traumatised and withdrawn – not to mention her poor physical condition, which will take months to overcome. She has some medical knowledge from her time in Russia and she could work for me as a nurse. My problem is that she is going to see some shocking sights, which I am not sure she can cope with mentally and it puts her at risk of infection, but it is better than her being confined. We will have to find a nursemaid for the child and she will have to feed her during the day. Then she will only need to be confined at night.'

'She won't be confined at night; she will be in my bed.'

Kohl stepped backwards in shock. 'Are you bloody mad, Herman? There are over 2000 French troops out there, with more arriving daily. You will have a riot on your hands if you forcibly take her as your mistress. For God's sake you are a married man with two children to start with and she is a married French Catholic woman with a child. What makes you even think she will agree to become your mistress? If she was prepared to risk death to get back to Paris to find her husband, she is not going to replace him with you. Besides, she is not the type to take orders from any man; she has a whole load of Russian stubbornness and courage in her character.'

'I know – she already gave me a black eye when I searched her body for weapons. However, she is also a prisoner and horse thief and for that alone I could have her executed.'

'Have you thought of the risk you are exposing her to with her own side? They will consider her a traitor and if they get hold of her she will almost certainly be raped and possibly even murdered. If you put her in front of our firing squad I wager you, they would not be able to shoot her. She has the beauty and charisma of Joan of Arc; men would fight just for a smile from her. She is very clever, and she would be capable of using you, far more than you would use her.'

'I don't give a damn as long as I possess her body.'

'Herman, believe me she is in no fit mental or physical state to cope with this. The sensible option is to despatch her to the nearest convent.'

'I am not prepared to lose her. I want her for myself; I could soon make her love me and forget her husband.'

'So, when we return to Germany you intend to take her back home and explain to your wife that you now have a French mistress and child moving in with you.'

'No, I would set her up in her own house. I don't intend to dispose of my wife.'

'The thought that your wife might not want anything to do with you, hasn't even crossed your mind, has it? Not to mention that the military might not be too pleased about you bringing a French spy into their midst. For God's sake Herman, either your wife or the government would shoot both of you. You need to think this through very carefully. I need to return to the hospital now.'

Reissman watched the doctor go and he put his head in his hands in despair. He had no idea why he was so determined to possess Marie as he had only just met her. Maybe he was so sex starved that she had unlocked a surge of passion and desire that he had managed to keep under lock and key so far. He had to admit that if he had been faced with executing Marie, he could not have done it. The irony of the fact that, had his horse not stumbled, he would have killed her, did not even register with him.

After dinner he could bear it no longer and he went over to the hospital bay to check on his prisoner. There appeared to be nobody around, so he quietly opened the door and walked in. She was asleep and so was the baby in the cot next to her bed. He sat down in the chair next to her, fascinated by her. Her hair had been unpinned and lay in a halo of auburn curls on the pillow. A bruise was starting to form between her left ear and eye, where the bullet had skimmed. Her skin was lightly touched by the sun and she had a sprinkling of freckles across her nose and cheeks. Her mouth was a beautiful shape and it took all his strength not to lean down and kiss her full on the lips. Just as he was debating whether to kiss her, he noticed her eyes flicker open.

She was startled to see him there and said, 'Ah my gaoler, have you come to lock me up for the night?'

He smiled, 'No madame, I have just come to enquire of your health. I hope it will not be necessary to lock you up whilst you are here, but your actions will determine how I deal with you. You must also remember that you are a very beautiful woman and any man who sees you will desire you. I have here over 2000 French soldiers who haven't seen a woman for a long time and over 500 German troops as well. Your safety is my primary concern and so you must do your bit to ensure your welfare and not take any risks.'

'What would you have me do sir, wear a veil to hide myself away?'

'No madame, that would be a shame, but I could offer you my personal protection.'

'So, are you offering to escort me to Paris yourself, to find my husband?'

'No, I am afraid not; as you will see I have a lot of work to do here and it may be some time before any withdrawal by Germany or the release of French prisoners. However, if you were to bestow sexual favours on me I would ensure your safety whilst in my care.'

Quick as a flash, she sat up in bed and he never saw her right hand until it had slapped him soundly across his right cheek. 'How dare you suggest I become your mistress. I am a happily married Catholic woman and I expect you have a wife of your own. I am also a prisoner of war and expect to be treated as such.'

He now stood over her with both hands around her neck, pushing her back onto the bed. 'Madame, your husband will almost certainly be dead, and I am offering you a mutually convenient arrangement to suit both of us and your child. You are not just a prisoner of war, you are also a horse thief and I could execute you now for that crime alone. France has a long history of producing beautiful women as mistresses. I suggest you consider whether you would rather become the mistress of one man or would prefer to be passed round my men every night for their pleasure, after I have finished with you. Finally, you have hit me for the second time in a day. Do it again and I will kill you.'

She spat at him and shouted, 'You bastard German son of a bitch. Go to hell!'

As he turned away he saw Dr Kohl standing behind him, who said, 'I suggest you go before either of us does something we regret. You have had your answer. I will take over their care from now on; I consider you relieved of that duty.'

Reissman stormed out of the room, furious with himself for losing his temper and threatening her. God, she was such a fascinating brave woman and she had shown no fear of him throughout the entire episode. Whatever made him say he would pass her round his men when all he wanted to do was love and protect her? The last thing he wanted was to force her into being his mistress; he wanted her to love him, not hate him. Now he had ruined everything.

Dr Kohl went to Marie and held her hand. She had tears running down her cheeks but made no sound. 'I am so sorry that Reissman said those things to you. It is totally out of character; he is usually an honourable man. The problem is, I suspect, he has fallen in love with you. You seem to have this effect on men Marie and unfortunately, you now find yourself surrounded by them.'

'Dr Kohl, do you think men can separate the acts of love and sex? Is it possible to love one woman but have sex with another at the same time?'

'Marie, if you need spiritual guidance we have a Catholic priest in the camp and I will see he visits you tomorrow. Yes, I do think men can separate sex from love. Men do have a problem with faithfulness and some men will take sex when and where they can without necessarily wishing to dishonour their wives. However, I don't think it is just that easy for women.'

'No Dr Kohl, both Charles and I are Catholics, but we do not believe in some of its practices. However, we both believe in the sanctity of marriage and in being faithful. Charles waited six months during our engagement and one night, two months before the wedding, I conspired to seduce him, and he would not take me. He said I was his gift from God and he would not tempt fate by taking me before we were married.'

'He sounds like a very honourable man, Marie and he obviously loves and cherishes you.'

'Before he left me in Belgium he said that he knew that men would find me attractive and desire me and he told me to choose life over death. Do you think he would forgive me if I let another man have sex with me to protect myself and Marie-Ann? Was that his way of granting me permission to be unfaithful?'

Kohl gathered her up in his arms. 'Oh, my poor child, you have to do what's best for you and Marie-Ann. Your husband may already be dead, and he probably realised that was a possibility before the war began. He thought you would be safe over the border in Belgium, but he didn't ever envisage Paris being invaded by Germany and troops entering via Belgium. You don't have to concede to Reissman's wishes. I will do my utmost to protect you here in the camp. I do not think he intends to harm you and I will not allow him to pressure you any further.'

'I know Charles is not dead. I would feel it in my heart if he was.'

'Let's hope you are right. Now try and get some sleep; you have had a very trying day.'

10

Marie woke the next day feeling refreshed but with a slight headache. Marie-Ann was just starting to stir in her cot. She saw a mirror in the room, so she went over to inspect her appearance. Her cheek and her eye socket were starting to bruise and for the first time she realised just how close to death she had been. Had the bullet exploded as it grazed her, she would have died instantly but the impact had still been strong enough to unseat her from the horse. She felt pain in her left shoulder and pulled the nightgown down and she saw the bruising starting on her shoulder blade, which must have been from her first contact with the ground.

Dr Kohl came in and smiled at her. 'How are my two patients this morning? Let me have a closer look at your shoulder.'

Marie allowed him to examine her shoulder and he said, 'I can't believe it did not break in the fall; you have no flesh to protect the joint.' He ran his finger over her cheekbone and eye socket. 'I don't think anything is broken there.' He looked into those beautiful sapphire blue eyes and realised that if he did not step back from her now, he would be another man to drown in their depth. He saw the flash of recognition across her face and he knew she was testing her power. He walked over to the crib and picked Marie-Ann up; she gurgled at him and reached for his nose.

Someone knocked on the door and a young woman entered.

Dr Kohl said, 'Ah Sylvie, this is Madame Duran and her daughter Marie-Ann.' Turning to Marie he said, 'Sylvie has a son about the same age and she is going to take care of her during the day while you assist me in the hospital. Reissman has made one of his own rooms available and we have found some toys for Marie-Ann to play with. She will be safe with Sylvie and you will take your meals together under my supervision. Have you fed her this morning?'

'No, not yet', Marie replied.

'Sylvie, can you take Marie-Ann for her breakfast and then bring her back for madame to feed? Perhaps you could bring some clothes for her as well.'

Marie pushed herself between himself and Sylvie saying, 'Dr Kohl, can I trust you with my precious daughter? Promise me you will not take her away from me.'

'Madame, you have my word that no harm will come to her.' He handed her over to Sylvie and she left the room.

'Dr Kohl, I need to keep breastfeeding Marie-Ann.'

He turned to her, 'I know that Marie, but she

needs to be on a proper, solid, high protein diet. At fourteen months old she is very underweight and already suffering from rickets and a lack of calcium. You can still feed her yourself, but I need to raise your weight by at least two stone as you are malnourished too. Currently, your reproductive system has shut down and you aren't ovulating, but you need to tell me immediately if that changes as your nutritional level rises. You are in no fit state mentally or physically to sustain another pregnancy.'

'I am well aware of that, Dr Kohl.'

'Good. There is a bathroom across the corridor with a lockable door and even some fluffy white towels. Why don't you go and have a bath and by then I may have some clothes for you to put on and I'll take you to Marie-Ann. You can have your breakfast with her and then join me on my rounds.'

She was overjoyed to have a real bath again and to wash her hair. She felt like she was in an expensive hotel when she wrapped herself in the generous towel. She returned to her room to find a pile of clothes consisting of a chemise, drawers, wool stockings, a simple black dress, a white full-length apron and a white cap. She dressed quickly and although it was still wet, she plaited her lustrous auburn hair into a long plait and then pinned it around her head. She put on the white cap and pinned it to her hair. Dr Kohl returned and studied her appearance with approval.

'Good – you look the part now Marie, but I

must remind you that you are still a prisoner. You will not have long conversations with the other prisoners. Your language skills will be useful as we appear to have both English and Italian prisoners in the camp. I hardly need to warn you of the dangers of over-familiarity with the patients as regards your own personal safety. Please keep those beautiful blue eyes lowered away from the men. Do not leave the medical building under any circumstances. You may only return to the room where Marie-Ann is being cared for, unaccompanied. If you disobey my orders Reissman will have you locked up permanently and I am sure you would not want that to happen.'

They set off and when she reached the room where Marie-Ann was, she was amazed at the food laid out on the table. There were boiled eggs, toast and marmalade, slices of ham and cheese and a jug of steaming hot coffee. Dr Kohl smiled at her surprise.

'Yes, Marie, that is all for you and I need you to eat as much as you can to build up your strength.'

Marie needed no further encouragement; she tucked into the food with relish. She sampled the ham first, having had no meat at all for over twelve months. Dr Kohl sat at the table with her and poured himself a coffee and ate a slice of toast. The door opened and Reissman appeared. He approached the table in his usual brisk fashion.

'Madame Duran, I am pleased to see you are well this morning and enjoying your breakfast. Dr Kohl, do you not think this is a little soon for madame to be working on the wards?'

Dr Kohl replied, 'No, or she would not be here. The sooner she starts, the more used to me she will become.'

Reissman said, 'I would like to speak to madame alone.'

Dr Kohl barked, 'Not now. I need her to accompany me on my rounds. I will send her to your office after 6 p.m.'

Marie could sense the friction between the two men and she took the opportunity to take her coffee over to the other side of the room and scooped Marie-Ann up and settled in a comfortable chair to feed her.

She could see Reissman having a heated conversation with Dr Kohl and knew he was objecting to her feeding Marie-Ann. However, he stormed out of the room and it looked as though Dr Kohl had won the argument. She knew she would have to concede to Reissman's desire at some point, but she did not want the added risk of pregnancy complicating the situation. She knew he would take her by force if he had to, but she was planning to do it on her own terms.

Dr Kohl showed her the way to the medical centre and specifically pointed out Reissman's bedroom and office on the way. She hardly dared look at him but knew he had done it as a warning.

As they went into the medical block she was whisked upstairs to his office. From an internal window, she could see the ward below set out with fifty beds, all of them occupied. Two doctors entered the room, aged in their late twenties. She was introduced to them and she remembered to keep her eyes lowered to the floor. They were both made aware by Dr Kohl that she was always a prisoner and had to be supervised.

They went downstairs to the main ward and as she swept through the door with the doctors, the background noise ceased instantly. She could feel fifty pairs of eyes boring into her and a shiver of fear ran up her spine. She could already hear the crude whispers of the men who assumed she was German.

The first bed Dr Kohl stopped at was occupied by a soldier who had a massive leg wound, judging by the size of the bandage below the knee. There was total silence in the room and she could hear the men straining to catch the scene.

'Marshal Marcon, may I introduce Madame Duran, a French prisoner who is going to be working on the wards. As you are the most senior officer in here I would like you to convey to your men that the first person who touches or speaks to her inappropriately will find himself in a cell. She is here to attend to their medical needs, not their sexual needs, and I would like you to make that very clear.'

Marie could feel herself blushing, but she kept her eyes fixed on the floor. Marshal Marcon replied with a laugh and leant forward, took and kissed her hand. 'Madame Duran, may I welcome you to the camp. God must have answered our prayers and sent an angel to tend to the wounded. Rest assured, madame that my men will behave honourably as only Frenchmen could.' His words were met by cheering and clapping from the men. The two young doctors looked astonished but at least Dr Kohl was smiling.

He said, 'Marshal, I need to remove this bandage. Perhaps madame could provide a distraction by chatting to you while we do it.' He signalled one of the doctors to fetch a chair and he placed it level with Marcon's waist but facing away from his leg and motioned Marie to sit down.

'Madame, please tell me how you came to be captured and became the first female prisoner in camp,' said Marcon.

'I stole a horse from the stables here to take me and my daughter to Paris. I made it as far as Sainte-Agathe and unfortunately ran into Reissman and two guards. I escaped but he fired his pistol and it narrowly missed my left ear then exploded and knocked me from my horse. I was dressed as a man with my daughter hidden under my cloak and he recognised the tack, so he knew it was one of his horses.'

Marcon winced. 'How the hell did you get the horse out of the stables unchallenged, and why risk taking one from here?'

'There are no horses or donkeys alive within a ten-mile radius. I had to risk taking a German horse, but I am an expert when it comes to horses. I made covers for his hooves, selected him well in advance so I knew his temperament and made sure he had no significant markings. I took him out by the turnout paddock and jumped the wall by the light of the moon.'

Marcon swore as the bandage was finally removed from his leg. 'Pardon, madame. If only I had men with your brains, courage and resourcefulness, we wouldn't be on the losing side.'

Dr Kohl said to Marcon, 'This leg is looking much better; we seem to have stopped the infection. Marie, do you think you could put a new bandage on the leg?'

Marie hesitated and said, 'I only know how to bandage a horse's leg if that will do.'

Her comment was met with spontaneous laughter from the men in adjacent beds and the two young German doctors. Marcon howled with laughter and said, 'Kohl, you have pulled a master stroke here; this beautiful woman will save more lives than any of your pills or potions. She's an absolute breath of fresh air and she can tend my wounds anytime.'

Marie had already been given the bandage by the junior doctor and he had applied a fresh linen strip onto the leg, with ointment. Deftly, she bandaged Marcon's leg and as she finished, loud applause and cries of 'Bravo!' filled the ward.

Nobody had been aware of the approach of Reissman in all the excitement. His voice rang out,

'What is going on here, Dr Kohl? Why is the ward in uproar and men out of their beds?'

Dr Kohl replied, 'They are merely observing Madame Duran's first wound treatment class – and what an admirable job she has done.'

Marcon said, 'Reissman, you are supposed to inform me when any French prisoner is admitted. I wish to know your plans to ensure Madame Duran and her daughter's safety, which I should have been consulted on.'

Marie and Dr Kohl exchanged horrified glances in case Reissman made a comment about taking her as his mistress.

Calm and controlled as ever, Reissman replied, 'Well, that's why I am here now, Marshal Marcon – to inform you that Madame Duran is going to serve in the hospital whilst her daughter is being cared for in my quarters by a nursemaid. I shall ensure madame's safety is my top priority.' The room was deathly silent.

Marcon pointed at Reissman. 'Harm one hair on madame or her child's head and you will have the biggest riot you have ever seen on your hands. Frenchmen treat their women with the utmost respect and madame will have nothing to fear from my men. Can you say the same about your men?'

'But of course, but to ensure maximum security I am taking personal responsibility for their safety.' He marched back out of the ward without further comment. Marcon grabbed her hand and pulled her down close to his face. 'Madame, if you have any fears for your safety, let me know or pass a message via Kohl.'

Marie whispered, 'I thank you Marshal for your concern, but I think I can handle Reissman.'

Marcon whispered, 'Be careful; he has a ruthless controlling streak and he would not hesitate to kill you or your child if you posed a threat.'

11

At lunchtime, Marie left to check on Marie-Ann and spend some time with her whilst eating their lunch. She managed to get her to eat some sausages and potatoes followed by strawberries and raspberries with fresh cream. She got down on the rug with Marie-Ann and played with her, something she hadn't done for a long time. Dr Kohl joined them and ate a quick lunch.

'You were magnificent this morning, my dear – you have your men eating out of your hand. Marcon's threat of a riot will have registered with Reissman and may just make him back off.'

'I doubt it Dr Kohl, I have seen that look in men's eyes before; he is like a lion stalking its prey. He is going to have me with or without my permission.'

'He is very attracted to you, Marie. Your beauty and bravery appeal to his German mind. You are so very different from German women; you must have fostered your independent streak in Russia.'

'If I negotiated a deal with him do you think he would abide by my conditions?'

'In principle yes, but if you push him too hard he could just as easily kill you. Could you really let him make love to you without having some feelings towards him? You don't strike me as that type of woman. It won't be once a week, you know – it will be every day and maybe several times a day. Are you attracted to him enough to put up with that? He will never release you if that's what you are hoping. He may not even allow you to return to Paris when it's over; he may want to take you back to Germany.'

Marie exploded, 'Surely not, he will want to return to his own wife and children and I certainly don't want to live in Germany.'

'But if he is besotted with you and wants to keep you as his mistress he could force you to go with him.'

'Then I would have to kill him before he kills me.'

'Believe me, Reissman has a lot of experience in killing and he could strangle you with one hand in your current physical state. If he tired of you, or you became a problem to him, he would not hesitate to do it.'

'Dr Kohl, I have experience in killing too. Perhaps he has the edge on strength, but I have the edge on surprise.'

'Then perhaps you are two of a kind and that's what attracts you to him, but you are playing a very dangerous game. Reissman is a master tactician; he has not been elevated to his current position in the army by chance. He is always on top of his game and he would not let his feelings for a woman prejudice his judgement.'

'Ah, but he has always fought men; he does not understand how women think or react.'

'Marie, you are playing with fire and likely to get burnt. He has a desire to get you pregnant, you know.'

'What? Dr Kohl, please explain to me why it is that men want to procreate with me.'

'Well that's very simple my dear, just look in the mirror. What man could not desire you?'

They returned to the ward, where Marie spent the afternoon shadowing Dr Jager and mainly changing wound dressings. Dr Kohl said he would spare her the operating theatre on her first day, to her utmost relief. She felt exhilarated – at last, she was doing something useful and communicating with people – she had been so alone for a long time. Despite Dr Kohl's instructions about physical contact, when she felt the need to give comfort she held patients' hands and she saw how much relief it gave them. She chatted to them about their families, their injuries and their lives, trying to give them hope that there was going to be a future. She met an Englishman who had married a French girl and owned a small baker's shop near Montmartre. He had joined up only six months ago when the war had escalated, and Paris was threatened. He had heard of Charles and knew his studio; she could easily have purchased bread from their shop. He told her gruesome tales of the Paris siege and how they had been reduced to eating rats, cats and dogs. Would Charles have survived being starved for the second time in his life?

At 6 p.m. Dr Kohl appeared to take her to Reissman's office.

'Time to go, Marie, and see the lion in his den. Be brave and don't give in. Fight for what you know is right. Take courage from your own countrymen; use their strength to back up your own.'

Reissman dismissed Kohl immediately and was not prepared to include him in their discussion. He went over to the dresser and produced a bottle of wine and two glasses, which he filled, then passed one over to her side of the desk.

'I think you may need a drink after witnessing some of the scenes in the hospital today. Please join me. You appear to have been accepted by the prisoners as a nurse even though your qualifications do not entirely fit the bill. As long as you carry out your duties as a nurse you may continue. However, my spies are everywhere, madame and if you step out of line I will have you locked up permanently. If I see any unrest in the prisoners I shall have no hesitation in hanging you in front of them for being a spy. I don't believe you are the wife of a lowly Paris artist. I think you are much more likely to be a member of the deposed French aristocracy, who has just got caught up by accident. Perhaps your husband was captured, and you are trying to return to your chateau in France.'

Marie could scarcely believe what she was hearing

but kept calm, took a drink of wine and replied, 'I am flattered you consider me to have aristocratic heritage but if you are judging me by my looks and education I regret I have no connection with the French court. I was reared in the Russian court for fifteen years but regrettably, not as a member of the Romanov dynasty. My father was there to teach music in St. Petersburg and I was educated there, not in Moscow. If I was a member of the French aristocracy, why would I be risking my neck stealing a horse from the mighty German army? Surely, I could have afforded several of my own and servants to do my bidding, as well.'

'I made you a proposition last night and I want an answer.'

'You mean the one of becoming your mistress? I recall giving you an answer. I would have thought that was a fairly clear refusal as I can't see any advantages in this arrangement for me, only for you.'

'But surely a comfortable lifestyle and my protection to ensure the life of yourself and your daughter are reward enough?'

'So, you expect me to break the marriage vows I gave to my husband, whom I love with my heart, body and soul, to be your bedtime plaything. You must be mad! I will face death with honour knowing that I tried to do everything to keep my daughter alive and return to him. Put me in the pens with the French soldiers; not one of them would harm me.'

'If your husband is still alive and in the National

Guard I can assure you that even as we speak, German troops are marching into Paris with orders to kill anyone who defends it – man, woman or child. There will be no prisoners; they will all die, and Paris will burn.'

Desperately trying to control her emotions and fighting to stop the scene he described from penetrating her brain, she took a deep breath and said, almost in a whisper, 'I know you can overpower me at any time and take me without my consent but if you do I will kill you and if I can't achieve that, I will kill myself!'

Reissman jumped up, ran around the desk, dropped to his knees and took her hand. 'Marie, can't you see I don't want to hurt you? I am falling in love with your beautiful body. I just want to protect you for the rest of your life.'

This time she stood up and snatched her hand out of his then grabbed him by his shirt collar, leaning threateningly over him.

She screamed, 'My body is not mine to give, or yours to take, it belongs to my husband as sanctified by God and the laws of the Catholic Church on the 22nd September 1868. Those whom God have joined together let no man put asunder!' She followed this with a resounding slap to his face and pushed past him and ran out of the room.

She ran to the room where Marie-Ann had been but found nobody there. Perhaps she had been taken for a bath. She threw herself down in the chair and sobbed from the sheer frustration and anger she felt. It was a full ten minutes before she realised that she had slapped Reissman for the third time and he had threatened to kill her if she did it again.

She heard his leather boots stomping down the corridor, but she didn't hear any more footsteps or clanking of armour. He flung the door open and marched in. She jumped up and turned her back on him.

'Yes, I have only just realised that I hit you yet again but if you are going to kill me then grant me leave to choose my own method of despatch. I do not want to hang like a common criminal. I would prefer to be beheaded by a Frenchman's sword and you have plenty to choose from out there.'

She heard him moving towards her and for one moment she thought he may be intending to carry out her wishes although she hadn't heard him unsheathe his sword. He turned her round, took her hand and dropped to his knees.

'Madame, may I offer my sincere apologies for my vile, threatening behaviour towards the most beautiful and bravest woman I have ever encountered. I surrender to your superior intellect and whiplash tongue and promise never to touch your divine body or harm one hair on you or your child's head but beg you to allow me to be your friend and confidante whilst we await our countries' fates.'

Marie was too astonished to speak; she just looked at him in amazement and he continued. 'May I also request you refrain from hitting me in the future? It really sullies my reputation as an officer to have a woman's handprint across my cheek.'

Marie roared with laughter and retorted, 'Don't worry, you are in a long line of men that I have dealt the same blow to, including my own husband, Edouard Manet, several Russians (including one who pushed his luck and I murdered) along with a few Frenchmen who forgot their code of chivalry.'

'Perhaps we could call a truce and over dinner you could tell me the story of this unfortunate mens' club of which I have now reluctantly become a member.'

There was a knock at the door and the nursemaid appeared with Marie-Ann. She informed her she had eaten well all day and was ready for her bedtime feed. Marie moved further down the room to the comfy chair, unlaced her chemise and pulled the dress down to feed her.

Reissman picked a book off the shelf and sat down in another comfy chair, directly facing her. He pretended to read his book, but she knew he was watching her feed Marie-Ann very closely, with an expression that she recognised as she had seen it on her husband's face when he had watched Freya feeding Louis. The dawning realisation that Reissman was observing her not just in a male lascivious sexual way, but openly declaring his intention to mate with her, made her gasp for breath. How long was she going to be able to keep him at bay? He may have pledged to leave her alone and even meant it sincerely, but what would happen when he got drunk or his sexual frustration overwhelmed him? The longer he waited, the more chance there was of her fertility returning.

She could not bear the prospect of being reunited with Charles and carrying another man's baby; it would kill their marriage instantly even though it would not have been her fault. Supposing she produced a male child, would Reissman be satisfied to take him back to Germany? Could she even contemplate handing over her baby for someone else to rear… and would Charles even allow it? The hopelessness of the situation overwhelmed her, and tears started pouring down her cheeks. She kissed her daughter's head to hide her tears.

Reissman noticed and said, 'Marie, are you, all right? You appear distressed.'

She summoned her inner strength and replied, 'I am fine, just a little tired and emotional from seeing so many wounded men. Why do men fight wars over stupid pieces of land? Is it just to show strength and dominance? I can't even recall what the justification was for this bloody war. Surely people matter more than land?'

Before he could answer, the nursemaid returned for Marie-Ann. Marie handed her over and the girl said, 'Madame I will settle her in her crib in the room that has been made ready in Major General Reissman's quarters.'

She replied, 'But I thought I would be staying

over in the medical centre?'

Reissman said, 'No Marie, you are not safe sleeping in the medical centre; someone could attack you. Remember I promised Marshal Marcon that I would oversee your security personally.'

She felt the noose tighten around her neck by one notch. She vowed she would go and see the Huguenot priest tomorrow. There was no point in approaching the Catholic priest; she would never make him understand her predicament.

12

There was a knock at the door and one of the servants appeared with a tray full of food and wine and set the table for two.

Reissman came over to her, 'Come, Marie, let's eat. I have had the kitchen locate some grapes especially for you. May I undo your hair? I do like to see it flowing free.'

She was rather taken aback by this but muttered, 'Yes, provided that is all you undo.' She gave him a withering look to warn him off stepping over the mark.

He carefully unpinned her long plait and ran his hand through it to release the strands. She remembered when Charles had unpinned her hair at Lille Academy, when she had been sitting for her portrait. But Charles had unpinned her curls and then plonked a delicate kiss on her forehead.

She moved over to the table and for the first time, realised she was hungry. There was a large piece of battered cod and some new potatoes and fresh peas. She knew she could not refuse the food because she needed it but felt like she was part of a horse breeding experiment. She would have to keep all her wits about her to keep him at arm's length, so she resolved to chat and be sociable without flirting.

Reissman said, 'Now tell me about all these men you have slapped across the face. I'm pleased to see your husband features on the list. Did he try to impose himself on you prior to the wedding?'

A surge of anger swept through her and she answered sarcastically, 'No, he did not attempt any such behaviour; he is a perfect gentleman. In fact, it was me who contrived to tempt him eight weeks before our wedding, and he declined.'

Reissman's eyebrows shot up and he retorted, 'There aren't many men who would do that with a stunning beauty like you.'

'Precisely my point – my husband is a very special man and it was important to him that his bride was a virgin on her wedding day and untouched by any other man. That is why there is a string of men who thought they could take advantage and they all got slapped, but only you dared to offend me three times. The Russian who tried a second time, I stabbed to death at the age of fourteen.' She saw the slightest twitch of his mouth. She knew she had better back off or she would end up fighting with him again.

'You killed a man when you were still barely a child? Did you get away with his murder? Does your husband know you did this?'

'I didn't plan the murder, but I covered my tracks very well. There were several other possible suspects, and who would expect a child to kill a man? I did not tell my husband, or my parents for that matter. I knew I would never have any cause to punish my husband.'

'But by your own admission you said you did slap him.'

'Yes, but it wasn't just a slap. I knocked him unconscious because forty-eight hours after our wedding he stood as "second" in a duel that Manet had been called out for and was unable to fight as he had fallen from his horse and was concussed and unable to see.'

'Surely the challenger would have waited for Manet to recover? It need only have been postponed a week.'

'Unfortunately, the idiot that called him out, who was very much like you in character, would not postpone and then he insulted Charles and insisted on going ahead.'

'Did he win?'

'Yes, he shot him dead with a pistol. I was only told after the duel had started and as I heard two shots go off I assumed he was dead. Thankfully, he was winged by a bullet through his shoulder. When I got to him I was so incensed that he had risked his life and our future so foolishly for another man's cause, I knocked him out with one blow. I then turned on Manet and slapped his face as well leaving a sizeable imprint.'

'God, Marie what a little tiger you are when someone crosses you.'

'Exactly, so be warned. I know I am hot tempered and impetuous, and I never think of the consequences of my actions, which is probably why I am sitting here now. My husband will be mortified at the danger I have put myself and our daughter in.'

'No, he won't Marie. He will be the proudest and luckiest man on earth to be reunited with you.'

'I had already bitten him on our wedding night as it was.'

'Why? Was he rough with you?

'No, of course not. My husband has only ever given me pleasure and is the most attentive lover any woman could have.'

'But why did you bite him, then?

She laughed and blushed. 'You probably won't me believe me, but it was because he didn't make love to me on our wedding night. He made me wait until the following morning and he was right, believe me it was worth the wait! What he has taught me about sex has resulted in a marriage of mind, body and soul.'

Reissman roared with laughter. 'So, it is really true about French men being the best lovers.'

'Absolutely!'

'And do you expect your husband to have been faithful to you since you have been apart?'

'But of course, and I would know in an instant if he lied to me, as he would know if I lied to him. We have such a spiritual connection, that's why I am convinced he is still alive. I feel it in my heart.'

'But Marie, he is an artist working with women all the time and I assume he paints nude women.'

'Yes, but he *can* look but not touch, unlike 90% of the male population.'

'Well let's hope you are right. If marriage is so important to you, why do you have no wedding ring on your left hand?'

'Simply because I sold it to buy food for us to stay alive; I don't think my husband will blame me for that. He kept my engagement ring for safety and I would have no qualms if he had to sell that to keep him alive.'

They finished their meal and Reissman showed her to her new room, which was literally next door to his. As she entered, her heart sank – there was a big, wooden, canopied bed right in the centre with Marie-Ann's crib at the side. Aware of Reissman watching her face closely she tried not to react, but she saw the flicker of amusement in his eyes. However, he bade her goodnight, told her if she needed anything to let him know tomorrow, bowed and left the room.

She sat down on the bed and sighed. How long was she going to be able to keep this cat and mouse behaviour up? She knew that sparring with him was dangerous – it only needed one wrong word and her cause would be lost. She got changed and found she even had a bathroom at her disposal. She wondered whether this may have been his own room and he had given it to her as he knew he would be back in it within days, with her as his sex slave. She looked at Marie-Ann and decided not to wake her as she seemed fast asleep. She may not even wake for a night time feed now that her diet had increased, and she was on solid food. She tried to stay awake, consciously listening for his footsteps or the door opening, but she was so tired that she fell asleep within minutes. The night passed uneventfully, and she woke at 6 a.m. to the sound of the *reveille* calling the prisoners to their roll call.

Marie-Ann stirred, and she fed her as she was feeling uncomfortable as she had not fed her during the night. She could tell that in only forty-eight hours, the effect of the food had increased her milk supply… but was it enough to suppress ovulation?

After she had breakfasted alone in the sitting room, Dr Kohl arrived and had some coffee and toast. 'I am glad to see you are starting to eat, madame. Please continue, as it is vital for both of you.'

She spoke quietly although nobody else was in the room. 'How much weight do I have to gain to become fertile again?'

'I really do not know, Marie. In some women it may be two stone, in others just a small amount. It depends how fertile you are normally.'

Well, let's put it this way – I conceived Marie-Ann probably within forty-eight hours of my wedding day. However, we did have a month's honeymoon here in Lille of all places, to make certain. I never had regular courses, so it was very difficult to tell. I could miss two months and then start and miss again for another two months. The first person to suspect was my darling husband and he kept quiet until morning sickness started at eight weeks and finally my thick brain got the message.'

'How did he know?'

She blushed and whispered, 'He said I tasted different!'

Dr Kohl responded with a roar of laughter. 'Oh Marie, you are such a delight. I haven't heard of that being a scientific diagnosis of pregnancy before, but I love the graphic description.'

Marie put her hand on his and said, 'Dr Kohl, is there any way I can prevent conception without a man knowing?'

His faced flushed with anger. 'Has he taken you, Marie?'

'No, not yet. He has apologised for threatening me and promised not to take me and says he only wants to be my friend. But he watched me feed Marie-Ann last night and I saw the same look in his eyes as I did when my husband watched his sister-in-law feed her baby. Charles had never shown any interest in babies until after the wedding and then he was driven by a desperate desire to have a child. Reissman has already told you he wants a son from me and he is just biding his time until I am fertile again and then he will pounce. He has installed me in a large bedroom with a huge bed right next to his bedroom. What happens if he gets drunk one night and his sexual desire takes control?'

'I see your point, but I don't know the answer…
I will revert to my textbooks and see what I can find.
Unfortunately, I do not have a magic pill that can
help you; I may have to resort to herbs. Let's hope we
have a bit of time yet and hope you may be released
before he gets his hands on you.'

'I would like to see the Huguenot priest today.'

'But you are a Catholic, aren't you?'

'Yes, but what I need to discuss would not receive
much sympathy from a Catholic priest as all he will
do is tell me to recite 100 Hail Mary's for thinking of
breaking my marriage vows. I don't need confession
and absolution, Dr Kohl. I need help from someone
who recognises my impossible situation.'

Dr Kohl replied, 'Very well, I think it would be
better if you were to go over to the small chapel,
as Reissman's spies are everywhere. I will have you
escorted there by a guard or Reissman will kick up a
fuss about your safety, but he can't deny your religious
rights. Father Bauman will respect your privacy and
he will not report back to Reissman. The Catholic
priest, however, will.

Do you think you are up to seeing my most
seriously ill patients? I think you will have a huge
impact. Some of them are severely mentally
traumatised but if anyone can drag them back into
reality it may just be you. I am not saying it will be
easy for you Marie as you're not in the best emotional
state either. I will ensure Dr Jager is with you all the
time; you just need to talk to them. Some have given

up communicating at all and the sight of you may just make them turn a corner.'

Marie replied, 'Well if you think I can offer them some help then I am willing to try.'

After Dr Kohl had done his rounds and she had tended to any wound dressings that needed replacing, he took her through the locked door into the psychiatric ward. She took a deep breath, unaware of what she might encounter. The first patient was a young French boy who had been hit by shrapnel in the head. The wound had healed but he had not spoken since he arrived at the hospital, although Dr Kohl was sure he was aware of his surroundings. Dr Kohl introduced her and told him she was a French prisoner but acting as a nurse. He looked younger than her but when she approached, he sat up in bed and looked at her very closely. She said hello and asked him where he was from.

He reached over and grasped her hand, kissed it and very quietly and hesitantly said, 'Enchanté, madame. You are very beautiful.'

Dr Kohl's face was a picture and he asked him, 'Have you now found your voice to speak to us?'

'You are the enemy and so I don't speak to you, but she is like me – a prisoner.' He was the only one she got through to, but several were aware of her presence and over time she hoped they might begin to trust her.

Dr Kohl called her – one of the guards had come to escort her to the chapel to see Father Bauman.

It meant going through the French compound and she attracted a lot of interest. Her escort became perturbed when several men congregated and made some lewd comments, and he put his rifle in both hands. However, a loud voice shouted at the men.

'Get back, you rabble and wash your mouths out. Have you forgotten your manners in front of a French lady?'

Marie turned and gasped when she saw this man in the flesh. He was in his early thirties, had deep brown eyes and stood over six feet tall with thick, long brown hair… and he possessed a very athletic body.

'Madame Duran, I presume.' He took her hand, bowed and kissed it. 'The description of your beauty was sadly lacking; you are more beautiful than a Greek goddess. I am Capitan Fabien Laurent of the Hussars and I am at your service.'

Marie was overcome by his introduction and was on the verge of replying when one of the men he had chastised shouted, 'She may look like a goddess, but she is warming Reissman's bed every night.'

She gasped in horror and must have gone bright red and shouted, 'That is a complete and utter lie. I am a married woman with a child and I am a prisoner just like you and I share my bed with no man.'

She turned to the Capitan and said, 'I would be grateful if you would convey my innocence of this accusation to your men.'

He replied, 'Madame, accept my apologies

for this unfortunate incident. I will defend your honour to my fellow soldiers. May I escort you to your destination?' Without waiting for a reply, he took her hand and led her away from the men. He bent down and whispered in her ear, 'Madame, I appreciate your delicate situation here and only wish I could defend you on the other side of that fence.'

They had now arrived at the chapel door and he kissed her hand, bowed and walked away. Her German guard took up position outside the door. The chapel was very small but laid out with an altar at the far end and enough seats to accommodate twenty people for a small service. There was a high window at the far end and sunlight was streaming through it and bathing the altar in light. She remembered her wedding day in the beautiful Norman church where the sun had refracted through the rose stained-glass window and produced multicoloured patterns over the altar and wall. Charles had wanted to paint it as it was so beautiful. She walked up the aisle and knelt at the altar rail. There were no religious icons on the altar, just a simple wooden cross on a plain white tablecloth – no embroidered altar cloth or rich icons in this chapel.

She asked God for help to keep them safe and to reunite her with her dear husband after the war. She asked for forgiveness for putting Marie-Ann in danger but thanked God for keeping them alive. She asked him for help with her predicament of trying to keep her wedding vows and keeping Reissman at bay.

She prayed for the safety of her family and friends.

She heard a noise and Father Bauman appeared from the vestry door at the side of the altar. He wore just a plain black cassock and looked around sixty years old. He came towards her and halted in front of her, then offered her his hand to help her stand.

'Madame Duran, how can I be of service to you? Shall we take a seat?' He led her to the front pew. 'Well Madame, Dr Kohl has acquainted me with your situation and I have every sympathy with your plight. I appreciate you are in a cat and mouse predicament with the outcome balanced on a knife edge.'

'Father, would it be considered adultery if I was forced to have sex with someone other than my husband? When he left me in Belgium where he considered my daughter and I would be safe from the war, he told me that my beauty would be a danger and to choose life rather than death. Do you think that was an indication that he would forgive me if I broke my wedding vows under duress?'

'Madame, you could not be blamed for submitting while your life was being threatened as that would be considered rape. However, if you became pregnant as a result you would have an even more difficult decision to make regarding the rearing of that child. Without knowing the parties involved personally, I cannot say whether your husband could be strong enough to rear another man's child as his own. Some men can do it, others think they can but never forgive their wives even though they may have been raped, and some men could not tolerate it at all. If your love for each other – and your marriage – is strong enough then it should work, but I don't underestimate the difficulty of living in that position in any way. Have you come to me rather than the Catholic priest because you would consider abortion?'

'No Father, my personal beliefs would not tolerate such an action, but suicide may be an option.'

'What of your responsibility towards your daughter, especially if your husband does not survive the war? Could you really contemplate suicide and leave her an orphan?'

'Not by choice, but how can I rear two children alone? I am only nineteen.'

'With the same courage, bravery and resourcefulness you have shown so far… and a woman as beautiful as you will have several men willing to marry you and take on the responsibility of both children. Dr Kohl says that in your current medical condition you are unlikely to conceive easily. The war may be over soon, and prisoners released. I suggest you carry on rejecting these demands as long as possible.'

'Do you know Reissman well? Can you give me some insight as to his character so that I can appeal to his better nature?'

'He is a complex character and likes to control situations and it may be that he has fallen in love with you and that just may stop him from going one step too far. He wants to be an honourable man, but he is also only human. A woman as beautiful as you would be hard for any man to resist.'

'My countrymen already think I am warming his bed willingly, and that makes me a traitor in their eyes. I have defended my innocence but for how long I can survive, I don't know.'

'Madame, the prisoners have nothing to do all day and when they see Reissman even look at you, they can tell he desires you and automatically assume he has taken this further.'

'But Father, this is exactly the problem. They watch him covet me, but I do not return his advances.'

'All I can advise you is to carry on resisting and even if you fail you will have done your utmost to prevent it in God's eyes, and your husband's. Do not contemplate suicide, madame. Your husband told you to choose life before death, and he was right. Now come and kneel at the altar rail and I will bless you and pray for you and let's hope the Almighty is listening.'

She felt a strange calmness come over her as she prayed with the priest's hand on her head as he blessed her, and the sunlight shone through the window and illuminated both of them. Charles had always maintained he had been guided by the light, so maybe this was a sign that God was listening.

Marie returned to the hospital and carried on with her work with renewed vigour. At least she was making a difference to some people. She had now been with three patients who died from infection and she held their hands while they took their last breath and although very frightening at first, she was proud that she had been able to do it. She even assisted Dr Kohl in the operating theatre and she had coped with seeing some horrendous amputations. For the first time in her life she felt she was giving rather than receiving, and it felt good.

She had not forgotten the impact that meeting Capitan Fabien Laurent had on her, either. He was stunning and had the same sapphire blue eyes as her. He resembled Charles in many ways but never had she felt such an instant sexual attraction to a man. If he had been in Reissman's place she knew she could not have resisted; her body would have melted at his first touch. What that said about her marriage, she did not know. She just knew that she desperately ached for the physical contact and intimacy that having sex gave her. Perhaps this meant that her fertility was returning, which was a dangerous prospect. However, the chances of her being in close contact with the dashing Capitan were unlikely. At least she had experienced what men felt when they looked at her. She was unnerved by the intensity of her feelings.

13

Marie returned to her bedroom after an affable meal with Reissman, who seemed to be in an ebullient mood. However, he had gone back to his office rather than his bedroom, saying he had some work to finish before morning. She settled down into her bed to go to sleep after a hard day.

She woke to the feel of fingers caressing her hair and as she opened her eyes, she saw Reissman leaning across the bed. He had his shirt and breeches on and had switched the light on. She gasped and tried to sit up, but his hand was pinning her to the pillow by her hair. She could smell the drink on his breath and her heart sank. The scenario she had feared most was finally unravelling before her eyes.

'What in God's name are you doing?'

'I want you and I can't wait any longer.'

'But you promised you would leave me alone and we would just be friends. You know I cannot give myself to you; I belong to my husband.'

'It is only sex and you are no untouched pious virgin. You are a beautiful woman with a body like Venus, made for loving. Only we will know about it. If you return to your husband, he need never know.'

'But he will know when he looks at me; our minds are connected, and what's more, God will know.'

He leant over her and said menacingly, 'You madame, have a habit of using God for your own cause as and when it suits you.'

'But you said you loved me and would never hurt me.'

'I won't hurt you. I will make it as pleasurable for you as it will be for me.'

Just at this point, he relaxed the grip on her hair and she twisted away to the right and tried to escape from the bed. His hand was too quick, and he had hold of the back of the collar of her nightdress. As she pulled away it ripped to her waist and she fell to the floor. His hand was round her neck as he pulled her to her feet and with the other hand, he ripped the nightdress off her body.

'We can dispense with that. Now stand still!'

He surveyed her naked body from the front, with his hand so tightly round her neck, she knew he would strangle her in seconds if she attempted to move. He ran his hand down her back and then round her right buttock and then between her thighs. The thought flashed through her mind that she could offer him oral sex, but she knew that would inevitably lead to full sex and then she would have revealed her skill.

She felt his hand move from between her legs and to her horror, she could feel him undoing his belt.

She cried out, 'No, please tell me you are not

going to thrash me as well as rape me.'

'Don't give me ideas, my beauty. No, I am just going to secure those deadly hands of yours.' Within seconds he had secured both wrists with the leather belt and he pushed her back against the bed. As she fell back, he pulled her round until her head was on the pillow and he pulled her hands up and secured the belt strap to the bedhead. He undid his breeches and forced her legs apart as he lay on top of her.

Sheer terror overcame her, and she begged him to leave her alone. She could not scream as Marie-Ann was within inches of the bed and she could not bear the thought of her waking up and seeing her mother being raped; she had seen enough dreadful sights in the last year. Who would come to her rescue anyway? She was in his quarters; there was nobody else about.

He was attempting to kiss her, and she was twisting her head away. He held her neck and he forced her mouth open by holding her nose. As he put his tongue in her mouth she bit him. He slapped her across the face and real tears ran down her cheeks. She made one final attempt to appeal to him.

'If you rape me I will kill myself. I cannot live with the shame.'

'I won't hurt you if you lie still and relax, my darling.'

His mouth was now at her left breast and his hand was on her right. She felt he was fully erect and knew there was no escape. She had tested the belt on her wrists and knew there was not enough slack to get her hands out or undo it.

He moved down to her navel with his tongue and his right hand slid between her legs. She braced herself for the inevitable but to her surprise, he concentrated on giving her oral sex with his tongue. To her horror, she realised that her body was responding to the stimulation and she was close to climaxing. He pulled away and moved up her body.

'Do you want me now, Marie?'

She could feel he was on the verge of penetration and she was on the verge of climaxing and for a split second she hesitated before she was able to shout, 'No!'

Suddenly, she heard Marie-Ann stirring in her cot. She cried out and both of them froze.

'Then we shall both remain dissatisfied. I will not take you without your consent.'

She was so emotional, she burst into tears. She could not work out whether it was fear, frustration or relief that was causing her to sob uncontrollably and her whole body was shaking.

He undid the belt and released her hands. He gathered her up in his arms and whispered into her ear.

'I am so sorry, my darling. I didn't mean to frighten you or hurt you. I do love you and thank God I was able to stop in time; it was the drink that drove me over the edge.'

Marie jumped out of bed to check Marie-Ann and thankfully, the cry had been in her dreams and she had not woken up. Reissman joined her and the full realisation of what he had intended to do hit him hard and sobered him up instantly.

'Marie, please forgive me. I don't know what devil possessed me to do such an abominable act.'

She looked at him in disbelief, with tears pouring down her cheeks, shivering in the cold. 'You promised you would not take me but like all men, you wanted to possess me regardless of my feelings.'

'Please Marie, you are freezing. Get back into bed with me. I swear I won't touch you sexually. I know I have broken my word and been an absolute bastard, but I need to tell you something.' He took her hand and she followed him back into bed. He pulled the covers over them and held her tight until her sobs receded. 'Marie, you know when Commander von Rixdorf came here recently, he was on his way back from Paris and he called to tell me of what transpired when we seized control. After all the fighting had ceased, Bismarck had come from Versailles to lead the victory parade up the Champs-Élysées. The few French National Guard soldiers who were captured were lined up to be executed in front of the Arc De Triomphe.' Marie shuddered in his arms as she realised the probable fate of her beloved husband, had he managed to survive the initial fighting. 'However, there were so many of the world's press and foreigners watching and when they realised Bismarck's intention they shouted and jeered, and he decided he could not do it while the world was watching. Instead, he imprisoned them and did not execute them. He told me himself that the National Guard was made up of the ordinary citizens of Paris including shopkeepers, office workers, firemen and policemen and a ragged band of artists who were defending the Louvre.'

Marie cried, 'That would have been Charles! He would have defended the Louvre with his life to protect the works of art within it, he knew every single painting inside it.'

'The prisoners were then rounded up and marched out of Paris and they are being sent here.'

Marie gasped, 'But it is 125 miles from Paris to Lille and those men were starved during the siege. They wouldn't be capable of marching here even if they were uninjured in the fighting. You had control of the railways; it would have only taken three hours for them to reach Lille by train.'

He turned his head away from her, unable to look her in the eyes. The realisation dawned on Marie and she rounded on him.

'You bastards! You never intended them to get here; you knew they would all die of exhaustion long before they reached Lille. Not only that, you nearly raped me tonight and you knew that there was a slight possibility that my husband was still alive. How could you?' She followed this up with another resounding slap across his face.

He pulled her close and said, 'Marie, you know when you said that Charles believed you were his gift from God? He survived the duel after your wedding and maybe God has kept him safe through the war. I nearly killed you, but my horse stumbled and I missed, and I nearly took you tonight. You feel he is still alive, just pray God is still watching over him. I will despatch a scouting party tomorrow to see if there is any sign of them. Even if they had all died, the troops would have reported here anyway.'

When she had calmed down he leant over and kissed her and apologised for his abysmal behaviour. She lay motionless and her eyes did not connect with him. He left her alone, deep in her thoughts, wondering whether Charles could still possibly be alive.

14

Napoleon woke on the third day after his surrender at Sedan. He was under house arrest at the German headquarters and had a very small single bedroom, lounge and bathroom as his suite. He was under heavy guard and his only royal privilege was his own manservant to attend him. His other generals were also housed in close proximity. So far, he had been treated reasonably well and had not faced any outward signs of hostility. The senior commander in charge of him was General Fritz Dammeyer, who had declined to discuss the terms of his surrender as it was not in his remit. He had been told they would return himself and General Marshal MacMahon to Paris, into the hands of Otto von Bismarck, prime minister of Prussia.

A servant appeared with his breakfast and he ate sparingly as his appetite was reduced. He had been suffering from constant back pain since he reached Sedan, due to long hours in the saddle and his arthritis having flared up in all his joints. He heard loud footsteps approaching and General Dammeyer was ushered into the room with two guards.

'Your transfer with Marshal MacMahon to Paris

has been arranged and you will leave today by train. You may take one manservant with you and select one other person to accompany you. Do you have someone in mind already, who you would wish to take?'

Napoleon sighed, thought for a moment and said, 'Yes, I would like to take Lieutenant Henri Croizette from the Hussars. I know he was captured alive and assume he will be imprisoned here.'

Dammeyer replied, 'Very well, I will make enquiries and, in the meantime, if you would prepare to leave, your train departs at midday. Are you content to take the manservant you already have here?'

'Yes General, André has been in my employ for the last ten years.'

An hour later, he heard steps approaching and General Dammeyer returned with Henri under armed guard. He took one look at Henri and saw his black eye and bruised jaw. He had seen him limp as he came into the room and his jacket and shirt were torn at the shoulder.

'General, this man had no mark on him three days ago. Am I to assume that the rest of my men are in a similar condition?'

'Sir, I understand from my officers that he fell down a flight of stairs.'

Napoleon interrupted, 'You mean he was pushed. Would you send a doctor to attend his wounds immediately?'

Dammeyer marched out and said he would do so immediately.

Napoleon turned to Henri. 'Sit down lad, and rest until the doctor arrives. You must have severe bruising all down your left-hand side. Is the rest of your troop alive?'

'Yes, sire. I objected to some rough handling of one of my men and I was hit by a rifle butt and knocked down some stairs. I don't think I have broken anything. Why am I here?'

André came in with a glass of wine for Henri and a bowl of hot water.

Napoleon replied, 'I was told I could take André and one other man back to Paris and I chose you. Your sister made me promise to look after you and you served me well last Christmas... and your language skills could be useful during the negotiations. I hope I can bargain for your release once we reach Paris.'

'Sire, I will serve you as long as you need me.'

'Henri, I am no longer the emperor of France and the best I can hope for is exile with my family, but where I go depends on the Germans. Promise me you will do nothing to risk your life when we are moved to Paris?'

The doctor appeared, and André helped remove Henri's uniform, so the doctor could examine him. He was bruised all down his left side, particularly on his shoulder, hip and knee. The doctor confirmed there were no broken bones and he cleaned up wounds where the skin had been broken. Henri was in a good, fit condition and should soon recover once the swelling subsided. He gave him some painkillers to take on the journey.

oOo

The train drew to a halt and Henri looked out. They were not in a town or city, just the countryside. The guards came and escorted all three of them to the door and they stepped onto a deserted platform. Their luggage was quickly unloaded, and they were bustled to the end of the platform where a carriage was waiting. A troop of six cavalrymen accompanied them on their journey.

Napoleon said, 'It looks like we are not going into Paris, so where are we being taken?'

Marshal MacMahon said, 'I heard that Bismarck seized Versailles as his headquarters, so we are probably going there.'

Half an hour later, they drove through the gilded gates of Versailles. Napoleon heaved a sigh of relief as he had wondered whether he was going to be murdered after they left the train. They were led into the palace and in the massive mirrored hallway, they were met by a welcoming party of officials who advised that negotiations would start in the morning when Bismarck returned from Paris. They shown to Napoleon's impressive designated suite of rooms. To Henri's surprise he had been given a smaller suite with a double bedroom, bathroom and a salon on the floor above. He had been told dinner would be served in Napoleon's suite and was advised he would be fetched. Then he was left, and the door locked, and a guard remained outside.

Henri checked the rooms for any possibility of escape, but the windows had been shuttered and locked. He inspected the lounge and found a huge fruit bowl and he tucked into an orange for the first time in many months. A young Prussian officer arrived with a suitcase, carrying his sword belt and sword. He spoke in perfect French.

'Lieutenant Croizette may I introduce myself, I am the Comte Hans von Brixenhof. Here is a suitcase sent by your barracks in Paris to provide you with uniform and suitable clothing to serve the Emperor. Your sword has been retrieved from your captors in Sedan but will obviously remain with us for the time being. I thought you would be pleased to know it has been returned as I see it is of Russian origin and set with jewels on the handgrip. You may also be pleased to know that your horse was also put on the train along with Napoleon's stallion and will be sent here tomorrow.'

Henri was close to tears and said, 'I never thought I would see Jester again. Why has he been sent back?'

The young officer smiled. 'I understand your horse has been highly trained for battle by you and knows how to unlock stable doors. He has deposited three Prussian cavalrymen, causing broken bones in two cases and has also undone the stable doors of a troop of twenty-five horses overnight, causing chaos.

General Dammeyer is an avid horse breeder and when he heard Napoleon had chosen you as escort, he thought your horse would be safer returned to Versailles along with Napoleon's stallion. You have him to thank for this kind gesture.'

'Will I be able to see him?'

'That will depend on the result of negotiations between Otto von Bismarck, Emperor Wilhelm I and your Emperor, Napoleon. I cannot see you would be denied the opportunity to exercise, under guard of course. Do you require any medication for your injuries?'

'No thank you; I was given some before I left Sedan. I am pleased to make your acquaintance, Comte von Brixenhof and thank you for your warm welcome.'

'May I ask a question, Henri?'

'Of course.'

'Why did Napoleon pick you from all his military staff in Sedan?'

'He has taken an interest in my career and although I have only been in the Hussars for eighteen months I was posted as his personal bodyguard last Christmas and we got on well. I speak five languages (although unfortunately not fluent German) but he thought I may be useful as a translator.'

'I will leave you to prepare for dinner and would advise you to change into some clean clothes.'

Henri went to the bathroom, ran himself a luxurious hot bath and eased his bruised and aching body into it. He was confused by what had happened in the last few hours and just lay in the warmth of the soothing water and reflected on this sudden turn in his fortunes. He opened the suitcase he had been given and was delighted to find several white shirts in both silk and cotton, three pairs of breeches, jackets, drawers, stockings and an evening suit and tailcoat. Whether these were the clothes he had been given when he was acting as bodyguard he didn't know, but the pair of long leather boots and two pairs of shoes were his from the barracks.

He was collected by a guard promptly at two minutes to 7 p.m. and escorted to Napoleon's suite. Already at the table with Napoleon were Marshal MacMahon and the Comte von Brixenhof. Henri was delighted to see the quality and quantity of food available and yet felt guilty that the men he had left behind in Sedan would be lucky to receive any food. They even had wine available and finished with port. However, within thirty minutes Henri's head was throbbing and he was desperate for sleep.

He turned to Napoleon. 'Sire, may I please be excused? I need to lie down. I think I should not have over-indulged in the wine and food.'

Napoleon replied, 'Of course, Henri; you must still be sore from your fall and the long journey cannot have helped.'

Le Comte stood up and said, 'Allow me to escort you to your room, Henri?'

As he was walking along the corridor he

stumbled, felt dizzy and grabbed a door handle for support. Le Comte put his arm round his shoulder and supported him to his room. As he went through the door, Henri shouted an apology and ran into the bathroom and threw up all the wonderful food and wine he had consumed. He removed his jacket and shirt for fear of soiling them and when he had finally stopped retching he made his way to the lounge, carrying a glass of water. He was startled to see Le Comte sitting in one of the chairs.

'My apologies, Comte von Brixenhof. I thought you had gone. That will teach me not to be so greedy in the future, but I am sure a good night's sleep will make an improvement for tomorrow.' He was conscious that he was standing bare chested in front of his captor and was feeling decidedly vulnerable. He knew Le Comte had noticed the bruising from his shoulder to his waist.

'Would you like me to help you off with your boots?'

'No thank you sir, I will be fine.' He realised he had answered too quickly and betrayed his fear. He noticed an amused glint in Le Comte's eyes and cursed himself for his stupidity.

'Very well Henri, you sleep as long as you can. Don't worry, my staff will bring you some breakfast and I will check to see how you are at around 10 a.m.' He strode out of the room, not waiting for a reply.

Henri struggled to undo his boots, cursing

himself for over-indulging in food and wine like a teenage boy when he had existed on a meagre diet of dry bread, berries and cheese for the last few months. Finally, he extracted himself from his boots, removed the rest of his clothes, put on the silk nightgown he had found in his wardrobe and tumbled into the bed. He was fast asleep in minutes.

15

Henri woke quickly when he heard the main door open but could tell it was someone bringing breakfast, so he remained in bed trying to focus his eyes. A servant brought a tray in and he indicated to them to leave it on the dresser as he wasn't sure whether the servant spoke German or French. He slowly sat up in bed and was relieved the banging headache had ceased. Carefully, he stood up and went to the bathroom. He cleaned his teeth and swilled his mouth out and was waiting to see if his stomach would start to churn now that he was vertical. He looked at his face in the mirror. Although he was pale and bruised, he did not look or feel feverish or nauseous. He took himself back to the bedroom and inspected the tray. He decided black coffee and a slice of bread with a small amount of butter was all he dared risk now. If he kept this down for an hour, then he might be more adventurous.

After he had eaten, he wandered round all his rooms, inspecting every drawer and wardrobe to see what he could find. On the top shelf of the wardrobe were a few books and he found Alexandre Dumas's *The Three Musketeers*. Reading was not a pastime he had pursued since he joined the cavalry, so he thought he would take it back to bed with him; if he was going to be shut up all day, he would read it. The prospect of being incarcerated did not sit well with him as he was now so used to living outdoors full time. He would feel like a caged lion if he was forced to remain indoors permanently. He needed to get outside to survey the land and plan an escape. The restricted view from his half-shuttered window gave very few clues as he was obviously overlooking the back of the building, not the front.

After an hour he ate a little more and decided he had better get into his new uniform in case he was needed at the meeting with Bismarck. He was hoping he would not be required as what use would he be in surrender negotiations? He was concerned that at some point he was going to be threatened by his captors, but what could he tell them? He had never been privy to military strategy and anyway, France had lost. He contemplated what he could reveal and what he should not inform them of his activities. He knew they were already scratching their heads at Napoleon's choice anyway. His age alone and the fact he had only been enlisted eighteen months was unusual. To be promoted to lieutenant so quickly would also be unusual. His thoughts were interrupted by the sound of approaching footsteps. Le Comte marched in and looked him over.

'Henri, you must be feeling better this morning?'
'Yes, thank you sir. I just over-indulged last night

on both food and drink and paid the penalty.'

'Bismarck has requested you be there at the start of the meeting if you are well enough?'

'Yes, I will be fine, sir.'

'Then if you are ready, please follow me.'

He was marched into the corridor with two guards behind him and Le Comte in front. They were obviously heading for the front of the building and they descended two flights of stairs, went through the Hall of Mirrors and into a large room set up with a round table for a meeting. The room had several doors, which opened directly into the gardens of Versailles but were firmly closed. Napoleon came over as soon as he entered. 'Henri, have you recovered from last night?'

'Yes sire, I just ate and drank too much for my own good.'

Napoleon pulled him away from Le Comte and whispered, 'Has Le Comte been questioning you?'

'No sire, I would not have any information to give him.'

'Be sure to tell me if he starts bothering you.'

The doors at the other end of the room opened and in swept a party of six men and one woman. Henri worked out which was Emperor Wilhelm I of Prussia, and then, Bismarck. Panic struck him as it appeared they were being lined up for a formal introduction. Should he bow to the Prussian emperor, and what should he say? Thankfully, he followed Marshal MacMahon; he gave a respectful bow to

Wilhelm but just shook hands with Bismarck. Le Comte was doing all the introductions and suddenly he was facing the Emperor. He bowed and offered his hand and then was facing Bismarck who looked him up and down, fixed his gaze on his black eye and cheekbone and asked him in German how old he was. He assembled his wits and managed to reply in German but dreaded him asking anything else. Thankfully, a group formed, and Napoleon indicated that Henri could be dismissed.

Le Comte replied, 'That's fine. I have a few questions to ask Lieutenant Croizette.'

Napoleon interrupted, 'Henri was never privy to any military strategy; he took no part in the battle as he was delivering messages between myself and Marshal MacMahon. He has already met with injury whilst he was imprisoned at Sedan and I do not wish him to be subjected to any further abuse.'

Bismarck intervened, 'Sire, you have my word that no harm will befall the young man, will it Comte von Brixenhof?'

Le Comte replied, 'Of course not, sir.' At the same time as flashing Henri an angry scowl, he marched towards the door and Henri took a deep breath and followed him.

When they got through the double doors and were heading through the Hall of Mirrors he fought to keep his voice steady. 'Sir, please could we go outside for some air?'

He didn't reply but marched towards the front

entrance and out into the garden, towards the massive fountain.

'Sir, have I upset you?'

'Your bloody emperor did, insinuating I would harm you. Just exactly what is your relationship with him? Are you his illegitimate son from one of his many mistresses?'

Henri laughed with relief. 'What in God's name gave you that idea? I told you I was his bodyguard for eight weeks over Christmas last year and maybe I do remind him of young Louis, but surely you only have to look at me and know that we have no matching characteristics.'

'Are you homosexual?'

Henri stopped walking and could feel the anger rising as he parried straight back with, 'No, are you?'

The two of them eyed each other and then Le Comte smiled and said, 'Well, at least we both know the answer to that question. I think we need some physical exercise to settle our differences.'

Le Comte set off at a brisk pace, with Henri desperately trying to make a mental note of his surroundings. They came out of the garden and into a long single-storey building, which was set up as a training room. There were six roped-off boxing arenas and then six fencing areas, divided by mats. Several were occupied by fighting couples. Le Comte marched him down to the end of the room where there was a changing room. He found two white vests and told him to change out of his shirt and remove his boots. He complied whilst desperately thinking of how he was going to play this situation. Much as he would have liked to beat the hell out of Le Comte, he would have to be careful not to show his skill at either discipline.

Le Comte barked, 'Boxing or fencing? Your choice.'

'Fencing – sabre by preference.'

Le Comte grinned. 'Henri, there's no way you are getting your hand on a sabre. It's épée or maybe wooden swords.'

'Well it will have to be épée then.'

Le Comte went and found the épées and two fencing masks. 'Best of twelve then Frenchie, I will avoid going for your current weak spots.'

'Oh, don't you worry about that sir; you won't get anywhere near them anyway.'

Henri took the épée in his left hand in an effort to slow himself down. His right hand was his sword hand, but he could put up a creditable performance with his left and would not look as if he was holding back. Several men were gathering round the room to watch this bout and one offered to referee and score.

They stood "on guard" and then they were off. Henri advanced and lunged immediately for Le Comte's chest and made the first hit as he needed to assess how fast Le Comte's reaction was. Within five minutes Henri had scored six points and Le Comte still only one. Basically, he just wasn't defending his body as he was exposing his entire chest – his foot position was totally wrong. Henri let him take two points as Le Comte moaned that he was moving too much. When the score was 10-3 to him, Henri moved up a gear and this time went in for the kill. He knew Le Comte's grip was tiring and within two seconds of the start he had Le Comte's épée flying across the room.

'How the fuck did you do that, you bastard? That must be an illegal move.' The men watching were howling with laughter over Le Comte's defeat and bright red face. One of them asked him where he had learned to fence, and he told them in Russia. The man replied in French, 'But the Russians are the best fencers in the world.'

Henri laughed, 'Well they should be; they have plenty of time to practice indoors in the freezing winters.'

Le Comte laughed and said, 'Christ Henri, you're as light on your feet as a ballet dancer and you have lightning reactions. Where did you learn to fight like that?'

'Well, I did start in Russia at the age of seven and I was taught by some incredible swordsmen but my timing and speed, I have perfected since I joined the cavalry. Your problem is your foot position as you are not standing sideways on but exposing your full chest to your opponent, giving him double the area to attack. Correct your foot position and increase your agility and fitness and you will improve markedly as well.'

'I suppose I should have chosen boxing instead but no doubt you would have knocked me out cold.'

Henri grinned, 'I am more than willing to continue with twelve boxing rounds now if you wish.'

'Fuck off, arsehole. One humiliating defeat is enough for today!'

oOo

Over the next three days, negotiations continued between the two sides and although Henri was not included in them, he was summoned by Napoleon every evening before dinner and was told every detail and his opinion sought. He was astonished to learn that the Germans had not taken Paris yet because the French were still fighting each other! The people had rejected Napoleon's surrender and were fighting on, but the more militant "Communards" were turning on the official French troops and burning, looting and pillaging government buildings, the royal palaces and destroying any trace of the old monarchy. The Germans had Paris surrounded and were controlling entry, as they had during the six-month siege of Paris. All the sea ports were under German control, as were the railways. They were positioned on the left bank of the Seine, overseeing the city centre and occasionally firing cannons over the river, but as Bismarck said, there was no point in risking his men while the French were still killing each other. 'Better to sit and wait and then ride in triumph, as conquerors, up the Champs-Élysées.'

Another interesting situation was that the Empress Eugénie who was acting Regent of France in Napoleon's absence at war, had mysteriously disappeared two weeks ago when her son the fourteen-year-old Prince Imperial had returned from campaigning with Napoleon in Metz, for his own safety. None of her ministers knew where, with whom or how she had got out of Paris. They suspected she had fled to Spain, but Napoleon knew Eugénie would not be welcome in her homeland due to the French opposition to Prince Leopold of Hohenzollern becoming King of Spain. He suspected she would have attempted to go back to England where they had spent their previous exile, but he had no idea who would have advised her. Obviously, her safety was compromised if revolutionaries were burning the city. Napoleon was relieved she and Louis had escaped and promised that Henri would take on the mission of finding her, if ever they got the chance.

Napoleon's own negotiating position was considerably reduced by these events as a Third Republic had been declared in which he would have no part. He was no longer Emperor of France, just a deposed failure and his death would be imminent if he set foot in Paris. Currently, he had the protection of the Germans at Versailles... but for how long? The best he could hope for was being released but he could not claim sanctuary anywhere in Europe – he would be a marked man wherever he went.

Fortunately, Wilhelm I and Bismarck admired him as a person but now that he had no power or influence in France, they had no need to negotiate with him.

16

Henri found it difficult to sleep as his mind was actively trying to piece together a solution to extract Napoleon and himself from the Germans and find Eugénie. He knew that he could survive as a fugitive with just a horse, living off the land, but not with sixty-year-old, sick Napoleon. He thought about offering to act as a spy for the Germans from inside Paris, but why would they trust him?

It was now after midnight and he was still tossing and turning when he heard the slightest sound of the key being turned in the main door of his suite. Instinctively, he jumped out of bed, shoved a pillow in his place and hid in the wardrobe near the door. He could hear the faintest sound of footsteps but knew whoever approached was barefoot. His eyes were one of his most useful assets and he could practically see in pure darkness. There was a sliver of moonlight coming through the shutters and a mirror on the wall that would give him sight of his visitor.

The door opened carefully, and he saw it was a woman wearing a hooded cloak, which concealed her face. She tiptoed towards the bed and was within three feet of it when he said in French, hoping she would understand him, 'Stay exactly where you are madame, do not turn around and tell me what you are doing in my bedroom at this hour.'

She stopped dead and spoke in fluent French, 'I have been sent by Le Comte von Brixenhof to amuse you.'

'I doubt that very much madame, more likely to kill me than fuck me, I think. But for my amusement you can very slowly remove that cloak and drop that chemise to your feet. It would be foolish not to see the goods on offer.'

She undid the cloak and said, 'But sir, I have no weapons and neither do you and surely you would not harm an innocent woman?'

Her hood discarded, he recognised her as the woman in the group of Prussian diplomats. 'I don't need a weapon to kill you, madame. I can do it with just my bare hands.' The chemise had now hit the floor. Her blonde hair fell to her waist and she had pert buttocks. He moved directly behind her and he could feel his sexual interest rising. She could see him in the mirror and as he put his left hand round her neck, he felt her shiver and he deftly kicked her left foot away and pushed her head down.

'Pardon me madame, for this necessary imposition.' He put his right hand between her legs and felt for any concealed weapon as well as checking the inside of both thighs before pulling her head back up.

'Was that really necessary when I told you I was

unarmed?'

'Absolutely, madame. I am no fool. Would you like to ask me your questions now or after we have sex?'

'Let's take our pleasure first; I imagine you have been a long time without a woman in your bed.' She put her hand back and touched his right buttock.

He pushed her forward over the bed and said, 'Apologies madame, for my boorishness but I need to take you now, but I promise I will attend to your needs afterwards.' He ran both hands over her ample breasts and kissed the nape of her neck and as he entered her, she sighed. Normally, he was a master of restraint but not this time, but his wits were still alert and before he reached a climax he withdrew and moved away from her on his knees.

She turned around and sat on the bed and touched his face. 'Why did you do that, Henri? It was totally unnecessary.'

'Madame, I am not going to father a child with you. I will decide who I procreate with, in my own time, with a woman I love and within the sanctity of marriage.'

'Ah Henri, you can't be a devoted Catholic if you just wasted your seed. You will have to seek absolution tomorrow.'

'Madame, I have seen from experience how hard life is for a woman rearing a child alone in abject poverty and I won't impose that on any woman. Come, let us get into the bed – it's cold and I hope

I can make amends to you for my impetuousness.'

They jumped in and he pulled the covers over them and then took her in his arms and kissed her for the first time. She was demanding so he allowed her to lead and she insisted on being on top. However, her ruse to keep him inside her as he neared climax failed, as his superior strength was no match for her.

'Bastard, Henri, your damned self-control is admirable.'

Henry laughed and propped himself up on the pillows. He took a strand of her hair and said, 'Now, madame, perhaps you will reveal your name and we can make a formal introduction?'

'No, Henri, you may have eyes like a cat, but I would like to see your body in all its toned glory. Turn the light on and I will tell you my name.'

He leant over her, smiling and reached for the light switch.

As the light flooded the room and their eyes adjusted, she ran her hand down his chest. 'Sergeant Anya Berinsky at your service, Lieutenant Croizette.'

'And your job, madame?'

'Probably the same as you do for your government and the military.'

'Now what does Le Comte want to know, considering I have told him most of what he wants? I am not Napoleon's love child or his whore or Empress Eugénie's lover. I hope my performance tonight may have dispelled any possibility of homosexuality now, if that is why you were despatched to my bed.'

'All we are looking for is the reason why Napoleon chose you out of all the military at Sedan to take with him.'

'Look, I spent eight weeks as his bodyguard last Christmas in Paris and he found me to be good company and an excellent man to have watching his back. My language skills in Italian, Spanish, Russian and English were useful to him at court. I played chess with him and dared to beat him. We talked military strategy, horse and dog breeding and I took him hunting. I share his love of art and music and enjoyed going to the opera, ballet and concerts with him.'

'It makes sense Henri but somehow I think there is more to it than that. I was there when he demanded your safety.'

'For Christ's sake, the evidence of what your guards did to me at Sedan is still showing, so maybe he had good cause for concern.'

'Henri, you need not fear for your life; nobody wants to do you any harm. Le Comte holds you in high esteem; he is not your enemy.'

'Perhaps not, he did after all send me you as a comforter. Now I would like to sample the goods once more before you return to your master, so I can give him a glowing reference for you.'

His mouth went to her left nipple and then his tongue explored the rest of her body until he had to put a pillow over her mouth to stem the scream of ecstasy when she reached her climax.

The following morning, he woke with a jolt as the memories of Anya surfaced. Had it been a dream? He knew it hadn't when certain areas of his body were sore that had not been used for the last eighteen months. At least it had drained some of his pent-up energy. He decided he needed an urgent bath as his heightened sense of smell told him he smelt of sex.

After he had eaten his breakfast, Le Comte appeared and gave him a sheepish grin. 'Did you enjoy my gift, Henri? I persuaded my superiors that we needed to know where your sexual preferences lay, and Anya admirably volunteered for duty.'

'You will never know how close you came to losing her. You risked her life for something as trivial as that?'

'Now you need to be in your best uniform this morning. Bismarck and Wilhelm want to see you.'

'Without Napoleon or Marshal MacMahon present?'

'Yes, Henri. You are, believe it or not, our bloody prisoner! Keep your mouth shut about last night's treat unless you want all your privileges withdrawn.'

He changed again, and Le Comte spotted his book on the table.

'*The Three Musketeers.* I have read that. Which one do you identify with, Henri? It draws many parallels with your life.'

'I don't see how. I am untried in battle yet, I would hardly have risen to the height of a musketeer.'

They made their way downstairs through the Hall of Mirrors to the large room he had met Bismarck in the previous week. He scanned the room and saw Bismarck, Wilhelm and Anya, obviously taking notes. They both avoided eye contact and he concentrated on Bismarck as the man fascinated him. He was invited to sit down, and he tried to remain as calm as possible.

Bismarck said, 'Henri, you may wonder why we have been speculating on why Napoleon chose you, a very young raw recruit to the cavalry, to be his escort here.'

'Sir, I have answered all your questions truthfully. I don't know why Napoleon chose me but surely you should be asking him, not me.'

'We decided to do some investigating ourselves. Comte von Brixenhof ventured into Paris yesterday and retrieved your military record from your barracks and this gives us a clearer picture of Napoleon's reasoning.'

Henri kept his eyes fixed on the table, trying to avoid showing any concern whatsoever. Le Comte was sitting directly opposite him and he ventured a glance at him and saw he had his record open in front of him.

Bismarck said, 'Perhaps you would oblige Hans, and read out some of the extracts from the record.'

'Henri joined the cavalry on March 29th, 1868. The following are some of the comments made on his record within his first year of service.

'The most natural horseman I have ever encountered. His knowledge of caring for and training horses is remarkable. He has the lightest hands I have ever seen and refuses to use a whip or spurs on a horse. He can calm a terrified horse by touching it with one hand. He never over rides a horse and is the quietest man in the saddle. I have seen him train his own horse without the use of a saddle or bridle. He deplores the use of the term "breaking a horse," and he can achieve more in one day than others can in six weeks.

'Croizette is highly intelligent, an ardent, diligent trooper with a genuine love and empathy for horses. He has the rare quality of being both a team player and a lone wolf and can master both disciplines. No challenge is too big for him and his ability to assess situations is way beyond his years. There is no arrogance in his manner and he will help other men to improve their skills.

'Croizette's sword skills are unbelievable. He started fencing at the age of eight in Russia and his speed with a sabre is as fast as lightning. As his training increases he can beat everyone that challenges him. He has started retraining with his left hand to increase his skill, so he can use two weapons at the same time. He shows no arrogance or cleverness, just strives to improve.'

Henri heard the inflection on the word "left," so he knew Le Comte had realised what he was doing when they fought.

'Croizette's shooting skills are amazing. He can hit a rifle target with a bullseye from up to 150 yards away. His pistol shooting is even more accurate. He can bring a running deer down with a shotgun from over 100 yards away. Apparently, he learnt hunting and tracking skills in Russia - recommended for scout training.

'September 9th, 1868 – Trooper Croizette volunteered to undertake training as a field doctor in a new initiative. The doctor who trained him said he should be a surgeon, not a soldier – he is so bright.

'November 8th, 1868 – Croizette completed his scouting course with honours. He survived two weeks living rough with no food provided, while being pursued by his own troop. They never saw him once and could find no visible tracks, but he was within 500 yards of them the whole time. He caught small animals with a bow and arrow to protect his cover. On the last night, his horse undid the main rope of the tethered troop horses, unassisted and Croizette led them back to the barracks. They did not realise they had gone until the next morning.'

There was outright laughter from both Bismarck and Wilhelm.

'November 28th, 1868 – Croizette convinced General Centiere that scouts should be sent out in civilian dress with no identifying military paraphernalia on horse or rider as it was detrimental to the task. Croizette was given permission to carry a short-handled axe attached to his waist, to use in his left hand. He was also given permission to ride with no reins whilst charging.

'December 1868 – Napoleon required a bodyguard over Christmas after an imminent death threat. Croizette was chosen due to his ability to speak five languages, his perfect manners, classic education and his outstanding sword and shooting skills.

'January 1869 – from a letter from Emperor Napoleon III; "Henri Croizette is an exceptional young man. His knowledge of military history is outstanding, and his manners and behaviour are impeccable. The attention to detail with which he applies himself to his work is commendable. There is no arrogance or clever attitude with him; he is honest, trustworthy and the best rider I have ever seen. His ability to train horses is a talent the cavalry should use, and his tracking and hunting skills are par excellence. This young man should be consulted on military strategy as he can sum up a situation in a heartbeat. The speed of his reactions when sword fighting are exceptional. Henri fenced against some of the best swordsmen in Europe whilst he was at court and beat them all. I have had the pleasure of meeting his family, who are all talented in the arts. Henri can play the piano and violin and has a good tenor voice. He does not over-indulge in drinking and neither is he a womaniser. Do not challenge him to a game of chess as he can win in three moves! He has mastered courtly skills and although he turns many of the ladies' heads with his good looks, he has perfected the art of being able to reject a lady without offence. I recommend you promote him immediately, despite his age and lack of battle experience."

'February 1869 – Trooper Henri Croizette promoted to lieutenant in the Hussars and assigned to No. 5 troop.

'April 1869 – From Chief Veterinary Officer: "Lieutenant Croizette's ability to spot shortness of stride in a horse before lameness occurs has saved the working lives of five horses in the last month. They were taken out of service and treated before the lameness became apparent. He has personally attended colicky horses throughout the night and saved them all, then led his troop out the following day. He has recommended we use horse shoes that have studs screwed into the shoe to help horses grip better in the mud. His passion for the welfare of horses is commendable and his suggestion that three-year-olds are only backed and turned away for the summer and not started in full work until they are four, needs to be implemented."' Le Comte closed his military record.

17

Bismarck spoke first. 'Henri never have I seen such high praise for any young man entering military service in Prussia. You should be very proud of your achievements in such a short time. However, I was sent a report from Colonel Schlesinger who witnessed the Battle of Sedan first-hand.' He nodded at Le Comte, who read from the handwritten report.

'1st September 1870 – from a report by Colonel Frederic Schlesinger at the Battle of Sedan: "The battle took place on a slope, with the French defending the hill and the Prussian cavalry ranging across, attacking uphill in five lines, with infantry behind. The young French officer on the black horse appeared from the small copse on the right-hand side of the hill. He was galloping at full speed, but his reins were looped and tied over the horse's neck. He charged into the fifth line of cavalry from behind them and took out two men, one with his sword on the right and the other with a short-bladed axe on the left. He forced himself into the fourth row as both men went down and warning cries were shouted. A Prussian turned around and advanced towards him, but the Frenchman sliced him with his sword, through the neck. He charged into the third row, aiming for a small gap, and was accosted by a Prussian from the left whom he slashed in the chest with the axe; the force felled him from his horse. The first two rows of Prussians were now fighting the French in close combat. The Frenchman carved his way through both lines with his sword and axe and reached Napoleon before the Prussian cavalry. He attempted to grab the reins from the nearside, to turn the horse away from the encroaching Prussian troops. Napoleon's stallion would not turn and reared up, sinking his teeth into the black horse's neck as he landed. He pulled his horse round to the right and went slightly up the hill, turned him back facing downhill and cantered up to Napoleon's stallion and vaulted onto him. His horse turned back and as a Prussian rider spurred to reach Napoleon with his sword raised, the black horse ran in front of the stallion and caprioled, kicking the Prussian rider clean off his horse. The Frenchman had now succeeded in turning the stallion back up the hill and away from imminent danger. Never have I seen such outstanding bravery, horsemanship or swordsmanship; every blow that young man wielded with both sword and axe, killed.'''

Henri sat with his chin in his hand, wondering whether he would be dragged outside and executed immediately.

Wilhelm said, 'Henri, were you under orders to rescue Napoleon?'

'Not exactly sir, but then nobody told me my

orders of December 1868 had been revoked either, so I felt I was duty bound to carry them out.'

Bismarck and the Emperor twitched with laughter and Le Comte gave him an admiring smile.

Bismarck asked, 'Where were you when the battle started?'

'I had been scouting and carrying messages and when I ascertained the strength and number of the Prussian army, I reported back to Marshal Mac-Mahon and suggested that surrender was the only option. He sent me with a message to Commander de Wimpeffen but after I set off I saw the battle start from the other side of the valley. I spotted Napoleon in the front cavalry ranks, where he should never have been in the first place. There was no time for me to go around and approach from the French side, so I broke through the Prussian cavalry ranks as it was the quickest route available. How many men did we lose in the battle?'

Bismarck turned to Anya, 'I believe you have the figures?'

Anya said, 'Yes sir, from the 122,000 French troops, 3,220 were killed, 14,811 wounded, and 104,000 captured along with 558 guns. We had 200,000 troops in the field, of which 1,310 were killed and 8,543 wounded.'

Wilhelm asked, 'Henri, what did Napoleon say when you reached him?'

'Well it wasn't the best welcome I have ever received, and some choice language was used.'

Wilhelm's mouth twitched, and he carried on, 'What exactly did you say that finally persuaded Napoleon to withdraw?'

'I suggested he would be better negotiating surrender rather than ending up dead. But I was wrong because I never expected his own countrymen to depose him. So, in effect I denied him an honourable death and left him in a far worse predicament.'

Wilhelm smiled and said, 'Henri, nobody could ever have predicted this outcome; you did your utmost to fulfil your duty to your emperor and your courage and bravery were indisputable. I would have you protect my back any day; you were truly outstanding.'

'Sir, I do have a suggestion to make to resolve the situation.'

'Well go ahead. Napoleon told us to listen to your strategy.'

'Bearing in mind what you have heard about me, I would expect you to throw me into a cell and forget about me as I would be such an arsehole to contain, so a quick death by firing squad would be preferable. However, if you let me and my horse leave in a civilian capacity I could go into Paris and endeavour to find out where Empress Eugénie has gone and contact her. If you required me to survey the scene and report back, I would do so. In return you would grant Napoleon and me safe transport to the nearest port or border, so he can enjoy an honourable retirement with his wife. This gets you out of a difficult situation with a deposed emperor on your hands who now has little value – and leaves you free to negotiate with the leaders of the new Third French Republic once they have been elected. I assume you are not intending to occupy Paris permanently and no doubt you will require a hefty payment to secure Paris' freedom, which is going to take some time.'

Wilhelm said, 'A very fine solution which we need time to discuss but I am sure we can negotiate a suitable agreement. You also need have no fear for your life; as far as I am concerned you have earned your freedom by your devotion to duty. If you choose to return to Paris after you have seen Napoleon settled, then you would make a valuable contribution to rebuilding the devastation caused by this war. In the short term I ask you to be patient and remain in captivity without being an "arsehole," and Le Comte will grant you access to your horse and the fencing and training grounds within the perimeter of Versailles. Perhaps, Le Comte, you would take Henri out for some fresh air and we will reconvene this meeting at 2 p.m. I expect your complete silence on what we have discussed today until an agreement is reached.'

'Yes, sir and thank you for listening to my proposal. I hope you will allow me to proceed.' He stood up, feeling slightly weak at the knees and Le Comte escorted him out of the room.

As they left the room and went through the Hall of Mirrors to the main entrance, Henri felt as though he had been trampled by a herd of wild horses. He headed for the nearest seat in the ornamental gardens and threw himself down, unable to stem the tears that fell silently down his cheeks. Le Comte followed and sat quietly next to him, patiently waiting for the torrent to subside. He proffered him an exquisite, white silk handkerchief, monogrammed with his initials.

'Henri, I cannot quite believe what you did at Sedan and if it hadn't been witnessed by a man I know and admire I would dismiss it as total fantasy, but I want you to know that I have the utmost respect and admiration for you. Did you once even consider your own safety?'

'No, not for one moment. It was Napoleon I was concentrating on; it was as if I was in another world. My hearing and sight were heightened, and I just fixated on getting through to him. I have never raised a sword or axe before intent on killing a man as it was always on dummies, but it was as if reality was suspended. The first three men never saw me coming and they just disappeared once I had struck them and I was already sizing up the next opponent. I had no control over the speed of my blow; it was like lightning.'

'Did you command your horse to capriole and kick the man off his horse?'

'No, I was too busy trying to wrestle with Napoleon

and turn his horse round. I saw Jester make the turn back to me and I have trained him to follow me as I have practiced vaulting from one horse to another several times. He must have realised I was in danger and intercepted in the only way he knew how. I have taught him to capriole in close combat fighting, so he may just have done it instinctively when he saw the other horse coming up behind him.'

'And you, little shit, fought me with your bloody left hand and still disarmed me.'

Henri smiled and said, 'I could have done it a lot sooner because you were giving me your whole body as a target. With an axe I would have killed you with my first strike.'

'But Henri, why use an axe?'

'Because the Vikings fought with just an axe and a shield – usually without any armour – and cut through their opponents' defences in minutes. An axe is a silent killer and invaluable if you are out scouting to kill game, or even a man. I can track a man in the dark and slit his throat in total silence. That is why you shouldn't have sent Anya in to me like you did. Thankfully, I was not asleep and heard her before she even got the outer door open, but had I been sleeping, and she had made it to the bed and had I woken up, I could have broken her neck with one blow. I don't need a weapon to kill, Hans. I can do it with my bare hands if I have to. My brain and body are so toned and sharp I am as dangerous as any wild animal when out on a mission.'

'Jesus, you are a fucking killing machine then, Henri.'

'Precisely!'

'I need to take you back inside now, but I promise you tomorrow you can see your horse and if we sort out giving you some more freedom then you will be able to come and go as you please.'

18

The next morning, Le Comte appeared after breakfast to accompany Henri to another meeting. He reassured him that his request had been granted. He had dressed in plain breeches and a jacket, not his uniform, ready to be reunited with Jester. He was ushered into a small office on the third floor where already seated, were Bismarck and Anya.

'We have agreed in principle to release you to carry out your mission and will provide you with whatever weapons, provisions, money or clothing you need. Anya will procure them. We require you to report back to us on the situation in the capital between the military and the Communards. We agree to the safe transport of Napoleon out of France, but we will not be involved in direct negotiation with the government of whichever country is affording him sanctuary. Comte von Brixenhof has volunteered to accompany you if you wish. I cannot guarantee your safety should you be apprehended by Prussian troops, but I doubt you would allow that to happen. You will be free to wander at will around Versailles, provided you carry no weapons. I hardly need to inform you that if you harm anyone here, both your life and Napoleon's will be forfeited.'

'Sir, I accept your terms and thank you for granting my request. I would prefer to act alone as my covert surveillance skills and knowledge of the terrain are sufficient to achieve my aims alone. If I need any help I will get a message back to Versailles. I would appreciate any knowledge you have of the geography of the centre of Paris as my activities will be centred on the Tuileries Palace.'

Bismarck rose from his seat, proffered his hand and said, 'May I wish you success on your mission and you have my utmost respect and admiration for your exemplary conduct. Napoleon is aware of what you are doing and wants to see you later today. I expect you will be with us for a day or so yet and I would like you to dine with me this evening.' He shook his hand and swept out of the room.

Le Comte remarked, 'High praise indeed from our leader, Henri. Do you want to see your horse now? Then we will sit down and devise a list of what you need.'

Henri jumped up and headed for the door, pursued by the pair of them. They walked briskly down towards the stables but Henri, with his excellent eyesight, spotted Jester being led from a field to the stable area when he was at least 150 yards away. Despite having no white markings on him, Henri knew it was Jester purely by his shape and movement. He stopped dead, put his fingers in his mouth and let out a high-pitched whistle. Le Comte nearly collided with him.

'Jesus Henri, what on earth are you doing?'

'I've seen him and summoned him.'

Le Comte looked in amazement and, in the distance, could see a black horse galloping loose along the track and scattering both men and horses in his path. 'You must have eyes like a bloody hawk to recognise him from here.'

Jester soon appeared and started to whinny as he got closer to Henri. He shuddered to a halt within inches of his master and Henri grasped his nose in one hand and fondled his ear with the other and kissed him between the eyes.

'I never thought I would see you again, Jester my boy.' He took the trailing rope, knotted it on the other side of his head collar, grasped a lump of mane and vaulted onto his back. 'I just need to have a few minutes alone with him and then I will bring him back to the schooling arena near the stables.'

'Fine, I will sort you some tack out.'

Henri laughed, 'I don't need any tack!' He spun Jester round, reared up and then galloped off, whooping with joy.

Anya and Le Comte watched in open-mouthed amazement as Henri galloped Jester down the steep grass verge without even picking up the rope. He halted in a quiet spot, leant over his neck and hugged and patted him. They continued walking towards the stables and followed Henri to the schooling area at the back.

Henri dismounted and meticulously inspected Jester all over his body from his nose to his tail, scrutinising each leg. He then jumped back on and walked him round the arena and then into trot, steadily reducing the size of the circle and changing the rein frequently. He then moved him into a slow, collected canter and moved him sideways across the arena, both at trot and canter, still without picking up the rope.

Le Comte shouted to him, 'How do you do that without a bit in his mouth?'

'I just use my legs because I may be using my hands with a weapon. As long as he is balanced and under control I can make him go forwards, sidewards and backwards. At this speed I can fire a rifle at a moving target and all Jesters' movements are controlled by my legs.' He then pulled his knees up and stood up on the horse's rump. 'Now I control the direction with either my voice, or pressure from my feet.' Jester cantered round in a small half circle, with Henri standing up.

Anya said, 'But why would you need to stand up on a horse?'

'Because if I want to climb over a high wall, up a tree or gain access to a building I can do it by standing up on him; he knows that if I get off him he has to move away and then I control him by whistling if I need him back.' He trotted over to them and jumped off. He spoke quietly, and Jester lay down on his left side, Henri got on and he jumped up. 'I have taught him to lie down in case I am unhorsed in a fight and too injured to vault back on.'

Le Comte said, 'God forbid, Henri. How long did it take you to get him to do all this? It's incredible.'

'Not long, just over the last six months or so. One movement leads to another but the real reason he does it is because of his perfect trust in me. I never pull his mouth about or lose my temper. I am balanced in the saddle and I never use spurs or a whip. My life depends on him and his on me.' He then rode up to the gate and made Jester bow to them.

A ripple of applause broke out among the people who had collected around the arena to watch Henri's fascinating display.

'Have you taught him to deposit other riders?' asked Anya.

'No but because I ride him so lightly, and often without a bit at all, if someone gets on and shouts or pulls at his mouth or kicks him in the ribs, he won't tolerate it. I could put a child on him and provided they didn't do any of those things, he would accept them. I don't use voice commands now because surveillance and tracking work requires total silence. I have also taught him to stay silent, as a horse on its own will often whinny if he hears other horses approaching and if he did that then I would be a dead man.'

Le Comte said, 'I can't believe you can be so balanced, bareback. You never move.'

'I started riding at six in Russia and you are not allowed a saddle until you can execute all paces competently. Besides, you learn far more about your horse the closer the contact between you. I'm not saying that I would relish riding twenty miles a day without a saddle though.'

Anya said, 'But you are not just using your heels to control the pace, are you?'

'Well spotted, Anya. No, I am using my inner thighs, calves, and heels and distributing my weight in the saddle, but he must be collected underneath me. It takes a bit of practice but pays dividends.'

Anya laughed, 'Well I can certainly verify you are extremely well-muscled and strong in all those areas.'

Henri laughed and turned to Le Comte, 'Are you a good enough rider to risk him bareback?'

'I would love to try.'

Henri jumped down as Le Comte came through the gate. 'You can hold the rope but don't pull on it, use your voice and put your leg on his side carefully, sit very still and relax.' He gave Le Comte a leg-up onto Jester and talked soothingly and patted his neck.

Jester walked on slowly and after half a lap, Le Comte sent him forward into trot. As they approached the first corner there was a loss of balance, which Le Comte fought hard to retain. At the next corner he sent him up into canter and maintained the collection and his position. Le Comte lengthened and shortened the horse's stride in canter and gradually became more confident.

Henri said, 'Bravo, Hans, you are a better rider than a swordsman.'

'Only because I have been doing it longer; I played about bareback as a child but never rode any distance. Tell me how you get him to move sideways?'

Henri moved closer to Jester and placed his hand on Le Comte's leg and put it in the correct position on the nearside and then went around to the offside and placed his other leg. 'Now ride him forward but put more weight on your right buttock and close your hand on the rope but nudge him quietly with both your heels. This will block him from going forward and he can only move sideways, away from your leg.'

Le Comte rode Jester sideways and he could feel him crossing his back legs over and see him crossing his front legs. He shouted with joy. 'Henri, this is just bloody wonderful; you must teach me more. To have this level of control over the horse in close contact combat gives you such an advantage over your enemy.' He jumped down from Jester and patted him. 'He is a superbly schooled mount, Henri; he might not have the looks or paces of a Spanish stallion, but he is so light to ride.'

'Ah, but he is the perfect horse for surveillance work. He is nearly pure black, so he blends into the background. He is not a stallion and therefore looks no different from the average cavalry mount, but his knowledge and temperament beat a stallion hands down. Remember, he has to cope with all my instructions while all hell is going on around him, so he cannot be highly strung and frightened. He has to charge against cannons and keep going back time after time when naturally, a horse will flee from noise and fire. We ask too much for a horse to fight against cannons as there can only be one outcome.'

Henri led him towards the stable and the groom who had been fetching him in from the field appeared to collect him and said, 'Monsieur, what a special horse he is and he obviously loves you deeply. I have had to tempt him to eat by hand as he was pining for you. But look at his bright, happy eyes now he has been reunited with you.'

Henri thanked the boy and told him Jester's name and that he would be leaving shortly and asked him to prepare him by not grooming him or trimming his mane and tail but by getting as much hay and feed down him as he would eat. The three of them then went back into Versailles and Henri detailed what equipment he needed with Anya whilst Hans left for a meeting with Bismarck.

After Le Comte had left and they were alone, Anya leaned across Henri and kissed his cheek. 'Henri, you are one special man with a mind as sharp as a blade, killer instinct, loyalty and courage, all combined with a pure heart. Don't let the horrors of war change your idealistic and romantic ideology.'

He nuzzled her ear and whispered, 'Don't distract me from my work, Anya. I have a lot to do to prepare for this mission. How good are your sewing skills?'

Anya laughed, 'Definitely not high on my list of accomplishments, why?'

'I need some pockets sewing into the black cloak to hold my weapons and some hemp laced boots making to cover Jester's hoofs.'

'What weapons do you intend to take?'

'A rifle and cover attached to a non-military saddle. I have dismissed taking my own sword as it is too ornate to pass as an everyday sword. I will need a pistol, two short daggers and a short-handled axe. I will personally sharpen the blades of all the weapons and I will have to settle for a military sword.'

'As we are at Versailles there may be an axe, daggers or sword that date back several years in the armoury store. What about clothes?'

'Well, as I want to appear as a civilian: dark breeches, a jacket, dark shirts and a hat. I may need one white shirt when I go to the Tuileries Palace, so I can mix in with the servants, but white is too noticeable in the dark.'

'Where will you house Jasper?'

'I don't know. There will be plenty of deserted houses with stables that I can use, or if he's very lucky I might be able to slip him into the palace stables or even take him back to my barracks. Don't worry, his safety is my top priority. I will take half a bushel of oats as I imagine hay will be non-existent, but I could take him to my brother-in-law's house if he is still alive... but it is on the left bank of the Seine, which your troops occupy.'

They finished writing the list and then Anya took him to the armoury to see what weapons were available. Henri was amazed at some of the historic swords but in the end, he opted for a modern, lighter sword, which he could sharpen himself. He did select daggers that were at least a hundred years old and to his delight, he found a short-handled axe that had been designed as a weapon that was very light, which would do the job perfectly.

On his return to the house he went to search out Napoleon, arriving as he was being served afternoon tea. Napoleon ushered him in and sent the servant for more tea and cake.

'Well, Henri you certainly made an impressive debut at your first battle scene. Bismarck says you killed eight men in ten minutes, which historically must be a record.'

'I doubt it sire; the Vikings probably achieved more than that. I am not exactly proud of killing men because I do actually value life. The first three never saw me coming so I had no resistance to overcome. I was just lost in some sort of dream world where all my senses were in overdrive and having trained for so long on dummies, I could not believe how easy it was to slice my way through five lines of cavalry. I just had surprise and speed on my side.'

'That is quite a normal reaction, Henri. I never saw you coming either as I was concentrating on the fight around me. I apologise for the unwelcome reception you received from me.'

'I know, sire. I should have left you. I deprived you of dying in battle, which shows just how bloody stupid I was – definitely not the military genius you all seem to think I am.'

'Henri, you were doing what you had been trained for, which was protecting my arse. Nobody could have anticipated that my people would refuse to surrender and would depose me within days. Your solution to both mine and the Prussians' problem was extremely succinct and well-devised. However, you are putting yourself at considerable risk in trying to execute it.'

'Sire, my life is of little importance and it is the least I can do considering the circumstances. I need some help from you as to who to approach at the palace who may know where your wife has gone… and any clues you may have as to her whereabouts.'

'Not easy, Henri. My wife, as you well know, has a definite mind of her own. She may have disappeared of her own volition, with no intention of being reunited with me. Indeed, she may be as disappointed to have you turn up, as I was at Sedan. She would not have left Paris unless she was under threat and possibly when I returned young Louis, to protect him she decided to abscond.'

'But why would the empress not want to be reunited with you, sire?'

'Jesus, Henri I have hardly been a good, faithful husband to my Spanish princess, have I? I never lived up to her very high standards of how a king should behave but I love her all the same. She was the only woman who would not bed me before I wed her and her strong Catholic views on marriage probably prevented her from seeking solace elsewhere when I took mistresses. Women are difficult creatures to understand at the best of times; don't follow my reprehensible lead on this subject, whatever you do.'

They chatted for another half an hour and then Henri took his leave. Napoleon hugged him and wished him luck on his mission.

19

Henri dressed for dinner with Bismarck, while reflecting on why he would want to dine with an inexperienced enemy soldier of no standing and wondered who else would be there. Le Comte appeared and knocked on his door before entering, which rather surprised him.

'Well, Henri, are you ready?'

'Why does Bismarck want to dine with insignificant me?'

'He admires and is fascinated by you – we all are.'

'Bismarck fascinates me too.'

He was surprised that the dinner was being held in a small dining room on the ground floor and there was only Bismarck, Le Comte, Anya and himself present; it was very informal. In fact, he felt overdressed for the occasion. Bismarck questioned him about his education in Russia, his affinity with horses and his sword skills. He was keen to know why he had selected an axe as his secondary weapon. The food and drink were excellent and although he was careful not to over-indulge he probably drank a little too much, but he had relaxed now he knew his life was not under threat. Bismarck informed him that he had ordered amended maps of the Tuileries to guide him on his mission, as the area had suffered from cannon fire and had been damaged by the Communards.

After the meal, Le Comte suggested they partake of a particularly fine bottle of brandy he had purloined from the Versailles wine cellars. Henri's first thought was to decline but it was only 10 p.m. and he would not be starting on his mission until everything was ready. Anya seemed keen to go with them. Le Comte's room was on the third floor and had a massive bed. Henri couldn't resist.

'Jesus Hans, how many women do you entertain in that bed every night?'

Hans laughed, 'As many as I can persuade to join me but regrettably, Versailles has a shortage of women in residence, so I have to make do with erotic dreams on most nights – especially when Anya is unavailable.' He kissed Anya on the cheek as he passed her a glass. 'Anya tells me you were very wary of her approaches the other night.'

'I had every reason to be; she could have been an assassin. Remember Hans, the female of the species is deadlier than the male.'

Anya said, 'Very true, Henri, but now I would like to get a better view of that excellent body of yours. In fact, I would like to take both of you on a sensuous journey you won't forget in a hurry. Ah Henri, your guard slipped then, and I saw a flash of concern flicker across your eyes. Do not worry, no harm will come to you and you might just learn a few tips that will ensure when you have found your future wife, she will remain in your bed forever.'

Anya approached both of them and told them to remove their jackets, waistcoats and boots. Hans complied immediately, and Henri hesitated, but Le Comte whispered to him, 'Just do as she says. Believe me, you won't regret it.' Anya was now sitting at the end of the bed, removing her silk stockings.

'Both of you come and stand here.' She pointed to a spot about three feet from the end of the bed. 'Now Hans, you undo my dress and help me out of it.'

Henri desperately tried to avoid watching and fought to control his breathing as all his senses were on high alert. The message to flee was running through his brain but he felt like his feet were stuck to the carpet. Hans did an expert job of removing her dress and hooped petticoat, for which he was grateful, as for all his agility he knew he would have struggled with the laces of the dress. In return, Anya was removing Hans's silk shirt and cravat and running her tongue around both nipples.

Henri's brain had managed to recall a conversation he had heard in the barracks from two soldiers who had gone to the local whorehouse and shared a woman between them, as they hadn't enough money for one each. They had described their activities in graphic detail and a shiver of fear ran down his spine as to what her next move would be. Hans picked up the dress and deposited it carefully over the back of a chair and returned to his side.

Anya beckoned him over and he forced his legs to move forward. She told him to remove her chemise and drawers. The fastenings for the chemise were at the front. He avoided her eyes as he carefully undid the chemise and pulled it down over her shoulders and let if fall to the floor. The sight of her ample breasts raised his blood pressure and something lower down responded as well. He undid her drawers and slid them down over her waist and as he touched that blonde, downy pubic hair he felt like he had received an electric shock. As he bent down to retrieve the underwear he realised his nose was within inches of her crotch and she laughed in delight. She pulled him to his feet and divested him of his cravat and shirt and then pulled him close.

'Relax Henri, switch off your brain and make all those senses move down here.' She ran her hand between his legs. She pushed him away, so he was back in line with Hans and they only had their breeches left on. She walked behind them and then came back in front of them and undid Hans's breeches and drawers and pulled them down in one swift move, then did the same to him.

Anya sat on the bed and surveyed the two men in front of her very closely. She walked round to the back of them and he was thankful he could watch her in a mirror. Thankfully, she didn't touch either of them.

'So, what have I got here in front of me? Two excellent male specimens that any woman would desire; one a 32-year-old Prussian count, well educated, moves in court circles, sexually experienced (thanks to my excellent tuition), good looking, great body – although carrying too much flesh at present. Or a 22-year-old French cavalry officer with a fantastic body, mind as sharp as a knife, kills with his bare hands, can track like a wolf, controls horses with his fingers, but is sexually inexperienced. Which one deserves to go first? You were reared in Russia, Henri. What would a Russian do in this situation?'

Henri looked straight into her eyes and said, 'A Russian, madame, would have fucked you twice by now and then slit your throat.'

Hans roared with laughter and Anya grinned. 'I told you to switch your brain off and concentrate on your body. I have other uses in mind for that sharp tongue of yours. Come here, Henri. You Hans, can wait for further instructions.'

Henri went to the bed, pulled her to her feet and kissed her passionately. They kissed and explored each other's bodies for a while and then she made Henri kneel facing her on the bed as she leant over the bottom of the bed. She started to give him oral sex. After a while, she called Hans over and he entered her from behind and the fun began.

oOo

Henri's eyes flickered open and he recognised he

was in his own bed… but how he had got there, he couldn't remember. He groaned as his brain flashed back to some of the images of last night. He moved and though he expected to feel some pain in his nether regions he could not understand why the muscles in his right calf were killing him. At this point, the outer door opened, and he assumed his breakfast was being delivered. He heard the tray being left in the lounge and then to his horror, Le Comte appeared in his bedroom.

'Morning Henri, just checking you are alive and well after last night's sport.'

'Fuck off, Hans. If you are here to crow about last night I will punch your head in. If I have partaken in the scenes my brain is replaying in my head now, I should be taken out and shot.'

'Rubbish, Henri. You were just taking your pleasure at Anya's request and relieving her sexual tension. It would have been rude to offend a lady in such distress.'

'From what I saw you were more than capable of doing that; why did she need me?'

'Anya has a voracious appetite and needs constant attention and stimulus and besides, she is fascinated by you. Believe me, last night was tame compared to some of her erotic fantasies. You got off very lightly indeed, young man.'

'Trouble is, I can't even remember what exactly happened; it's just all a blur of arms and legs. I can't understand why my right calf is killing me. I know

I was in some very unusual positions last night but how did I hurt my calf?'

'Well, when I was just getting into my stride on top of Anya, you disappeared off the side of the bed and got cramp in your calf and started screaming in pain. We had to cease our pleasure in order to shut you up; Anya massaged your calf whilst I smothered you with a pillow. We thought Bismarck and the King had retired but thankfully, they were still downstairs playing pool.'

'Oh God, Hans, how embarrassing. Did I make an utter fool of myself?'

'Do you remember the round of applause both Anya and I gave when you achieved your first orgasm and never attempted to withdraw?'

'Oh, God forbid. What sort of debauchery did I partake in? How can I ever look Anya in the eye again? But you said, "first orgasm," how many times did I do it?'

'Henri believe me, Versailles will have seen a lot more sex and debauchery going on here over 100 years ago than the minor amusement we indulged in last night. Believe it or not I wasn't exactly counting how many times you had sex, but as a conservative estimate it would have been at least four times. You appear to be fixated on breasts whereas I find more pleasure in the lower half of the female anatomy, but Anya made sure we both had our full share of intercourse.' Henri groaned in embarrassment and mortification. 'Now for God's sake you young stud, get out of bed, get dressed and eat your breakfast. I need you in my office to go over the maps Bismarck has had done for you and to brief you on your barracks by 9:30 a.m.' He then pulled the covers off him and left the room.

Henri forced himself out of bed and limped to the bathroom. When he looked closely at his chest in the mirror he was horrified to find he had a line of love bites from his throat to his crotch. He could only hope and pray they had been inflicted by Anya. He ran a bath to remove the odour of sex from his body, in the vain hope that scrubbing himself clean would absolve him from sin. He dressed in plain breeches and a white shirt and jacket, then ate his cold breakfast, pulled on his leather riding boots and ran down to Le Comte's office, bang on time.

20

The cartographer was already there as Henri arrived. He described the damage inflicted by either cannons or fire in the area around the Tuileries Palace and Luxembourg Gardens. Finally, he was able to blank out thoughts of the previous night and concentrate on the task facing him.

Le Comte talked him through what was left at the barracks as it was he who had raided it to obtain his military record. There was only one troop in residence and they went out patrolling daily. There appeared to be only one officer in charge and a few clerks in the office. The main gates were guarded but access could easily be gained in several areas surrounding the barracks.

He set off down to the stables to check out his weapons and sharpen them in the blacksmith's forge. Hans had told him Anya was already down there preparing his saddlebags for the journey. He walked through the main stable block and was attracted by the crashing, banging and shouting he could hear. He discovered that all the noise was coming from the large corner box and the noise was made by a horse kicking against the bolted shut top and bottom doors. He tried to converse with the two men who obviously only spoke German and ascertained that the occupant was Perseus, Napoleon's stallion who was the source of the controversy. Thankfully, the French groom who looked after Jester spotted him and came over.

The cause of the problem soon became obvious when he learnt that the horse had been confined to his stable since his arrival at Versailles a week ago. He had become increasingly stressed by his confinement and needed some exercise. The German grooms said they daren't turn him out in a field as if he jumped out he could cause havoc and would be impossible to catch as he had taken to biting and kicking anyone who entered his stable. Henri despatched Jasper's groom to find a saddle and bridle as he was not prepared to risk trying to ride bareback after last night's activity.

He spoke soothingly through the closed top door of the stable and was pleased to note that Perseus had stopped rearing and striking the door with his front legs. He unbolted the top door a fraction and the German grooms fled as Jasper's groom returned with a military saddle and bridle. Perseus was pawing with his near fore and snorting as he pushed back the top door, his beautiful grey coat lathered in sweat. Henri took the bridle from the groom and carefully opened the bottom door, all the while talking softly to the stallion. He walked confidently up to the horse, slipped the reins over his head and patted his lathered neck. He popped the bit in his mouth, put the bridle over his ears and quickly did up the noseband and throat lash. He called the groom to bring in the saddle and put it on the horse. He kept a tight hold of his offside rein and as the groom fastened the girth, Perseus tried to whip round and bite the groom. Henri was far too quick for him and for the first time raised his voice and shouted, 'No!' He moved directly in front of him and made eye contact with Perseus and the horse stared back at him. Henri knew that one flicker of fear in his eyes would lose him the battle. Perseus held his gaze but after a while averted his eyes and backed off, away from Henri. The groom had finished girthing him up and motioned for him to leave the stable. He rubbed his hand down the horse's neck, talking to him in a quiet voice. He held both reins under his neck and led him to the door. Perseus suddenly tried to run for the open door but again, Henri was too quick for him as he shouted, 'No!' at the same time as administering a sharp slap across his nose. The stallion looked visibly shocked and allowed Henri to lead him out into the yard and towards the exercise paddock.

At this point Le Comte arrived, breathless. 'Oh God, Henri. One of my men ran into my office claiming the mad Frenchman was about to be killed by Napoleon's stallion.'

Henri laughed, 'Well I am still alive at the moment, but time will tell. I am glad you are here. How much experience have you had of riding

Barbary stallions?'

'Well I have never had the pleasure of owning one, but I have ridden a couple.'

'Well watch and learn because you will be riding him daily once I have gone. All he needs is some exercise and work; shutting him up in a stable is going to drive him as mad as locking me in a cell would.'

Henri closed the door of the paddock and turned to mount Perseus; he felt a flicker of movement as Perseus lined him up for another bite but this time he didn't need to slap him or say anything as he stood still and allowed him to put his foot in the stirrup and mount. Very carefully, he adjusted the stirrups to his length and avoided taking up any contact with either the reins or his leg. The horse stood still, and the flicking of his ears suggested he was waiting for the rider's instructions. Henri used his voice to command him forward into trot but kept his reins loose and did not make contact on the horse's sides with his legs. Perseus went forward into trot and Henri made him take small circles around the arena, slowly putting pressure on with his legs. When he was sure Perseus was accepting the contact, he asked for canter. The horse was visibly relaxing as he had nothing to fear from Henri's light hands and he started shortening his stride in answer to Henri's legs. Henri asked him to halt and used his weight in the saddle to lean back very slightly. Perseus dropped from canter to halt in one stride.

The audience, collected around the arena, clapped in appreciation and as Henri asked for canter from halt; he executed it perfectly. As Henri lengthened the stride and cantered full length down the arena, the horse bucked for joy but never attempted to drop his head or twist to the side.

He halted him at the gate. 'Note I did not punish him for that exuberance but chose to ignore it. Now he is listening to me, I will see what he can do.' Henri took him to the bottom of the arena in canter and then asked him to half pass to the opposite side and he was able to continue the movement across the arena with the horse changing leg as he re-joined the track each time. He halted him again at the gate and vaulted off. 'Your turn now, Hans. Believe me, he is a dream to ride. The more freedom of rein you can give him, the lighter he becomes. Don't take too strong a contact with your legs whilst he gets used to you. You have naturally good, light hands anyway, but he will teach you how to perform the advanced movements, provided he trusts you.'

Hans approached Perseus and Henri bent down to give him a leg-up. Perseus nuzzled his jacket sleeve and Henri blew softly on his nose. He adjusted the stirrup length for Hans and then stood back, away from the horse.

'He is all yours now; you must assert your authority without fighting him. If you give an inch he will take a mile. Show an ounce of fear and he will deck you every time you ride him, just for his own amusement. You must be one step ahead of him at all times.'

Le Comte took charge in the same quiet way as Henri. He wasn't as still in the saddle, but his position was good, and he knew to keep the horse going forward into his hand. He soon had him performing half pass at trot and canter and managed enough collection to achieve a few steps of passage. Henri was delighted Hans had done so well; it would be one less worry for him whilst he was away.

Anya approached. 'God Henri, the empathy and touch you have with horses is remarkable. I have all your weapons ready now so if you want to sharpen them in the blacksmith's forge, they are ready. You may wish to try out the rifle on the range as this is Prussian, not French. The French rifles captured are still in Sedan.' Le Comte, having returned Perseus to his stable, joined them.

'If you are going to try that rifle Henri, I am coming to watch.'

Anya showed him the Prussian rifle, which was a lot chunkier and heavier than the newly designed breech loading French Chassepot rifle and had an attached bayonet. Henri had been equipped with the Cavalry Carbine model, which did not have a bayonet attached as the cavalry had their own swords. This made the rifle lighter than the infantry rifle and for his type of work, was better suited. When he was scouting he needed to shoot from long distances to either hit game or pick off enemy troopers or guards.

They went across to the rifle range and Henri tried out the Prussian rifle. Le Comte demonstrated it first and he was an excellent shot at over 100 feet but struggled at 150 feet, although the Prussian rifle had never been designed to perform at that distance.

Henri's skill with any type of rifle had been honed by his time in Russia, shooting game and he adjusted quickly to the weight of the Prussian rifle. He could still hit the centre of the target at 150 feet but found it easier from a prone position rather than standing. Le Comte and Henri discussed the feasibility of the weapon and they both came up with the solution that for the mission Henri faced, which was as a lone scout, he would just remove the bayonet. He was much more likely to need to use a sword, pistol, dagger or axe rather than a rifle. If he got into his barracks under cover he may be able to pick up a Chassepot rifle anyway. Le Comte agreed to have some of the captured French rifles shipped to Versailles from Metz or Sedan.

They then went to the blacksmith's forge and Henri sharpened the axe and sword on the stone wheel. Le Comte watched in awe as Henri carried out the sharpening and tested the blades with rope and horsehair. The axe was sharpened until it would slice through a strand of human hair.

They returned to the stables, where Anya was busy packing his saddlebags. Le Comte went to talk to one of the grooms. Anya chattered away, telling him what she had packed and then she produced the cloak and threw it over his shoulders. Instinctively, he pulled her closer and bent his head to kiss her hair. To his utter surprise she pushed him away and faced him, wagging her finger.

'Henri, don't you dare fall in love with me. That was never my intention; we both have jobs to do and although I am content to have a sexual relationship with you, there is no way we can have a future together.' She saw the desolation in his eyes and she pulled him close and put her head on his chest. 'Henri, don't be disappointed. Whilst we are working together I will be your friend, lover and confidante, but we can never be any more than that as we are on different sides and will be parted soon. God willing, you will return safely but we both take severe risks in our working lives and both of us know the odds are stacked against us. It was a miracle you survived Sedan and your covert work puts you at even greater risk. I will come to your bed tonight sweetheart, to say goodbye, but you must switch your affections away from me now and go back into survival mode.'

As she turned away and left the room he saw tears glisten in her eyes. He walked back up to Le Comte's office for his final briefing, with a heavy heart. After they had discussed his mission, Henri proffered a question to him.

'What exactly does Anya do and who does she work for?'

Hans shook his head. 'Henri, just don't go there. You know you should not have asked. All I will say is, don't misconstrue the privileged treatment you have received at her hands. She is just as capable of ripping your balls off with her bare hands as you are of throttling her. If you step out of line she will kill you without a backward glance. She is a consummate professional soldier and rarely fails on a mission. Don't think you will be unobserved out in Paris, either. Be warned and stay alive, my friend.'

oOo

Henri enjoyed his last dinner with Le Comte and Anya and this time he moderated his drinking as he needed a clear head for tomorrow's challenges. At the end of the meal a servant came in with a message for Anya. She read the note and then proffered her apologies and stood up. She touched him on the shoulder and then whispered in his ear that she would see him later.

After she had gone, Hans said, 'Looks like she is going to give you her own personal send-off. God, I will be glad to be rid of you, Frenchie; I am not used to sharing my women.' Henri noticed the smile, so he knew he was only joking.

Henri snapped back, 'And is she mistress to Bismarck, too?'

'He is effectively her commander and if they choose to have a sexual relationship that's entirely their own business. Anya allows no man to control her heart; she permits sex for her own pleasure but would not be stupid enough to fall in love with anyone as she wants to remain alone and unattached. You concentrate on the job you have to do and if you make it back she may still be here. However, if Bismarck wants to send her on a mission she may not be; just as I may not be here either when you get back.'

'You will look after Perseus for me? I would hate anything to happen to him.'

'If I go, I promise to oversee his welfare. I may be able to move him to Napoleon's stud once we occupy Paris. On the other hand, I might just get him shipped back to my estate in Bavaria. He is a magnificent animal and just the stallion I need for my mares.'

'I don't care as long as someone who understands him looks after him.'

'Be careful where you leave Jester in Paris; the people are still starving, any horse is at risk, especially one unprotected by armed troopers.'

'I know. That's why he would be safer in the barracks or palace stables, but I can't go back to my troop as they will expect me to return to my duties.'

'Well, you will find somewhere. Perhaps you can pay someone to look after him?'

They both left the dining room and made their way upstairs to their rooms.

oOo

It was after midnight before Anya appeared at his bedside. He desperately wanted to ask her if she had come from Bismarck's bed, but he did not want to row with her on their last night and he knew that it was none of his business. She could not have made that clearer to him than she had at the stables.

He pulled her close to him and she sensed his urgency and let him take the lead. He made love to her with such passion and intensity that when he reached his climax he had to stifle his cry with a pillow and he fought to stop the tears welling up in his eyes.

'Steady on, Henri. You will give yourself a heart attack if you try to keep that pace going.' She pulled him close and stroked his hair until his breathing had returned to normal. 'I maybe should not have awakened your sexuality so much; I only wanted to give you some release from the frustration of your captivity, but it seems like you are getting to like it too much. Don't ever think that some doe-eyed inexperienced virgin will be any good to you as a wife. You need an experienced woman who is as intelligent and clever as you, who will be content to rear your children alone. She needs to understand your craving for adventure and your strong bond with nature and animals and be confident enough to let you get on with it and leave the rearing of children to her.'

'Why do I need someone like that?'

'Because Henri, you will never be content to stay at home and curl up by the fireside until you are in your dotage – only then will you settle down and breed horses and be a father to your grandchildren. You need the excitement of solving problems and living new experiences. The fact you chose an axe shows you have a lot of Viking principles in you. But what are the chances of you reaching old age with the risks you take – about a million to one? One day there will be a bullet or a sword with your name on it. You will just want a wife to come home to for rest and recuperation so that you can breed again and rock the cradle of the last baby you left her to rear. In fact, a widow would be the perfect answer. You have a generous, gentle nature; you could rear another man's children and that would be a perfect solution. You are too young to settle down yet but, in your thirties, it would be ideal. There will be a lot of widows around in France after this war ends. Marry for love Henri but appreciate the responsibility you are heaping on a wife. She has got to be strong enough to be able to wave you off on your travels with a smile on her face, knowing that one day, you will not be coming back.'

'I understand what you are saying because I have seen the harsh reality women face in rearing children single-handed and I am amazed at their dedication and resilience. Women are far stronger, mentally, than men because they must be to deal with the cards that life deals them. They have no choice in how many children they have, and the Catholic Church makes their lives even harder.'

'You will never be faithful to your wife either,

Henri. You will succumb to temptation as and when it crosses your path. You have animal instincts no different from a wolf. If a woman shows an interest you will bed her without a second thought. Let's face it, Henri – what woman would not want to tumble with you due to your stunning looks and muscular body? You proved that the other day when you took me, even though you knew I might have been out to kill you.'

Henri pushed her onto her back and said, 'Now I will prove to you that your teaching has given me the carnal knowledge to please women in bed and I will give you a demonstration to remember me by.'

oOo

The next morning, Henri was up by 7 a.m. and dressed in his civilian clothing, ready for the start of his mission. Anya had left his bed straight after their passionate lovemaking, suggesting he needed to get some sleep. He collected the last items he needed from his room as his saddlebags were down at the stables. He went down to the main dining room where breakfast was served buffet style, as he wanted to eat more than coffee and toast; he knew it might be the only food he would eat that day. He got some strange looks from the Prussians due to his mode of dress but thankfully, as he sat down with a plateful of food, Le Comte turned up.

'Partaking of your last decent food are you, Henri?'

'Yes, you said it was going to be difficult to obtain it in Paris so even stealing it may not be worth the risk.'

'What will you do if your own men recognise you? They will automatically assume you are a deserter and clamp you in irons.'

'I will have to do a lot of talking my way out of trouble as I cannot operate confined to the barracks or in a cell. I have no idea who is left at the barracks so anything I do there will have to be covert. I will have the same problems at the palace if they recognise me from when I was there as a bodyguard. It could work either way, as an advantage or a disadvantage.'

Le Comte took him to his office to give him the money and a safe passage from Bismarck, should he get caught by Prussian patrols. Le Comte got called away by one of his men for a few minutes, so Henri took the opportunity to give Anya a small gift.

'There was an old French tradition when knights fought in exhibition tourneys or went off to war that they carried a "favour" from a woman, which generally consisted of a ribbon in her heraldic colours. Young and unmarried knights generally wore the ribbon of the wife of the master of the house in which they served, attached to their sword belt. It was believed to protect them in battle and ensure they returned safely.' Henri knelt down on one knee and took her hand, kissed it and placed in it a thin strand of blue ribbon. 'I would like you to accept this gift from me and wear it to guide me safely on my journey. I have the other half of it fastened to my sword belt.'

Anya replied in a choked voice, 'I would be honoured, Lieutenant Croizette. May God keep you safe and protect the bravest and most chivalrous French knight I have ever had the pleasure to meet.' She kissed him on both cheeks and they set off down to the stables, where Le Comte re-joined them.

Jester's groom was waiting with Jester fully kitted out with his saddlebags, a rifle and sack of oats already attached to the non-military saddle. He wore just a plain bridle with a metal bit that had been covered in muslin cloth to prevent any noise if Jester chewed it. Henri checked all Jester's legs for any problems. He noticed that although the groom had not brushed him for three days he had removed any bedding from his mane and tail. The groom led him out and Henri pulled on his boots, cloak and hat.

He turned to Le Comte, shook his hand and said, 'I wager you're glad to see the back of your arsehole of a French prisoner?'

'Not especially, Henri. You have been great company and served as an inspiration in what true duty and courage to your country means. Maybe, after the war is over you would come to Bavaria to see my horse breeding farm and show me how to train my horses?'

He refrained from kissing Anya as they were in full view but bowed to her before he mounted. He trotted off towards the gate with their good luck shouts ringing in his ears. As he reached the gates, which were opened by the guards, he walked through then turned Jester, asked him to rear up and he took his hat off and bowed to the guards and waved to Anya and Hans. He took a deep breath and cantered off.

21

Henri's first destination was to be Charles and Marie's house on the left bank of the Seine. He came off the road and used the woods as he did not want to run into any Prussian troops. He reached the chateau in half an hour and even from a distance, he could see it was deserted. There was no activity in the fields and no horses in them either. He went through the gates, straight to the stables and found the barn had been boarded up. The stables were empty and had been for a long time, so he put Jester in one for a moment, with a bucket of water. What fate had befallen Marie's mare Favorit, the two ex-cavalry horses he had given them as a wedding present and Marie's two Borzoi hounds? He hoped they hadn't been slaughtered for food. It didn't take him long to check out that nobody had been in residence for a while. He found a loose window that would grant him access but he did not intend to use it as he needed to be in the centre of Paris.

Henri got across the Seine using a bridge that merchants and traders were using. He checked there were no guards at either side and he entered a wartorn Paris for the first time. He headed to Montmartre to see if he could locate Charles at his studio. Across the street from Charles's studio he slipped into an overgrown garden, checked the house was deserted and left Jester to eat the grass in the garden while he continued on foot. To his delight, he found one stable at the back of the house, so thought he might be able to use this for Jester if needed; he hid his tack and luggage in a cupboard.

People were stirring, and some shops were open but very few had food supplies. He tried the door to Charles's studio; it was locked. He went into one of the alleyways further down the street, climbed up onto the buildings and made his way to the back of the studio at first-floor level. Again, everything looked deserted. He headed towards the Luxembourg Gardens and Palace. The beautiful gardens and lake were overgrown and neglected, and the palace had been boarded up. There was evidence of cannon fire in the gardens, which he assumed must have come from the Prussians.

He took the direct route to the Tuileries Palace, to find that the east wing had been ravaged by fire. It opened access to the quadrangle and he could use the charcoal ruins for cover. He made his way very gingerly up to the top floor, which gave him an excellent vantage point. He settled down to observe all that was happening around him. He knew from experience that until he had observed his surroundings he could not risk attempting to go any further. He could see the Palace Guard patrolling the other parts of the palace, but they were thin in number and there was little activity at the main entrance. In the far distance he could see the barricades and units of the National Guard in their grey overcoats. He watched some horse-drawn wagons unloading supplies to the kitchen and decided to make his way over there, undercover. He intended to pose as a merchant if he was challenged. He got into a position close enough to hear the men chatting while unloading the wagon with the kitchen staff. To his delight, one of the chefs Mario who he had got on well with, came out of the main door and wandered off to have a smoke. Thankfully, there was enough cover for Henri to reach him unobserved and he was far enough away from the supply wagon. Mario was leaning on one of the pillars, with his back to him. Henri approached stealthily and then grabbed Mario from behind and put his hand over his mouth, whispering in his ear and raising the axe to his throat with his other hand. He pulled him back into the darkness but was talking to him soothingly in Italian. After the fear and shock had left his eyes, Mario led him into the wine cellar.

He told Mario he was working undercover and wanted to know the whereabouts of Eugénie. Mario assured him nobody knew where she had gone or with whom and there was a whole host of rumours but none of them could be verified. Henri asked whether there had been any indication that she intended to flee, and he said no. She had not taken any servants with her, just disappeared one night with Louis, without saying a word to anyone – including her political advisers. When the young prince came back to Paris she had been overjoyed and she had gone, taking him with her, within forty-eight hours of his return. The one significant piece of information he gained was that Carolus-Duran had visited Eugénie a week before the prince came home as Mario had seen them talking in the palace garden. Mario had been involved in preparations for the meal for the Arts' Ball and he remembered Charles and Marie being principal guests and had seen the newspaper coverage in Le Figaro, so he was certain it had been Charles. There had been no sign of Marie, though. Before he left, Mario supplied him with a basket of food as he said he would have little luck finding anything substantial in the Paris shops.

Henri slipped away from the palace and made his way back to Montmartre, to Charles's studio. He found a suitable spot where he could observe from street level. He saw, in the twilight, a tall man in a National Guard grey overcoat come to the door, unlock it and enter the studio. Henri assumed this must be someone Charles knew as he had a key. He decided to go and check on Jester and then come back and observe from first-floor level.

Jester was pleased to see him, and he put him in the stable and fed him for the night. There was no sign of life in the house or in the other two houses on both sides, so he hoped that Jasper would be safe.

He returned to Charles's studio and climbed up

to first floor level, so he could observe through the windows. He could see into the kitchen window due to a faint light. A man was preparing some bread and cheese. To his utter surprise he approached the window and looked out and Henri recognised Charles for the first time. He had lost a huge amount of weight and the only discernible features Henri could recognise were his eyes and nose. Henri was shocked at the state of him and realised he was the man he had seen in the grey coat. He waited to check that Charles was alone and then went back to street level and knocked on the door. Charles came down but demanded to know who was there before he opened the door. When he answered, the door was quickly unlocked, and Charles threw it open.

'Henri, is it really you? I thought you may have succumbed in battle.' He threw his arms round him in a bear hug and locked the door behind him. Tears were running down Charles's cheeks as he observed Henri.

'God Charles, how have you survived? You look half the man I remember.' He pulled the basket of food that Mario had given him from under his cloak and continued, 'At least I come bearing gifts of food.' They went back upstairs to the small salon and Henri told Charles to eat whatever he wanted from the basket whilst he opened the bottle of wine that Mario had sent. 'Where is Marie?'

The reaction from Charles was pitiful. 'I don't know, Henri. She was in Lille, but I have no idea whether she and Marie-Ann are alive or dead.' Unable to control his emotions he sobbed, and all Henri could do was kneel beside him and stroke his hand while the sobs subsided.

'God forbid, Charles. Just eat some of the chicken and then we will talk. Do you have to return to duty for the National Guard tonight?'

'No Henri, not until tomorrow night.'

After Charles had eaten and the wine had warmed him through, he started to tell his story. Henri just sat back and listened. It was obvious that Charles blamed himself for putting Marie and Marie-Ann at great risk in Lille as the Prussian army entered France via Belgium and set up camp from Lille. He bitterly regretted not sending them to England, especially as he had been pivotal in securing the safety of France's art treasures – with the help of the British. Monet had moved to London and was surviving well and had a new appreciative audience to sell his work to. Eventually, Charles asked Henri what he was doing back in Paris and he told him about being at the Battle of Sedan and being selected as Napoleon's aide. He did not tell him the part he had played in the battle by rescuing Napoleon but confirmed that his major work had been as a scout and messenger (he avoided mentioning his spying missions).

Eventually, Henri raised the question of Eugénie's disappearance and admitted that he was now on a mission to reunite her with Napoleon in exile and needed to know where she was. Charles volunteered that he had been to the palace to see her to warn her that her life was in danger and had advised her to get out while she could. However, she refused to leave immediately; she wouldn't go without her son. When young Louis was sent back from Metz, she contacted Charles and he had arranged for them to be escorted to Normandy by Manet and to escape via a fishing boat to England, assisted by Monet at the other end. Charles had previously advised her to remove the two Velázquez and three Goya paintings she owned personally, to safety in London. They were now in the care of Paul Durand-Ruel, the art dealer who had fled Paris and set up a gallery in London. The whole operation was done in total secrecy and apart from travelling with Dr Evans her American dentist as an escort, Eugénie had left France with just one small bag containing some of her jewellery, and minimal clothes. Manet had accompanied her to London but intended to return to Paris and Charles expected him back soon.

It gave Henri a huge boost to have found out where Eugénie had gone, with relative ease. If Manet was due back he would either suggest they both return to England, so he could meet her, or if Manet could not go back, he would go alone. He remembered what Napoleon had said about Eugénie possibly not welcoming him, so he could not leave it to anyone else to do.

Charles insisted Henri stay with him and fetched him some bedding for the large sofa in the salon.

He told him where Jester was, and Charles thought he would be safe enough where he was. It was close to midnight when Henri insisted Charles rest as he was exhausted. They would have time to catch up whilst they were waiting for Manet's return. He was relieved to hear that his parents had also gone to Italy to avoid the danger, as their chateau was within five miles of Versailles. He thought about the fate of Marie, but he could not offer Charles any help now until his mission for Napoleon was complete. Then he might be able to go to Lille and search for her, but Charles was in no fit state to go looking for her now as Prussian troops had Paris surrounded. It would give him a breathing space to find out what exactly was going on in Paris, to fulfil his side of the bargain and report back to Bismarck.

oOo

At dawn the next morning, Henri left a note for Charles and slipped out to go and feed Jester and let him out into the garden. On his return, Charles was still asleep and only started to stir when he heard Henri banging around in the kitchen. He brought them both coffee and the last of the bread rolls and cheese. He looked at Charles closely and reckoned he probably only weighed around ten stone now, which was far too little for his 6ft 2 inches frame.

'Charles, when did you last eat a decent meal?'

'God, Henri, I can't remember! I haven't eaten meat for a long time except the odd bit of pet meat that was available. I have existed on bread and jam during the siege. The less you eat, the less you crave food.'

'But have you noticed how deprived your body is? You are half starved.'

'Of course, I know I have no energy. I can hardly walk, never mind fight. Even holding a rifle is a huge effort, never mind wielding a sword. It isn't just my physical strength that's gone; it is my mental strength too. I know I have gone into a deep depression at the loss of Marie and Marie-Ann and I blame myself entirely for leaving them in such danger.'

'It wasn't your fault, Charles; you could not have known. You were doing your best to protect them. I have a close bond with Marie and I feel she is still alive, and you know how resourceful and clever she is. She may have left Lille ages ago and got out of the country with Marie-Ann and be safe.'

Charles turned and gave him a haunted look as he replied, 'Do you really think Marie could go unnoticed anywhere? With her looks alone she will have become the target of men and God only knows what fate may have befallen her. I don't care if she has been molested by another man or is even carrying a child; I just want her back in my arms where she belongs. Having seen with my own eyes the children starving to death during the siege I suspect I have no hope of seeing my beautiful daughter alive again.' Shuddering sobs engulfed him, and a waterfall of pent-up emotion poured out of him.

Henri knelt and put his arms around him to offer some comfort.

'I promise you, as soon as my mission is completed for Napoleon, I will do everything I can to find her. When I get back to Versailles I will ask them to help me find her and I promise to bring her back to you. You must do everything you can to stay alive when the Germans enter Paris. You must hide, not be at the forefront on the barricades.'

'You are suggesting that I desert my post and become a coward. I never expected someone with your integrity to suggest something as outrageous as that.'

'Charles, explain to me why you signed up to the National Guard in the first place. You have never been a warmonger; you have always been a peaceful man. The Germans are just biding their time across the Seine, watching Frenchmen destroy their own capital city. Why in God's name did it come to this, why didn't the people accept surrender? More Frenchmen could be killed by their own countrymen here in Paris than those killed in battle by the Germans. Why have the people done this when Napoleon was an elected emperor, not a monarch?'

'Don't you think I have asked that same question myself? It is a topic that Courbet and I discuss all the time when manning the barricades. He has always had revolutionary principles but even he cannot answer that question. The world has gone mad, Henri and I joined up purely to protect the works of art in the Louvre from anyone that wishes to destroy them. The fact that some of them are my own countrymen leaves me sick to the core.'

22

Henri rose before dawn and went to collect Jester, then rode out of Montmartre to his barracks. Jester was full of energy and glad to be out and Henri was careful to keep off the main roads so as not to draw any attention to themselves. He approached the barracks from the fields behind. Protected by the cover of a copse, he cautioned Jester to remain silent, stood up on his back and climbed up a tree, to survey the scene. As he had hoped, by coming this way he could gain access via the isolation stables and paddocks. In the nearest field there were six cavalry horses grazing contentedly. They were obviously a group of horses who were recuperating from various stages of lameness. He knew the isolation yard of twelve large stables was controlled by one senior groom and only visited by vets when necessary, to avoid cross-infection from the main stables. It was totally out of bounds to troops and other grooms.

He noticed movement from the stables and an elegant grey stallion was being led out by a groom towards a small, well-fenced arena and he was literally bouncing on the spot or rearing up and giving the handler a very hard time. The groom made it to the arena and unleashed the stallion and he jumped back behind the gate and shot the bolt across. The Barbary stallion dived onto the grass and rolled over several times, leapt up and set off, bucking and kicking around the arena. This convinced Henri that the groom must be on his own or he would have asked for help in moving the fractious stallion. He shimmied back down the tree, called Jester back to him and jumped into the saddle. He had decided to take the most direct route to the stables, which meant jumping in and out of the field of invalid horses. The fence was a substantial four bars high, but this would be no problem for Jester. He urged him into a fast canter and approached the fence in the middle, away from where the group of horses was grazing. When Jester realised he was being asked to jump the fence, he bucked with delight and surged forward, giving it a good six inches' clearance. He kept cantering in a straight line to set up for the next fence. The other horses, disturbed by the sudden appearance of Jester, galloped off down the field. Jester took the fence out of the field and Henri let him canter towards the stable-yard. Suddenly, the groom came running out of the stables as Henri entered the yard. He must have thought the stallion had jumped out of his paddock. Henri pulled Jester up and to his utter delight he realised the groom was Andy, a young English lad who had been an apprentice groom whom Henri had supervised. He knew had a depth of knowledge of dealing with injured horses.

He addressed him in English as he dismounted. 'Andy, it's Lieutenant Croizette. I need your help.'

The boy reeled in shock. 'Nay sir, I thought tha' was a woman with all that hair... and where is your uniform? But I know that's Jester all reet.'

'I could not wear it coming into Paris with all the German troops around. I am here on a mission and you must keep my visit a secret. I have come to deliver a message, but I don't want anyone to know I am here as that could delay my return. Does anyone else come down here?'

'Nay, I'm on mi own down here looking after the lame uns and there is only one troop still stationed 'ere so no one bothers me.'

'You look like you have got your hands full with that stallion out in the paddock.'

'Aye, that be "Apollo," Colonel Matisse's stallion an' he's been an absolute bugger to nurse. He's had more bites out of me than I care to count, but it was mi own fault for opening mi big mouth and saying I could cure 'im. I told those vets and commanding officer that there was no need to shoot 'im he would be reet as rain when I had cured him. I told them you had shown me how to poultice wounds and it would just take time.'

Andy opened a stable door for Jester and Henri untacked him. He fetched him some sweet-smelling hay and Jester dived into it with relish.

'Well you had better show me what miracles you have performed on Apollo then.'

Andy's face lit up and they walked out to the paddock where Apollo was grazing. His head shot up when he saw another person with Andy and he moved away from the gate and eyed Henri with suspicion.

'Just be careful sir, 'e mebbe thinks you are coming to ride 'im and he can be so quick with them damned teeth and 'e kicks like a mule. Let me get ho'd of him first before you come in.'

Andy opened the gate and advanced towards Apollo, chatting quietly in a reassuring voice. The stallion whinnied quietly in greeting but kept his eyes fixed on Henri. When Andy clipped on the rein and brought him over to the gate, Henri slipped in and closed the gate behind him. He walked confidently up to his shoulder and he could see the stitched wound snaking from the horse's wither past his shoulder and round to his chest. He raised his hand, but Apollo spun away and whipped his head round to snap at Henri. Henri spoke soothingly to him in a low, melodic voice and put his hand on his side. Slowly the horse relaxed, and the tension flowed out of him. As Henri finally got within touching distance of the livid red scar he moved in closer and rubbed his hand on Apollo's muzzle. He didn't touch the scar directly but ran his fingers over the muscle and skin around it.

'Jesus, Andy you have done a remarkable job with this wound. Did you stitch it yourself?'

'Aye I did, you may remember mi mam is a

seamstress and mi nan is an herbalist healer in Yorkshire. It took three other grooms to 'old 'im still and the stitches held except over the shoulder muscle, so I packed it with comfrey, calendula and turmeric and it healed slowly. I had to slart it on daily and his majesty weren't too pleased with me, as it must have stung him but eventually he stopped biting me.' Apollo was now nuzzling Henri's jacket while he scratched his ear. 'I knew you had healing hands, sir. Look at him; he's acting like an old dog wi' you, he trusts you completely. Colonel Matisse was real shook up when he got back with 'im, there was so much blood he was sure he would die. He was with a small group of four and they ran into a German scouting troop of five. They were engaged in close contact fighting and a German sliced at Matisse with his sword and although he deflected the blow with his own sword, it bounced off and then sliced downwards into Apollo.'

'They were very lucky; one inch further and it would have severed Apollo's jugular vein, he would have gone down immediately, and Matisse would never have made it back. Thank God your mother married a Frenchman and brought you over here, Andy.'

'It was 'ard leaving God's own county – Yorkshire – but at least I am caring for some decent 'osses now rather than cart horses and cows.'

They returned to the stables and Henri questioned Andy on who was likely to be about when he went

240

over to the stables. He donned his cloak and hat and walked over to the barracks, keeping to the trees and bushes.

It was two hours later when Henri returned to the stables. Andy was busy putting straw beds down before bringing the horses in.

'Don't you leave the horses out overnight now they are roughed off?'

'Jesus sir, ye can tell ye haven't been in Paris during the siege. We daren't leave any 'oss outside for fear of it being nicked for riding, or worse to eat. I see tha's helped thissen to a rifle on your trip yonder?'

'You don't miss much do you, Andy?'

'No sir, but in Yorkshire "we see all but say nowt," so don't worry thissen. Might you be returnin' to us in due course?'

'I have no idea where I may end up Andy, but you take care of yourself because the Germans will be here soon. Don't try any heroics; they will always want good nags men and you could tell them I trained you and that just might secure you a job and keep you safe.'

'We also say in Yorkshire that "a man cannot serve two masters" so whatever ye are up to sir, watch your back and keep that wonder 'oss of yours safe as well. I ain't niver seen a man as good with 'osess as thee and it would be a crying shame to lose ya. I thought tha might need a bit of decent jock, so I have fastened a plucked pheasant to your saddlebag.'

It was three days later, before dawn, when Henri woke to an urgent knocking downstairs on Charles's studio door. Charles was on night duty and so Henri slipped down and asked who was calling. He was transfixed when the answer came back. He quickly opened the door and Manet looked as shocked to see him as he was to see Manet.

Manet recovered first while he locked the door. 'God Henri, both Charles and I thought you would not make it through this war but here you are as large as life. What are you doing here?'

'Surprisingly, I have been waiting for you to return from England because I need you to take me there to find Empress Eugénie.'

'What makes you think I have a clue as to her whereabouts?'

'Charles says you know the right people to ask in London.'

'But why? She would be foolish to set foot in France ever again.'

'I have been sent to find her so that Napoleon can join her in exile as the Germans have him captured at Versailles and as he is no longer the head of state, they are prepared to release him into exile.'

'I doubt that would be the view of the new revolutionary government. I would expect they would prefer his head hanging above the gates of Paris.'

'And is that your opinion too?'

'I have never been a fan of Napoleon and I got

myself labelled by the government as "trouble" when I painted *The Execution of Emperor Maximilian,* but I have always respected Eugénie and appreciate that Napoleon was an elected emperor rather than an imposed monarch. I will help you as best I can, for Eugénie's sake.'

They chatted about the war and Henri said he was very concerned about Charles and asked him if they could take him to Le Havre as he was sure that the Germans would take the city in the next few weeks. Manet said he thought that Charles would refuse to leave Paris, but he would willingly try.

oOo

Henri sat back and let the sea breeze blow his hair away from his face and relished the smell of the sea as the fishing boat pulled out of the harbour. He and Manet had taken two days, riding mostly at night, to get to Le Havre and he had left Jester at Manet's, being guarded by Leon armed with a rifle, under orders to keep their horses safe whilst they were away.

He felt a pang of unease at Charles's refusal to leave Paris with them as he feared for his safety once the Germans claimed the besieged capital. All he could do was pray that he managed to hide rather than fighting to the death on the barricades. He could do nothing until he got back to Paris... and now he had to concentrate on finding Eugénie.

Henri and Manet hid in outlying barns during daylight hours. They slept for a few hours and then he hunted for food with a homemade bow and arrow. He had always managed to bring something to the table, even if it had only been stolen eggs. Manet did the cooking and they chatted over their meal.

Henri asked Manet about his fascination with Marie and was genuinely surprised to find that he hero worshipped her rather than seeing her as a potential sexual conquest. Having learned from Charles of Manet's fascination for women he had assumed that he lusted after Marie and wanted a sexual relationship. However, although he admitted that he would love to paint her, he harboured no illusions of her ever bestowing her delectable body on him.

Manet told him about Charles's first trip to England to negotiate the loan of artwork to the Tate Gallery for exhibition. He was desperately seasick during the crossing by fishing boat whilst Manet, who had trained as a sailor on cargo ships and smaller craft, loved the rough and tumble of the sea. It took Charles two days to recover after he reached London, before he could meet with officials at the Tate. He and Monet had investigated the capital whilst Charles slept off his sickness. Charles never crossed the Channel again and did his negotiating from Paris whilst Monet and Manet represented the French in London.

Henri was looking forward to seeing London although there would be little time for sightseeing as he needed to return as quickly as possible. He wondered whether his captors had considered that he may just disappear and fail to carry out his task. However, he would hardly leave Napoleon in dire straits when he had volunteered for the task. He just hoped that when he found Eugénie, she would want to be reunited with Napoleon. During his time as a bodyguard at court he knew they tended to live separate lives. They only appeared together at official state functions when necessary. Eugénie maintained her own private court and operated entirely separately from Napoleon. She would have nothing to do with any of his mistresses and none of them were permitted to dine or socialise within the inner sanctum. Eugénie devoted herself to her religion, art, education and campaigning for women. She had never taken any lovers although she enjoyed the company of men. Her main interest had always been her son, Louis. She had overseen his education and had ensured he remained grounded and was fit to be the young prince. She had not pampered him or kept him locked up in an ivory tower, which as it turned out, would equip him well in the future as he would have to make his own way in the world now. He had met him while at court. Louis had been studying at the Sorbonne. He spoke Spanish, English and German but military history was his natural subject. With Napoleon I as his great uncle and Napoleon III as his father he had two great battle strategists to follow, but life was not going to be easy for him now that his father had been deposed.

On the train up to London, Henri was fascinated by the changing scenery. One minute, they were going through rural villages and the next, they were in heavily industrialised towns. He was surprised to hear that Victoria Station was only one of several stations in the City of London. He was pleased that Manet knew where he was going and had decreed their first port of call would be Durand-Ruel's gallery. After announcing them at reception, Paul Durand-Ruel came out to greet them and ushered them into his office.

'Manet, how can I be of service to you? Have you some paintings you wish me to sell?'

Manet laughed, 'When do you think I have the chance to paint? Believe it or not, there is a war on in Paris and some of us are fighting for our country. We are here to track down Empress Eugénie as Henri has some news from Napoleon and King Wilhelm of Prussia.'

Durand-Ruel replied, 'Well as far as I understand, she is living with her son at 1C King Street, which is the house they leased here when he was in exile last time. They still maintain the lease on the property.'

Henri said, 'Is the British Government aware she is residing here?'

'Well I would have thought so, as it would be difficult to keep quiet.'

Manet said, 'So where are Monet and the rest of the French artists?'

Durand-Ruel replied, 'Oh, Monet has just

opened a studio and gallery here, which he shares with Pissaro and Sisley when they are in town. He seems fascinated by the Thames and its changing weather patterns and has done several paintings, which are selling well.'

Manet jumped to his feet shouting, 'Fucking hell, so Monet is sitting painting quietly by the Thames while Paris burns. Explain to me why the only artists who are defending their country are Duran, Degas, Courbet, Renoir (who has been stricken with dysentery and unable to fight) and me. Also, Frédéric Bazille and Henri Regnault, both promising artists aged twenty-eight, have died in battle defending their country. What exactly does this say about the courage of Frenchmen? On top of that, we are now fighting each other while the Germans sit on the left bank of the Seine, watching in disbelief.' Both Henri and Durand-Real stared at him in shocked silence. Manet continued, 'Shit, Paul. I didn't mean to offend you as if you hadn't moved over here after buying paintings from me, Cézanne and other French artists, we would have starved six months ago.'

'No offence taken, Manet. I can fully understand your anger and frustration with your colleagues.'

They left with friendship restored and Durand-Ruel offered them accommodation with him whilst they were in London.

23

As Eugénie was in London, Manet suggested that they part company and Henri go alone to meet her as he didn't expect to be party to the messages from Napoleon. He wanted to go into the art galleries to see some of the famous masters' work.

Henri set off to find the house and when located, he observed it from the other side of the road to see if he could detect any activity. He was just about to approach the door after seeing no movement for fifteen minutes when a hansom cab pulled up and a man and woman got out. He crossed the road quickly and recognised Eugénie. He intercepted her as she moved towards her front door.

'Your Majesty, may I speak with you?' He bowed and removed his hat.

She looked startled and then she recognised him. 'Henri, what on earth are you doing in London? Come on in.'

Her male companion looked perturbed at his intervention but made no move against him. She led him up the stairs to the first-floor apartment and was surprised to find there was only a maid in attendance. She dismissed her companion as they entered the salon.

'Henri, I am relieved you survived the fighting but what are you doing here?'

'I bring you news of your husband and a proposal from King Wilhelm of Prussia.' She looked at him in amazement and gestured for him to sit down. 'I have come from Versailles, where we have been held, with an offer to release your husband into exile with you, provided he complies with the demands of the Prussians and remains banished from France.'

'Oh, Henri, why did he surrender? He should have died honourably in battle.'

'Madame, we were outnumbered two to one at Sedan and the generals knew that within hours of the battle commencing, as I was out scouting and saw them bringing more troops into position. I believe dying on the battlefield was your husband's intention, but it didn't happen, and he had no alternative but to surrender before more Frenchmen were slaughtered in vain.' Henri shuddered at the part he had played in this but had decided it should be up to Napoleon to divulge the truth to Eugénie if he so wished. 'The Germans thought you may have fled to Spain, but your husband suspected you would return to England as you still have the lease on this apartment.'

'Yes, Charles Duran came to me and warned me that my life was in danger from the Communards, but I wouldn't leave without Louis and then when he was sent back from Metz I followed his advice and fled, telling nobody but escorted by Thomas Evans. Duran gave me Manet's address in Le Havre and he arranged a boat to England. Has Paris been taken yet? I have only what the English press print, for information.'

'Not yet ma'am, but I suspect they will move in within the next two weeks or so. There is still fierce fighting going on between the two warring factions, but their patience is running out.'

The salon door was flung open and fourteen-year-old Prince Louis Napoleon swept into the room. He looked at Henri as he rose from the chair.

'By Christ it's you, Henri Croizette, my fencing and shooting tutor and the best horseman in Europe. Have you come with news from Paris? Has it fallen?'

Henri bowed. 'Yes, Your Highness – with the good news that the Germans will release your father into exile here to join you. Paris is on the brink of invasion and in a very sorry state.'

Louis answered, 'You can cut the titles, Henri. I am no longer a prince. How were you allowed to travel over here?'

'I am a prisoner, just like your father, at Versailles along with his other generals and have been given the task of finding you. As your father is no longer the head of state and not in the best of health they have agreed to his exile, but it will have stringent conditions attached.'

'So, if you are returning to Paris then I can come back with you.'

Both Eugénie and Henri shouted an emphatic, 'No!' simultaneously.

Henri said, 'Louis think about it, all your family will be banned from entering France again and whilst they may allow your father to leave, there would be no such leniency granted towards you. They would have no hesitation in killing you, as you remain a threat to both the Germans and the new French Republican Government when it is formed.'

Louis threw himself onto the sofa next to his mother and she took his hand and said, 'You will have to accept that you will be unable to return to Paris and will settle here in England and continue your education.'

'But Mama, I am French and want to live there, not England.'

'Louis, you will be grateful that the English Government is prepared to offer us sanctuary here in Britain.'

Henri spoke. 'Ma'am, how are you managing for money since you arrived?

'Thankfully, we still had a bank account here in England and Duran took three Goya paintings and two Velázquez paintings of mine and shipped them over here to Durand-Ruel; he is holding them ready to sell when the need arises. I don't need an army of servants and we will cut our cloth according to our means. I came here with some jewellery and my precious son and that is all I need for now.'

'I don't expect you will receive any money from

the government as they will have a huge sum to raise if they want the Germans to leave Paris. I imagine that they will insist on the return of their territories in Alsace and Lorraine as well. This will all take time as the new government has not been elected yet. However, they may release your husband before the negotiations are finalised.'

Louis said, 'Will they release you to accompany my father to England?'

'They have agreed that I can have safe passage to accompany him into exile, but I will be expected to return and report back to them. I am still their prisoner and they will want to use some of my skills to their advantage.'

The maid brought tea and afterwards, Henri took his leave and Louis escorted him to the door.

Henri hugged him and said, 'Louis, you have to look after your mother and continue your education here. I know it must be very difficult to be a prince one moment and then become an exiled refugee overnight but you're clever and resourceful and if you study hard you can forge yourself a bright career in whatever area you want.'

'Oh, Henri since you came to court as bodyguard to my father two years ago I have only wanted to be like you – a great soldier – but now I cannot even fight for my country.'

'Politics and governments change quickly, Louis; you may find your exile ban lifted in the future, but don't get yourself killed trying to go back to France.

The Germans will have you under surveillance from the minute your father is released, and I can assure you they are excellent spies. At the first sign of rebellion from you or your father they will kill you. Stay safe and bide your time and hopefully I will see you again soon.'

Henri returned to Durand-Ruel's apartment above his gallery and he treated them to dinner at the Savoy and gave them clothes to wear. They had a wonderful meal and had plenty to drink and enjoyed the luxury of the hotel. They were about to leave when a commotion occurred in the reception and a man ran into the dining room shouting, 'The Germans have taken Paris!'

All three men sat in silence as the news sank in. Henri's first thought was of Charles because he knew he would not have taken his advice to hide. Manet's first thought was whether his studio and home had survived and Durand-Ruel also wondered whether his office and gallery had survived. He had brought his wife and children with him to London but there were still relatives living in and around Paris. Durand-Ruel paid the bill and they walked back to his apartment, engrossed in their thoughts. Manet and Henri had already been planning to leave the next day.

oOo

Henri had a difficult night having vivid dreams about the fate of Charles and what damage the Germans were wreaking in Paris. He had not been privy to any inside information at Versailles and certainly, Anya had given him no hints. He knew Bismarck would have posted troops on all the major routes in and out of Paris, so anybody who thought they could escape would be disappointed. They took the first train back to Dover before dawn had broken and were relieved their fishing boat was still bobbing in the jetty. They decided to aim for Le Havre and if German boats were patrolling the harbour, they would say they had been fishing overnight. Henri bought a box of herring and a loaf of bread, so they could pretend they were gutting if they were challenged. If they couldn't get back in at Le Havre, Manet would sail them round the coastline to find a deserted cove further north. Thankfully, they were in a small boat; if they had gone in a larger vessel some of these options would not have been available.

Henri left Manet to sail while he cooked four of the herring for their breakfast. They chatted about their options and although Henri suggested Manet would be safer staying in Le Havre, he announced he was going back into Paris with him in search of Charles and Courbet and to see if he could get them out to take them back to Le Havre. Henri suggested Manet dress as a civilian, although this would not necessarily guarantee the German troops would treat him any differently.

To their utter delight, about two miles from Le Havre they spotted a small fleet of five fishing boats heading back into port. They caught them up and Manet asked one of them if they could come into port under their cover, and whether Germans were in the harbour. The men did not know Paris had been taken when they set out, so they had seen no troop activity when they left. Manet manoeuvred their boat into the middle of the formation and they sailed into the harbour. Immediately, they could see a small German patrol boat moored at the main jetty. Thankfully, they were heading to the far side of the harbour where the fishing boats unloaded their catch. Although the Germans watched them file past they made no attempt to stop them. Both Manet and Henri heaved a sigh of relief. They thanked the fishermen profusely and gave no explanation for their journey. Leon appeared as he had seen them sailing in from the cliff top. They went back to Manet's and prepared to leave as soon as darkness fell.

Henri was grateful that Jester had been rested for a week and was well fed so that if he had to put him under pressure, he should stand up to it. Manet's horse was in good condition too, so if they had to flee from a pursuit they would have some speed. Manet packed some herring in ice and prepared a pannier of food as hunting might not be an option depending on what they encountered along the way. Henri had gone into survival mode and all his senses were on high alert. He checked his rifle and pistols were in full working order and checked the sharpness of his sword, daggers and axe.

They left at 7 p.m. and Henri was grateful to have Manet with him as he knew all the short routes through the villages, avoiding the main roads. They were lucky that there was a three-quarter moon to give them some light as there was no way they could risk using any light, for fear of detection. They were keeping within a mile of the road and had seen very little traffic. Suddenly, they both heard a horse whinnying in the distance. Henri commanded Jester to stay quiet and whispered to Manet to take cover in the woods with the horses and he would check out the area on foot.

His suspicions proved right as, camped off the road, was a German troop of twelve with eight pack horses. He stealthily crept up to a wall where the packs had been unloaded overnight. To his surprise they weren't full of weapons, but food and they must have been heading into Paris to either relieve the starving citizens or ensure supplies for their own troops. Quickly, he made his way back as dawn was only an hour away and he wanted to put some distance between them and the troop. They rode on for another hour and then pulled over into a deep wood and dismounted to rest the horses and – hopefully – to sleep themselves.

They slept for six hours and then Manet made a fire and cooked them eggs and bacon for breakfast. Henri saw to the horses, rubbed them down and gave them plenty of oats and cut them a pile of fresh grass to eat while tethered. He fetched water from a nearby stream. They studied the map and planned their route for that night. Henri had already decided to approach Paris from the south west side (around the area the barracks were), as it offered plenty of natural cover. He would scout and check whether the Germans had taken over the barracks and if not, he planned to leave their horses in Andy's care and hope they would pass as invalids if the Germans did move in. Andy would be bright enough to put a stone in one shoe to make them look lame in the field if required. It was 111 miles from Le Havre and Henri expected to do twenty-eight miles each night, but it would still take them four days. They were basically following the Seine into Paris and he had contemplated using a boat to get there quicker but he did not want to leave the horses as they would need them, to get out of Paris. Henri knew that Le Comte had been to the barracks, so he would know it was an ideal spot to base the horses operating in Paris, so he expected to find them in occupation when they got there.

24

They arrived two miles from the barracks on the fourth day, having experienced no further problems. Henri left Manet and both horses in the woods and took up an observation post in the trees at the back of the isolation unit. He could tell immediately that the Germans had moved into the main site as their flag was flying and it looked as though they had over 100 horses based there. It was a hive of activity as they were preparing to go out on patrol.

The isolation block still only had the horses that he had seen earlier. He spotted Andy making his way down to the yard alone. He checked around and decided he would make his way down to the stables. Andy was busy making feeds for all the stabled horses before they would be turned out. Henri crept up quietly and as Andy turned around with two buckets in each hand, he stood in the doorway.

'Jesus sir, you gave me an 'eart attack. Tha's gonna have to stop appearing like a ghost; it's bad for mi nerves. Tha' knows we are occupied by the Germans on the main yard?'

'Yes, I can see. They must have about 100 horses based here but I expected that, as they already knew exactly how many of our troops were here and it's too far from Versailles for them to operate daily. Have they left you to get on down here? Did they shoot their way in?'

'They sent a small group of forward scouts who crept in and soon disarmed the few men 'ere without a shot being fired and then they marched in with full force and within an hour there were over 100 'osses filling the yard. Senior officer here at the time was Lieutenant Cassell and fortunately, he can speak German. They rounded us up and left us locked in the hay barn and then an hour later marched us out and I thought mi time 'ad come when they lined us up but instead of shooting us, Lieutenant Cassell read out names of ten of us and told us we were to remain 'ere and they loaded the other fifteen onto a hay wagon and off they went to God knows where. We were told to carry on with our jobs and we were to serve as grooms to the Germans. Lieutenant Cassell told me I was to remain down here looking after the invalids. They brought with them a pack of 'ounds from 'ell, some of 'em German Shepherds and a bigger, stronger type that 'ad teeth the size of a tiger. They are using them to patrol the site so tha' mun be careful wi' your comings and goings, sir.'

'I have a friend with me and I would like to leave Jester and his horse with you while we do some investigating. Do the Germans know how many horses you have down here?'

'Nay, one of them came down and saw some of

'em in't field but he soon scurried off when Apollo took a lump out of his arm when he looked over 'is door. I brought down extra hay and feed when you warned me to expect 'em in case they decided our 'osses weren't getting any food.'

They both rushed to the door as they could hear noise; the Germans were setting out in troops and leaving the barracks. Henri slipped back through the field and after checking from a tree top, he went for Manet and they jumped their way through the field and into the yard. Andy had two stables ready for them with hay racks filled and two buckets of feed prepared.

In view of Andy's warning about the guard dogs, they skirted round the fields and avoided going near to the main yard. Henri updated Manet on the situation at the barracks and they made their way out into the streets. There appeared to be no damage to any buildings round the barracks and people were out on the streets. They both wore black cloaks and hats with their weapons concealed underneath and hoped to blend in with the crowd. Henri decided to keep pushing on towards Montmartre and the Tuileries.

It took them half an hour to reach Montmartre and the crowds on the streets got bigger. A troop of Germans trotted past, but Henri looked to see if Le Comte was in evidence – to no avail. They reached Manet's house and studio, which he was visibly relieved to see intact, as many of his paintings were in the cellar. They did not pause but pressed on to Duran's studio. This remained just as Henri had left it and Manet found the key in the flowerpot and they went in. It looked as if the last time anyone had been in residence was at least a week ago. Milk had gone off in the fridge, as well as some fish. Both men sighed and remained silent. Henri suggested they make their way to the Louvre and start questioning shopkeepers for information. Manet suddenly remembered that there had been some American female artists who had helped with the copying in the Louvre and they had been living in Mary Cassatt's studio, which was in the same street as Charles's, as she had gone back to the USA.

They left quickly and were soon knocking on the door. It was opened by a woman in her late twenties and she was shocked to find Manet on her doorstep.

'Monsieur Manet, what a surprise! Do come in. How can I help you?'

'Mademoiselle, I apologise for not knowing your name, but I understand you were one of the artists working for Duran in the Louvre. This is Henri Croizette his brother-in-law and we wondered if you had news of Duran and Courbet?'

'My name is Amy Freeman and my friend Sonia, and we did indeed work as copyists for Duran. Please come in and let me make you some coffee and I will tell you what happened when the Germans invaded.'

They were ushered into the studio and Manet noticed several of Mary Cassatt's paintings still adorned the walls. She confirmed that both Courbet and Duran had been on the barricades in front of the Louvre, defending it from Communard sympathisers who were trying to gain access. A troop of Germans had arrived, and both sets of Frenchmen had soon been captured and disarmed. The National Guard was marched off and she identified Courbet and Duran among the ranks of prisoners. The next morning, Bismarck had paraded up the Champs-Élysées with around 150 French prisoners and had intended to execute them all. She had been in the crowd along with several American, British and French spectators and they had protested vigorously when they realised Bismarck's intention. Thankfully, there were many journalists in the crowd and troops were sent to control them, so Bismarck ordered the prisoners to be marched away. She got as close as she could as they were marched in pairs and she confirmed that Duran and Courbet were among them. Where they went, she had no idea. The joyous relief on both Henri and Manet's faces was evident. However, Henri knew that Bismarck would not be best pleased about his victory parade being hijacked by the press and wasn't convinced that he hadn't carried out his original intention somewhere else. They left Amy Freeman, who was obviously a devotee of Manet; they were invited to return if she could be of any further help.

They made their way to the Louvre, but it was all locked up and guarded by a full troop of soldiers, along with the Tuileries. The palace had taken some more cannon fire but apart from the library wing in the Louvre, it looked intact. Manet smiled and reflected on whether the Germans had discovered that over 150 of the masterpieces that could be physically moved had been sent to London and were now in a highly acclaimed exhibition at the Tate. He had not worked full time copying, as his job had been moving them to Le Havre and shipping them over to England. However, of the two Velázquez paintings in the Louvre, he had been honoured to be asked by Duran to copy his *Rokeby Venus,* while Duran had done the *Equestrian Portrait of Philip IV.* He had gone to Spain in 1865 to study Velázquez and his work had been influenced by what he had learned during that time. It had been a memorable two days working alongside Duran at the Louvre and at the same time, Rodin was copying the statue of Venus de Milo. The original had been crated up and hidden in the basement of the Prefecture of Police.

The crowds were increasing, and the German troops were lining the streets, anxious to move people away, so they followed the crowd that was being shepherded into the Luxembourg Gardens. They paused and rested on a stone wall, considering their next move. Henri decided that he would return to Versailles and report on his mission to England and would have a better chance of finding where Duran and Courbet had been imprisoned; he hoped he may be able to have them released. Manet intended to check out his house and paintings and then return to Le Havre. He intimated that he might spend the night at Mary Cassatt's studio, with the delectable Amy. They made their way back to the barracks, retrieved their horses and came back together. Then, Henri skirted the centre and headed for a secluded bridge over which to cross the Seine and head for Versailles.

25

Marie woke early and knew she would be unable to get back to sleep. Marie-Ann was sleeping soundly. She felt she wanted to go to the chapel to pray for Charles's safe return. She couldn't ask Reissman, but she could go through the hospital and ask whoever was on duty to call a guard to escort her. She quickly dressed, as quietly as possible, then went to the hospital. Dr Jager was on duty and he summoned a guard to take her through the compound to the chapel. There was nobody about until she got close to the chapel and saw that Capitan Laurent was sitting on the steps leading up to the chapel. She was astonished to see him.

He jumped up and said, 'Do you need spiritual guidance, madame? The priest will not be there for another couple of hours. Perhaps I could be of assistance?'

She smiled, 'Yes, I would like to share my problems with you.' He held out his hand and led her up the steps to the door. She turned to her guard and said, 'Please allow me to pray with the Capitan alone.' The guard indicated with his rifle and they went into the chapel. He remained outside. The room was lit by candles on the altar as well as by four more, one in each corner of the room. They went and sat together on the front pew.

Laurent said, 'What brings you here so early with such a troubled countenance, Marie? Has Reissman finally forced himself on you?'

'Nearly, but I threatened to kill myself and this may have registered in his drunken stupor as he managed to control his desire. I was inches from my baby's cot and dare not scream in case I woke her.'

'You poor girl. I have been very concerned for your welfare but powerless to do anything.' He gathered her in his arms and planted a gentle kiss on her forehead. Marie clung to his strong body for comfort and then told him what Reissman had revealed about the possible fate of her husband. He listened attentively, stroking her hair with devoted tenderness. After she had finished, he tilted her chin towards him.

'Marie, if you find yourself a widow and unfortunate enough to be carrying Reissman's child, I will marry you and take on both children when this war ends.'

Marie looked into his eyes and put her hand to his cheek. 'Thank you, Fabien. I am honoured that you would consider following that path, but let's just see what happens in the next few weeks.' She kissed him full on the lips, then quickly stood up, went to the altar rail and knelt in prayer.

He stood up and said, 'Marie, I will be here for

you if you need me, but I sincerely hope you and your husband may by some miracle be reunited.' He walked back down the aisle and out of the chapel.

She completed her prayers and then left the chapel with her guard. The camp was just waking up and she was met by the prisoners, but nobody commented. She was relieved that nobody had directed any nasty comments towards her as she was in no state, emotionally, to cope. As she was returning through the compound she saw a troop of six German soldiers riding out and leading an extra horse. She prayed to God that they might find her husband alive and bring him back to her.

oOo

She returned to her room, where Marie-Ann was just waking up. She picked her up and looked her over before feeding her. She was filling out now both in her face and body and she had lost the pale complexion and even had rosy cheeks. She had also grown considerably in height and could run and dance. She was saying a few words now, but the poor child was speaking in both German and French. What would Charles say about his daughter being reared in captivity by Germans? But at least she was still alive, and she had done her best to keep her safe. Reissman had always been good with Marie-Ann and had spent time with her, playing and showing her the dogs and the horses. Marie-Ann had fallen for his German Shepherd bitch Marte, who had been reared with his two children back home, and she was very gentle with her.

She dressed Marie-Ann in the pretty clothes Sylvie had brought in from her neighbours. She felt that if Charles should be found alive, he could not chastise her about the health and wellbeing of their daughter. She had now regained nearly two stone of her own lost weight and she had some flesh covering her bones. Dr Kohl had checked her over only a week ago and warned her that she may start to ovulate soon. She realised that she would have to be careful if Charles was found alive and well; the last thing they would need was a pregnancy resulting from their reunion.

She went to the lounge, ate her breakfast and gave Marie-Ann her breakfast. Dr Kohl joined them, and she told him of her night of terror with Reissman, and that the troops had gone out to search for her husband. He said they had better discharge patients from the hospital to the compound to make some bed space for the injured. She carried out her nursing duties but kept one eye on the prison gates, waiting with anticipation and hope of her husband returning.

Just as her shift was ending she heard shouts in the compound. She ran out of the ward door and saw the small troop returning. All six horses had riders, but one horse had two. Dr Kohl was at her side and he grabbed her hand. The troop galloped through the gates and up towards the hospital. She had spotted two men in grey uniform, one being held round the chest, slumped to the left in the saddle, barely conscious, in a shredded grey coat. She uttered a scream.

'Charles?'

His body straightened in the saddle and he called out, 'Marie, my God is that you?'

The other prisoner shouted, 'Marie, it's Gustav Courbet. Is that really you?'

She was rooted to the spot as Dr Kohl and Dr Jager ran down the steps with a stretcher, to Charles. They lifted him from the horse as he had now lost consciousness again, and gently lowered him onto the stretcher. Reissman arrived at her side and took her hand as he saw tears slowly falling down her cheeks. As they came level with her with the stretcher they stopped, and she put her hand out and touched Charles's face. Then she fainted; thankfully, Reissman caught her before she fell across her husband. As the stretcher party made its way into the ward, the patients who had crowded round the open door stepped back but all the men were silent. Charles was taken into the examination room. Reissman carried Marie to an empty bed and laid her gently down. Gustav, supported by his German guard, was helped onto the next bed.

Marie started to come around and she struggled to sit up. Reissman said, 'Marie, just let Dr Kohl examine Charles and just take a minute to come around.' He gathered her in his arms and pulled her close to his chest.

'I need to be with him.'

Marie struggled to her feet and he supported her into the examination room. Charles lay on his front whilst both doctors were gently removing his clothing. When they got to his shirt, Marie gasped. As the doctors carefully cut it away from his pitifully thin body there were lines of scars running from his shoulders and after they had cut his breeches off she could see they went right down to his buttocks in jagged lines. Some were old, but some were open, weeping, infected wounds that had been made more recently – probably by a long horse whip.

Marie screamed, 'You miserable German bastards. How could you do that to a human being, you scum?' She grabbed a scalpel from the tray, raised her hand and lunged upwards towards Reissman's face. Dr Jager was able to deflect her blow, but it still caught Reissman across his cheekbone. Dr Jager twisted her hand, removed the scalpel and held both hands behind her back.

Dr Kohl shouted, 'Marie, for God's sake! Your husband is alive, and you could have sealed your own death warrant, you impetuous child.'

He took a muslin cloth and gave it to Reissman, to staunch the bleeding from his cheek. He strode to the door and shouted for the guards. Two of them ran in. He looked at Reissman, who appeared to be in shock. He shouted to the guards to take Marie to her room and told one to remain outside her door.

He spoke softly to her.

'Marie, leave us to treat these wounds; it is too painful for you. When I have assessed his full condition, I will come and tell you. I need you to be strong enough to do all the nursing that will be required but now I am going to heavily sedate him to treat these wounds and he won't be conscious until tomorrow.'

The guards marched her away, leaving Reissman leaning against the wall with the cloth covered in blood. Dr Jager brought a bowl of hot water and cleaned the wound. It would need a few stitches but overall it was a glancing blow. Dr Kohl told him to stitch it. Reissman said nothing; he just gazed down at Charles, seemingly unable to take it all in. Dr Kohl motioned him towards the chair and Dr Jager made him sit down before he started stitching.

Dr Kohl returned to Charles and with a bowl of hot water mixed with alcohol, a cotton swab and a scalpel, he painstakingly followed the line of each scar, removing any debris, which ranged from infection to clothing and soil. To ensure his patient felt no pain, he injected strong painkillers and a sleeping drug into his arm. He guessed that Charles weighed around ten stone, which for someone of his stature was nothing. He had prominent sores on his hips, shoulders, knees and ankle bones and his feet were covered in blisters. He would set Dr Jager cleaning those when he had finished with Reissman. Looking at Charles, he gave him a 20% chance of survival due to the danger of infection – and that's before he had even assessed his major organs. He did have one thing in his favour, and that was having his wife at his side. If anyone could bring him back from near death it would be her and their strong bond. Maybe Marie was right, and God was watching over them.

Reissman left the room and was accosted by Marshal, who was waiting outside. The room fell silent as the patients surveyed the scar across his face.

Marshal said, 'How is her husband? Why have you Marie under guard?'

Reissman replied, 'He is not good, but Dr Kohl is working on him and if anyone can perform miracles in nursing him through this, it will be his wife. Marie is under guard for her own safety – and mine – until he is conscious. She became overemotional when she saw the extent of his injuries and acted irrationally. I do not intend to have her flogged or shot, if that is your concern.' Quickly, he marched out of the ward and a wave of prisoners' voices rose to a crescendo as he left the room.

26

Having been marched to her room, Marie threw herself on the bed, unable to take in what she had just witnessed. Her anger had yet again erupted and stirred her into a frenzy; she had nearly killed Reissman. She had never thought of the consequences had she succeeded but she had always been impetuous and hit out if someone hurt her and the sight of her husband's wounds had caused this violent reaction. She heard the guards talking outside the door and it appeared that they were deciding who was going to stay outside. She heard one of them leave.

Marie wanted to speak to Courbet but now she was trapped here. He could give her more information about what had happened, but she would have to wait until she was released. She heard Reissman's boots approaching and she wondered what fate awaited her. Perhaps he had come to rape her now, just to prove to her that he was dominant and to shame her in Charles's eyes.

Reissman entered and walked over to the bed where Marie was lying on her front with her head averted.

She said, 'Have you come to rape me now just to show me you are superior and to ruin our marriage?'

Reissman gasped, 'Marie, how could you think that? I am not a monster. I love you! When will you understand that I do not want to hurt you even though you seem to want to do me harm?'

Marie sat up, put her hand out and indicated that he should sit next to her on the bed. 'I am sorry. I did not mean to harm you; it was my wicked temper. I know you weren't the one to harm Charles personally, but I would not have expected that level of cruelty to be shown to a prisoner of war. You saw how thin he was – how he managed to walk the 100 miles, I will never know.'

'I know, Marie. It appalled me as much as you. I pray to God he lives; he did not deserve that but at least he wasn't executed in Paris.'

Marie sobbed, 'I know that infection is going to be the biggest threat to his life. I have seen some men with large areas of infected bone and tissue that have survived, and others with only a small wound, who died from it. But he has no strength or stamina left to fight it off. I fear he will die after all he has been through.'

'You can only do your best as a nurse alongside Dr Kohl as a doctor, to pull him through. You will have my complete support and I have told them to bring him here after they have finished treating him. He is too poorly to be on a ward and he will have you at his side to nurse him back to health. I will engage the nursemaid to look after Marie-Ann at night if you want?'

'Thank you, that will be helpful as the risk of infection from other patients is an ever-present problem. May I go and speak to Gustav Courbet now, to find out more?'

'Who is Courbet?'

'An artist who, like my husband, is also a Velázquez worshipper and a good friend of Charles.'

'I don't see why not. Are you safe to be released from your guard? Do you promise me to keep those wretched hands away from my face?'

'Thank you and I will promise to behave myself.' She touched his cheek to inspect the wound and for the first time ever, she kissed him lightly on the lips.

Reissman was both shocked and pleased by her kiss. He remembered the night he had tried to force her to kiss him and she had bitten him badly. She was like a wild horse, impossible to break, and she only allowed intimacy on her own terms. He could feel his hopes of ever possessing this beautiful woman being dashed like waves on a rock face, but her show of affection warmed his heart.

Marie went back into the hospital, where Dr Kohl was still working on Charles. She had a quick word with Dr Bauman, who informed her Courbet had a bad head injury from the butt of a rifle, which had caused some damage to his brain – he reported blackouts and memory loss. Marie shook her head once again at the cruelty of war.

Courbet was resting but as she was about to leave him he opened his eyes and said, 'Who can I see? Is it an angel from God or is it you, Marie?'

She knelt beside his bed and took his hand. 'Gustav tell me what happened in Paris to both of you.'

'Marie, please do not ask Charles what we were doing. It is too dangerous to speak about when you are surrounded by the enemy here. We cannot discuss this until we are released and safe. Suffice to say we have been protecting the Montmartre district and the Louvre from thieves, communards and the Germans. The Communards set fire to the Tuileries Palace, which adjoins one side of the Louvre, and the Richelieu Library was destroyed but we prevented it spreading any further into the Louvre galleries.'

'Charles has been badly beaten, Gustav. Did all the prisoners receive this same horrific treatment?'

'Yes, if you failed to keep up the pace and Charles was very weak from the siege. I told him every night that he had to keep going because of you and Marie-Ann. Thankfully, he managed to keep going.'

At this point, Dr Kohl appeared from the examination room, spotted Marie and called her over. She rushed to his side and he ushered her into the room. Charles was laid face down with a large muslin sheet draped over his back, which was covered in an ointment made up of honey, turmeric and calendula, and he was unconscious.

Dr Kohl said, 'I won't lie to you, Marie. You know the dangers he is facing from infection and his deplorable physical state is not going to help matters. Another day would have been too much; his hips, knees and feet would have given up. I have done the best I can with his open wounds and time and rest will be the greatest healer, but we must get him eating again as his major organs are in danger of failing. It is going to be the biggest challenge both of you have had to face yet, but you can do it with the help of the love you share, your strong physical and mental bond and your absolute belief in God.' He hugged her tightly and she cried huge, raking, heartfelt sobs into his chest.

'I don't think I can do this, Dr Kohl. Even if we can improve his physical state, infection could still claim him weeks later.'

'I know that sweetheart, but you have to put that out of your mind and live from day to day. It won't be an easy journey for either of you, but you have both faced death alone several times and survived and now you have each other.'

Marie looked at Charles's still gaunt body and she moved to touch his face and run her fingers through his very long hair. He looked to her like the many religious paintings she had seen of Jesus Christ. She took a deep breath. 'Well, if God spared him, then I am not going to fail him in fighting for his recovery.'

She started gathering bandages and the instruments she would need into a basket. Dr Kohl said he had already asked the kitchens to prepare a beef broth and to produce a mashed fruit drink. Getting sufficient fluids into him would be vital.

He sent two orderlies with a single mattress to put on Marie's bed to ensure that his bones were sufficiently supported and protect the bed from weeping wounds. He told Marie what to expect in the next twenty-four hours and told her to come for him during the night if she had any worries. Charles should have the muslin cloth over him only until the wound dressings had dried. Then, he should only have a light cotton nightgown over him. She would need plenty of pillows to prop him up, so that she could get water and liquid food into him. He wasn't to attempt to stand for at least another forty-eight hours as he would be so unsteady on his feet due to the drugs that had been administered. She was to inject him every eight hours with a high dose painkiller and he would drift in and out of sleep. He warned her that Charles might panic when he came around, and that there was a possibility that he might not recognise her; he could even be violent.

She went to turn her bedroom into a hospital room: she cleaned every bit of dust from the walls and carpet, changed the sheets and cleaned the bathroom thoroughly with alcohol. Finally, at around 10 p.m. the orderlies brought Charles in on a stretcher and she and Dr Kohl transferred him face down onto the bed. As she put a pillow under his head and turned his head to one side, he stirred slightly, and his eyes opened. She saw a flicker of recognition and she kissed his cheek and then she observed silent tears running down his cheek. She leant over and said,

'You are safe now, Charles and I am here to nurse you back to health. Marie-Ann is here and safe too; we have all survived.'

The nursemaid brought Marie-Ann in for a final feed and she sat in the chair close to his bed so that if he did come around, he would see them both. However, he was sleeping and breathing soundly and showed no movement at all. She decided she would curl up beside him on his other side and change his head position to face her. She unpinned her hair because she knew he loved to run his fingers through it, but she kept her chemise on instead of changing into a nightgown, so that she could dress quickly if she needed to fetch the doctor. She kissed his cheek and whispered goodnight, then she lay facing him but holding one hand so that she could sense any movement, should he stir. She left one bedside light on, so that she could see instantly if he had moved. She banished fearful thoughts from her head as she knew she needed to sleep now as he could come around later and have her up all night.

At about 3 a.m. she woke to the sensation of fingers stroking her hair and as she opened her eyes, she looked straight into his eyes. He had turned onto his side and he was half-raised on his elbow above her. She pulled him close and finally, their lips touched. He gave her a lingering kiss on her lips whilst caressing the back of her neck.

He whispered to her, 'My darling wife, I never thought I would find you again.' She returned his kiss with delight and pulled him close to her chest, burying her head in his hair. After a while he groaned and said, 'I need the toilet, now where is it?'

She pushed him away saying, 'You are not to put a foot out of bed for two days. I'll get you a bed pot; stay right there.' She leapt out of bed and brought the pot she had ready and waiting. He filled it and she took it to the bathroom. She checked there was no blood in it before she flushed it and was pleased that his digestive system seemed to be working. When she came back, she asked him if he was hungry or thirsty and he declined. She rearranged his pillows to prop him up on his left side. She gave him the painkiller injection and followed it up with a kiss to his arm. As she got into bed next to him, he tugged at her chemise.

'Marie, would you lie naked next to me? I need to see you and feel skin contact with you.'

Marie laughed, 'God, you are a demanding patient. I hope you don't think I let all my patients take liberties with me.' She pulled off her chemise and lay down facing him.

He kissed her cheek and said, 'Now turn on your side like we used to do so I can get as close to your body as possible.' He traced his finger down her ear, neck, shoulder blade, elbow, hip and round to her thigh. Before he could go any further she said,

'No, Charles you go no further, sex is not permissible until your body is ready. You may think your mind is capable, but you have a weak heart and

I am taking no risks.'

'But I have dreamt of this moment for countless nights away from you. You can't deny me your body now.'

She turned around to face him. 'Do you recall our wedding night?'

'Yes, I have relived it in my mind nearly every night.'

'You made me wait until the following morning. Pleased as I am that your body is working sexually, this is not the time to waste what little energy you have on sex.'

'Does that mean I can have you tomorrow?'

'No, it certainly does not! I am under strict doctor's orders to abstain from sex until Dr Kohl considers you fit and well enough to resume.'

'But he doesn't know how my body feels and how my mind has been dreaming about you since we were apart.'

Marie leant down and kissed him. 'Charles, believe me, I have also dreamt about you nearly every night, but we need to wait just a little bit longer. Now settle down and go back to sleep or I will remove my naked body from the bed.'

'There are other ways of satisfying our bodies without sexual intercourse.'

'Forget it, Charles. They still have the same risks such as raised heart rate and blood pressure. You can speed things up by getting your body fit and well again by doing what we tell you.' She rolled over and took his right hand and laid it across her right breast, which was the position they had always adopted when they slept together.

27

The next time Marie woke, it was daylight and she felt Charles running his fingers through her hair. She turned over and kissed him and he returned it passionately. They lay in each other's arms and Charles' lips moved to her breasts. She checked the time; it was 6 a.m. and she knew that from 7 a.m. she would have Marie-Ann to feed.

She said, 'Charles, don't think of going any further. I need to get up and see to your wounds, give you your injection and get you ready to greet Marie-Ann. The doctor could come in to see you before his breakfast and even Reissman may come to check on you.'

He reluctantly released her as he was anxious to see his daughter. He wanted to go to the bathroom, but she would not hear of it. She fetched him the pot and a bowl of hot soapy water and produced a toothbrush and towel. She would have bathed him herself, but he assured her he was quite capable. She retrieved her chemise and put it on.

She made him lie face down as she gently removed the muslin sheet from his back and saw it had stuck to him in several places. She was as gentle as she could be, but he couldn't hold back the occasional wince and gasp of pain. The fact that she was even doing this amazed him. He would never have expected her to take on nursing duties as she had always been spoilt and had never had to cater for the needs of others before, except with her animals. He knew she was not squeamish like many women. She must have been a stronger woman than he gave her credit for. This was not Marie, the girl anymore – this was the adult Marie who had finally learned to empathise with people and put someone else's needs before her own. If this was the one thing that war had taught her then it was a huge step. She allowed him to get up out of the bed whilst she straightened the covers and plumped up the pillows. She gave him a soft, white cotton nightgown and helped him put it over his head. She allowed him a few steps around the room and asked how he felt. He did have a headache and he was a bit dizzy and his knees were very swollen, painful and stiff. She ushered him back to bed and fetched him some of the fruit drink.

A knock came at the door and Sylvie came in with Marie-Ann still in her nightie. She rushed to take her over to the bed and Charles's face was a picture. Tears were already forming as she handed her over to him and Marie-Ann was already reaching out to him. He cradled her in his pitifully thin arms and with his finger, he traced the outline of her face.

Charles said, 'Her eyes are mine, but the button nose and mouth are yours. Her hair has your colour and thickness and her skin and complexion are like you. My little darling, I never thought I would see you alive again.' He kissed her, and she grabbed a handful of his long dark hair and wrapped it in her little fingers. She twisted round to stand up and grabbed his nose.

She put her finger to his eye and said, 'weinen,' which meant "crying". As Marie climbed into the bed she reached out with her hand and said, 'muttermilch' ("breast milk").

Charles watched speechless as his little daughter clambered over to Marie and undid her chemise, shouting, 'Milch, Mama'. His precious French daughter was speaking in German, the language of her captors. Marie saw his hurt expression.

'Charles, she still speaks French with me. You cannot expect her not to pick up German when she is surrounded by it every day. Her nursemaid does not speak French and she is not allowed to mix with the prisoners. Only Dr Kohl, Reissman and Dr Jager are fluent in French. Remember, I speak four languages and have picked up German whilst I have been here, but I am still French.'

'I'm sorry Marie, what am I thinking of? It was just such a shock and I wasn't prepared for it. I should be thanking God that she is alive and thanking you for keeping her safe.' Marie-Ann was busy feeding. Charles leant over and grabbed Marie's left hand. Searching for her eyes he said, 'Marie, why have you no wedding ring on your hand?' His breathing stopped while he waited for her answer.

'Please forgive me, Charles. I had to sell it for food.' He knew instantly by the look in her eyes that she was telling him the truth and he started breathing again.

'Oh, sweetheart, we can replace a ring. I feared you had removed it because you didn't love me anymore or worse still loved someone else.'

Marie responded angrily, with tears in her eyes, 'How could you think that Charles, when I vowed to love you and remain faithful to you forever? I meant it.'

Charles said, 'I am sorry, I just feared the worst.' He struggled out of bed and picked up one of his boots. He knelt beside her at the bed, took her hand and carefully placed her sapphire engagement ring in the palm of her hand.

'I kept this ring on me the whole time; you were in my thoughts every day. I wanted to have it on me to give it back personally if I found you and was willing to risk losing it if I died in the meantime. I left you a letter and my will locked away in my studio underground, with all the paintings and drawings I had done of you along with your sapphires and the emeralds Napoleon gave you. I could feel in my heart that you were still alive, but I will never forgive myself for putting both of you in such danger. I left you in Lille thinking you would be safe there and away from the fighting, yet Whistler had offered to take both of you to England and I turned him down.'

Marie put the ring on the third finger of her left hand and said, 'Charles, you were not to know what would happen. Nobody would have thought that Paris would have been besieged and taken by the Germans – but it was. Your experience and suffering outweigh mine by a mile. Yes, we were hungry but not as badly as you must have been during the siege.'

Marie-Ann had noticed the ring and tried to grab it off her mother's hand, saying, 'Jolie bande'.

Marie laughed and said, 'I told you she had some French in her.'

At this point, Sylvie returned, and Marie got out of the bed, handing Marie-Ann to her father. Charles chatted to her in French, kissed her and then handed her over to Sylvie, who took her off for her breakfast. Marie put on her black dress and white pinafore and brushed her hair through, plaited and pinned it up and clipped her white cap into place. Charles watched her in total admiration. He could not believe the change that had occurred in Marie. Had the war or the Germans tamed his wild Russian tiger?

Breakfast arrived, and he was delighted to see a full jug of black coffee and a plate of toast and croissants on the tray. He did not need any encouragement to eat this time. He had plenty of questions he needed answers to from her, but he would take it very slowly because some of them, he probably did not want to know the answers to. She had not challenged him on his fidelity yet, but he had remained true to her. He knew that Marie had stayed true to him in mind, but he was not so confident about her body, which as he well knew could easily have been ravished without her consent. Dr Kohl arrived and was staggered to see his patient sitting up and eating.

'Well, this is a transformation I have never seen happen so quickly before'.

Marie removed the tray, indicated that Charles should lie face down and gently eased up his nightgown. Dr Kohl examined the wounds and muttered in German to Marie.

Charles intervened, 'Now let me make one thing absolutely clear. The state of my health is primarily my business and I want to be involved in my treatment every step of the way. Both of you will speak in French and neither of you will withhold any information. Do not think that not telling me the truth will work because Marie, you can't lie to me.'

Dr Kohl said, 'Apologies Charles, you are perfectly correct; we are a team and we need to all be aware of that situation. We think that later today we need to introduce some maggots to the dead areas of skin on your back to clean up any infection.'

Charles groaned, 'I wish I had never asked. I don't like maggots at the best of times.'

Dr Kohl asked, 'Now I want you to tell me exactly how you feel?'

Charles complied, 'I have a blinding headache and some dizziness, my knees and feet are swollen and stiff and my back bloody hurts but I have been living with that pain for a while. I know I am tired and weak but compared to when I arrived, I feel stronger. However, the good news is that my sexual appetite and function have returned with a vengeance, but my wife informs me that you have put a ban on any sexual relations. I have walked 100 miles to get here because I thought my wife may still be alive and now I have found her again.'

He watched in amusement as Marie blushed from her forehead to her neck and gave him a look that could stop a charging bull.

Dr Kohl had difficulty keeping his face straight and replied, 'My main concern was that your heart was weak and would not cope with the extra demands sex requires. But if you think you are ready to restart your conjugal relationship then I think it can only help speed up your recovery. Would you like me to add this to your treatment plan, perhaps once a day and then increasing this to four times a day in a fortnight?' Marie gasped in shock and horror and turned crimson as both men laughed.

Charles replied, 'Well, that gives me a challenge to aim for and I will do my best with Nurse Duran's help.'

Dr Kohl turned and left the room with a big grin on his face. Marie was still in shock at what she heard but Charles was already out of the bed and standing next to her.

'Now, you heard what the doctor ordered. Get on that bed. I need to know that I can perform but

I will have no control over the timing as it has been so long since I experienced it. Allow me to fulfil my desire now and I promise I will make it up to you tonight. I need you now Marie, no time to remove any clothes. Just lay over the edge of the bed.'

She knew he was desperate, so she did as she was told, pulled her drawers down and knelt over the bed, hitching up her skirt and apron. He had no time for any foreplay and she winced as he entered her but started to relax and enjoy it before it was all over in less than five minutes.

After their frantic passion, she insisted Charles get into the bed and revert to being the patient and obey her instructions on eating, drinking and resting. She told him he could only get out of bed to go to the bathroom and not to attempt to leave the room as if Reissman found him he would be shipped back to the hospital. She had to go and help Dr Kohl with an operation and prepare the hospital for the rest of the prisoners taken from Paris.

Charles was left alone and was pleased to have the chance to reflect quietly on the last two days. There were so many unasked questions they both needed to ask but he felt that Marie was not ready yet. He could not help wondering if she had been forced to succumb to Reissman in the same position he had just taken her in. He drifted off into a troubled sleep.

The next time he heard the door open, he was surprised to see Courbet coming in. He could tell by his face that he was troubled.

'Charles, I do not wish to be the bearer of bad news, but I have to tell you some of the things the prisoners are saying about Marie and Reissman.' Charles's heart missed a beat and he gripped the sheet tightly. 'I have spoken to several prisoners who tell me that Reissman took Marie as his mistress within days of her capture. They have seen him take her out on rides away from the camp, show her round the horses and the dogs in the kennels and seen him hold her hand, put his arm around her, kiss her as he lifted her down from her horse… and his eyes follow her every move. They say he is besotted with her and acts like a teenager in love with his first girlfriend.' Gustav paused as he saw the haunted expression on his face.

'But Charles, I have also questioned the men and none of them report her reciprocating his affection. Marshal Marcon swears that Marie has no affection for him but has been forced to comply to protect herself and Marie-Ann. The good news is that none of the men have seen him do anything improper with Marie-Ann. He has two daughters of his own and he has behaved as a substitute father and been seen playing with her and letting her play with his dog and has made a swing for her and ensured she has been kept in complete safety. I am told that the closest confidants to Marie have been Reissman, Dr Kohl and the Protestant priest, Father Bauman.'

'For pity's sake Gustav, are you now telling me that as well as becoming another man's mistress my wife has changed her religion?'

'This may not be true; the men say that the Catholic priest would have reported everything Marie said back to Reissman, but Father Bauman would not. You must remember she was in a very poor emotional and physical state and her life was in danger. Marshal says Reissman's orders were to only take women to work in the camps and to shoot any children, and he did not do that. She also stole a horse and he could have executed her for that alone and he did not. The men have also said that on several occasions Reissman had Marie's handprint across his face, so they knew that she was fighting her corner as best she could. They did not want to believe she was a traitor to her country.'

'Gustav, how many men are imprisoned here?'

'Marshal says around 2000 French prisoners and 500 German soldiers.'

'God, Gustav, how could my beautiful wife end up being a prisoner among so many men, all of whom would desire her body?'

'Charles, you and I discussed this very thing during the long nights manning the barricades in Paris. You told her before you left her that her beauty would be her downfall, and to choose life over death. You said you could live with the fact that she may have been unfaithful and could even be carrying another man's child, provided you got her back. Surely you are not going to reject her now; you cannot lay any blame on her if she was taken by force. There is no evidence whatsoever that she consented to this arrangement. Marshal says Reissman does have some honourable qualities and he may tell you the truth. He said Marie never confirmed to him that she was being forced by Reissman. Please discuss it with her before you make any accusations; she had your child to protect. She may have agreed to sex if he would spare Marie-Ann's life.'

'Gustav, I don't know what to think anymore except it was me who left her in grave danger when I could have sent them to England with Whistler and they would have been totally safe. You know we would not have survived the siege of Paris without the help of the English food and weapons we received. They came to our aid when the rest of Europe abandoned us. We survived being executed by the Arc de Triomphe purely because of the dissension of the foreigners watching, many of whom were English and American.'

28

The door opened, and Marie and Dr Kohl entered, bearing a bowl full of maggots that were going to have their lunch, courtesy of Charles. Gustav left and said he would see him later. Dr Kohl said he was going to get Marie to draw his back and then they could plot the infected areas where the maggots could be used to best effect.

Charles laughed, 'Dr Kohl, an artist usually likes to draw something that appeals to them. I don't think my wife will relish drawing my back in its current state.'

He turned over and lay there while Marie did a pencil sketch of his back and Dr Kohl distributed the maggots. He was surprised that he couldn't feel anything but that was because the flesh was already dead. However, when Dr Kohl started on newer areas he could feel that and winced. Marie noticed, and she held his hand in comfort and as it was her left hand with her engagement ring back in its rightful place, he kissed it. He took his mind off the pain by contemplating how close her thigh and if he could risk running his hand up her skirt, but he thought better of it as he wasn't up to receiving one of Marie's famous right-hand punches just yet. He was fascinated to find that they counted the number of maggots placed in each section, so they could be certain of retrieving them all after they had fed.

Dr Kohl asked, 'How is the dizziness and headache?'

Charles replied, 'Improved now I am eating and drinking more.'

Dr Kohl said, 'I would like to get you back on your feet and walking again. Would you feel up to taking a walk outside every day to keep your knees and hips working? You may need some sticks for support at first and you are not to walk alone; someone must be with you.'

'Well I managed to walk 100 miles from Paris to here, so I guess I should be capable of that.'

Dr Kohl said, 'It won't be for a couple of days as the men in your troop are due to arrive tomorrow and I need Marie in the hospital with me to help with their treatment.'

'That's fine with me. They will need her more than I do. Doctor, how did you turn my wife into a nurse? I would never have thought my little firebrand would turn her hand to nursing people; she only ever had experience of nursing animals.'

Dr Kohl smiled, 'There's not much difference if you think about it and she was not the sort of squeamish woman who would faint at some of the awful things she saw. She has been an excellent pupil, treating injured soldiers but also those who have been mentally damaged. The empathy she has for animals has helped her bring some of those traumatised by the battlefield, back to life. Three of my patients had never spoken until Marie came along and touched them. She was also an immense comfort to the dying; to have a woman as beautiful as her holding their hand in their final minutes on earth was a great comfort to them, but I am also aware of the mental energy it took from her.'

When they had finished their treatment, he was left alone under instructions to sleep but his mind kept wandering to Marie being Reissman's mistress. Surely, she would not have willingly allowed him to have her? But, he knew that she may have been pressured to do it to save her own life or Marie-Ann's. He would say nothing and see if she brought up the subject. He would make love to her that night and he would know instantly if she did something he had not taught her.

He was just drifting off when he heard heavy footsteps coming closer and he knew it was Reissman. He did not recall seeing him when he had arrived as he had only had eyes for Marie until he fainted. Reissman approached the bed and their eyes locked.

'Monsieur Duran, I hope you are feeling a little better than when you arrived, and that you are being taken care of.'

'I presume you are Major General Reissman, my wife's captor. I would be grateful if you would enlighten me on your contribution to my wife's four-month stay here. I was not aware that women and children were considered prisoners of war.'

'Your wife gave me no option. I encountered her dressed as a man, having stolen one of my horses and trying to escape from two of my guards whilst I was returning from Lille. I chased after her and shot her from a short distance with my pistol. Luckily for her, my horse stumbled as I pulled the trigger and the bullet missed her head but passed her ear and then exploded. She was thrown to the ground and fell unconscious and it wasn't until I reached her that I found your daughter hidden under her cloak. I brought them both here to undergo treatment for their severe malnutrition and the blow to her head she sustained in the fall. I can assure you that I have treated your daughter as if she were mine and have done everything to ensure her safety and wellbeing.'

Charles interrupted with an icy stare from his big brown eyes.

'But what about my wife?'

'Well of course, I did the same and ensured she was given the treatment she required. She only weighed seven stone when she was captured, and she was malnourished and showing signs of severe depression. Your daughter was fourteen months old but only weighed as much as a nine-month-old baby. Your wife hardly had any milk to feed her and they were both starving. You must appreciate that I am commander of a prison camp with 2000 French prisoners and 500 of my own troops and now had a female prisoner in my midst who was so beautiful that every man who laid eyes on her wanted her body. For her own safety I had to ensure she was protected and kept away from the prisoners and my men.'

Charles interrupted, 'Her safety amongst the Frenchmen was never in doubt; none of them would have touched her. This was proven by her nursing them in the hospital, as not one of them stepped out of line.'

'Are you suggesting that I should have thrown her into the compound and left her to protect herself?'

'Why not? The only person she needed protection from was you. You wanted her as your mistress and from what I have heard, that is exactly what you did. What vile deed did you threaten her with to keep her compliant in your bed?'

'Monsieur Duran, you dishonour your wife and myself. I admit that I became infatuated with Marie and nothing would have given me greater pleasure than to have her in my bed, but your wife made it very clear that she would not allow me or any man to touch her.'

'So, did you take her with a knife at her throat every night?'

'Certainly not! You of all people must know what a dangerous hellcat she is once provoked. Yes, I could have taken her by force, but I would have needed two men to hold her down every time.'

'And that did not appeal to you, so you threatened her with death, or my daughter with death, in order to silence her.'

'No, I did not, Duran. If you want proof of your wife's fidelity, then I can give it to you. She is a remarkable woman and we both said things that we did not mean. I threatened to hang her in the prison compound in front of the entire garrison and she was brave enough to demand that she did not want to die like a common thief; she wanted to be beheaded by a French swordsman.'

Charles gasped at this revelation. 'She must have been terrified.'

'No, she wasn't, she knew very well I could not have killed her; I was in love with her. I only wanted her if she wanted me. I admit we both played mind games and she is indeed a brilliant tactician. I have nothing but admiration and respect for her. She has a man's mind; she only reacts impetuously like a woman if something threatens her. She threatened to kill me if I took her and if she could not do that she said she would kill herself because she could not bear the shame of being unfaithful to you. Whether she would have done it, we will never know.'

Charles interrupted, 'But you were seen by the prisoners taking her out of camp on rides, holding her hand, kissing her cheek.'

'But nobody saw her return my affection. You must understand my position here, Charles. Marie was a threat to me because she could have caused the entire camp to riot if they rallied behind her. You know the effect she has on men. She does not need to touch them; they will follow her blindly into battle. She has the same charisma as Joan of Arc. We negotiated a deal to suit both of us. I did not want to lose her as a friend even though she would not have me as her lover. I had to make the prisoners believe I had taken her because the whole camp's safety was at stake. She did not like being thought of as a traitor to the French but when they saw my slapped face they thought she was at least fighting back.'

'So, you wanted the men to think you had forced her into submission.'

'Yes, if you think about it I could not let one single French woman keep me at bay when I had 1500 French men in captivity. What impression would that have given the prisoners? I had to appear to dominate her just as I ruled the prisoners.'

Charles turned and fixed him with his gaze. 'Tell me truthfully, have you had sexual intercourse with Marie?'

'No – I admit I wanted to and after one night's drinking I did come to her room with the intention of taking her. That is the only time I touched her, and I apologise for being drunk but I did not rape her, and she never once gave me permission to touch her. She is the bravest, most honest and incredible woman I have ever known and her loyalty to you never wavered for one moment. I hope you have remained as faithful and loyal to her as she did to you, because I would hate to think her hero let her down.'

'You can rest assured that I have never touched another woman since I met Marie and would never break my marriage vows. Where she found the courage to stand her ground in such difficult circumstances, I will never know.'

'Charles, you are a very lucky man to have found your wife and daughter alive. Please do not punish Marie for a crime she never committed. Do not let it spoil your relationship. If God is watching over you, then you owe it to him to live your lives in peace and happiness together.' He turned and left the room.

Charles felt as if he had been run over by a herd of wild horses. What Reissman had revealed had shocked him to the core. He had no reason not to believe him. He had spoken with sincerity and courage, probably to spare Marie having to relive what had taken place. The fact that she had fought tooth and nail to remain faithful to him despite the obvious danger she had been in, made him love and respect her all the more. He understood what Reissman meant about him having to appear to have dominated Marie and that if she had appealed to the prisoners for help it could have ended in a bloodbath for them all. If she had caused a riot, then Reissman would have had no alternative but to kill her but several brave Frenchmen would have died as well. Perhaps his little firebrand was finally learning to consider the consequences of her actions. He drifted off into a restless sleep, picturing the awful scene that had transpired between Marie and Reissman.

At 5:30 p.m. Marie bustled in, with Marie-Ann skipping behind her. She ran up to the bed shouting, 'Dada up!' He swept her up in his arms and put her beside him and could not stop the tears running down his cheeks.

Marie turned to him, 'What is the matter, Charles? Why are you crying?'

'She called me "Dada" for the first time, that's why. Although she managed one word of English and another in German; the poor child probably does not know where she is.' He smothered his daughter in kisses and held Marie's hand. 'My beautiful brave girls – I am here to protect you now. Nobody will ever harm you again.' Marie eyed him suspiciously but did not question him further.

He cuddled and chatted to Marie-Ann, tickling her tummy until she squealed. He asked Marie if she could bring him some paper and pencils, so they could draw together next time she came to visit. He had lost twelve months of his daughter's life and he was determined to spend as much time as he could to repair the damage that had been done. He knew that they would be imprisoned for quite some time, so he would do his utmost to get to know Marie-Ann while he had the chance.

Marie had prepared his next injection and said to Marie-Ann, 'Now Dada is going to have an injection to make him better. Do you think he will be a brave boy and not cry?'

Marie-Ann said, 'Dada est un brave garçon et ne

weinen pas.'

Marie gave him the injection and whispered to Charles, 'Don't mention the German word.'

Sylvie came to collect Marie-Ann to take her for tea and as she left, he turned to Marie.

'Come and sit next to me sweetheart, I need to be close to you.'

Marie did as he asked and leant over to kiss him. 'What's wrong, Charles? Something has unsettled you.'

'It's nothing ma cherie, I just had a bad dream this afternoon and it shook me up a bit.'

'Do you want to tell me about your experiences? Dr Kohl said I was not to push you into remembering but I am here for you when and if you are ready to talk to me about them. Please don't think you have to spare me the gory details. I can't talk to you about Paris whilst we are in enemy hands sweetheart, but I will do when we are safe.'

'Charles, have you any news of my parents?'

'Yes, they are both safe and well in Rome. They left about four months ago because it was getting unsafe at the chateau with the Germans occupying Versailles.'

'Have you any news of Henri?'

'Yes, sweetheart he is alive and well and I saw him only three weeks ago. He was captured at Sedan and was promoted by Napoleon to accompany him to Versailles after he surrendered.'

'Oh, thank God for that. I have prayed he would

survive and, as with you, I could feel he was still alive somewhere. Hopefully we will be reunited soon. What of Manet, Antonio and Jacques?'

'Manet joined a cavalry regiment patrolling between Paris and the French coast that was responsible for transporting food supplied by Britain into Paris during the siege. Antonio and Jacques stayed in Paris until the last month before invasion and then escaped to Rome. He will keep Jacques safe and perhaps you can persuade Reissman to let us visit his parents to tell them he is safe – under guard, of course. What of my father, have you any news of him? I know my mother passed away and it grieved me I could not get to the funeral.'

'I have been careful not to reveal his existence while I was here for fear the Germans might raid the farm. When I last saw him, he was fine, and he had some young horses safely hidden. I went to see him to see if he had one I could use but the oldest was only an unbroken three-year-old grey filly and would not have been suitable for my purposes.'

'Any news of Gustav, Freya and Louis? Are they still in Lille?'

'Yes, they left six months ago for Sweden and they have a daughter now, called Charlotte. They offered to take me and Marie-Ann but like a fool, I refused.'

'Have Gustav and Freya settled down together now?'

Well as Freya admits, they will never be as close in marriage as you and I are, but Gustav followed your advice and supported her during her pregnancy and it brought them closer together. Freya still has a soft spot for you though Charles, she still thinks of you as her knight in shining armour.'

'Oh, what I would give to have my "fire and ice" girls to ravage together in here.'

'Hang on a minute, husband; are you admitting coveting your sister-in-law as well as your wife?'

'Nothing wrong in dreaming about it Marie and while I had some spare time I did recreate the painting of you both together. I drew you depicted as Diana the goddess of hunting and left Freya as a Viking warrior.'

'I hope you put me some clothes on in this picture.'

'Of course, dear I would not exhibit you in the nude. However, I would like to study your nude body tonight in bed.'

'May I remind you that we are expecting what's left of your troop in here tomorrow and I am going to be very busy, so I need as much sleep as possible.'

The maid entered with their evening meal and they both ate in quiet contentment. Charles removed his dish of strawberries and jug of cream from the tray on the pretext that he would eat it later as he was full after his fish course.

Sylvie brought Marie-Ann back in her nightie, ready for bed and her final feed. He watched Marie feed her in the chair and marvelled at how much bigger her breasts were than when Marie-Ann had been a baby. Not that he was complaining in any way at all. He went to the toilet and on his way back, dropped a delicate kiss on his wife's head and unpinned her luscious hair. He bent down to his daughter and kissed her head.

'She reminds me of Louis Odin Duran. He was a combination of a Viking prince and a French king, with a temper to outdo both.'

Marie laughed and said, 'He was four when I last saw him, and his blonde curls and his blue eyes were a delight but when he is mad he shows a terrible temper. Freya took his pants down and smacked his bottom when he was naughty one day and he was furious.'

Charles smiled, 'Oh, little Louis Odin would not like that. Freya needs to be careful or her head could roll for insulting a royal prince.'

'You're desperate to have a son aren't you, Charles?'

'I would be lying if I said no but we have plenty of time, ma cherie when we get back on our feet. You have taken enough of the responsibility for Marie-Ann's life on your own as it is. Two children would not be ideal at this time. I don't know what state Paris will be in and whether our studio and rented home will even be standing when we return. However, please do not ask me to abstain or withdraw from intercourse Marie, when I have only just got you back in my arms; I could not do it.'

She leant over and kissed him. 'Don't worry, I won't. I will ask Dr Kohl's advice, seeing as he recommended sex four times a day on your treatment plan. The least he can do is come up with some form of contraception.'

29

Sylvie arrived for Marie-Ann and she kissed her Dada goodbye but cried when she was removed from the room. Her attachment to Charles had returned already and she was going to get more demanding. Perhaps she should remain in their room soon.

Charles pulled Marie up out of the chair, hugged her and undid her chemise, so it fell to her feet. He undid the button of her drawers and they too, fell to her feet. He reached down, picked them up and tossed them onto the chair.

'Now madame, you are no longer bossy Nurse Duran; you are my wife and will do as I wish. Stand still so I can examine that beautiful body with my artist's eye.' He walked round her, admiring the view from every angle. 'I am thankful I made you breastfeed Marie-Ann from birth as I know it wasn't easy for you, but I never expected you to continue till she was fourteen months old… but if you hadn't, Marie, she would have died. I have so much respect and admiration for your courage and bravery and sheer determination to find me. Did you never think of leaving the country by sea or fleeing to another country? Only my beautiful impetuous wife could get herself imprisoned surrounded by 2500 men. You are like a moth drawn to a flame where danger is concerned. You pitched yourself against the might of the German army and won, but you could so easily have lost. If God is really watching over us, as I have faced death twice and survived and you have faced it once; he is going to run out of guardian angels to protect us soon.'

'Not whilst you were still in Paris. I knew in my heart you were still alive, but I could not have left France without you.'

'Oh, my beautiful wife. What am I going to do with you? Just get into that bed now and let me ravish you.' Marie jumped in and Charles went to the dresser and brought his plate of strawberries and jug of cream into bed with him. He placed the cream jug on the bedside table and said, 'Now you want me to eat all this precious fruit up to make me stronger, don't you?'

'Yes, of course I do!'

'Well lie back in the bed and don't move.'

He took a strawberry and bit a piece out of it and then placed it on her right nipple, followed immediately by another one on her left nipple. He then placed them in a line from her cleavage down to her pubic bone. He then selected a large one and slipped it between her legs. Marie was astonished… and then she saw him with the cream jug in his hand.

'No Charles, not the cream!'

But it was too late; he was already dribbling it down her cleavage.

'If you don't want the cream running over the bed you had better lie still until I have finished my pudding.' He proceeded to remove each strawberry after dipping it in the cream and ate them slowly, one by one. His tongue was everywhere, sending a myriad of sensations throughout her body. When he had licked the cream off her pubic hair, he burrowed his tongue inside her to retrieve the last strawberry, she was so sexually aroused that she was already demanding him inside her. He obliged with delight and this time he was determined to control his timing and intended they should have a simultaneous orgasm. Just in time, he remembered she had a habit of screaming when she came. He just got the pillow over her mouth before she screamed loud enough to summon the entire camp, never mind Reissman in the next bedroom.

He removed the pillow and she demanded, 'Don't you dare move now, I want you to stay inside me as long as you can and when you have recovered sufficiently, do it again! You are wonderful, Charles. You were near death twenty-four hours ago and now you have turned into a rampant sex god.'

'That's because you are back at my side, angel, but don't you ever give this treatment to any more of your patients to speed their recovery or I will beat you severely.'

He kissed her passionately on the lips and moved

down her body. By the time he had reached her navel he was fully ready for action again. He whispered in her ear, 'You get on top of me but watch my back.'

She complied with pleasure and this time she controlled the proceedings and managed to refrain from screaming at the height of her passion. Afterwards, they lay in each other's arms, recovering from their exertions.

Charles kissed her and whispered, 'Thank God I have got you back my cherie, I love you so much. I don't know how I would have lived if I had lost you.'

oOo

The next morning, Marie awoke and tried to sneak out of bed without disturbing Charles. Just as she was about to get out, his arm pulled her back by her waist and he said, 'Where do you think you are going, madame?'

'I have to get moving now. Your unit will be here soon, and I have more lives to save. I have done as much as I can for you; now it is up to you to get your body better.'

'Very well, madame but you are not leaving this bed until you have given me a long, lingering kiss and I have kissed your body in all the areas I covet.'

He lay across her body, so she could not escape and proceeded to kiss her and run his hands all over her. She would have loved to stay, but she knew today was not going to be easy.

She got bathed and dressed quickly, gave Charles

his injection and told him she would ask Sylvie to bring Marie-Ann in to him for an hour, so they could draw together. He asked her to get Courbet to come and tell him who had made it back in his troop, when they had arrived. Courbet was now in the compound with the other prisoners as they had emptied as many beds as they could in the hospital. Marie left to go and feed Marie-Ann and promised to be back for his afternoon injection.

His breakfast arrived soon afterwards, and he tucked in with vigour as he had Marie's portion to eat as well. He was beginning to like his food again and loved the croissants with butter. Today's fruit treat was a bowl of cherries and he put them to one side for later. Unfortunately, Marie would probably not be as receptive to a repeat performance after work today. He laughed at last night's antics, but he knew he would have to work hard to prove to Marie that he was worthy of her love and eradicate the fears she had about what Reissman had done to her. He would not mention it to her but would let her tell him in her own good time.

He could hear movement outside, so he knew the troop had arrived; he was on the verge of plucking up the courage to go and see if Reissman had a book he could read when Reissman himself entered the room.

'Good morning, Charles. I trust you are recovering a little more strength each day.'

'Yes, I am, thank you. I was wondering, since I

have lost my devoted nurse today, if you may have any books I could read.'

'But of course, I have a small library in my study with one or two French titles. Perhaps you would like to come and choose one yourself.'

'I will have to come in my nightgown. I have no clothes worth putting on.'

'That's fine. There's nobody about; my men are busy with the arrival of your troop. I will ask Marshal Marcon to sort you out some clothes.'

Charles got out of the bed and Reissman even offered him a hand as he was struggling to get his knees to bend. They walked down the corridor to his office and Charles selected a German book featuring all the works of art in German museums, and one French novel. He made his own way back and heard the German commander of the troop come into his office. This was the bastard who had inflicted some of the whip marks on his body, so he was in no need of a reunion with him. He tried to listen at the door, but his German was not up to translating at speed yet.

He had been reading the art book for about half an hour when Courbet appeared. They had a long chat about who had made it to Lille. There had been 107 of them who had been marched out of Paris a month ago and only forty-eight of those had made it. Sheer exhaustion, lack of energy from starvation and wound infection had been the major causes of death. Charles was very saddened to think that so many good men had been lost unnecessarily. The futility of war was a mystery to him. Man's inhumanity towards man was deplorable. He and Courbet reflected on their capture and being marched up the Champs-Élysées. They had known that they were facing death, but both had remained calm. He had pictured his wife and child in his mind whilst silently praying they were still alive and asking God to watch over them. Now, he felt guilty about being spared when others had not, but he wasn't sure he would have made the twenty-five miles extra that he had been spared. Courbet told him that Marie and Dr Kohl were operating on young Francis Pliette, who had tried to escape on the march and suffered the same beating as Charles. Courbet said he would come back later in the afternoon with more news.

A few minutes after Courbet left, he heard a commotion in the corridor and heard Reissman rushing out of his office, down the corridor and into the hospital. He could hear a barrage of angry voices and then the door was flung open and Marie was marched in by two guards. God forbid, what was going on now? He held his arms out and she ran to him, sobbing. He heard Reissman and another German arguing in the corridor, but he could not understand what was being said. They moved off into Reissman's office and continued the argument.

'What is the matter, sweetheart? What have you done now?'

Marie replied, choking with sobs, 'We operated

on the 18-year-old young man in your troop that had tried to escape and been whipped by the same German bastard that attacked you. Unfortunately, he died on the operating table. The bastard that did it came into the ward and laughed when he was told he had died.

Charles groaned and said, 'Oh, Marie, what did you do?'

'I slapped him across the face and called him a cruel, vindictive bastard. He grappled with me and then had hold of me round my neck and threatened to have me flogged. Dr Kohl intervened and told him to leave me alone, that I was under his authority as a nurse and to get out of the hospital. Several of the French wounded had left their beds and were coming menacingly towards him, including Dr Kohl and Dr Jager. Someone had gone to tell Reissman and he appeared. They had a furious row and he ordered me to my room under guard and they are in his office, still rowing.'

Charles opened the door and checked there were no guards. He motioned to Marie to join him and they moved down the corridor to the office door. He could not understand what they were saying but he heard his name mentioned more than once. Marie listened to the argument and tears ran down her cheeks. After a few minutes the voices calmed down a little and he thought they had better get out of the corridor.

When he got back into the room he looked at his

distraught wife and said, 'Tell me exactly what was going on now, Marie. Do not spare me any of the detail.'

'He insisted he wanted me flogged in front of the prisoners for attacking him but Reissman said that would cause a riot in the camp as Frenchmen do not like their women disrespected. He had heard the rumours that I was Reissman's mistress. Charles, it was not true.'

He put his arms round her and said, 'Marie, I know it's not true. Reissman himself has revealed the full extent of your ordeal. I know he has not had intercourse with you and he confessed in full about the night he got drunk.'

Marie looked even more shocked. 'The officer then said that he was delighted that Reissman had been enjoying me in his bed, while he had been marching you from Paris. He assumed that after four months Reissman had left me with a German child in my belly, which along with the marks he had inflicted on your back, would make a wonderful souvenir of the war for both of us.'

'Marie, you were the victim. There is no way that you have broken your marriage vows to me; you did everything to prevent him taking you. I told you to choose life over death because I knew your beauty would be your downfall. I would have forgiven you if you had voluntarily become his mistress to protect our daughter and were carrying his child, because none of it would have been your fault. I didn't tell you what Reissman said because I wanted to let you come to terms with it in your own time. I have him to thank for the lives of you and Marie-Ann. I cannot hate him because he loved you and wanted your body; he backed off from raping you, which is all that matters to me.'

'But Charles, it will be all round camp that I am pregnant with Reissman's child. What will the Frenchmen think of me?'

'Oh, Marie. I don't give a damn what they think. The three of us know the truth; that's all that matters. We can both handle the deception until we are released and if it takes longer than six months, they will know you are not pregnant. Unless of course, I mess it up and get you pregnant in the meantime.'

They heard Reissman's boots walking down the corridor and Marie pressed closer to Charles and he put his arm around her.

Reissman entered and said, 'Marie, I am here to reassure you that you have nothing to fear for your impetuous reaction with Colonel Dittmar. I have persuaded him to reconsider his idea of flogging you in front of the entire camp and causing a riot. I do beg you once again to keep your hands to yourself and consider the repercussions of your actions before you carry them out. However, justified your slap may have been in your mind, you put yourself into danger yet again. Unfortunately, Dittmar has also heard the camp gossip that you are my mistress and he has assumed that as this was over the last four months, you could also be carrying my child. We both know this is not possible, but it gave him some amusement to think that whilst he was marching your husband out of Paris I was violating you and leaving your husband with the dilemma of raising another man's child. It was his warped idea of justice. I know this will be difficult for you to reconcile what your countrymen think of you, but under the circumstances I ask you to neither confirm nor deny these allegations in camp. I have already told your husband the truth and absolved you from any blame whatsoever.'

Charles replied, 'For my part, I don't give a damn what anybody thinks. I am just grateful to have my wife and daughter alive, but my wife may see it differently.'

Marie answered, 'They are going to consider me a traitor, albeit under duress, but at least their sympathies will lie with Charles, so they will hopefully refrain from raising the issue direct.'

Reissman replied, 'You are free to return to the hospital if you wish. Dittmar is leaving to return to Germany by train later today. Yet again Charles, I apologise for this unfortunate incident, but I have done the best I can to limit the damage. Thankfully, I could pull rank on him.' He left the room and returned to his office.

Charles said, 'Marie, only go back to the ward if you are mentally up to it. You have suffered enough trauma today.'

'I will go back in a few minutes. Just give me a big hug. At least I have you to protect me now.'

He took her in his arms and hugged her tightly. 'I just wish I could have been here before to support you. You really have seen the horrors of war, which few women would be able to cope with. You are a very brave woman and still only nineteen.'

oOo

After lunch, Marshal Marcon came in with a bundle of clothes for him. He had managed to find him a hussar uniform that should fit him and two decent cotton shirts, leather boots and two pairs of navy breeches.

'I heard what happened this morning. Your wife is as brave as a lion, Charles.'

'Yes, but one day it will be her downfall. She doesn't consider the consequences of her fiery temper. If Dittmar had flogged her she could have been responsible for causing a riot and losing more French lives.'

'Your wife has been an example to us all. She would be welcome in any regiment and her tactical skills outweigh that of most men. She has played a very dangerous game with Reissman, but she has come out the winner. She kept her daughter alive and her honour intact and buckled down to tackle a job she had no training in and made such a difference to some of the men. She comforted them when they were dying, brought some of them out of their depression and nursed some back to health. How many women could do that? She told me you have the Chevalier de la Légion d'Honneur, but she deserves one too.'

'Probably, but many women are the unsung heroes of war and never get recognition.'

Marshal continued, 'You are a very lucky man to have her as your wife. You can imagine how she has been the talk of the camp since she arrived. There have been some misconceptions among the men as to her behaviour with Reissman, but it pleased them to see him with hand marks across his face. It reassured them that she was fighting back. Under someone else's command she could have suffered a worse fate.'

'You don't need to remind me what could have befallen her. I have to give Reissman his due for his restraint, but I can also understand his reasons for appearing to dominate her in front of the prisoners.'

'Charles, none of the other men know. Marie only confided in Dr Kohl, Father Bauman and me.'

'Ah, yes that reminds me – she appears to have changed religion since she arrived here. I must speak to her about that.'

As Marshal prepared to leave, Sylvie arrived with Marie-Ann, complete with a sketchpad and coloured pencils.

Charles said, 'Ah, my little girl who needs some drawing and French lessons. She keeps speaking to me in German and I can't do with that.' Marshal and

Sylvie left the room together.

30

Charles settled on the bed with Marie-Ann, with the sketchpad propped against his knees. He decided that the best way of teaching her would be to draw something and see what word Marie-Ann came out with to describe his picture. He started with a cat and she pointed to it when she recognised the drawing and said, 'le chat'. With the dog she said 'hund,' but he remembered that she had played with Reissman's German Shepherd. She referred to the horse as 'cheval,' so two out of three in French was not too bad. He expected that she would use more German words for everyday objects. He let her have her own go at drawing and while she couldn't produce more than a few lines, squiggles and circles he could not expect more from a fourteen-month-old child.

She kept asking him for more pictures, so he used Reissman's book and showed her some of the paintings and when he pointed to a tree or an object, he got some more words out of her. He was pleased that she recognised God, Mary and Jesus in some of the religious works. He told her the names of some of the Greek and Roman gods. He managed to find one of Diana, the hunting goddess and Marie-Ann immediately said 'Mama'. He located the *Birth of Venus* by Botticelli, which he had seen in the Uffizi Gallery in Florence, but because she had blonde hair, Marie-Ann did not refer to her as Mama. Titian's *Venus with a Mirror* was also a blonde with an ample figure. He found a whole section of French kings, mainly pictures of Louis XIV. When he let her turn the pages herself it was always the horses and dogs that caught her attention. Maybe she would have her mother's gift with them.

When she became bored of looking at the pictures he sat her on his knee and tried to recall some of the nursery rhymes from his childhood, but he could only remember "Mary Had a Little Lamb" and "This Little Piggy Went to Market". He recited the latter using her fingers and when he got to the little piggy running all the way home he tickled her tummy and she laughed with glee. After this he managed a creditable story of "Little Red Riding Hood" and played down the part of the wolf for fear of frightening her.

He realised how little he knew about rearing a child and realised that because of Marie's upbringing, she must have had even less knowledge when she became a mother. No wonder Marie had felt out of her depth when Marie-Ann was born. She had no role model to follow to teach her parenting skills and she had returned to work part-time in his studio before Marie-Ann was six months old.

Marie appeared at the door looking very tired

and pale. She smiled when she saw them surrounded by paper and books – trust Charles to start his daughter drawing at fourteen months old. He gave her a tender kiss and Marie-Ann grabbed hold of her, chanting 'Mama milch.'

She sighed and said, 'See, she only sees me as the woman who feeds her. I am not a real mother to her.'

'Oh, Marie that's not true. She knows you are her mother; you have done everything in your power to protect her since she was born.'

'But I am not a natural mother Charles, like you are a father. I find it difficult to relate to a child. I suppose I am too wrapped up in myself to understand a child.'

'Rubbish, you just haven't had a role model to teach you. Now you give her a feed and I will run a bath for you, so you can have a good soak before dinner arrives.'

Marie took her pinafore and dress off and sat down to feed Marie-Ann in the chair with just her chemise on. He stood behind her unpinning her hair, so he could run his fingers through her curls. Just as she had finished feeding, Sylvie arrived to take Marie-Ann for her tea.

Marie was just sitting there, deep in her own thoughts and he led her into the bathroom, removed her chemise and drawers and helped her into the warm water. 'Now, would you like me to wash your hair for you?' He was concerned when this simple question was met by a wall of tears from Marie.

'What is the matter, sweetheart?'

'Oh, Charles I do love you. You have no idea how good it feels to have you back. I feel as if we have been apart for twelve years, not twelve months.'

'You need to talk about your feelings now I am here. Bottling everything up is not good for you. Is it the death of Francis Pliette that has hit you so hard?'

'Yes, of all the prisoners he was the youngest at eighteen and should have survived. He wasn't suffering from malnutrition and he hadn't as many whip marks on his body as you do. Dr Kohl thinks it was his heart that failed.'

'I think he tried to escape, and he misjudged it; he was too inexperienced to plan it carefully enough. Dittmar would have taken great pleasure in capturing him and whipping him. He was an evil bastard. From the moment he captured me, he was intent on killing me. I punched him off his horse when he hit Gustav over the head with the butt of his rifle for no reason. As I had humiliated him in front of his men, my fate was sealed. That was the first of several whippings by him. When they had us lined up to execute in the Champs-Élysées, he moved into position straight in front of me. He was apoplectic when Bismarck ordered them to cease fire and I gave him such a beautiful smile when he lowered his rifle.'

'Weren't you frightened of dying, Charles?'

'No, I didn't want to leave you because I knew you were alive somewhere, but death didn't hold any fears for me. But I am no hero, Marie. I was not involved in any battles; I just fought to save the Louvre from being ransacked or burnt because it mattered to me as an artist that the precious masters' works within survived. I wasn't doing it out of loyalty to France, even. As you well know, most of the masterpieces in there are Italian anyway; that was another reason Antonio stayed for so long. If what I contributed to the war means that they survive then I consider my job well done.'

'Did you actually kill anybody, Charles?'

'A few perhaps, but I was rarely on the front line, only taking night watches when we were down to a few men. I had duties elsewhere, which I cannot discuss with you now.'

He finished washing her hair and she dipped under the water to rinse it off. He fetched her nightgown for her and rubbed her dry with the towels. She still seemed withdrawn, but he knew she must be exhausted after her work in the hospital.

When dinner came he made sure she ate as she said she was not hungry but once he got her eating she was fine. They looked together through Reissman's book and then she gave him his final injection and they settled down for an early night. He gave her lots of cuddles and tender kisses, but he knew to avoid any sexual advances; she was too exhausted for that. He cuddled her on her side with her back to him and knew she just wanted his comforting presence.

The next morning, they were awake early, and Marie turned over and kissed him.

'Thanks for your support for yesterday. It was good to have someone to share my thoughts with. It has been so long since I have had someone to talk to.'

'Marie, I never want to be parted from you again. If this war has taught us anything it is the importance of love, family and life. I am going to start walking today and will gradually build up my fitness again, provided my knees will allow me. Courbet will help me round the compound; you carry on with your work. Is there a barber in the camp? I could do with getting my hair cut; it is longer than yours.'

'There must be. Ask Marshal; he will know. Don't get it cut too short. I rather like you with longer hair. When I first saw you after Dr Kohl had cleaned your wounds, you reminded me of the many portraits of Jesus I have seen.'

'That does worry me darling, I can't possibly live up to his reputation… and didn't he die when he was 35? That doesn't give me very long to live. I thought I might visit the Catholic chapel as well, to thank God for my survival.'

He watched her face, but she made no comment, so he let it be. He would do some investigating of his own. He would give her time to talk to him when she was ready.

The door burst open and Marie-Ann ran in, shouting 'Dada!' at the top of her voice. Marie grabbed her, scooped her up into bed and told her to be quiet. She was already unfastening her mother's nightgown, so he plumped up the pillows for them and lay next to them, watching his two girls interact. He remembered watching Freya feed Louis and how desperately he had wanted a child, and now he had a daughter of his own who could have been lost due to the ravages of war.

After breakfast he had a bath, washed his hair and tried on the uniform he had been given. Marie had found him a silk vest to put under his shirt to protect his wounds from rubbing and chafing. The novelty of having a clean shirt and breeches compared to his badly torn guard's uniform raised his spirits. He brushed his hair through, which was down to below his shoulders. He tried on the leather boots and was pleased that they fitted well. He thought he would ask Reissman's permission to leave his room as he was still a prisoner, so he knocked on his door.

Reissman looked slightly shocked as he didn't recognise him at first, fully dressed. Charles asked, 'I thought I had better ask your permission to go over to the compound to take some exercise, hopefully get my hair cut and visit the chapel as I am officially your prisoner.'

'Well of course you may. I am delighted your recovery is progressing so well. I hope Marie has not been too upset by yesterday's events? When she arrived here Charles, she was in a fragile mental state and Dr Kohl advised me to talk to her and get her to communicate. I must say I managed to coax probably a little too much information about her private life, which included you, as she was surprisingly honest with me about her past. She told me she had killed a man in Russia when she was only fourteen because he "overstepped the mark," as she put it, and admitted she had not told you.'

Charles replied, 'It does not surprise me. There were many aspects of her life in Russia, which puzzled me. Her relationship with her mother was one that concerned me. I did question her brother Henri and he skirted the issue by saying Marie got herself into several scrapes that she had to fight her way out of, but he didn't refer to any murder. Her history tutor seemed to delight in trying to frighten her with too much detail.'

Reissman said, 'He was obviously ex-military himself as he taught them about the battle strategies of war as well as their history. Marie certainly took it all in very seriously. She thinks like a man, but the problem is she lets her temper fly when she is hurt or threatened. I think we have both been on the receiving end of her hands at one time or another.'

'Did Marie discuss religion with you?'

'Marie used religion as a weapon against me as and when it suited her. She was very quick to quote her marriage vows and the expectation of the Catholic Church on fidelity. However, I am aware that she saw Father Bauman the Protestant priest rather than the Catholic priest. I would not concern yourself too much about that; I suspect it was on the advice of Marshal Marcon as he knows I can't get any information out of Father Bauman, but I can from the Catholic priest. I also suspect that she may have thought she would get a better reception from Father Bauman than the Catholic priest.'

'Why? She has done nothing wrong and even if you had raped her, she would not have been guilty in the eyes of the church.'

'For a country with such a history of mistresses the suggestion did not go down well with your wife.'

'Precisely. We entered our marriage, vowing to remain faithful "so long as we both shall live". It would have been a complete shock to her that you could propose such a thing.'

'Oh, don't worry, she told me several times that her body was not hers to give as it belonged to you. What I can't understand is why she married you when she could have made a far more aristocratic marriage that would have given her more money, status and freedom. I honestly thought she was from a deposed branch of the French aristocracy due to her arrogance, manner and education.'

'You can't understand why Marie married me because you have never been properly in love in mind, body and soul. Believe me, we are. I know that every man who sees her raw beauty desires her, but it was me she chose to marry, and I can only remain ever grateful to her for that. She has never understood why men find her so sexually attractive.'

'Ah, but she has found someone that she finds sexually attractive, so my spies tell me. You may want to check out a certain hussar by the name of Capitan Fabien Laurent; your wife has spoken to him in the compound. On the day you returned she spent an hour with him alone in the Protestant chapel.'

Charles replied angrily, 'I do not know exactly what you are alleging here but my wife would not have been unfaithful to me in the first place, and certainly not in a house of God – of that I can be assured.'

'I am not suggesting that she was, but I am informing you of what my spies told me.'

'Don't you dare judge my wife against your German standard of morals. It was you who wanted to take another man's wife, when you have one of your own!'

Reissman smiled at him, having sowed the seed of doubt in his mind. He replied, 'By the way, I wonder if you and Marie would care to join myself, Dr Kohl and Marshal Marcon for dinner on Saturday… provided nothing untoward happens in the meantime?'

Charles snapped, 'I will consult my wife and let you know.'

Charles left the room angrily, knowing that Reissman had deliberately dropped the bombshell to concern him, and that he had risen to the bait. He went through the hospital and chatted to some members of the National Guard troop he had been with who were receiving treatment. He went through to the compound and felt perturbed at being locked in, as so far, he had enjoyed special privileges and freedom.

He asked a young trooper where he may find Marshal Marcon and he showed him to his office. Marshal was thankfully alone when he found him.

'Ah, Charles, come in. What can I do for you?'

'Well firstly, I am supposed to get some exercise and have been advised to have someone walk with me, so I was hoping Courbet was around. I desperately need this mane of hair cutting and I also would like to meet Father Bauman.'

'Well I'm sure I can help you with all those things. You had better see Father Bauman first as he will still be in the chapel now and then I will sort you out with a barber and find Courbet for you.'

'Marshal, do you know Capitan Fabien Laurent?'

'I know of him but don't know him personally. He is not attached to my regiment; he is in the Hussars. Why do you ask?'

'It's just that Reissman has just told me that he spoke to Marie twice when she came to see Father Bauman, and he took great pleasure in insinuating that she found him attractive.'

'Well, I have to say that he is a good-looking fellow and would not have been one to walk past Marie without speaking to her, but I would hardly call that an attraction. Reissman is insanely jealous of you because you have returned and spoilt his own chances of courting your wife. I would not take anything he says on that score as true. Ask her yourself, Charles. she has always been totally honest with me and she fought so hard to keep Reissman at bay, I would hardly think she would have entertained Capitan Laurent.'

He left Marshal Marcon's office, relieved by what he had heard. He certainly wasn't going to ask Marie, or it would look as though he did not trust her, and that was the last thing he wanted.

He set off across the compound to the chapel. As he paused to go up the steps, he was aware of being watched. As soon as he saw him from a short distance of thirty feet away, he knew instinctively that this was Capitan Laurent. He carried on walking up the steps and into the chapel.

He saw the piano in the corner first; he missed playing so much. Father Bauman was changing the altar cloth and motioned for him to come to the altar rail.

He said, 'You must be Madame Duran's husband, and may I say how delighted I am to see you so fit and well after your long trek here. Your wife and daughter will be delighted to have you back.'

'Father Bauman, perhaps you could enlighten me as to why my wife appears to have changed religion since her capture?'

'Monsieur Duran, you must know that I cannot divulge any of my conversations with your wife as I must respect her confidentiality. I suspect your wife chose me because she had been advised of this and perhaps she did not think the Catholic priest would be as sympathetic to her cause as I would be. She found herself in a very difficult situation with a child to protect and surrounded by men who desired her, and she was not in good health, physically or mentally. She needed someone to confide in who would not judge her or criticise her; she just wanted guidance and to deal with her own conscience and religious beliefs. The sanctity of her marriage was uppermost in her thoughts and her belief that you would be reunited was very strong. She has neither forsaken her religion nor broken her marriage vows and for that you should be very grateful. You told her to choose life over death and that is the concept she was struggling with.'

'Thank you, Father Bauman. I will speak to Marie but only when she is ready to do so. I will not put her under any pressure; I am aware of how fragile her mental health is, and I have nothing but admiration and respect for how she has dealt with this untenable situation.' He shook Father Bauman's hand and left the chapel.

Courbet was sitting on the bench, waiting outside for him to show him to the barber's and accompany him on his walk. They went to the barber's first and he instructed him to cut his hair shorter but not above the nape of his neck, to obey Marie's instructions. He was amazed when he saw at least five inches of hair on the floor. He had not realised that it had grown so long.

Courbet accompanied Charles on his walk,

following a well-worn path round the boundary of the fence. He did not need any support as his hip was recovering from its stiffness. They stopped for a rest after his first lap and he told Courbet about Capitan Fabien Laurent – and Reissman's warning. Courbet told him to forget about it as there would be absolutely no truth in it if it came from Reissman's lips. Charles managed a second lap and then headed back to the gate. He thought he may have trouble getting out, but the guard opened the gate immediately.

31

As he was going back through the ward, Marie spotted him and ushered him into an examination room. She told him Dr Kohl was going to examine her tomorrow to check on her fertility. He insisted that he should be there when Dr Kohl examined her. Marie then presented him with a test tube, requesting a sample of his sperm for testing under the microscope, to check his fertility. He was told in no uncertain terms that he had to bring the sample back before 4 p.m. that day. He tried to point out that he would be able to produce it a lot quicker if she came with him, but she sent him back to his room like a naughty boy, to do her bidding alone.

When he got back to his room, within minutes his lunch arrived and for once he was hungry; the fresh air must have done him some good. He ate his lunch with gusto and realised that he was beginning to enjoy the sweet puddings that he normally would not eat. He decided to take a nap after lunch as he expected Marie-Ann to visit at around 3 p.m. If he napped now, he knew he would be less tired that night and already he was missing intimacy with his wife, even though it had only been forty-eight hours.

He went into the bathroom and thought about what he would like to do with his wife that night, and soon provided the sample required. He tiptoed along the corridor and went into the hospital. There was no sign of Marie, but Dr Jager said she was in another ward. He had the embarrassment of having to hand the test tube to Dr Jager and he took it graciously but could not conceal a smile.

He went back to his room, took off his jacket and lay on top of the bed for a snooze. He fell asleep dreaming of Capitan Laurent and what designs he may have had upon his wife. He was startled from his slumber by his daughter throwing herself at the bed and trying to climb up. He scooped her up into his arms and kissed her. She was clutching a rag doll and so he asked her who her baby was, and she said she was called Phoebe and Sylvie had given her the doll this afternoon. He helped her describe in French what the doll was wearing, going over the different colours of her dress. They played peek-a-boo and hid her in the bed and he pretended she was talking in a high-pitched voice, which Marie-Ann found amusing.

He took her over to the table, sat her down with the doll and attempted to draw Marie-Ann. He gave her a small piece of paper and pencil and told her to draw Phoebe and he propped her up against the wall. While Marie-Ann tried to draw her doll, he tried to capture Marie-Ann on paper. He managed the basic outline of her face and her concentrated expression, trying to emulate him. However, she would need considerable coaching if she was to even produce a shape. He drew two circles for her and roughly outlined the eyes and nose, all the while talking to her and encouraging her to draw the doll. Her French vocabulary was improving all the time now that he was spending time and effort encouraging her. He knew Marie would not have the patience to do this with her, but he was sure that when it came to teaching her about animals, she would be a great tutor.

Sylvie came back to take Marie-Ann for her tea and he tidied up the room and then resumed the drawing of Marie-Ann. The thought suddenly struck him as he worked on her face that she was possibly going to be even more striking than her mother. Her dark hair and pale complexion set off her beautiful blue eyes. As if it wasn't hard enough keeping Marie safe around men, how was he going to protect his daughter? The thought kept him fully occupied until Marie returned. She came over to look at his drawing.

'Do you feel ready to get back to painting again, Charles? How long is it since you last did a portrait?'

'I painted the dead body of the young artist Henri Regnault who was killed in the Battle of Buzenval during the siege of Paris in January. He was only twenty-eight years old when he died and had already produced some notable work.'

'Oh, Charles that must have been a difficult thing

to do. Did you know him well?'

'Not really, but I wanted to paint it to try and show the ravages of war encompassing people from all walks of life. He wasn't the only young artist to die – Jean Frédéric Bazille, an artist, again only twenty-eight and a good friend of Manet – was killed at the Battle of Beaune-la-Rolande in November after he took over command of the regiment when his commanding officer was injured. That incident was what provoked Manet into joining up.'

Marie gave him a hug and laughed at Marie-Ann's drawing efforts.

oOo

The next morning, Marie instructed Charles to come to the hospital for his check-up with Dr Kohl and her fertility examination. He knew she was mad at him for wanting to be present but as no female staff could be there, he felt he had every right to be present.

He decided he would go and do his exercising before his check-up, so went to find Courbet and challenged him to a fencing bout. They did ten laps of the compound as a warm-up and then he beat Courbet in a fencing match. He was delighted that his arms and legs were recovering their muscle tone and his reaction speed had improved dramatically.

He returned to the hospital and as it was nearly his appointment with Dr Kohl, he stayed to chat to some of the other men in his unit. He was delighted that all the men who had made it to Lille were improving now their sheer exhaustion and starvation had ended.

When they got into the examination room Dr Kohl said he would examine Marie first as he thought Charles's back would take longer. Marie removed her drawers but left her outer garments on, then climbed onto the examination table. Dr Kohl advanced towards the bed with his rubber gloves on, Marie pulled up her skirts to her waist and Charles was forced into moving to the top of the bed and patting her shoulder in support. The look she gave him should have turned him to stone and frankly, that would have been a relief. No man should be expected to endure the sight of another man with his hand inside his wife. Marie seemed perfectly calm, but he could tell she was gritting her teeth and her body was tense. She could not hide one painful grimace as the doctor pressed down on her stomach with his other hand. It probably took all of two minutes but to him it felt like ten minutes. He could not fathom why he was so bothered as when Marie had been in labour, both he and Henri had examined her, but there had been a perfectly good reason for that. His examination over, Dr Kohl removed his gloves and Marie pulled down her skirts.

'Marie, everything seems fine and I would expect you to be ovulating very soon. Have you had no sign of your courses returning yet?'

'No, but I am still breastfeeding Marie-Ann

morning and night.'

'Then if you do not want to become pregnant immediately, you are going to have to be careful. I don't think it is enough to suppress ovulation. The problem is, you could conceive as soon as you produce an egg, provided fertilisation occurs, and then you would not start your courses anyway. Do you know how quickly you conceived with Marie-Ann?'

'I was exactly fourteen days from my last course on my wedding day, but they have never been monthly anyway.'

'So, you could have conceived on your wedding night then?'

Charles could not resist. 'No, she didn't because the marriage was not consummated until the day after.' Marie gave him another withering glare. Dr Kohl raised his eyebrows and tried to avoid a smile. Charles continued, 'We went on honeymoon here in Lille for a month and to be fair, we were at it like rabbits the whole time.'

Marie gasped, and he stepped back quickly, wary of her lethal hands.

Dr Kohl replied, 'Well I expect you succeeded very quickly Charles, in the first few days, so you could have saved yourself a lot of time and energy.

Charles responded, 'Perhaps, but I would not have wanted to miss the sheer pleasure and experience.'

Dr Kohl answered, 'However, that brings me conveniently on to your fertility result, which considering your physical condition, is excellent. You have a very high fertile result and the sperm mobility is 90%. This means that you are going to have to be very careful if you want to avoid pregnancy. With a sperm count like that you could soon repopulate Paris.'

Marie exploded, 'Dr Kohl, don't you dare give him any encouragement. He already thinks he is God's gift to women, especially when you are insisting he leaves me alone.'

Dr Kohl replied, 'I am merely making you aware of the situation and trying to offer a solution and advice.'

Charles said, 'Well what is the solution? Because I cannot contemplate abstaining from sex, as we have only just got back together.'

'It would only need to be until she has her first bleed, then you would only need to abstain from day twelve to day nineteen. You could use the latest rubber sheaths, which are relatively safe, but I have none here to give you.'

Marie exploded, 'Dr Kohl, it would be a sheer waste of time. He is a Frenchman and they are genetically wired to spread their seed far and wide to procreate and are conveniently aided and abetted by the Catholic Church.'

Charles intervened, 'Marie, that is hardly fair.'

Marie turned to Dr Kohl, 'If you have finished with me now, I need to go and assist Dr Jager.'

Dr Kohl replied, 'That's fine Marie; I will see to

Charles's wounds.'

After Marie had left, Dr Kohl apologised to Charles for causing an upset. Charles explained that they had already discussed that it would not be a good idea to have another child until they were back on their feet in Paris. He had no idea what state Paris would be in now and his studio and his rented house may have been lost completely. Dr Kohl warned him to ensure he had a doctor engaged when Marie did give birth to her next child, which would be bigger, as she might struggle to give birth naturally without assistance. He also warned him to be careful using the withdrawal method of birth control as it required precision timing and could be compromised by contamination via his own hands. Dr Kohl said Charles's wounds were all healing successfully, with no sign of infection. However, it would be some time before the scarring healed and he must ensure that Marie continued with the treatment.

Charles made his way back to his room for lunch. He felt that Marie was slightly irritated by the revelation of his fertility results and it concerned him. Was she angry because she did not want to become pregnant too soon, and Dr Kohl advising her of her returned fertility improved her chances? He was sure it wasn't because she did not want any more children; it was just the timing of them that was uppermost in her mind. He would have to speak to her about the subject and get to the heart of what was concerning her. After all she had been through, he felt she should be the one to decide. He would just have to ensure he complied with her wishes. If it meant abstaining from intercourse, then he would just have to do it.

When they were in bed that evening he plumped up the pillows and told her he wanted to talk to her. She flashed him one of her inquisitive looks and he saw a flicker of amusement in her lips. He put his arm round her and pulled her head onto his shoulder.

'Tell me, Marie. Why you were angry at me over my fertility results?'

'I wasn't angry with you personally. I was just concerned that now is not the time to bring another child into the world when our lives are in such a mess.'

'I thoroughly agree with you darling, and if you want me to abstain until your courses return to avoid sex during your most fertile time then I will agree to do it. Your health and wellbeing are more important to me than my own. I do not want to push you into becoming a mother for a second time until you are ready.'

'I don't want to deny you the intimacy you crave because I desire it too. I have missed that part of our relationship so much since we have been separated. However, we must be sensible, and Dr Kohl has just confirmed how potent you are. We will have to find ways to relieve the desire without risking pregnancy.'

'Very well, sweetheart. I will see what I can dream up. However, let's start with a good kissing.' He leant down and kissed her urgently on the lips and she responded enthusiastically. Within minutes he had moved from kissing her lips to her breasts and down to her navel, using his tongue to stimulate her beautiful soft skin. She was soon lost in the depth of her feelings and she forced his mouth towards the ultimate goal. She was soon close to climax and it was her who reached for him. 'No darling, not now, after what we have just said.'

She groaned with frustration, but he continued until she had reached her climax alone. He remembered to pull a pillow over her face just in time. He realised that he was close to climaxing just watching her pleasure, so he ceased all movement while their bodies lay entwined. He reflected that keeping their new rule was going to be frustrating and difficult for them both.

32

The next day was Saturday and that evening, they were dining with Reissman at his personal invitation. Marie only spent the morning in the hospital and so in the afternoon, they took Marie-Ann into the compound for some exercise. She proved to be a magnet as the prisoners had not been in contact with her before. Charles was pleased as it gave Marie-Ann an opportunity to listen to French conversation. They received many compliments regarding her beauty, and good wishes that they had both found each other alive after so many setbacks due to the war. Several men who had been patients of Marie's came up to chat to her and thank her for her nursing.

They visited the gym and Charles was pleased to learn that they had recently been given fencing foils, so they could practice fencing as part of their fitness regime as well as boxing. Charles declared that he would start doing both disciplines to improve his fitness. They could set up extra fencing areas outside as well.

Finally, they went to the Protestant chapel and introduced Marie-Ann to the ritual of prayer and they sang 'The Lord's My Shepherd' to introduce singing as well. As they came out of the church, Capitan Fabien Laurent was waiting on the bench outside. He stood up as they came out and he approached Marie.

'Madame Duran how delighted I am that you and your husband have been reunited.'

Charles watched the expressions of both very carefully.

Marie replied, 'Capitan Laurent, thank you for your kind words and may I introduce my husband Charles Carolus-Duran and my daughter Marie-Ann.'

Charles extended his hand to Capitan Laurent and asked him, 'Capitan Laurent, are you another of the patients my wife has treated?'

'No, not exactly. I met your wife when she came to visit the chapel and I did my best to support and befriend her during her imprisonment.'

Charles watched Marie's reaction to Laurent's response and observed she deliberately avoided direct eye contact with him and physically distanced herself from Laurent. Laurent was careful not to register any emotion on his face, but his eyes gave away his feelings towards Marie. How often had Charles seen men smitten by Marie before? But this time he felt uneasy... for what reason, he could not explain. As they moved on, he turned to Marie and gave her a chance to explain.

'Is he another of your many admirers, Marie?'

Marie blushed and said, 'You may be surprised

to learn that I now know what it feels like to be attracted to another man but as a married woman, I was not in a position to pursue my feelings. Yes, I found him attractive, so I now understand what men feel like when they desire me, but that does not mean I am going to take it any further.'

'I am pleased to hear that sweetheart, as I would not like to find I had another rival for your affections.'

'Charles, it is no different than your attraction to Freya or any other woman. Like you said before, you can look but you can't touch.'

He was pleased with her honesty and that she had not tried to hide or lie about her feelings… and she was right that most women would have fallen for the charms of Capitan Laurent; he was particularly handsome in his uniform and quite the dashing French hussar.

They returned to their room and Charles suggested Marie have a nice long hot bath and he would amuse Marie-Ann until Sylvie came to take her for tea. Marie jumped at the chance to have some time to herself while he attempted to finish the picture he had done of Marie-Ann. When she had become bored of drawing, Marie-Ann clambered onto his knee and chatted to him.

He moved over to the bed with her and played with her, pleased to see her little body was filling out, particularly her arms and legs. Her abundant dark hair was now down to her waist and fell naturally in ringlets. He plaited her hair into two plaits and then pinned them around her head. She loved the attention and sat very still for him. As he looked at her, he wondered what the future held for his little girl. He was determined she would receive an education, which he had always felt lacking in himself as he had been painting since he was eight years old; he wanted to ensure Marie-Ann received an all-round education the same as any boy.

Marie came out of the bathroom in her wrap and joined them on the bed. Marie-Ann saw the opportunity of a feed, so Marie agreed to feed her now as they would be dining later. Charles watched with interest as his two girls interacted and they discussed whether it was time to stop feeding her altogether now she was back on a normal diet. Surprisingly, Marie was in favour of continuing her night feed if she wanted. He thought that if she stopped feeding then ovulation would return, and they would at least know where they were in a monthly cycle. Sylvie took Marie-Ann for tea and so he stripped off, ready for his bath. He could not resist coming back to the bed and giving his wife a sexy kiss but when she realised he was looking for more than just a kiss, she ordered him into the bath while she attended to her hair. When he returned, she was starting to dress her hair and he asked her to leave most of it loose, so she only pinned the top and sides up. She went to the wardrobe and pulled out the two dresses Reissman had given her and asked which she should wear.

'Definitely the red one my beauty, as you will be

the only woman present amongst five men; you will make a real impact in red. The blue one, I would have chosen had we got your sapphire necklace with us. Shame I will have to wear uniform, as I have no alternative.'

'But I like you in uniform, darling. I have got used to it now.'

Charles could not resist saying, 'Ah, but will I turn your head as much as Capitan Laurent does?'

In the reflection from the mirror, he saw the flash of anger cross her face, but he had not spotted her right hand fling her hairbrush at him, which caught him on the chin. She ran over, full of apologies and he made her kiss him better.

He helped her into the dress. To his delight, it was low cut over her breasts and slightly too tight, which gave her an ample top line. Charles suggested she tighten the lace of the chemise to give her even more cleavage, and it certainly gave her a buxom look. Had she had a corset, she would have looked sensational. Charles was delighted as he knew the effect it would have on the men, particularly Reissman. He wanted him to see just what he was missing out on now that he had reclaimed his wife. Marie looked wonderful as the fitted dress showed off her slight waist and hips. Thankfully, they had now filled out and there was a covering of flesh on her hips.

As he got dressed, he realised he must be putting weight on as he had to loosen his breeches by one hole. His legs and arms were also fleshing out now and the scars were becoming less noticeable on his back. He wondered how long it would take until they faded into silvery scars – probably a long time.

Marie made the final touches to her hair. He bent down and kissed the top of her head. 'You look beautiful, my angel and I am so proud of you.'

Marie replied, 'And you my love, look as handsome as ever.'

They went to the dining room where Reissman and Dr Kohl were already partaking of an aperitif. Dr Kohl reacted with delight at Marie's dress and he bowed and kissed her hand. Reissman held back but his eyes studied every detail of Marie's appearance and Charles noticed the pause when he looked at her breasts. Marshal Marcon and Dr Jager arrived together, and both men were dazzled by Marie's appearance. Charles took great pleasure in knowing that every one of them was captivated by his beautiful wife but that only he had the pleasure of her in bed. Marie was determined to make the dinner a pleasing affair and she went into hostess mode and chatted to make all the men feel at ease. Reissman and Marshal were in uniform, but the two doctors were in dinner suits.

They sat down, and he noticed that Reissman was at the head of the table with Marie to his right and himself to his left. He did not think Reissman would spend much time chatting to him, but he supposed he could hardly have banished him to the far end of the table. Dr Kohl was sitting at the bottom of the table, facing Reissman. There was a menu for a four-course meal and he was delighted to see that steak was the main course and the description was in both German and French. Marie had taken the lead as far as the conversation went and she spoke in French, which was appropriate as he and Marshal were not fluent in German. The starter, which was goat's cheese in a small, round pastry base, was light and very tasty. The conversation was on the theme of education and it appeared that German schooling was biased towards science, maths, languages and history whilst the arts did not seem to feature. Charles asked how potential musicians, artists and writers learnt their craft, but nobody could give him a reasonable answer. Obviously, these areas were not considered important in German culture. This did not surprise him as he could only name one German artist he would consider a master, and that was Hans Holbein who had spent much of his time as a portrait artist at the court of Henry VIII. He could not resist dropping this into the conversation. However, he received a frown from Marie who under normal etiquette rules would have classed this as sleight to their German hosts. Reissman had a dig at Charles's lack of education but when he agreed with him it rather took the wind out of his sails. He got his own back by pointing out that he had received a much wider education by studying in Toledo and Madrid in Spain and Rome, Venice and Florence in Italy. He had received the benefit of studying their culture, religion and history, as well as their art, first hand.

They discussed the education of girls and Charles pointed out that he thought girls could be equal to men in medicine, art, law and teaching if only they were permitted to aspire to higher roles. He pointed out that Empress Eugénie as Regent in Napoleon III's absence at war had insisted that women should be admitted to the medical schools to train as doctors, provided they had the qualifications. Marshal thought it unlikely they would be able to join the military academies, but Charles defended women's rights to attain the highest qualification in their chosen subject. Reissman said women were too emotional to be entrusted with war. Charles responded that there wouldn't be any wars if women were in charge because they would not allow wars to happen in the first place. Marie backed him up by saying if the European queens had been able to rule instead of their kings then half the wars already fought would never have happened.

Dr Kohl asked Charles what his most difficult project in Italy had been. He told them about the wall mural that he had been asked to do as part of a religious theme for a main hall in the Vatican. The project employed over thirty different artists, working on different areas of the fresco. He had been shocked to discover he had to paint six virgins along with another Italian student and they were both only nineteen at the time. The virgins consisted of daughters of the ruling house of Savoy aged between thirteen and sixteen, who were carefully chaperoned throughout the sittings as they were to be painted nude. The first sitting was done in a studio and the master positioned each girl in the background setting, with half of them standing and half sitting. He could remember the initial shock as his eyes surveyed the scene. Their job was to capture the scene on paper and then it would have to be recreated and scaled up onto the wall fresco. He admitted that it was one of the most difficult paintings he had ever done. Three of the girls were sisters and the resemblance in their facial features was startling, although one girl was blonde and the other two brunettes. Reissman asked if he had been able to touch them and he admitted they had only been allowed to pose them back into position after breaks in painting... and two of the girls deliberately required repositioning every time, just to embarrass the two young painters.

Dr Kohl said, 'And what did that teach you, Charles?'

Charles thought and replied, 'A respect for women, a better understanding of anatomy and nature at its best. There was no embarrassment by the girls; they had been chosen to do the job, which they considered an honour, and we were there to capture it for posterity. It helped me as a portrait artist in my work now, to take the time to talk to my subjects and find something of their character that I can portray in the portrait. Some women are very shy and have been dominated by their husbands but even the plainest woman can be made to shine if you take the trouble to find out what they are really like. Take Marie's portrait; it was perfect for her to be painted on horseback because I was able to portray her complete empathy with the horse and her riding skill. When we selected Jacques as a scholarship student he painted her hunting bears in Russia and was able to capture her spirit, along with her affinity to nature. I learnt very early on that I had to have the final say in what my subject wore. Some people are incapable of knowing what colours and styles of dress look good on their bodies. I have been known to have dresses designed for women and have cut and pinned them into place if they do not fall correctly. A woman does not have to be nude to be sexually attractive to men. Some of my best portraits of women have been of them fully clothed. Marie in a black velvet riding habit was sensational. Freya my sister-in-law in a dress I slashed from her thigh to her ankle, was another. I got into trouble with my mother for that one as she thought I was coveting to my brother's wife!'

Dr Kohl asked, 'When did you realise that Marie was the girl for you?'

Charles laughed, 'She flirted with me throughout her two-day sitting with those deep blue eyes and then she challenged me to a horse race along the beach, knowing I hadn't a hope in hell of beating her on the horse I had, plus I had to get on after she had galloped off. My forfeit for losing was to give her a kiss and that gave me hope that I had a chance. When I came down the stairs at the ball in full dress uniform with my Légion d'honneur sash, she watched me and came over and gave me the most beautiful deep curtsy and congratulated me. That was the moment I knew she had to become my wife; she made me feel like a king.'

Reissman turned to Marie and asked, 'And was this the same for you, Marie?'

Marie smiled, 'I had to be forward with Charles to let him know that I was interested in him. If I had waited and behaved like a demure French girl I would have lost him. I fell for his beautiful brown eyes, his dashing good looks, his natural humour, patience, gentleness, tenderness, artistic ability and the fact he loves every bone in my body.'

Dr Kohl asked, 'Tell us how your brother came to deliver your child?'

Marie told them how Henri had a habit of turning up when she was in trouble and had always been her guardian angel. Dr Kohl was interested in the concept of training soldiers to be medics on the battlefield. He thought it was an excellent idea as immediate medical attention could save the life of a patient. Dr Jager thought it would be very distracting for the soldier. Charles confirmed that they were soldiers first, not medics. They could be court-martialled if they attended to the wounded without permission. They were also at considerable risk if they were dealing with patients on the battlefield as they would be an easy target for the enemy.

They had now reached the main course of steak after a fish course of smoked mackerel. Charles noted that Marie was being careful in her consumption of wine and this surprised him. Perhaps she was finally beginning to have a more mature attitude towards life. Charles found the steak was excellent and just melted in the mouth. He could not remember when he had last had any beef at all.

The conversation drifted towards the characteristics and temperament of European men. Charles pointed out that when it came to charming women, the Italians were at the top of the tree. However, he did point out that they spent too long talking about themselves and could find the women drawn towards French men, who know how to flatter women and get them into bed. Charles nominated Spanish men as being the most family orientated, with a healthy respect for their older generation. English men were considered too reserved and showed little emotion when it came to flirting. German men were too stiff and formal to be attractive to women. Marie pointed out that sometimes the most attractive men could be the most selfish lovers. Marshal said he regretted pursuing an army career as he had completely missed out on socialising with women. Reissman asked Charles if he considered himself to be an average Frenchman.

Charles replied, 'God, no. I have broken all the rules of French etiquette and am definitely not your average Frenchman. It wasn't until after I married that I realised there were all these stupid unwritten rules of behaviour and that is why Frenchmen have mistresses; they are not allowed near their wives for most of the time. Some of this has been perpetuated by women themselves to rid them of the presence of a bad husband. This idea that as soon as pregnancy is confirmed, the husband should be banned from the marriage bed until six weeks after birth is ludicrous. I enjoyed watching the process of pregnancy in Marie and would not have missed it for the world. This myth that it is dangerous to continue intercourse once a wife is pregnant must have been issued by women, not men!'

Dr Kohl replied, 'Exactly, there is no reason to suspect that a woman will miscarry if sex continues during pregnancy; it is just not physically possible to cause any damage.'

'Charles retorted, 'Precisely, we had a wonderful sexual relationship right up to days before the birth and we certainly resumed it long before the six weeks was up afterwards. I was in severe disgrace with my mother-in-law, mainly because I insisted that Marie breastfed, which is another etiquette faux pas as she considered her grandchild should have been fed by a wet nurse. I cannot see the point, having created a child within a loving marriage; you would then consider handing over the child to a stranger to rear. If you want your child to have your values, then surely the mother is the best person to rear the child within the family unit. This idea of the French aristocracy not seeing their children until they are in their teens is a complete mystery to me. As a father, I want to be involved in every aspect of my child's life. Being away from Marie-Ann for over a year has been very difficult to deal with.'

Marie interrupted, 'But you Charles are one in a million; not many men have your patience or empathy with children. You make me feel inadequate sometimes because I don't have the maternal feelings some mothers have towards their children. Again, in Russian high society, women do not feed or rear their children and that was unfortunately the background I was brought up in.'

Charles replied, 'Marie, you do yourself an injustice. The only reason you struggle is that you don't have a role model to follow. The Italian and Spanish families have a perfect set-up in that all members of the extended family help rear their children.'

Reissman countered, 'I leave all the decisions regarding my children to my wife. That's her job and I would only intervene if I thought I was justified.'

Charles asked, 'But what about important decisions such as education and religion? Surely you must discuss that together?'

Reissman replied, 'No, not especially, my wife knows what my wishes are in those areas anyway.'

They had now moved on to the pudding course and Charles was delighted to find it was a raspberry meringue, which, considering the difficulty of obtaining sugar during the Paris siege, was a blessed treat. Marie ate half of hers then passed her plate over to him and swapped it for his empty one.

The conversation switched to talk of when the prisoners would be released and what would happen to them. Reissman assumed that they would be sent back to Paris by train. There was hope that it would be within the next four weeks, but the French government had still not paid over the money agreed in the treaty. Charles was concerned that they probably did not have the money, but he said nothing.

Marie asked Reissman if they could visit Jacques' family in Lille under German escort. He said he would personally escort them with a small guard tomorrow. Charles wasn't so sure Jacques' parents would relish a German troop arriving at their house.

33

Henri was determined to make it back to Versailles undetected, as a matter of principle, even though the area was swarming with German troops. He made a further detour and approached Versailles from the east side. Guards were positioned at all the gates, so he risked riding up to the main gate where two troopers on horseback cantered out to intercept him, 100 yards from the gate. He was stopped at gunpoint and asked to dismount. He advised them in German that he was returning from a mission for Comte Hans von Brixenhof. One of the men recognised him from his time in captivity at Versailles, so he was permitted to remount and escorted through to the stables. His arrival caused a stir and Jester's French groom came running out to greet him. He handed Jester into his care after he had given him a good pat and a hug. He was escorted by the two troopers to Le Comte's office. He was not surprised to be told that he was out in Paris but to his sheer delight, Anya swept into the room and dismissed his guards. After the guards were out of the room, she ran to him with open arms.

'Henri, thank God you are safe and well. I feared

you may have been caught up in the initial seizure of Paris.'

Henri pulled her to him and gave her a long, lingering, passionate kiss. 'Well you knew I would come back if only to see you again, ma cherie. Anya, I need your help to track down Charles Duran. He was one of the prisoners that Bismarck marched up the Champs-Élysées, intending to execute. Where were those prisoners taken and can you get him released for me?'

She pulled away from him and took her place at the desk, motioning to him to sit down. 'Henri, I will find out where he is, but I can't promise you his release – that would be down to a higher authority than me.'

'I appreciate that Anya, but it was thanks to his help that I was able to find Eugénie so quickly and he was in a bad physical and mental state when I left him, having begged him to get out of the firing line.'

Anya picked up her pen and smiled at Henri. 'First things first, my beautiful French musketeer, your report on your mission please and then we can concentrate on your emotional and physical wellbeing. I read *The Three Musketeers* while you were away, and I think you are most like young D'Artagnan.'

Henri blushed and laughed at the same time as he had just been considering whether to attempt to make love to her over her desk. He gave her a summary of his mission, which she took down in shorthand and asked some further questions.

'Now Henri, I suggest you go to your room and have a leisurely bath, which believe me, you desperately need. Bismarck and Le Comte won't be back from Paris for at least another two hours. I will join you as soon as I can.'

'Delighted to oblige, madame. I shall be ready and waiting.' He picked up his saddlebags and left the room. He saw nobody on his way up to his room but knew they would all likely be involved in the occupation. He ran a hot bath, stripped all his smelly clothes off and dived in, relishing the hot water easing his aching bones from nights in the saddle and days sleeping rough.

He had just finished washing his hair when he heard the outer door open and Anya appeared. She picked up a large towel and offered it to him. Henri got out of the bath, gave himself a quick rub down with the towel, discarded it and then picked Anya up in his arms and carried her into the bedroom.

'Madame, yet again I apologise for my boorishness, but may I have your permission to ravish you now and relieve my sexual appetite and then do it again to relieve yours?'

'Oh, Henri you can do what the hell you like to me; with a body like that no woman could ever refuse you.'

Henri took her with the same intensity he had on their last night in Versailles, his passion fuelled by pent-up energy. His possession of her body gave him a combined feeling of safety, serenity and comfort. After an hour of numerous passionate couplings, Henri finally admitted defeat. He lay in her arms and she stroked his still wet hair.

'I am going to have to get back to my office before they all return. You have a sleep, my love and if you aren't down for dinner I'll send Le Comte to wake you.'

Henri kissed her nipple and reluctantly released her body, so she could get up. He was now physically exhausted and was mortified to see his hand was shaking uncontrollably and he could feel his heart pounding in his chest. He threw the covers over himself and within minutes, he was in a deep sleep.

He woke to see Le Comte at his bedside. 'Jesus, Hans, how did you get so close to me without my hearing you? God is it dinner time already?'

'Calm down Henri, you have half an hour. Anya suggested I come and wake you as she suspected you were exhausted. She tells me you succeeded on your mission and managed not to kill anybody, which must be a first for you.'

'Yes, but I could have killed your side for ruining my one and only night in London by invading Paris. I had to return far too soon; I would have loved more time to investigate London.'

'Little shit, we didn't send you on your bloody holidays, you know. You were supposed to be working, not playing. Get your lazy arse out of that bed and get down for dinner.' He smiled at him indulgently and then left the room.

Henri joined them for dinner and was surprised by the warmth of his greeting from Bismarck and Wilhelm. Napoleon was overjoyed and hugged him, visibly tearful that he had returned safely. Over dinner, Napoleon asked about the devastation in Paris and Henri asked Le Comte for permission before he responded.

'Sire, Paris is indeed in a very sorry state due to fire and cannon shot, particularly around the Tuileries Palace and Luxembourg Gardens. The Louvre library has been partially destroyed but the rest of the building is still intact. The Hôtel de Ville is in ruins; it is just a burnt-out shell. The National Guard and French troops are weakened by lack of food and the residents have been starving for a long time.'

Bismarck interrupted, 'I trust you are not blaming us for all this devastation as much of it has been self-inflicted, as you are aware, Henri.'

Henri decided to keep his mouth shut as he knew he might need Bismarck's goodwill to extract Charles from captivity. Wilhelm rescued him from his predicament by changing the subject. He expected to see Napoleon alone tomorrow and would update him then.

After dinner, Le Comte purloined a bottle of brandy and he, Anya and Henri returned to his room. He told them in greater detail about the state of his brother-in-law and his missing sister and niece.

He showed them the newspaper cutting of the Arts' Ball. Le Comte was immediately taken with Marie and her similarity to Henri.

'God, Henri your sister is stunning; no wonder they called her "la belle étoile de Paris."'

Anya said, 'Never mind your sister, I would welcome in my bed all three men in that picture. No wonder French artists have got such a reputation as womanisers. Come on, Henri, tell us about them.'

Henri laughed, 'My brother-in-law Charles is one of the nicest men you could ever meet. He is a perfect gentleman despite coming from a humble background. He is a competent swordsman, horseman and musician. He is a brilliant portrait artist and teacher of painting. Edouard Manet is from old French money, a distinguished respected artist… but he suffers abuse from the public, critics and his peers for his modern style of painting. Charles says he is a genius but will never know that in his own lifetime and is very much a tortured soul. He is very attracted to women and has slept with most of his models. He has the morals of an alley cat although he worships my sister as a goddess. Claude Monet is ten years younger than the others and he is attractive to women but recently married one of his ex-models and they now have a son. I really don't know much about Monet, but I do know Manet was angry that he was painting the Thames in London whilst Paris burned.'

Anya replied, 'Imagine what I could do with the

three of them stark naked lined up next to you two.'

Henri roared with laughter. 'Believe me, Manet would not wait patiently in line for any woman. He met an American girl today who he has gone back to bed, tonight.'

Le Comte said, 'A man after my own heart who gets his priorities right.'

Anya said, 'Right, I have to go – Bismarck wants me.'

Henri moaned, 'Oh no, I wanted you to sleep with me all night.'

'Forget it my little musketeer; Bismarck needs my calming hands. He is certainly showing signs of stress since the invasion. If you want me to plead for your relatives, leave me to smooth the path to his heart as only I know how.'

Le Comte said, 'That does it, with super stud musketeer D'Artagnan back in town and Bismarck now making demands, I am going to pick up my own little French girl and smuggle her back here for my personal pleasure. I could lock her up in a stable and nobody would know.'

Anya came over, bent down and kissed Henri on the lips, whispering, 'You get some sleep, Henri and I promise to make some enquiries about Charles tomorrow.' She gave Le Comte a kiss on the cheek. 'Behave yourself Hans, or I may suggest to Bismarck you head up a troop and remain on duty in Paris.'

As she left the room Le Comte said, 'That might not be a bad idea; I could enjoy the Paris nightlife.'

'Forget it Hans, believe it or not there isn't any nightlife; everything has closed down – including theatres, hotels, restaurants and cafes. However, London looked full of promise and I had to leave it, thanks to you. When I take Napoleon there I am going to spend a week investigating the London social scene. The meal and wine I had at the Savoy were outstanding. No wonder Manet left me to see Eugénie alone; he will have been finding himself a rich lady for his own amusement.'

'Right, well I shall demand to escort you and Napoleon to London and then we can both hit the town running.'

oOo

Anya started to make enquiries as to what had happened to the French troops that were captured when Bismarck entered Paris. She located the commanding officer who had been there, down at the stables, and was surprised to discover that they had been despatched to the prison camp at Lille. She assumed they had been sent by rail but to check, she located one of the soldiers who had been in Bismarck's troop that day. To her horror, she discovered that as Bismarck had been so angry that his plans to make an example of the French troops manning the barricades had been thwarted, he had insisted that they were marched on foot under escort, with Colonel Dittmar in charge. Anya groaned as she knew what a hard man he was. Henri had told her about the physical and mental state Charles had been in when he found him. She knew that the chances of him surviving a 125 mile walk to Lille were one in a million. How was she going to explain this to Henri? He would be devastated.

As she arrived back at the Palace, Le Comte was just coming out of the main door, dressed in uniform.

'Anya, Bismarck wants me to do some scouting. I will be away most of the day.'

She returned to her office and searched through the lists of prisoners held in Lille, which were updated every two weeks. Each prisoner was recorded from the date of capture and a record kept of their time in captivity. She selected the latest list, knowing that there would have been little chance of the troop arriving there when this was compiled two weeks ago. Under the section of "new prisoners" there were no entries, but she cast her eye over the list of French prisoners and found a reference to a "Michel Croizette," captured in July for "theft of a horse". He was now listed as working as a hospital orderly as he possessed medical skills. She had no idea how common Croizette was as a surname, but she was surprised that there was only him captured, as to pull a stunt like this from within the camp would have indicated a collective attempt at breakout by more than one prisoner. She looked back over previous records and noted that Michel Croizette had not been listed as a prisoner before July. She found him on the list of new prisoners for 18th July, but no French regiment was recorded in his entry. There came a knock at her door and Henri entered.

'I have been with Napoleon, reporting on my visit to London. He is delighted that Eugénie and young Louis are safe and well there.'

Anya replied, 'Henri, how common a surname is Croizette in France?'

'Not very popular. I was the only Croizette stationed at my barracks in Paris, out of 600 cavalry. Why do you ask?'

'Sit down, Henri. I have some bad news for you. The group of prisoners that Charles Duran was captured with was despatched to the prison camp at Lille.'

'Lille? Why so far away? Do you not have a Paris prison camp?'

'Yes, although I expect it would be overflowing already.' She walked round the desk, knelt at his side and took his hand in hers. 'My brave musketeer, the National Guard prisoners were not sent to Lille by rail; they were made to walk and Colonel Dittmar was in charge and he has an odious reputation within the army.'

Henri jumped to his feet and turned on her. 'How in God's name were those Frenchmen expected to walk 125 miles? They were starving, shell shocked, physically and mentally exhausted and totally incapable of walking ten miles – never mind 100 miles!'

'Oh, Henri I am so sorry my love, but do not give up hope completely. Perhaps when Charles realised he was going to Lille where he had left Marie and his daughter, he may have summoned the strength to get there.'

'Shit Anya, you did not see him. I did. He wouldn't have made it on horseback in his condition, never mind on foot. But then you didn't intend any of them to reach Lille, did you? You bastards knew they would all die long before they got there. Was that Bismarck's idea because he didn't get to execute them as he wished?'

'Henri, what can I say? I cannot defend Bismarck's actions but there is a possible lead on your sister. In the prisoner entry for Lille, a "Michel Croizette" is listed as being captured for horse stealing in July and no French regiment was recorded in the log. He has been imprisoned there, working as a medical orderly since. Does your sister have any medical skills?'

Henri looked at her in shock. 'No, not with humans but she has cared for animals all her life. You think she may have been listed as Michel to hide her sex?'

'I do hope so, Henri.'

'But that will make it even worse as Charles will die before he gets there. Oh, why didn't I insist he left Paris with me when I went to Le Havre? Do you think Bismarck will allow me to go to Lille before I take Napoleon to England?'

'I don't know as they won't release him until

the terms of the treaty are met, and that could be a while.' She hugged him now he had calmed down a little. 'Why don't you go down to the stables and exercise that wonder horse of yours? You are confined to Versailles but there is enough space for you to go for a ride through the woods.'

34

Henri wandered down to the stables, still reeling from Anya's news. He could not bear to think of Charles having to walk to Lille. He knew that the chances of him surviving were virtually nil, but he had to hope. Jester spotted him coming into the stable yard and greeted him with a loud whinny. His groom came over and he asked if Napoleon's stallion was in the yard. He was told Le Comte had taken him out that morning with a small troop going to Paris. At least Perseus was working, which was all he needed, even though it was as a German cavalry horse. He suspected that Perseus would end up at Le Comte's stud in Bavaria as there was no way Napoleon would be able to take him to England.

Before he could tack up Jester, his groom came back accompanied by a German groom who wanted help with a sick horse. They left Jester and he followed the grooms to the sick horse's stable. A very dejected bay horse stood at the back of his stable with white sweat showing on his neck and shoulders. His eyes were rolling with pain and he was pawing at the bedding. Henri suspected colic immediately and asked the groom to summon a vet quickly, to administer a muscle relaxant. The horse was in desperate pain and could end up with a twisted gut if he started rolling around too much. Henri put a head collar on him and gave the rope to his groom, talking soothingly and calmly while he put his ear to the horse's stomach to check for sounds of movement. Thankfully, a young vet arrived and injected him straight away. Henri said he would check him when he got back from his ride.

He went back to a fractious Jester, who was desperate to go out for a ride and burn off some energy. Henri let him canter along the leafy pathways, deep into the wood. They disturbed a group of deer who set off out of the copse. He followed them and then headed up the hill, where he knew he could view the valley below. He observed the beauty of the land before him and compared it to the war-torn state of the streets of Paris and thought it impossible to believe that this was happening within ten miles of Versailles. He felt desolated that Charles may have died so close to the end of the war and with the possibility of Marie being alive. He was not generally a religious person, but he prayed with all his might that God would spare Charles.

oOo

That evening at dinner there were lots of extra guests, some of them from the French government, who were negotiating the peace treaty. He sat at Napoleon's table as both Anya and Le Comte were on Bismarck's table. It didn't look as if he would get chance to chat to either of them after dinner, so he retired early and for entertainment, started reading *The Three Musketeers* to find out what part D'Artagnan played. He had just settled down and turned off his light when he heard his door open. As Anya appeared in his bedroom, he switched the light back on.

'I didn't expect to see you tonight. I thought you would be busy entertaining. Are you staying with me and if so, can I undress you? You look beautiful in that blue silk dress.' He leapt out of bed naked and turned her round to face the mirror.

'I have some news for you D'Artagnan, but it will have to wait until we have both sated our desire. Certainly, one part of your body is pleased to see me. God, you do have an incredible body Henri and your long dark hair is touching your shoulders now. You are definitely my interpretation of how D'Artagnan looked.'

Henri had already removed her dress and was unpinning her luscious, long, blonde hair. He insisted on taking off her corset as she had already undone her chemise and removed her drawers. When she was naked, Henri held her in front of the mirror as he stood behind her.

'Manet would love to paint you, Anya. He loves curvaceous women and even Charles would have a hard time keeping his hands off you.'

'Don't be ridiculous, artists only paint nubile

girls. I am old enough to be their mother, never mind a muse.'

'Rubbish, Anya. Most men would rather tumble an experienced woman who knows how to pleasure them, than deal with an inexperienced virgin.'

'Steady on D'Artagnan, you are beginning to like your sex lessons a little too much. I might have to restrict you to a cell to rein you in a bit. You are starting to become an Italian stallion.'

Henri laughed, 'Rubbish, madame – as Charles says, Italian men are too busy charming women with their incessant flirting. Frenchmen would have a woman in and out of their bed long before the Italians.'

'I have to admit you Frenchmen are irresistible, especially with your "come to bed eyes" and a body like Adonis.'

Conversation ceased as Henri picked her up and took her to his bed. After they had both sated their appetite, Henri propped himself up on his elbow and ran his fingers through her hair.

'What's the good news?'

'I persuaded Bismarck to let you, me and Le Comte go to Lille to look for Charles and your sister. We had a letter from the French requesting the return of Gustave Courbet to face criminal damage charges, so if he is there we will bring him back as well.'

'God, Anya, how did you persuade Bismarck to do that when he was responsible for their plight in the first place?'

'Classified information, my little musketeer; you should know better than to ask.' She pushed him onto his back and straddled him. 'Stop becoming jealous of other men. I told you before, nobody owns me or my body. I take my pleasure with whomsoever I want. You would be surprised how much information men will give away when you bed them. Now much as I would like to remain with you tonight, I can't; Bismarck wants me back. However, tomorrow we are staying in Lille and I promise to sleep with you then, my little French puppy dog.'

As she got up from the bed, Henri threw a pillow after her and shouted, 'Don't think I am sharing you with Hans, either!'

She threw the pillow back at him and replied, 'Henri, you step out of line and I will horsewhip you. I am the master and you are my prisoner; forget that at your peril.'

oOo

They finally left Versailles by carriage at 3 p.m. after Anya had finished all her urgent paperwork and Le Comte had escorted Bismarck into Paris. Henri had teased him mercilessly about choosing Perseus as his mount to give him more credibility than Bismarck, who was not riding a stallion. They were dropped at the Gare du Nord, where they boarded the train for Lille. Anya was dressed in uniform as befit her military status as a sergeant and Senior Aide to Bismarck. They had a shared suitcase in case they stayed longer than the expected two nights. Henri opted for civilian clothes so as not to appear to be a prisoner of the Germans.

By 6 p.m. they were checking into the hotel at Lille and Henri was amused to find that Anya had booked a double room for them and a single room for Le Comte. He couldn't resist a dig at Henri.

'So how come D'Artagnan gets to sleep with you while I have to manage alone?'

Anya smiled at him, 'Because as I am the senior officer here, I am responsible for ensuring he remains in captivity and I thought you may like the freedom to find your own partner for the night.'

Le Comte replied, 'As if D'Artagnan would stray from your side; he's been acting like a dog chasing a bitch on heat since he got back. However, I will do my best to procure my own entertainment as seemingly, you two will be celebrating your reunion.'

They agreed to meet for dinner at 7:30 p.m. As soon as the porter had shown them to their room and left, Henri locked the door, threw off all his clothes and then started removing Anya's.

'Slow down, D'Artagnan, you'll give yourself a heart attack.'

'But we are alone with no interruption, especially from bloody Bismarck. So, if you think I am going to waste one moment of our time together you are very much mistaken.'

In the dining room, there were several Germans in various differing uniforms, eating at the hotel.

Anya prompted Le Comte to do some digging later, in the bar and see what information he could pick up on the prison camp. Henri raised the question of whether he would be allowed into the interview with Reissman. Anya told him he would not be able to be present. He ventured the question as to what Reissman would likely have done with Marie if she was within the camp.

Anya replied, 'I looked at his service record and he volunteered for the military from being a respected lawyer in his civilian career. He is married with two children, well-educated and lives in Dortmund and was chosen to run the Lille camp because he was a very fair-minded individual. He would respect the prisoners in his care and would be unlikely to inflict excessive punishment unless it was warranted.'

Henri replied, 'But what are the chances of him keeping his hands off my sister if she did attempt to steal a horse from the camp?'

Le Comte said, 'Well she is shown on the register as Michel, so he didn't execute her and he would have been within his rights to do so.'

Henri said, 'Hans, you have not seen my sister in real life. No man would be capable of shooting a woman as beautiful as her. Wanting her in his own bed possibly, but there is no way Marie would consent willingly to a sexual relationship with any man except Charles.'

Anya said, 'He's not a sadistic man so he would not rape or kill her, especially with 2000 Frenchmen in the camp. He would have a riot on his hands. He wouldn't dare leave her incarcerated with the French in case they lost control and raped her, so he would have had to keep her close to him.'

Henri replied, 'Charles told her when he left her in Lille to accept "life over death" because he knew how vulnerable she would be. If Marie-Ann was alive on capture, then she would have had to accept becoming Reissman's mistress.'

oOo

The next morning, they breakfasted at 7 a.m. so they would be at the prison camp early. Henri and Anya had spent the night celebrating their time alone together. Anya was becoming overly fond of her "D'Artagnan" but he was so special in many ways; she knew she could be forgiven for loving him even though she was twenty years older than him. Le Comte had arranged a coach to take them to the barracks. He reported over breakfast that he had done some digging amongst the locals and the army but had no confirmation of any sighting of Marie. Anya asked him if he had found suitable entertainment overnight but apart from a sly smile and shake of his head, he would not comment. However, Henri noticed the wife of one of the guests at a nearby table, who kept directing looks in Le Comte's direction. They teased him, but he refused to disclose her identity.

They arrived at the camp early, much to the

consternation of the guards. As the carriage passed the compound of French prisoners, they were all taken aback by the number of people in captivity. As the carriage pulled up at the main entrance, a rather harassed Reissman appeared at the door. As they walked up the stairs, he tried to assess who they were and what they were doing there. He spotted their uniform but was confused by Anya being in uniform, but not Henri.

'Gentlemen and madame, Major General Herman Reissman at your service.'

Le Comte responded, 'May I introduce Sergeant Anya Berinsky, senior aide to Otto von Bismarck, Lieutenant Henri Croizette of the French Hussars and I am Comte Hans von Brixenhof. We have been sent here from Versailles to locate Charles and Marie Carolus-Duran and Gustave Courbet.'

Reissman shook hands with them but was speechless when he realised they were looking for the Durans. Eventually, he said, 'I am pleased to confirm that all three of them are here and Madame Duran is working in our hospital.'

Henri shouted, 'Marie and Charles are here? Thank God. Please show me to them immediately.'

Reissman led them to the hospital wing and as they appeared in the main ward, Marie, who had been bandaging a wounded soldier's leg, leapt up and ran screaming to Henri and threw herself into his welcoming arms. The whole ward had gone completely silent, amazed by the spectacle before them.

Le Comte said, 'Major General Reissman, perhaps we could go to your office and leave Henri here to greet his sister.' He and Anya were fighting back emotion at the sight of Henri's unbridled joy, although both siblings were sobbing.

Henri hugged Marie so tightly that she was struggling to breathe. 'Oh God, Marie. I could feel you were alive, but what of Charles? Did he make it here from Paris?'

'Only just, Henri; he was more dead than alive when he arrived, but he has made a remarkable recovery over the last two weeks.'

'And what of Marie-Ann?'

'Oh, Henri, she is here alive and well and is one of the reasons Charles is recovering so fast. Come, I will take you to Charles now, but I must finish bandaging this man's leg.'

Dr Kohl and Dr Jager were approaching, and she introduced them to Henri as she finished bandaging. The whole room was buzzing with raised voices and delight for Marie, as all the men considered her their own special heroine.

Charles had been in his room with Marie-Ann when he heard the commotion of several people going down the corridor into Reissman's office. When he heard more people approaching and the door was flung open and he saw Henri in the doorway, he was speechless.

Henri ran over to him and hugged him. 'Charles,

how in God's name are you alive after that horrendous march? You don't know how I wished I had forced you out of Paris when we left for Le Havre. I came back for you, but it was too bloody late.'

He looked down at the beautiful little girl sitting across the table from Charles and instinctively recalled Marie as a baby.

Marie said in German, 'Marie-Ann, this is your Uncle Henri – your godfather and my beloved brother.'

Henri picked her up and cuddled her, planting kisses on her delicate pale cheeks and gazing into those deep blue eyes. He followed Marie's lead and murmured reassuringly to her in German, with tears flowing down his cheeks. He wept as he held Marie-Ann and looked at both Charles and Marie.

'What happened to you, Charles? How in God's name did you stay alive on the march to Lille?'

Marie raised her voice, 'Not only was he suffering from malnutrition and exhaustion but look at what one of those German bastards did to him.' She took Marie-Ann from his arms, went to Charles and turned him round and pulled up his nightshirt, exposing the vivid red whiplash scars from his shoulder to his feet.

Henri groaned in horror and tears ran down his cheeks. He finally controlled himself and said, 'When they interview you, tell them who did that to you and if they do nothing to punish him I promise you, I will. You are all safe now and we are taking you back to Versailles.'

35

Reissman was about to be interviewed by Le Comte and Anya.

'I don't see why I should be questioned by a junior officer, Le Comte. Any questions you have of me I will attempt to answer, but please dismiss Sergeant Berinsky.'

'But you misunderstand. She is the senior officer by virtue of being Bismarck's senior aide and my role is subordinate to her's on this mission.'

Reissman looked horrified and surveyed the anger on Anya's face. She placed an extra chair at her side for Le Comte and motioned to Reissman to sit at the front of his desk.

'Perhaps we can get started now?' She opened her black book and gave Reissman an equally black look. 'I wish to know the circumstances with infinite detail, of how Madame Carolus-Duran and her daughter came to be imprisoned here.'

Reissman realised he had been thwarted and had no option but to explain the capture of Marie and her four months as his prisoner. Anya let him tell his version of the story without interruption and made copious notes and asked only one question. 'Did you physically have sex with her, whether consensual or otherwise, at any time?'

'I would have liked nothing more than to have had a physical relationship with Marie, but as she repeatedly told me, she was a married woman and unavailable. I admit I fell head over heels in love with her, even to the point of thinking I would be able to take her home as my mistress after the end of this war. I also admit that I broke the rules by allowing her to keep her daughter by her side, but I did not sign up to kill women and children. I was mindful of their safety and kept her away from too much exposure to the prisoners. She proved to be an excellent nurse and conducted her duties with great empathy and courage. She refused to become my mistress but agreed to make it appear that she had, in front of the staff and prisoners. I have great respect too for her husband and have confessed to him of my love for his wife and apologised to him for my behaviour. Marie is an excellent strategist; she exploited my weakness and won. She threatened to kill herself if I took her and as she was emotionally in a very fragile state, she may just have carried out her threat. I was prepared to settle for having her as a friend rather than losing her. I have great respect and affection for her and do believe that the bond she has with her husband has been protected by some higher authority. Individually, they have both stared death in the face and survived. When I fired my gun at what I believed was a man, there was no way I should have missed, yet my horse stumbled. I examined that ground after I captured her and there was no slippery surface or hole that could have caused my horse to trip.'

This concluded his interview and he was dismissed from the room.

Anya looked at Le Comte. 'Do you believe him?'

'Yes, actually, I do.'

'We had better interview Dr Kohl next and see whether he verifies Reissman's story and then we will interview Marie on her own. Neither Henri nor her husband should be there.'

oOo

Henri brought Marie into Reissman's office and assured her that she could speak in complete confidence to Le Comte and Anya, then left.

Le Comte spoke first and asked her to confirm Reissman's story, which she did. She admitted that she had played mind games and flirted with him to get him to fall in love with her, so that she could control him. She had tried to keep him at bay with threats of suicide, which she assured them she would never have carried out as Marie-Ann was her priority. She confirmed that he had made a drunken attempt to force her into submission but that she had persuaded him not to do it. She admitted that she had welcomed him as a friend and he had been instrumental in helping her recover from the isolation she had felt before she had been captured. She had found working as a nurse a difficult task, but she admitted that she had needed something to focus on to stop her falling into depression. They all laughed when she told them she had asked if she could work in the stables but after her horse stealing success, she knew she would not be allowed that privilege. She had always felt that both Charles and Henri were alive. She told them of the appalling condition Charles had been in when Reissman's troop had found him and said she had never expected him to recover so quickly. Anya told her that Dr Kohl had also confirmed that Charles had been extremely lucky to survive and believed it was the special bond the pair of them had, which had accelerated his recovery.

They then prepared to interview Gustave Courbet and asked a guard to fetch him. As he was ushered into the room by the guard, Anya was shaken by his appearance. He was now fifty-one and suffering from the effects of the war, but he had a mane of thick, brown hair streaked with grey, and the most startling brown eyes. He looked at her as if he was a wolf deciding whether to eat her or mate with her.

Thankfully, Le Comte made the introductions as she had been thoroughly disconcerted by the look he had given her. She felt as though she was stripped naked in front of him. The sexual magnetism in his eyes completely threw her off guard. However, Le Comte was looking at her to take the lead.

'Monsieur Courbet, I understand you have been serving in the National Guard along with Charles

Duran.'

'Yes, that is correct. I rode back with the troop sent by Reissman as Charles was too weak to stay upright on horseback, he was in such an appalling condition. We had the pleasure of being Colonel Dittmar's prisoners on our journey and he is responsible for whipping Duran within an inch of his life.'

'What did Duran do to deserve such punishment?'

'He objected when I was knocked senseless by a blow to my head from a rifle butt, courtesy of Dittmar. Dr Kohl says I will have repercussions from this blow for the rest of my life. However, there was no excuse for Dittmar's treatment of Duran – that was downright cruel.'

'The French Government wishes to interview you about criminal damage to a fountain in the Place Vendôme. They consider you responsible for blowing it up. Did Duran accompany you on this exploit?'

'Certainly not, he would never destroy another artist's work.'

'But you did?'

'Madame, I am saying nothing because I don't know what you are talking about. I am an artist first and foremost and have been a soldier during the war.'

Le Comte added, 'The French say you are a revolutionary, intent on destroying the empire.'

Courbet grunted, 'I think Napoleon III did more than enough to destroy his own empire. He hardly needed my help; the writing was on the wall before the war started. As an artist I am renowned as the father of realism, not a revolutionary.'

Anya said, 'We are returning you to Versailles for questioning by the French, along with the Durans. I think you will find Versailles a more beautiful and peaceful place to be in captivity and it will give you time to reflect on the advantages of a monarchy over a republic.'

'Very well, madame. I accept your kind invitation to Versailles, but I warn you to keep Napoleon out of my reach, for his own safety.'

oOo

Marie, Charles and Henri had gone into the compound to speak privately outdoors, away from any German ears.

Charles said, 'What will happen to us when we go to Versailles? Will we be imprisoned there, and for how long?'

Henri replied, 'I don't know myself as yet. You will not be thrown in a prison cell and hopefully, you will be afforded the same privileges as I have been, your own room, meals in the main dining room with Wilhelm I, Bismarck and Napoleon in attendance and the freedom to go out into the grounds and stables of Versailles and ride within the perimeter. I don't know for how long; it all depends on the negotiations with the new French government. The Germans won't release the prisoners until the money is received and the peace treaty signed.'

Marie said, 'But Henri, we have no clothes to wear at Versailles. I have two borrowed dresses, that's all and Marie-Ann has been provided with clothing via Sylvie. Charles isn't even wearing National Guard uniform – what the prisoners had on them when they arrived was only fit for burning. He has been supplied with a cavalry uniform by Marshal.'

'Oh, don't worry about that. Anya will see you are all clothed suitably for Versailles. I will try and persuade them to release you back to your home, which is still standing although empty with no livestock. You hardly pose a threat to them and they can keep checking up on you if they want.'

Marie replied, 'Why are the Germans being so good to you Henri, when you are French?'

Charles interrupted, 'Marie, it is none of our business what Henri is doing so please do not ask or risk compromising his safety. Just be thankful he is alive and well and we are going to be freed from captivity. I will certainly relish the chance to recuperate in such beautiful surroundings and it will do Marie-Ann a power of good to be able to play outside, even if there are no other children there.'

Henri said, 'Courbet is being taken as well.'

Charles exclaimed, 'Why?'

'The French have asked the Germans to return him to Paris for questioning about the destruction of a fountain at the Place Vendôme. Please assure me you had no part in this, Charles?'

'Of that you can be absolutely sure, Henri. There

is no way I would ever destroy a work of art in whatever form. I have spent the war protecting art of whatever nationality, to preserve it for the benefit of future generations. Courbet and I spent many hours on the barricades debating his republican beliefs and we did have some common ground, but that is something I would never have done. However, Courbet and I will enjoy examining the art treasures of Versailles and will try to ensure the Germans leave it where they found it.'

That evening, Le Comte, Anya and Henri dined together back at the hotel. They had a table in the window with no other people around them, so they were able to talk freely.

Anya asked, 'What do you know about Courbet, Henri?'

'Very little really; he has a reputation for opposing the government, but he is a respected artist with a taste for the macabre and dark subjects. He is a renowned womaniser and adores female sexuality but does not treat his women with respect. Marie has never mentioned him directly to me, but she can sense danger a mile away and she would not welcome his attention. Charles would not leave Marie alone in his company. Let's say he is a predator as far as women are concerned but I don't think he is as revolutionary as everybody makes out. Like all artists, his work is his life.'

Anya said, 'Well he certainly made an impression on me. The way he surveyed me with those startling brown eyes, I felt as if I had no clothes on.'

'Believe me, you wouldn't if Courbet got you alone. Keep well away from him Anya; he is a sexual predator.'

'But I love a challenge, even if it is from a rogue Frenchman.'

Henri was concerned and replied, 'He will not treat you with respect, Anya.'

She flashed him a smile. 'He certainly won't have your superb, lean body Henri, but he will have fifty years of raw sexual experience.'

Le Comte roared with laughter at the look on Henri's face. 'Don't be so cruel with D'Artagnan; he can't cope with the rejection.'

When they retired to their room, Henri had drunk a little too much wine to compensate for Anya's sudden interest in Courbet. He was horrified that she should want Courbet as a lover instead of him. Determined to stamp his authority on her body, he initiated a fierce and passionate lovemaking session that left them both breathless and sweating.

As they lay together afterwards, Anya ran her fingers through his hair and said, 'Remember what I said, Henri. We are not in a relationship and you have no rights over my body.'

'I am just concerned for your safety; he will certainly want to dominate you and if you object, you could be in danger.'

'Don't you think I am capable of looking after myself, D'Artagnan? Or would you prefer to be in the room, so you can protect me if necessary?'

'That was totally uncalled for Anya, and not the behaviour of an honourable woman. Take Courbet if you are so desperate but don't expect the same treatment from him as you get from me!' He turned his back and threw the covers over himself.

oOo

Charles was awake early and was contemplating their move to Paris. He intended to allow Marie to say goodbye to Reissman on her own. He had done two pencil sketches of Reissman and Marie, which he would give him as a thank you for sparing his wife and daughter. He knew the outcome could have been a lot worse. He could be going back to Paris with Marie-Ann's life lost and Marie carrying Reissman's child, which would have been a far greater loss than he was now facing. Marie stirred next to him and he gathered her in his arms and hugged her.

'We are going home my darling, but to a very different Paris from the one you left. It will do you good to get away from the constant tension you have felt here. You must thank Reissman, Dr Kohl and Dr Jaeger as well as Marshal and the priest. I will not be present, so you can speak freely to Reissman. Much as I deplore what he did to you, he did not force you, for which I am eternally grateful. He treated Marie-Ann with the utmost care and attention and she is alive and well because of it. Perhaps his background as a lawyer and his moral code was strong enough to negate his sexual desire for you but you must thank him for that.'

As they finished dressing, Sylvie arrived, carrying a bundle of clothes.

'Madame, I understand you are moving to Versailles and as Marie-Ann has hardly any clothes, my sister has sent you some dresses and breeches that her daughter has outgrown. We cannot have her arriving at court in torn clothes.'

'Thank you so much, Sylvie and thank your sister for these clothes. You have looked after Marie-Ann so well.'

Charles came over and kissed her on both cheeks and thanked her for looking after Marie-Ann whilst she had been in captivity.

Marie left to see if she could locate Reissman to say her goodbyes; she took the rolled-up sketches Charles gave her. He was in his office taking his breakfast at his desk. He was delighted when Marie came in alone.

'Madame, you must be elated that you are being released from your prison. I imagine you will have far better facilities at Versailles to aid your recovery.'

'I just wanted to say goodbye to you alone as I have a lot to thank you for. I appreciate that you did not force me to become your mistress and it wasn't that I hated you, I just wanted to remain faithful to my husband.'

'Marie, I know that and much as I would have liked to, I am glad I did not pursue my feelings. You are an exceptional woman and the love you two have for each other as a couple should never be broken. I do think God is watching over you and I wish you both a happy future together. I admit to being in love with you and I know it was wrong, but you used it to your advantage and you kept me at bay.'

He came around from his desk and hugged her and she kissed his cheek, with tears pouring down her face. As he released her, she gave him the two sketches and he was overwhelmed.

'Your husband is a very forgiving man, Marie. I shall cherish this gift.'

Too overcome to speak, she turned quickly and left his office and ran back to Charles. She threw herself on the bed and sobbed while Charles held her hand until the sobs subsided. He said nothing to her as he knew that she had not harboured any desire for Reissman, but they had been good friends and had supported each other in many ways.

When she had composed herself she said, 'I didn't love him Charles, but I respected him and enjoyed his company.'

'Of course, you did, sweetheart. I don't blame you for that. I am just so thankful that he did the honourable thing. Not many men in his position would have done so and for that, I am forever grateful to him.'

They went together into the hospital wing as Dr Kohl had asked Charles to come for a final check-up on his back before he left. He examined his wounds, which were in various stages of recovery.

'I really don't understand how you did not pick up any infection. You were covered in open wounds that had been exposed to the elements and worse, and yet none of them succumbed. Do they still give you pain on movement?'

'Yes, sometimes but it is nothing compared to when I arrived. I will use my time wisely at Versailles and start fencing and boxing again to stretch the skin, but I am just so grateful to survive with my hands intact. At least I will be able to paint again.'

'Charles, you will be careful with Marie? When the pressure of living on the edge, as she has been here, starts to fade, she will need careful handling – both mentally and physically. She has been living on adrenalin for far too long and she could slip into depression if she has nothing to occupy her time. Try not to rush her into a second pregnancy too soon. Her mind and body need to recover.

'Dr Kohl, I am well aware of the knife edge that Marie's mental health is balanced on. She has lost a whole side to her character due to the trauma she has been through. I know how easy it is to fall into depression because I have been there myself. I am determined to try to get back the bright, cheerful, confident Marie that I married, and I will never leave her side again. If this damned war has taught me anything, it is that family is so precious and it's not until you have nearly had it snatched away that you realise how much you value it. I am mortified at the trauma that they have both faced and I will endeavour to make it up to them without stifling their independence.'

'You are a remarkable man, Charles. You have coped with horrific pain and suffering yet never once complained. All your attention has been centred on Marie and Marie-Ann. Your love for them has pulled you back from the brink of death. I think you have had some divine intervention too as when you arrived here I only gave you a twenty percent chance of survival. Take heart from that because if anyone deserves to survive this war, it is you. Go home and be the gifted artist you are and show the world that true love can conquer everything.'

Marie returned from saying goodbye to the patients, so he left her alone with Dr Kohl as he went to say his farewell to Marshal and the other prisoners. He met up with Courbet on the same mission and they embraced each other.

Courbet said, 'Well at least I might get to enjoy the hospitality at Versailles before I face the firing squad.'

Charles laughed, 'I am sure you can make a convincing case to the Germans that you are innocent; then perhaps they won't hand you over.'

'Well I will have to cultivate the affections of Anya as she has Bismarck's ear; perhaps then I can keep my freedom. She is one very highly sexed woman who will be well worth pursuing – both in bed and on canvas!'

36

As the carriage pulled away from the prison camp, Marie dissolved into floods of tears. Henri took Marie-Ann off Charles's knee while he gathered Marie in his arms and let her cry on his shoulder. Nobody spoke; they just left her to get it out of her system. Henri realised then just how close to breaking point Marie was and he leant across and held her hand.'

'Marie, you need have no fear now. Everything is going to be all right; I promise you that.'

On the train journey to Lille, both Marie and Marie-Ann slept. Charles held his daughter tightly, cradling her head on his shoulder.

Anya was astounded by the depth of Charles's love and protection for Marie and his daughter. He was no arrogant Frenchman full of his own importance; he wore his heart on his sleeve and was not afraid to show it. Sitting opposite Marie, she examined her features in detail. She could see why men found her so attractive. However, as Henri had pointed out last night, there was a desperate vulnerability emanating from her, which must have been due to her parting from her husband and the sheer responsibility of keeping her daughter alive. Her spirit had been diminished. Perhaps she would recover it when she was out of danger and her body relaxed.

As they pulled into the station, she designated Le Comte to find a carriage to Versailles and Henri and Courbet saw to the luggage as Charles carried his daughter through the smoke and noise of the station, whispering quietly to calm her through her broken sleep.

oOo

They arrived at Versailles and were ushered into a salon while Anya went to speak to Wilhelm and Le Comte collected the keys for their rooms from the housekeeper. Anya came back and said formal introductions would be made at dinner. Henri showed the Durans to their suite on the first floor and she took Courbet up to the second floor, to his room. On walking in and surveying the room, Courbet was pleased to see he had a double bed at his disposal.

'Well madame, this is hardly a prison, but I think I need some company in that big bed; so what have you planned for my entertainment?'

'You, Monsieur Courbet will do well to remember your manners whilst you are in the company of two kings and several generals. One foot out of line and I will have great pleasure in confining you to a stable in chains. You will find Versailles has few women in residence, so I would appreciate you not offending any of them.'

'Oh, don't worry about that madame; there is only one woman I want in this bed and you are more than aware it is you. We have a lot in common and it would be shameful to waste time. Why don't you just strip off and let me show you what you would be missing?'

Quick as a flash, she leapt forward and issued a resounding slap across his face, to which he neither flinched nor turned away.

He laughed at her and said, 'Never mind, madame. I can wait; your curiosity will have you in my bed sooner than you think.'

Blushing bright red, she turned on her heel and fled the room. That insufferable arrogant bastard had just insulted her but the sexual attraction she felt for him was overwhelming.

oOo

Marie had brought the two dresses Reissman had given her and she wore the blue silk shift dress. Marie-Ann had been given a pretty, pink silk tulle dress with a hooped skirt and some soft pink ballet shoes. Charles insisted on combing her hair through and pinning the top and sides into a band, leaving her long, dark curls to cascade to her shoulder. To their great amusement, Sylvie had taught Marie-Ann to curtsey on their last day together and she twirled round the room, dropping a curtsey at every corner. Marie laughed, and he was so glad to hear it that tears welled up in his eyes. It gave him some hope that buried deep inside her was the old Marie, not the tortured Marie he had found.

They made their way downstairs, where Henri and Le Comte were waiting for them. The introductions were going to be made in a small salon off the dining room. Le Comte told them that they would be introduced to Napoleon, King Wilhelm, Bismarck and some of the French and German generals. Courbet had arrived and so Le Comte opened the salon door. Marie grasped Charles's hand for support and he picked Marie-Ann up and carried her into the room. Le Comte led them over to the distinguished line of dignitaries, headed by Wilhelm as the highest ranking. Charles put Marie-Ann down and held her hand.

Le Comte said, 'Your Majesty, may I present Monsieur and Madame Carolus-Duran and their daughter, Marie-Ann.'

Turning to them he said, 'May I introduce you to King Wilhelm I of Prussia.'

The King shook Charles's hand as he bowed and then leant forward to take Marie's hand as she dropped into a low curtsey. 'Madame Duran, may I welcome you to Versailles – and your charming daughter too.'

At this point, totally unasked, Marie-Ann curtseyed and put out her hand to Wilhelm. He was astonished but took her hand and bent right down to help her up. At this moment, Marie-Ann spotted Wilhelm's old German Shepherd dog sitting watching the scene and mistook him for Reissman's dog.

She shouted, 'Papa, Deutscher Schäferhund is est Marte?'

The King called Fritz over and commanded him to sit in front of Marie-Ann. He gave her a paw in greeting and she giggled and grabbed his big paw in both hands. The effect on everyone witnessing this scene was evident. Charles was delighted at her love of dogs but mortified that she had spoken in German rather than French. Henri was in tears because his niece and goddaughter who had spent four months of her short life in captivity was now speaking in the language of her captors.

Napoleon was next in line and tears were running down his face as he shook Charles's hand and Marie swept into a curtsey before him. He offered her his hand.

'Marie Duran, my songbird and "l'étoile de Paris," thank heaven you have returned to us safely.'

Charles had to persuade Marie-Ann to leave Fritz and curtsey to Napoleon. All of them were affected by this beautiful child as they had all left children or grandchildren behind to fight this war. The fact that Marie-Ann was even alive was a miracle.

Marie kept her composure during the long line of introductions, but Marie-Ann pulled away from her father's guiding hand and went back to the King and his dog. He waved at Charles to leave her and sat her down on a sofa with him and let her stroke Fritz. After they had finished they returned to Wilhelm, who was telling Marie-Ann all about Fritz. Aware that they were back, she proceeded to tell them in German what the King had told her. Marie was amazed as she realised their daughter must have understood far more German than they had thought.

Le Comte went over to Anya; she too was silently crying. 'Whatever is the matter?'

'I left two children to be reared by their father and his family and watching Marie-Ann with the King highlighted the sacrifice I have made for this bloody war.'

Le Comte pulled her behind a pillar and mopped her tears with his silk handkerchief and gave her a brief kiss on the cheek. 'Now back to work, Anya. You will be required to escort Bismarck into dinner.'

As the salon door was opened and dinner was announced, Napoleon approached Wilhelm and the Durans. Just as Wilhelm was about to ask for Marie's hand, he intervened. 'Surely you wouldn't deny my right to escort l'étoile de Paris into dinner?'

Wilhelm hesitated but said, 'No, of course not Napoleon; but I claim the hand of her daughter if she will permit me.'

Charles leant over to Marie-Ann and asked her if she would walk into dinner holding the King's hand. She readily jumped up, took his hand and pulled him up off the sofa and said, 'Yes, but can Fritz come too?'

403

He laughed and said, 'Yes of course, my dear but we must hide him under the table, so nobody can see him as he is usually banned from the dining room.'

So, the procession to dinner led by a Prussian king, a French child and a dog, set off to the dining room in the Palace of Versailles, followed by Napoleon and Marie and then Bismarck and Anya. The remaining men followed in single file. Charles smiled as he thought, *Louis XIV would probably be turning in his grave in disgust.*

A chair had been boosted with cushions for Marie-Ann and she had her own waitress to cater for her every need. She was placed between her father and Uncle Henri. Marie was seated between both kings and was forced to make polite conversation even though she was extremely tired. However, by the end of the meal she was beginning to enjoy the novelty and welcomed the high-quality wine. Poor Charles oversaw Marie-Ann, but he smiled at Marie encouragingly, realising the effort she had to make after spending so much time alone. By the sweet course, Marie-Ann was rubbing her eyes, so Charles brought her to Marie and said he would settle her in bed and when she had dropped off to sleep, the waitress would remain with her and he would return if he could. Charles bade her kiss her mother goodnight and Wilhelm patted her shoulder as she set off.

Wilhelm said, 'Your daughter is divine, Madame Duran. I can understand why Henri was so concerned for your safety. You do have a definite look of your brother. I have a granddaughter a fraction older than her and it makes me realise how much I am missing my family too.'

Charles returned to the dining room after half an hour and the men had their port. Marie decided she would go up to bed as she felt exhausted, but she was happy for Charles to stay. Both Wilhelm and Napoleon chatted to him about his time on the barricades. Napoleon asked him about the siege and was genuinely horrified at how little food there was to eat. All the animals in the zoo had been killed as there was no food for them so they became edible targets. Many horses were stolen and slaughtered for food and dogs and cats became another easy target. Napoleon was horrified when Charles confirmed that rats had been openly sold in the shops.

oOo

The next morning, Charles woke to find Marie fast asleep next to him and it was Marie-Ann who woke first in her little bedroom next to theirs. She got out of bed and set off, investigating her surroundings. She was soon climbing into his side of the bed. He chatted to her in French about leaving Lille and coming to Versailles on the train. The first thing she remembered was Wilhelm's dog, Fritz. Marie-Ann could not resist poking Marie and she eventually came around.

Charles was concerned about her fragile state but

when she exited the bed and ran to the bathroom and was violently sick, his heart missed a beat. The only time Marie was ever sick was when she had been in the early stages of pregnancy. *Had he gone and done precisely what Dr Kohl had warned him not to do?* He hardly dared look her in the face, but she seemed convinced that it was due to over-indulging on the wine, so there was no point in frightening her at this point. He suggested he dress and take Marie-Ann for breakfast and she could either go back to sleep or have a leisurely bath and he would bring her coffee and croissants back to the room.

Never having dressed his daughter alone before, he was astonished by how much underwear a child wore. She had a simple chemise and drawers but then had a second starched chemise with layers of tulle to puff out her dress. She knew how to wash her hands and face and go to the toilet and she was still only sixteen months old. He found some clean, white long socks and drawers for her and put her leather shoes on in case they went outside. The hair he knew he could manage even though it was now below her shoulders. He had been taught to plait by his father, who plaited the farm horses. He combed her hair through and thankfully, she didn't object too much. He then divided her ringlets of auburn hair into three strands and made two plaits and secured them with blue ribbon to match the trimmings on her white dress. He found some tiny breeches and white shirts in her suitcase, which she would need to play outside in and visit the stables. He left her playing with some animal soft toys, which had been left in her bedroom while he washed and dressed.

To his astonishment, when he came back she was chattering away to herself and the animals in half French and half German. He knew he must spend more time on her French as she would cause huge consternation back in Paris if she was overheard speaking German. At least she would hear more French spoken here than back at the camp, as all the Germans spoke fluent French.

Marie had gone back to sleep and she looked very pale. He bent down and kissed her cheek and tried to forget the possibility of another baby being on the way. When they reached the beautiful main staircase, Marie-Ann insisted on walking on her own, holding the rail as she was fascinated by the gold leaf scrolls between each bannister. He accepted the slower pace as his daughter was showing such good taste. Halfway down, Henri caught up with them and they both roared with laughter when Marie-Ann curtsied to him.

Charles intervened, 'No, Marie-Ann, this is Uncle Henri, but he is not a king and you don't need to curtsey to him; only the man with Fritz the dog and the little man in blue uniform.'

Henri, by this time, was in hysterics and he said, 'God, Charles, she looks exactly like Marie did at that age. Where is her mother?'

'Sleeping off an over-indulgence of wine, so I am

nursemaid for the time being.'

'I'm sure Anya will let you have the nursemaid that looked after her last night. She will converse as much as possible in French with her but is also fluent in German.'

'Well, we will look into that after breakfast.'

As they approached the dining room, Fritz lay by the door, obviously banished from entering for breakfast. Marie-Ann ran towards him and Henri quickly ran forward and picked her up in case the dog attacked her.

'Whoa, my little niece, you have to learn that you cannot run up to dogs like that – they could bite you.' However, Fritz was busy holding a paw up to Marie-Ann, repeating last night's lesson. He allowed her to stroke him and shake his paw and then Henri carried her in to breakfast.

They joined Le Comte at a table set for eight. Wilhelm was dining with Bismarck, further down the room. The young waitress who had looked after Marie-Ann last night came over to serve at their table. Le Comte asked after Marie and reminded Henri that this was exactly what he did when he first arrived at Versailles and over-indulged at his first dinner.

He warned Charles about the fountains outside that were very deep as they supplied the water for Versailles; he was sure they would be an instant attraction to Marie-Ann. Unfortunately, Versailles was never intended to be the home of royal children;

they were not allowed there until they were fourteen or fifteen. Louis XIV's children were reared at the Tuileries Palace and his brother Philippe's children at Chateau de St-Germain.

Charles laughed and said, 'I was hoping to do some painting whilst I was here, but I am not going to be able to fit it in around teaching my daughter to ride, behave around dogs, swim and speak French! What other facilities does Versailles have to offer?'

'We have an indoor boxing and fencing gym, horse schooling paddocks and a shooting range. There is a beautiful chapel with Italian marble pillars, an organ and frescos to die for, several ballrooms, a huge library, heated Roman baths and a fully equipped music room with every instrument imaginable.'

'Well don't be in any rush to send us home; a few weeks here should soon restore our health and sanity.'

'I think after what you and your wife suffered in the war, you deserve as long a break as you need.'

Le Comte turned to Henri, 'Marshal MacMahon has been asking after you. I think he wants to ask you if you are interested in becoming a politician and standing in the elections.'

Henri burst into laughter. 'Can you really see me behind a desk permanently and becoming a republican politician? God forbid, I would die of boredom. Perhaps when and if, I reach the age of sixty, I might be ready for a desk job.'

Charles decided to return to check on Marie but

as they were on the ground floor, Le Comte showed them into the chapel, first. The opulence of the gold altar and the Gothic pillars reminded him of Italy. He held Marie-Ann's hand and walked slowly up the aisle to the top pew, drinking in the scene.

He sat her down and quietly explained where they were and that she had to kneel and say her prayers to God and be very quiet. She watched him kneel and then solemnly copied him and put her hands together and tucked them under her chin. At that precise moment a shaft of sunlight came through the stained-glass window above the altar and enveloped them both in a single ray of light. This shook Charles's composure as he realised that this may be a sign that God had granted him all his wishes when he had prayed for them to all be safely reunited. He gave his thanks in silent prayer and then picked Marie-Ann up and when he moved out into the nave he bowed and crossed both himself and her. He would come back alone to formally thank God.

When they arrived back at their room, Marie was sitting up in bed with a tray of food. She had managed a croissant and a slice of ham and cheese and drunk the coffee. Marie-Ann kissed her mother and asked for a piece of cheese and then ran into her room to play with her toys.

Charles tentatively asked, 'Are you feeling better now, my dear?'

'I feel fine. I told you it was just over-indulgence

last night.'

He breathed a sigh of relief and hoped she was right.

37

L e Comte asked Henri if he could offer a solution to sort out the recent bad behaviour of one of the stallions that was ridden by a German officer. Le Comte sent a groom to bring the horse out to a training paddock and they all walked round. He explained that this horse had got into the habit of rearing and had deposited two troopers and injured them and had come over backwards with a third one. He now repeated the habit as he knew he could easily remove his rider and head for freedom. He was an impressive chestnut stallion with plenty of height and bone.

Le Comte got on him in the paddock and rode him quietly around at walk and trot and he was biddable and willing. However, when Le Comte asked him to canter, he stopped dead and reared up. Immediately, Le Comte dug his heels into his sides and with a sharp crack of his whip behind the saddle, propelled him forward. The horse leapt forward into canter in shock and then, realising that Le Comte meant business, attempted to stop and rear again. This time he went higher in the air, but Le Comte gave him his head and stayed still in the saddle. As he came back down on all fours, he smacked him again and forced him back into canter. He did two more laps of the paddock and the horse was sweating as he was forced to accept his rider was not going to come off anytime soon.

Henri said, 'Well, that's all very well Le Comte, as he now knows he can't get away with being naughty whilst you are on his back, but it won't stop him trying it out with every other rider who gets on him. He needs to learn to go forwards not upwards and he needs endless schooling sessions to keep his brain occupied so he has no time to think of ways of ejecting his rider. The more you enforce him with the whip, the more resentful he could get. If he was mine I would ignore his rearing sessions to a point but insist he goes forward. I will hunt him on Saturday if you like; that should give him plenty to think about.'

Charles, Marie and Marie-Ann returned to the chateau as Henri and Le Comte had more work to do. As they walked back, Charles commented on both having rosy cheeks and remarked that they had clearly enjoyed their riding experience. Marie-Ann's new nursemaid appeared and offered to take her up to bed for a nap and look after her until bedtime. Charles took the opportunity to suggest they found a small salon to sit in and have a private chat, away from prying ears. Marie seemed concerned, but they found a suitable room and he led her to the opulent Louis XIV chaise longue.

'I wanted to explain to you what my role was in the war as I do not want any secrets between us, but

I will understand if you are not ready to hear it.'

'Will you tell me the truth? I will know if you are lying.'

'Oh sweetheart, of course I will and before I go any further, I want you to know that I remained totally faithful to you, as I vowed before God on our wedding day.'

Marie leant across and kissed him on his cheek. 'Oh Charles, I do appreciate that, as not many men would have been able to do that.'

'Marie, why do you consider it acceptable for me to have broken my marriage vows? Is it because I am a man and considered incapable of faithfulness, but a woman is expected to remain faithful? We jointly entered a marriage contract that should bind us both equally. I was in a war zone and just staying alive from one day to the next was my priority; I had no time for socialising and frivolity.'

He then explained to her about his role as custodian of the Louvre art collection, commissioning artists to copy the masters' works and arranging the exhibition of some of the original masterpieces with the Tate Gallery in London. The object was to remove them from Paris for fear of damage or them falling into the hands of the Germans and being forcibly removed from Paris.

Marie listened carefully with tears in her eyes as she would have loved to have been by his side to help him and would have been a huge asset. She was slightly concerned that most of the copyists he had used were women as most male artists had either fled Paris or joined the military. Mary Cassatt had rallied the remaining American female artists still in Paris, until she finally left for home. Rosa Bonheur had helped out on several copies where animals were depicted, from lions to birds, as her animal portraits were outstanding, and she was also a sculptor.

She only cheered up when Charles described how he and Manet had copied the two Velázquez paintings, working side-by-side for two days to complete their task, mainly in total silence and avid concentration. She sighed as it would have been a spectacular scene to have watched.

When she expressed her sadness about not being there to help him as she had been in Lille he replied, 'Sweetheart, I longed for you to be my side, but it was not easy. We were under fire from the German cannons across the Seine and during the siege, food was a real problem. I don't think Marie-Ann would have survived the starvation and sickness that struck the city; I saw so many children die. Believe me, you were both safer away from Paris and going back, you will find a very different city. It will take years to repair the damage caused by the war in the city centre alone. We can't even blame the Germans for all the devastation as the Communards were responsible too.'

Marie said, 'Now I have a confession to make to you, my love.' Charles's heart missed a beat and he froze in fear of what was to come. 'You know you said, "choose life before death" – did you mean that if my life was threatened I should succumb to another man's desire rather than die defending myself?'

Charles sighed and spoke slowly and carefully, 'I knew no man would find it easy to kill you Marie but knew many would want you. Yes, if it kept you alive I would have accepted it.'

'But that was the problem, Charles. Because you are such a kind, forgiving person you would have tolerated unfaithfulness and even taken a cuckoo into our family nest. If Reissman had succeeded in his rape attempt I just know I would have fallen pregnant with a boy and I could not have lived with the shame – even though you could. Every time I looked at the child I would be reminded of my betrayal and eventually I would have let it destroy our relationship. I am not the tolerant, kind person that you are. I know I can be an absolute bitch at times and I would have taken out my anger and frustration on an innocent child. You know I never loved Reissman, but I did miss our close intimate relationship and the security I feel with you and I admit I craved for someone else to take on the huge responsibility of keeping Marie-Ann alive.'

Charles pulled her into his arms and stroked her hair. 'Sweetheart, I can understand that totally. I can hardly forgive myself for leaving you in that situation. But we must live and learn from our experiences and put them behind us or they will dominate our lives forever. We have been given a chance to survive and we must move forward with no regrets, especially when so many others lost their lives.

oOo

The day of the hunt dawned, and Marie was up early, getting dressed for the day. Le Comte had asked King Wilhelm if she might ride astride and he had readily agreed. This would give her much more freedom to enjoy the chase and Henri had loaned her Jester and he would be a perfect mount. Had she ridden a young horse or a stallion she would have had to curb her enthusiasm for the chase. She was not exhibiting any signs of morning sickness, for which Charles was relieved. She was beginning to come out of the depression she had been in and was becoming the lively girl he had first fallen in love with.

The hunting party included King Wilhelm, Le Comte, Bismarck, Henri, Courbet, Anya, Charles and Marie, along with several German officers and hunt staff. Henri was having a difficult time with the unruly stallion; it frequented between galloping flat out and stopping and rearing. Its jumping ability was unproved and only Henri could have stayed in the saddle as it misjudged the fences. Standing still quietly outside the covert, waiting for hounds to draw was not on the stallion's agenda. The inactivity prompted him into threatening the other horses that were in close proximity.

Le Comte said, 'Come on now, Henri. Surely even your patience has run out? You are going to have to resort to a giving him a damn good hiding.'

'No, Le Comte, I just need to channel his enthusiasm in the right direction. Believe me, he will be as quiet as a lamb before the day is out, without my resorting to a whip.'

Marie suggested, 'Move him away from the group when we are standing still. He won't appreciate the isolation. Only let him come back to the group when he behaves and remains standing quietly.'

Hounds were now flushing deer out of the woods and they took off in pursuit. Jester needed no encouragement as with lightweight Marie in the saddle he had a speed advantage, plus she was intent on being up front. After a three-mile point in open country, jumping wire, wall and hedges, hounds held their quarry at bay and a huntsman despatched it by shotgun.

During the break while they regrouped, Marie noticed Anya joining Henri, who was standing away from the group, tussling with his horse. They walked into the cover of trees and Marie pulled Jester away into the woods and followed them. She made up the distance and was horrified to see Henri leaning over his horse and kissing Anya. This was no flirtatious kiss as the response between their bodies was mirrored. Only intimate lovers could respond as they had. Her attention had been so centred on them that she had failed to hear another horse approaching from behind until a twig snapped. She spun around, expecting it to be Charles but was amazed to see Courbet.

'Looks like your brother is fraternising with the enemy, Marie. Not that I wouldn't like to be in his place, enemy or not!'

Furious and unable to offer any defence for Henri, she spun a startled Jester round and cantered him out of the woods. The rest of the hunting party was about to set off again as hounds had picked up a new scent. Charles noticed Marie coming back out of the woods, flushed and angry, but had not seen Courbet. He came towards her but said nothing and urged his horse into a faster canter to catch up with the huntsmen.

When they returned to the stables, Charles noticed that Marie was distinctly cool with Henri and he had noticed her giving him some angry looks when they were riding back from the hunt. Charles decided to wait and see whether Marie mentioned what was bothering her, rather than saying anything himself.

When they got back to their room and she had stripped off her hunting breeches ready for her bath, he could see in the mirror that her temper was rising. She turned to him and angrily said, 'Did you know that Henri is conducting an affair with Anya?'

Charles sighed; so this was what she had witnessed in the woods. 'Marie, your brother is no longer a boy, nor is he a married man and whom he wishes to romance is entirely his own business.'

'So, you approve of him fraternising with the enemy but if I had succumbed to Reissman's wishes, you would have condemned me like the Frenchmen did, as a traitor.'

'Marie, that is an entirely different scenario; firstly, you are a married woman not single, and whilst some may have considered you a traitor, others would naturally assume you had no choice in the matter and see it as inevitable. Your brother is old enough and wise enough to make his own decisions and he may well be using her for his own ends – not pursuing her as a love interest but as a means of extracting information. I don't often forbid you anything, but I must insist you do not approach either Henri or Anya about this matter. It is none of your business and you stirring the pot could have serious repercussions for both of them.'

She glared at him angrily, flung off her riding shirt and stormed into the bathroom, slamming the door. He resorted to removing his clothes and decided to leave her alone to simmer and see how she was later.

At dinner that evening, she was sitting next to Wilhelm and he was complimenting her on her riding ability, but her eyes roved between Henri and Anya like a fox watching its prey. She was seething about him demanding she say nothing about the affair and she had been barely civil while getting dressed for dinner. Much as he loathed the icy atmosphere, at least it showed that she was thinking clearly. Why Henri having a lover should affect her so, concerned him. Was it just because Anya was German or was it because she did not want another woman taking her brother away?

When they retired to bed, she put on her nightdress and laid with her back to him. Determined he was not going to let her get away with sulking, he pulled her over onto her back and leant over her.

'I trust madame, that your behaviour and you wearing your nightgown is provoked by your anger at me for demanding you keep your nose out of your brother's affairs. Surely you can understand that I am absolutely right to insist you leave Henri to make his own decisions.' He ran his hand down her leg to pull up her nightie and was astonished to find she had drawers on as well. 'Are you denying me your body out of sheer spite, Marie?'

'No, you misunderstand, Charles. My courses have started after today's strenuous hunting and that is probably what has been bothering me all week.'

'You mean you are not pregnant – thank God for that!' He gathered her up in his arms and kissed her cheek.

Marie stared at him in shock and said, 'You mean you thought I was pregnant and now you are delighted that I am not? Jesus, Charles. I don't understand you. I assumed you desperately wanted another child.'

'Oh darling, of course I do, but not yet. Dr Kohl said you needed time to recover, mentally and physically. We need time to get back on our feet as well, as I am not earning a penny.' He pulled her close to him and stroked her hair. 'We will have a baby when the future looks brighter. I do not want to bring a second child into the family until we are all recovered from our ordeal. At least your fertility has returned, and we can monitor your recovery carefully.'

'I can see the point in waiting as we need to be certain we will have a sound financial footing and that art students will return to Paris.'

38

Anya left the dining room, relieved that Bismarck had told her he was going to play cards with the King and others and he would not need her tonight. She was just deciding whether to please Henri and grant him a night in his bed or whether to go to Le Comte, who had been strangely quiet after receiving a letter from home today. She sensed something was bothering him and intended to offer him a listening ear. As she descended the stairs, Courbet was lingering, looking at a portrait on the landing. He turned around as she approached.

'You said there were Roman baths here, but I haven't located them as yet.'

'Monsieur Courbet, please allow me to show you where they are now, so you can indulge at your leisure tomorrow.'

She turned and went down the magnificent staircase and he followed, meekly. The baths were underground and had been elaborately decorated with marble pillars to resemble their origins as closely as possible. This included murals and frescos, which took Courbet's eye immediately. With minimal sconce lighting in the main room, the pool was the size of a ballroom and reflected the pillars and the mirrored walls. There were smaller rooms equipped with plunge pools and baths off the main pool, as well as changing rooms. Anya leant against a marble pillar and watched Courbet absorb the scene around him.

'You are impressed, monsieur, as I was. Louis XIV certainly knew how to create an exquisite backdrop to pleasure his senses.'

'And you madame, enjoy the pleasures of the flesh too. I see you have taken young Croizette under your wing to further his education, so you cannot be immune to flirting with Frenchmen, either.'

'Henri Croizette is a very special young man and I considered it my duty to ensure that his sexual skills were on a par with the rest of his exceptional talent.'

Courbet advanced towards her and touched her cheek. 'He may be young and virile madame, but he does not have the experience to know how to pleasure a woman of your sexuality – but I do.' His mouth was on hers in seconds and he pushed her back against the marble pillar, restraining her hands behind it. After a short struggle she gave up and then he released her arms as she put one hand round his neck and pulled him closer and with the other, was undoing his trousers. Courbet smiled in triumph, knowing that her desire for him had been equally as strong as his for her. They were like two passionate wild animals, intent on satisfying their desire. He divested her of her dress, chemise and undergarments as she was ripping his shirt and trousers off. Finally, both stark naked, they each surveyed the other.

'You think I am just going to take you to satisfy my own desire, but you are mistaken, madame. You will have to beg me on your knees to take you when I have finished exploring every inch of your delectable body and sending you to ecstasy and back. I know how to pleasure a woman and I am not the selfish lover you think I am.' He picked her up and she expected him to take her to one of the many cushioned seating areas but with a wry laugh, he threw her into the pool and dived in after her.

It was an hour later before they emerged exhausted from the pool and Anya had been forced to beg him to take her after he had propelled her to heaven and beyond. The intensity of their lust and passion had driven them both to the edge. Courbet had been determined that she would not be the dominant partner, only submissive, and Anya had to submit if she wanted his body. Both had learnt new techniques in their shared art of lovemaking.

As they retrieved their clothes and Anya found some towels, Courbet laughed and said, 'Well madame, do you consider your sexual appetite thoroughly sated, and did I surprise you with my intimate knowledge of the female body?'

'Arrogant French bastard, do you expect me to award you marks out of ten? Then perhaps… a six for that performance.'

'Be careful madame, or you will not be receiving a

repeat performance and you wouldn't like that either. I was just testing Duran's advice that sex under water was a pleasurable experience. He and his delightful wife enjoyed the experience on honeymoon and it certainly has its advantages.'

'No doubt you would have preferred it if it had been his wife in the water with you rather than me. She does have a profound effect on men.'

Courbet grabbed her arm. 'Whoa, steady on, madame. That was not my intention at all. Marie Duran is unattainable as far as I, or any man is concerned. Duran has claimed her mind, body and soul and she will never be tempted from his side. She proved that in Lille; she is not interested in sex for its own sake or she would have accepted Reissman's offer. Duran released her sexuality slowly and carefully and she has no desire for anyone but him, the lucky bastard, and the fact he survived his ordeal to reclaim her is a miracle. I do not believe in God but if there is one then he pulled him back from the brink of death. Both Marie and her brother must have experienced something in Russia that influenced their attitude towards sex.'

Furtively, Anya led the way back to their separate bedrooms. She had no wish or inclination to continue her sexual antics; she was exhausted both mentally and physically. She lay in bed, reliving the scene in the pool and had to admit she had been wrong about Courbet. He was no selfish lover; he knew exactly what turned women on, but only on his own terms. She knew he would never tolerate a woman having the upper hand in bed, or out of it for that matter. He was a product of his generation, career, upbringing and nationality. They were both in their own way, sexual predators and they would never be able to sustain a relationship as they would tear each other apart. However, she was intrigued by his depth of understanding of women as he had summed up Marie Duran succinctly. He had also summed her up and she knew she would be going back for more sex with Courbet to assuage her passion and lust. Perhaps he had been right about Marie and Henri's experiences in Russia dictating their attitude to sex. She would see if she could find any evidence of this from Henri.

oOo

Charles was thoroughly enjoying the art treasures of Versailles. He had been allowed to enter the Royal Chapel Gallery to appraise the paintings on the Gothic vaulted ceiling. Three artists had been engaged to paint the scenes from both the Old and New Testament: Antoine Coypel, Charles de la Fosse and Jean Jouvenet. He was itching to get a closer look at the magnificent organ created by Robert Clicquot and would have loved to have been able to play it. Charles vowed that one day he would paint a ceiling in a church. He had dragged Courbet up to the gallery with him, even though he disliked anything to do with religion; even he had been silenced by the sheer beauty of the chapel. Whereas Charles revelled in the warmth and security of the chapel, Courbet felt threatened and exposed. He did not believe there was a God and so Charles could understand his reticence. Charles had begged Anya for some painting materials and was delighted that she had come up with paints, canvasses and easels, so he had immediately set up in the Hall of Mirrors, to paint the interior. He was fascinated by the way the external sunlight reflected off different parts of it throughout the day. Courbet was fascinated by the fountains, so he set up outdoors to capture the winter scenery.

Marie had discovered the library and was overcome by the sheer volume of leather-bound books available. There were many illustrated historical and religious books from every country and she spent time looking through them. She even found some Russian books with illustrations of places she knew in St. Petersburg and Moscow. She read through it and immediately, her knowledge of Russian was rekindled. She had also visited the music room and after a hesitant start, had begun to play the piano again. She found plenty of music to help her polish her skills and found that playing helped her release her emotion. She played Fauré's 'Cantique de Jean Racine' with tears pouring down her face, remembering how wonderful it had sounded on her wedding day. She was quick to realise that she needed to continue playing – as she did, the numbness that encased her heart began to melt away.

Le Comte entered Anya's office and noticed she seemed bright and cheerful on this cold, frosty morning.

'Where were you last night? I got roped into playing cards with Bismarck and the King and I knocked on your door when I finally got away from the gaming table, but you were not there.'

'Oh, Bismarck told me he was staying to play so I took the chance to have an early night and was probably fast asleep.'

'Well, you weren't in your bed at midnight and D'Artagnan had been with the Durans after dinner, so you could not have been with him. Where were you? Oh God forbid, Anya. You weren't in Courbet's bed, you fool? One day your desire for carnal knowledge will be the death of you.'

'Neither of us had any intention of killing one another; we took a far more sensual path.'

'Oh, when D'Artagnan hears about this there will be hell to pay!'

'Well, I don't expect you to go running to inform him. He knows I found Courbet sexually attractive and I warned him to keep his nose out.'

'And you think Courbet will keep quiet about it? If Bismarck gets wind of this Anya, you could be in trouble.'

'Had you ever thought that I may be doing this at his request?'

'Poppycock, Anya. Courbet is hardly a threat to

Bismarck, but you could find that when he does find out what you have done that he is handed over to the French for them to proceed with his criminal damage charges.'

'Let's just drop the subject. I am not in love with him, for God's sake, just interested to understand the character of the man.'

'You're playing with fire, Anya – and likely to get burnt!'

'You received a letter from home yesterday and by your quarrelsome manner today, I assume you had news that displeased you.'

'Yes, it was from my mother, reminding me that since my father died in September and this war is now over, she is expecting me back home to take up the reins of son and heir and I should be taking a wife, too. My brother George already has a son and daughter and she is sure she can find me the perfect German wife.'

'Oh, I can see how that did not sit well with you, Hans.'

There was a knock on the door and Henri came in. 'Sorry if I am interrupting but I wanted a word with Le Comte… but I can catch you later if you are busy.'

Le Comte replied, 'Oh come in, Henri. We were just discussing my letter from my mother, demanding I return home and head up the family and business and take a wife quickly. My brother George has produced two children already and he is four years younger than me.'

Henri replied, 'I can't quite see you willingly retiring to Bavaria just yet.'

'Exactly, and the prospect of marrying some German virgin fills me with dread. I want a more spirited and educated wife, preferably as close to your sister in looks and character as I can find.'

Henri laughed, 'Believe me; my dear sister is totally unique and furthermore happily married and reunited with her husband. I know you may be the eldest son, but why does that mean you necessarily have to head up the business as well as succeed to the title? Surely you could continue your career in the military and leave your two brothers to run the business and the stud? There must be enough money in running a large steel foundry in Munich to keep three families in the manner to which you have been accustomed.'

'Do you know D'Artagnan, you may have just come up with a workable solution. What did you want to ask me?'

'I want you to ride that young stallion I hunted, as I think I may have cured him of his bad habits.'

'You mean you want me to risk my life to find out whether you have been successful or not. Oh, go on then, I will have a sit on him in the school and then try him out on my next patrol into Paris. Don't expect me to be as forgiving as you if he tries any of his clever tricks on me. If I don't think he is cured, he will end up feeding the hounds as he could kill someone.'

Marie had been pursuing the answer as to why Henri was treated with such respect as a prisoner and despite casual approaches to Napoleon, Wilhelm and Le Comte, she had failed to gain a convincing answer. Eventually, Le Comte sought permission from Henri to tell Marie and Charles of his role in the Battle of Sedan. Henri did not want to discuss it with them but had agreed that he could tell them.

At breakfast, Le Comte had requested Charles and Marie to join him in his office at 10 a.m. and they both arrived, looking slightly perturbed.

Le Comte said, 'Marie, I know you have been asking questions about your brother and why we hold him in high esteem and have given him certain tasks and privileges whilst he has been here. For a start, Napoleon chose Henri to accompany him into captivity as Henri had served him at court as a bodyguard and was an admirer of his many exceptional talents. However, there is one very good reason why Napoleon chose him – and that was because he saved his life at the Battle of Sedan.'

Both Charles and Marie looked shocked and Marie exclaimed, 'But, why did he not tell us?'

Le Comte continued, 'Marie, you know your brother is no self-seeking show-off. Henri considers what he did to be nothing more than what was expected of him in the line of duty. I have a report that was written after the Battle of Sedan, which we revealed to Henri after his capture, and he has given us permission to read it to you. You must understand he had not been ordered to protect Napoleon. His role was as a scout and he was on his way to report troop movements when he saw the battle begin.'

As he read the report, he watched the effect of his words on both Marie and Charles. Marie's face went pale and she gripped the desk as his words penetrated her ears. Then, silent tears ran down her face and she grasped her husband's hand for comfort. Charles looked shocked but listened carefully, full of concern for his wife. When he had finished, Le Comte paused and waited for any questions.

Marie turned to Charles, 'I knew he was brave, but he usually weighs up the risks as well. Whatever made him think he could accomplish that and extricate both of them from the front line, alive?'

Charles replied, 'Marie, you know what a courageous man he is, and he acted on instinct to protect his king. Whilst he visited me in Paris to find out where Eugénie had gone, he had plenty of time to discuss it with me and he chose not to.'

Le Comte said, 'As a result of your brother's courage and devotion to duty, Wilhelm and Bismarck agreed that Henri would not remain a prisoner. Indeed, it was his suggestion that we released Napoleon into exile to join his wife and he volunteered to be the intermediary. Once he has achieved this task, he is free to leave. He has a promising future if he chooses to remain within the French military, although he has turned down the chance of becoming a politician. He has never spoken of it again as, honestly, he does not consider himself to be a hero in any shape or form. In fact, he was mortified that he had made Napoleon's life more difficult after he was overthrown. When he returned from England and discovered what had befallen Charles, it was Bismarck's high regard for Henri that resulted in your release from captivity in Lille. I would also like to add that I consider Henri to be an exceptional man. You are both exceptional riders and trainers of horses and if they were the only skills you learnt in Russia then it would be enough. However, it appears you are both multi-talented in a variety of areas, so you should both be exceptionally proud.'

Marie replied, 'Henri has always been my protector and guardian – always the sensible one, never the hot-headed one like me. He even turned up just in time to deliver my baby when I was in dire need. Nikolai was his hero and inspired him to become a cavalry officer. It was he who taught us both to ride, shoot and fence... but Henri has taken those skills to another level.'

39

The carriage pulled up at the main entrance to Versailles. After lengthy negotiations, Napoleon's release had been agreed and both Le Comte and Henri were escorting him to London and had been granted two weeks' leave with a proviso that they returned to Versailles before Christmas. The assembled party made their final goodbyes to Napoleon and he joined Henri and Le Comte to board the coach. A small escort of eight cavalry troops was to accompany them to Calais.

They arrived in good time for the ferry across to Dover and Anya had arranged and paid for accommodation in London at the Savoy at Henri's request for himself and Le Comte; they had both been given generous expenses to cover their trip. Henri had been asked by Charles to contact Durand-Ruel, Monet and any of the other artists he came across, to update them on the situation in Paris.

They travelled up to London by train and took a hansom cab to King Street. Henri knocked on the door and it was opened by Louis. The shock on his face to see his father and Henri, was visible. He ditched his court etiquette and ran and threw his arms round his father. They climbed the stairs to the salon, where Eugénie awaited them.

Louis turned to Henri, 'Perhaps you two gentlemen would prefer to wait here with me while my parents have some private time together?'

Henri replied, 'Of course Louis; that would be fine. May I introduce Comte Hans von Brixenhof.' Louis shook Le Comte's hand.

'Is he your Commanding Officer now, Henri?'

Le Comte replied, 'No, Henri is free to go where he wishes now. We both have decided to enjoy the delights of London before returning to Versailles.'

Louis turned to Henri, 'So what are you going to do, Henri?'

'I have no firm plans other than to continue my service in the cavalry. Marshal MacMahon has intimated that I would be due for promotion with the Hussars and that is where my skills are best employed. He tried to convince me to become a politician and stand for election to the new government, but I don't think it would suit me – do you?'

'Certainly not, Henri. You are an outstanding military officer; you could serve anywhere. I only wish I was not denied the right to serve France once I have finished my education here.'

'If you are determined on a military career Louis, have you considered whether you would be able to serve in the British military? I believe they are a formidable, disciplined army to fight against. Your grasp of military tactics could well be of use to them.'

'I will make an enquiry. That is an excellent idea,

Henri. What happened to Perseus? Was he killed at Sedan?'

'No, he survived unscathed and was shipped to Versailles along with my Jester, as he was causing so much trouble by letting horses out of their stables and untying his rope that the Germans wanted rid of him as well. Your father wanted to give Perseus to me, but I declined as I have no use or facilities to keep a beautiful, grey Barbary stallion. I could not be seen riding such a horse as a lower ranking officer and his looks would cause envy amongst other officers. Besides, he is hardly the best colour to go on scouting forays. However, Le Comte has a stud in Bavaria and he has offered to take him there and has promised to breed me a black stallion replacement in due course.'

The salon door opened and Napoleon and Eugénie emerged to say goodbye. Napoleon hugged Henri and told him to keep in touch and wished him well in his career. Henri fought to keep his composure as he was genuinely fond of him; he promised to keep in touch. They were shown to the door by Louis and Henri. Le Comte summoned a passing hansom cab.

On the way to the Savoy, Le Comte said, 'So now, D'Artagnan. Are we going to hit the high spots of London and find some available women to tumble? I just want to eat, drink, sleep and have sex non-stop for the next two weeks. How about you?'

'I have some planned sightseeing to do during the day, but I think I can concur with your idea of entertainment for the evening.'

'Too right, you are keeping me company. You are far more fluent in English than I am and with your dark good looks and my fair, we should attract plenty of attention from the ladies.'

Henri laughed, 'I thought you had come here to look for a suitable wife? And from what I have heard, English ladies do not jump into bed on their first date.'

'I am not looking for a raw virgin for a wife, Henri. I am perfectly happy to have a young widow with her own children who will produce my heirs as she will have to be content to be at home alone if I continue my military career.'

'It won't be easy tempting an English lady to leave her country to live in the wilds of Bavaria.'

'But why not? She will be a countess and will never have to worry about money again and will have me as an absent husband and father.'

'Do you honestly think any woman used to a court lifestyle would want that? She would soon be looking for entertainment from other male admirers and then you would not know whether the children she bears are even your own.'

'Oh, D'Artagnan, you are so bloody French. How is she going to manage to conduct extra-marital affairs living in the same house as my mother, two brothers and their entourage – not to mention the servants?'

'You underestimate the subtlety and cunning

of women, Hans. Hell, hath no fury like a woman scorned!'

The cab pulled up outside the Savoy and they were ushered into the huge reception area and then escorted to their rooms on the third floor. The porter took them into Le Comte's room first and as he surveyed the opulent lounge, bedroom and bathroom, he turned to Henri.

'You have good taste, D'Artagnan... maybe not quite up to Versailles's standard, but it will do.' He threw himself in the chair and poured himself a brandy.

After Henri had been shown into the suite next door, he returned to join Le Comte with a brandy.

'First stop Henri, is a tailor's. I need clothes suitable for London high society. Then you need to investigate ways of securing invitations to the right parties, even if it requires a little subterfuge and greased palms to get them. Find out how we can meet high class ladies without spending hours at the opera or ballet.'

'Hans, did you do any research on London before we set out?'

'No, why?'

'Because if you had, you would have found out that since Prince Albert died, Victoria has disbanded the court and fled to the Isle of Wight in deep mourning.'

'But that was eight bloody years ago, Henri... and isn't the Prince of Wales a serial philanderer and gambler? It is his court we want to be following, not hers.'

'Yes, I know. Bertie established his own pleasure palace, but not in London.'

'Well, where?

'In Paris, so he was out of sight and sound of his mother.'

'Well he won't be there now, will he? So, he must hold court here in London somewhere and with your aptitude for spying, you had better find out quickly.'

'Very well Le Comte, you go to find a tailor and I will make enquiries to secure the best entertainment for this evening.'

'Just remember to investigate a second option for if we fail to entice a woman to our bed immediately. I am not spending tonight alone; I am prepared to pay for one if not two ladies to join me, so find out where such services can be acquired.'

'Very well my lord, your wish is my command and I will do my utmost to fulfil your desires.'

oOo

That evening, they dined at the Savoy and then moved on to a prestigious London club for a 21st birthday party of a young man who had recently graduated from Oxford University. There were over 100 invited guests of both sexes and Henri had given Le Comte the details of their hosts and told him to say they were distant European cousins of the family, should anyone question them. He had acquired the details of the party from the hotel concierge, who was proving to be a mine of valuable information.

There were several beautiful girls there, but the majority were with fiancés or husbands and the single girls were heavily chaperoned. They did cause a flurry amongst the ladies with their good looks, and Henri's French accent was an added attraction. Le Comte was disappointed to find they were a little too young to fit his profile for a wife, but his attention was drawn to a young blonde girl who was dressed in black and obviously chaperoning her younger friend or relative. He sent Henri off to the bar to find someone who knew them. Whilst waiting, he found a convenient corner to observe the lady from, himself. She looked to be in her early twenties, had long blonde hair that was pinned in a tight chignon, green eyes and a delicate figure. Her dress was black silk, which indicated she could be in mourning, but she had a diamond necklace and earrings and was (to his delight) wearing a gold wedding ring with a large, oval diamond engagement ring. His interest increased minute by minute.

By the time Henri returned to him, he was already smitten. Agitated, he barked at him, 'Well, what have you found out?'

Henri chuckled, 'Calm down, Hans and stop looking at her; she is bound to see you. She is Mathilde Courvoisier, aged twenty-two and the recent widow of a French silk and spices merchant who was killed in action at the Battle of Beaumont on 30th August. She has two daughters aged two and four, was born in Germany and raised in England. She is chaperoning her sister-in-law here tonight. She lives in London in a house owned by her father-in-law, near Hyde Park.'

'Oh God, Henri. This is too good to be true! She will hopefully speak fluent German as well as English and French. How do I get an introduction to her? I can't just walk up to her and ask her to be my wife, can I?'

'Certainly not, the English are steadfast at observing etiquette rules. She is in mourning, so she cannot really partake in any social activities for at least a year. She should not really be out now, but I suspect her sister-in-law was anxious to come and there was nobody else in the household suitable to escort her. We'll just work our way around to them as there is some space and hopefully, we can get chatting to them. For God's sake stop looking at her like you want to devour her in one mouthful; she will run a mile if you continue to do that. Sometimes I think you should be the commoner and I the count. I will turn my attention to the younger girl as she is conveniently French and nearer my age, but you must be careful as there could be more of her family here than we think and she will not be expected to converse with a strange man, since her husband only died three months ago.'

Henri moved over to the corner of the room where the two women were engaged in conversation with another girl and her mother. He continued to talk to Le Comte about the delights of London in French, hoping they would become aware of them. However, at that moment a servant came into the room carrying a tray of hors d'oeuvres and as Mathilde stepped back to make room, she caught her elbow on the bookcase and dropped her glass of wine. Henri kicked Le Comte and whispered "handkerchief!" into his ear. Thankfully, he leapt into action.

'Madame allow me to assist you?' He proffered her his spotlessly white, monogrammed silk handkerchief and bent down to retrieve the glass, which as it had fallen on thick carpet, had not broken.

She was extremely flustered and embarrassed but was forced into accepting his handkerchief as the wine had spilt over her arm, though not, thankfully, over her dress. 'Thank you so much, monsieur for coming to my aid with such speed. May I introduce myself – Madame Mathilde Courvoisier – and this is my sister-in-law, Mademoiselle Claudette Courvoisier.'

Le Comte was swift to accept her hand and bowed over it and said, 'I am Comte Hans von Brixenhof and may I present Lieutenant Henri Croizette.' He moved to Claudette and bowed to her saying, 'Mademoiselle, what a pleasure to meet you.' Henri bowed to Mathilde. He then took Claudette's hand and bowed to her.

Claudette was quick to say, 'And what are two such distinguished soldiers doing here in London?'

'Henri and I are here on a brief holiday, staying at the Savoy, to get some respite from war-torn Paris.'

Mathilde said, 'But you sir, must be German… and Lieutenant Croizette, French… so surely you are on different sides.'

'Exactly, madame, but we have been working together on the peace treaty at Versailles and have become good friends. Now allow me to replenish your wine and then we can talk in more detail.' He whisked off to the bar and left Henri to do the talking in his absence.

Mathilde said, 'And have you seen action during the war, Lieutenant Croizette?'

'Yes, madame. I saw action in the Battle of Metz and the Battle of Sedan, where I was captured when Napoleon surrendered.'

'You are very young to be involved in negotiating a peace treaty.'

'Indeed so, but I don't get to make the big decisions; those are made by King Wilhelm and Bismarck, along with representatives of the new French Republican Government. Do you live permanently in London?'

Le Comte returned with fresh glasses of wine for the ladies.

Mathilde responded, 'I have been living here since war broke out in Paris but unfortunately, my husband was killed at the Battle of Beaumont in August.'

Le Comte responded quickly, 'My condolences,

madame. You are very young to have lost a husband.'

She avoided his gaze while she fought to control her emotions. 'We had only been married six years and I have two girls to rear alone now. It doesn't help either that I am German by nationality but was raised here in London and educated at court with the Queen's children.'

Le Comte took her hand and said, 'I appreciate it must be very difficult for you at present, madame.'

Henri asked Claudette, 'And you, mademoiselle? Have you finished your education in England?'

She replied, 'Yes, I have just completed my language degree at Oxford and am about to start looking for a job. I would love to return to Paris, but I think it will take some time for the city to be restored.'

'Indeed, it will, mademoiselle as the centre has been devastated by heavy shelling and the people are still suffering from the siege. It will be some time before commerce returns to normal.'

They chatted some more, and Le Comte managed to arrange a meeting with Mathilde in Hyde Park for the next day. A group of students arrived, and Henri guided Le Comte away as they could not be seen to monopolise the ladies for any longer.

They took their leave from the party at around 11 p.m. and Le Comte was delighted when he caught Mathilde watching him leaving the room. They walked back to the Savoy and Le Comte was so overjoyed at their first meeting, he was like a young boy dating his first girlfriend. Henri tried his best to calm him down and warned him not to raise his hopes as Mathilde's situation was extremely difficult, and she had put herself in danger by agreeing to meet him, as her husband's family would be furious if she was seen greeting a male stranger in the park while her young husband was hardly cold in his grave. Mathilde had insisted Henri was also present so that it appeared like a chance meeting during a walk in the park.

They had a drink in the bar and Le Comte insisted he needed a female in his bed that night or he would not be able to control his lust for Mathilde. Henri pointed him in the direction of the concierge, who he knew would be able to oblige him with a bed pal.

After Le Comte had departed to his room, Henri wrote a quick message and gave it to one of the waiters to give to the young waitress he had already singled out for his attention. She lived in an attic room at the top of the hotel and had been more than willing to keep him company when she was off duty. Henri smiled as Le Comte had no idea about his subterfuge. He had no desire to chase prostitutes for fear of contracting more than just sexual release. He had seen, first-hand, the devastating effects of syphilis on both males and females, while undergoing his medical studies at the barracks and it had frightened the life out of him.

40

The next morning, they set off to meet the two ladies in Hyde Park. Henri was very dubious about this as he was concerned that Mathilde was unaware of the risks she was taking by being seen in public talking to strangers. However, he was relieved when they reached the meeting place as it was not on one of the main public paths through the park. Le Comte had told him to see if he could persuade Claudette to go for a walk with him so that he and Mathilde could have some time alone.

The ladies arrived in ermine bound cloaks and hats to keep out the cold December chill. They were lucky it was not raining. The cooler temperatures ensured there were not many walkers, so they found a convenient bandstand to shelter in, out of the wind. After a little idle chit-chat, Henri suggested to Claudette that they take a stroll together.

Mathilde said, 'But I really must take my role of chaperone seriously.'

Le Comte intervened, 'But madame, Henri is a perfect gentleman and Claudette could not be in safer hands.'

Henri escorted Claudette, making sure he made

no attempt to touch her or behave in an inappropriate manner. As luck would have it, a troop of Household Cavalry appeared and were heading towards a large schooling area, so Henri was delighted to have the chance to witness this famous troop in action. Thankfully, Claudette was also a horse lover and so they leaned on the paddock rails and watched them having a lesson. These were obviously new recruits, and some had not yet mastered the finer points of riding. Their instructor had them doing sitting trot without stirrups and two riders fell off whilst going around the corner, much to Claudette's amusement. Her laughter only helped to shame the riders who had fallen off. It also helped the conversation flow and Henri was able to glean more details about the girls' lifestyle and piece together their family history.

After about half an hour, Le Comte and Mathilde appeared as she was obviously concerned about the length of time that Claudette had been away. However, when they saw what they had been watching, she calmed down and joined them.

That evening, Henri had arranged to dine with Durand-Ruel and Monet and had invited Le Comte to join them, but he had declined, sensing his presence would not be welcomed by the other Frenchmen.

Le Comte dined alone at the Savoy and then returned to his room, where he changed into black breeches, a dark shirt and a black cloak. He tucked a dagger into the secret pocket in the lining of his cloak and donned a large black hat to cover his blonde hair. He used a back entrance to exit the Savoy and slipped into the street outside.

He made his way to his destination, which took him ten minutes and then observed the house through the locked, wrought iron gates. He moved round to the back and climbed the wall and then shimmied down a drainpipe, onto the wall of a garden shed. He moved into the bushes close to the back door, checked his watch and waited. After about ten minutes the door was opened, and a cloaked figure came out of the back door and whistled. He checked nobody was in sight and slipped quietly across to the waiting figure and was ushered inside.

oOo

The next morning, Henri rose early after his night out with Monet and Durand-Ruel; they had wined and dined, but not to excess. He knocked on Le Comte's door as he went past but was not surprised when he received no response as it was only 8 a.m. and if he had been out on the booze the night before it was more than possible that he would be crashed out, fast asleep. He continued downstairs to the dining room and ordered his breakfast and a newspaper. He had just been presented with his sizzling cooked breakfast when to his astonishment, Le Comte appeared, carrying his cloak and hat, and joined him at the table.

'Good grief, Hans. Where are you going so early?'

'Not going, D'Artagnan, just coming back from an early morning ride in Hyde Park. I heard you can hire horses to ride in the park and I thought it would be a wonderful, brisk form of exercise to set me up for the day.'

'Really? You do surprise me, Hans. There are just one or two problems with that explanation.'

Le Comte poured his coffee and said, 'What are you on about?'

'Well, for a start, there is not one whiff of horses on your clothes and secondly, look out of the window and you will see it is still pitch dark! You may have been in the vicinity of Hyde Park and you may have even been riding – but it wasn't a horse!'

Le Comte's bottom lip quivered and he snapped, 'One day D'Artagnan, you will stab yourself on that sharp brain of yours and let's hope it is sooner rather than later!'

'If you have been where I suspect you have been, then you have been thinking with your balls and not your brain!'

Le Comte glared at Henri and said quietly, 'We will discuss this upstairs in private later. I need to have my breakfast in peace.'

Henri picked up his newspaper and used it to shield his face as he was close to laughing out loud at Le Comte's discomfort. The silence was welcome as he set his mind to calculating the risks Le Comte had taken in pursuit of his ardour.

After breakfast they returned to Le Comte's room

and he threw himself in a chair and motioned to Henri to sit down.

'Ok D'Artagnan, I will tell you exactly what happened last night as it will be seared on my soul forever.'

'Oh God Hans, what have you done? I can't believe you exposed both yourself and her to such danger. Neither can I understand how a woman of her standing would put herself in this position and risk both her and her children's future and reputation on a night of passion with you.'

'Oh, give me a break. I know I was foolish, but can't you see I am besotted with her and could not stop myself?'

'Did you ever ask yourself why she was so willing to romp with you in bed within twenty-four hours of meeting you, when her husband is hardly cold in his grave?'

'Yes, but she is as besotted with me as I am with her!'

'Rubbish, she seized an opportunity to net herself a count and guarantee herself a life of luxury at your expense.'

'But that's what I wanted from her anyway; a wife to rear my children as well as hers.'

'And no doubt you consummated this union several times last night and left yourself wide open to blackmail as she can claim you as the father of her next child? You idiot!'

'No, Henri, listen. She told me afterwards that

she had taken precautions to ensure there would be no repercussions.'

'Christ Hans, this gets worse by the minute. How does she know how to prevent pregnancy when she should never have had the need to? Does that alone not ring alarm bells in your thick head? How many other men has she been attempting to trap as her future husband?'

'She probably knows because she has lived in Jerusalem for four years as her husband's family have a house and business there trading in silk and spices from the east and selling French wine to them.'

'Well, that certainly answers a lot of my questions. No doubt she was the best lover you have ever slept with and drove you to ecstasy and back.'

'Yes, she was sublime and wonderful. She did things to my body I have never experienced before.'

'I bet she did, and you didn't wonder how she had gained this knowledge?'

'Well from her husband Ralf, he had been working in Jerusalem since he was eighteen and would have lost his virginity with local girls. They were married in Paris when he was twenty-two and then moved straight out to Jerusalem and she became pregnant very quickly and had their first daughter Brigitte out there, followed by Veronique two years later. I am certainly not complaining about her skill in bed, nor do I believe it was gained outside her marriage.'

'For your sake, I hope it was not! I know all about the sexual skill of women from the Holy Land. One of my troopers was born in Jerusalem as his father was serving out there. He used to regale us frequently with stories of the delights of Saracen women, by the campfire at night. But why is Mathilde so anxious to leave London and bury herself in your ivory tower in Bavaria, with her court upbringing? She is going to find it very cold and boring in Bavaria after the heat and delights of Jerusalem.'

'To be fair, her lifestyle was forced on her by her husband and was not one she craved for herself. She is not the experienced courtier you make her out to be and she did truly love her husband and children, so why would she look elsewhere? The children were in a bedroom adjoining her suite and the youngest one woke during the night. She brought her into her bedroom and breastfed her and she did it with such tenderness and love, all I could think about was her producing my son and loving him like she did her daughter.'

You're not the first man to be gripped by such a desire to procreate. Charles was the same when he witnessed his sister-in-law breastfeeding her son... not that he wanted her as the mother, he wanted Marie of course, and in fact he got her pregnant within the first week of their marriage. You know I am only pointing out these obstacles to protect you, Hans. I would hate to see you rush into this and find it all collapses around you.'

'She knew she was taking a risk having me at the house, but her parents-in-law and Claudette were at the opera and staying with friends, so they were out of the house. I invited her here, but she would not leave her children alone overnight. Brigitte still wakes crying at night calling for her father and she did not want to risk this happening when she wasn't there. You are not the only man that can enter and leave a house unseen D'Artagnan, and I did have some inside help.'

'But what about the servants, Hans? They are the ones most likely to use that sort of information to serve their own cause.'

'Rest assured Henri, nobody saw me enter or leave the house and I was in Mathilde's room the rest of the time. Did your trooper's knowledge extend to how to prevent pregnancies?'

'Yes, the usual one is a small sponge soaked in vinegar inserted at the entrance to the womb, but it is usually done well in advance of intercourse and left in place until the next bleed. You obviously didn't find it during your explorations?'

'No, I did not – I was too engrossed, concentrating on the delights lower down. Did you know that in Jerusalem both men and women shave all their body hair off to keep them cooler in the baking heat and Mathilde still practises this tradition? It really threw a whole new light on the female anatomy and I can highly recommend it.'

Henri grinned at him and said, 'I assume you are not going to be amenable to sharing her with me like you did Anya.'

Le Comte exclaimed, 'No I am bloody not, D'Artagnan! Besides, Anya oversaw that session, not me.' He picked up a book and sent it flying in his direction.

Henri ducked and smiled, 'Well tell me then, master horse breeder, how you are going to sire a son with her when she has only produced two girls so far?'

'That's an interesting concept. Perhaps I will have to adopt the practices I use to try and influence the sex of a foal. In horses, as humans, the male is responsible for determining the sex of the offspring. I don't usually bother about what sex a foal is as my interest is in the fillies for breeding and the colts to sell as riding horses or stallions. However, on the few occasions I have particularly wanted a male foal I have deliberately kept the mare from mating until she has ovulated.'

'I never realised it was so complicated. I would love to come and see it in action someday. Charles and Marie went to the Beauchamp Thoroughbred stud and they breed racehorses and hunters; they said the facilities were amazing.'

'Well if you think that's difficult then try breeding for colour only and you will find that twice as challenging. I will breed you a bay or black by Perseus if I can, but he may prove to carry only 100% grey colour genes as grey and chestnut are dominant genes.'

'I am delighted you are planning to keep in touch

with me then, even though I have expressed doubts about Mathilde?'

'D'Artagnan, I only allow you to do that because I consider you my friend and you have a quick brain and always look for the pitfalls in any situation. Mathilde wants us to meet her and Claudette in the park again at 2 p.m. Please come and meet her and you can ask her any questions you like.'

'Very well Hans, I will, but you are risking being seen by her family and it will not go down well.'

'Thank you D'Artagnan, now bugger off and let me have a bath and get some sleep. Wake me up at 1 p.m. for our walk in the park.'

Henri had been out window shopping and to a café for a quick snack and arrived back at Le Comte's room as scheduled. He had been thinking carefully about Mathilde and he was still concerned about her forward behaviour with Le Comte. There must be a reason why she wanted to get away from her French in-laws so quickly after the death of her husband. How they would view her remarrying and taking their grandchildren to live in Germany was another big issue. Le Comte had told him there were two younger sons also working in the business and the eldest one already had children.

41

Le Comte was elegantly dressed in his newly acquired London wool tail suit, a white silk shirt, cravat and yellow waistcoat, finished off with a new top hat and fur-lined cloak. Henri was slightly less formally dressed in suede breeches, a white shirt, a waistcoat and his black cloak and hat. They arrived in good time at the appointed spot and sat on a bench to await the ladies. There were not too many people about in the park as it was quite cool, but at least it wasn't raining. He saw the ladies approaching and was surprised to see that Mathilde was pushing a large perambulator and Claudette was holding Brigitte's hand.

After introductions were made, Le Comte suggested he and Claudette take Brigitte down to the swings, leaving Henri and Mathilde at the bench with Veronique asleep in her pram. Mathilde was obviously nervous, but she faced him with courage.

'Henri, I know you have some concerns for Hans and the speed of our relationship, but I can assure you I have no ulterior motive and am not trying to find myself a rich husband to replace Ralf.'

'Madame, all I can comment, as it is really none

of my business, is that I don't think many French ladies would be as quick into a new relationship within three months of the death of their husband and certainly, an English lady would not contemplate it. I am only concerned for Hans' welfare and future. I also wonder why a lady who has spent her youth in the English court would want to move to secluded Bavaria, unless of course the attraction of becoming a countess would outweigh the solitude?'

Mathilde blushed at his words and fought back her tears. 'I know I deserved that rebuke Henri and I can fully understand why you have come to that conclusion but in my defence, I feel I must stress that I did not choose to be raised in London or live in Jerusalem and I would welcome a quieter lifestyle back home in Germany – both for myself and for my children.'

'And how do you think your in-laws are going to feel when they find out you wish to remarry and take their grandchildren to be raised in Germany? To lose a son in a war is hard enough to endure, but to lose your grandchildren to a victor of that war requires extreme fortitude.'

'I know it is going to be difficult for them to accept but I do not intend them to have no contact with the girls and I am sure Hans would agree that they should remain in contact with their French family. I appreciate that the timing for this is perhaps inappropriate but then when love strikes, you have no control over it. Hans has told me he intends to retain his military career, provided he can come to some arrangement with his brothers regarding the business. I will not be seeking amusement elsewhere during his absence, if that is what you are concerned about. I was in love with Ralf and would never have cheated on him and I do not think he would have wanted to deny me the right to remarry. I admit I have been remiss in moving as fast as I have with Hans but that was exacerbated by your short time here in London, as well as our feelings for each other.'

'If you want my opinion I think you both need time to consider this drastic change in your lives very carefully; rushing in too soon could prove a disaster for both you and the children. If you are in love with each other then surely six months' wait would make no difference? Besides, Hans needs time to convince his family that he will be taking on not just a new wife, but two French stepdaughters as well.'

'Hans said you were wise beyond your years and certainly for twenty-two you are incredibly worldly wise and sensible, but you must surely understand that after going through the devastation and trauma of war, the chance to snatch happiness again feels irresistible.'

Veronique had woken, and Mathilde stood up and leaned into the pram to sit her up. Henri gasped when he saw her.

'Good heavens, Veronique is the spitting image of you being fair, blue eyed and German, whereas Brigitte is dark haired, olive skinned, petite and

French.'

Mathilde smiled, 'Yes, Brigitte does resemble her father and Veronique favours me. I would be honoured to bear Hans's children and I promise you I would be a dutiful wife and mother.'

Le Comte, Claudette and Brigitte were approaching, and so no further discussion took place.

After the ladies had departed, Le Comte flopped down onto the bench. 'Well go on then, what did you say to her?'

'Nothing that I haven't already raised with you and although I feel less concerned that she is after you for your money and title, I still think there is a reason why she wants to get away from her in-laws. I did not mince my words either when I accused her of being too forward in pursuing a new relationship so soon after the death of her husband. Her answer was that "when love strikes, you have no control over it".

Le Comte leapt up off the bench and shouted, 'She actually admitted to you that she loves me. Oh, hallelujah! Henri, you don't know how much that means to me!'

'Hold on a minute Hans, you have to decide whether she was telling the truth, or if in fact, what you are both experiencing is attraction and lust, but not love. You know very well how quickly that can burn itself out, but true love will last a lifetime. I suggested you both need time to consider the drastic changes to your lives that marriage would bring for all of you. If you are in love with each other then surely, waiting six months would make no difference?'

'What was her answer to that?'

'She said that after going through the devastation and loss of war, the chance to snatch happiness again was irresistible.'

'Well there you are, then. She must love and want me.'

'Not necessarily you Hans, but an opportunity for a new secure life for her and her children – certainly.'

'Oh, Henri, don't dash my hopes so. You know I want her as my wife, but you keep throwing a bucket of cold water on me.'

'That's precisely what you need! You accused me of pursuing Anya as if she was a bitch on heat, when you are now behaving the same.'

Le Comte wagged his finger at him. 'But you haven't had the delight of her making love to you and making you feel so happy, fulfilled and your whole body screaming in ecstasy like I have.'

'The question is though, is it love or lust? Only time will tell – so wait and see.'

oOo

Over the next two days, Le Comte did not see Mathilde and whether this was due to her being unavailable or Le Comte backing off, Henri didn't ask. They spent their days sightseeing and their nights wining and dining. Whether Le Comte had managed a night-time sojourn with Mathilde or not, he had no way of knowing. However, he knew he was not going to give up easily, as he was entirely besotted with her.

On the Saturday night they had booked to go to the theatre and afterwards, Le Comte seemed anxious and not interested in having an extended drinking session and claimed tiredness and a need to get some rest. Henri was not to be fooled and left his door propped open slightly and as they were on the third floor, he listened for the lift door opening. He put on his cloak and waited. Half an hour later, he heard the lift door open and two figures in black cloaks and hoods moved furtively down the corridor towards Le Comte's room. When they were within three feet of his door, he threw open his door and went out into the corridor.

Mathilde gasped and he said, 'You, Hans are playing with fire and you madame, risk losing your children if this liaison becomes public.' He then flounced past them and caught the lift downstairs. There was no way he was going to be in his room whilst they were cavorting next door. He went back outside and went to a bar down the road, took a table close to the window and bought himself a large brandy. He suspected that even Le Comte would not risk her being absent all night and he smiled at throwing yet another bucket of cold water on Le Comte's ardour. He had not seen any sign of them leaving by the front door when the bar closed but that did not mean they hadn't left by another entrance. He made his way to his room and when inside, listened intently for any sound from next door. All appeared to be silent.

The next morning, he knocked as usual on Le Comte's door at 9 a.m. as it was Sunday. To his surprise, Le Comte answered the door wearing only his drawers.

'You may enter only if you promise not to lecture me on my morals or behaviour last night.'

'Very well my friend, I will just glare silently at you whilst you get dressed and ready for breakfast and afterwards you are going to church to confess your many sins.'

'Oh, I couldn't possibly sit on a wooden pew. Everywhere aches and for once in my life I would be incapable of riding a horse or even sitting in a carriage.'

He failed to persuade Le Comte to attend a Catholic church to confess his sins, but they did look round Westminster Abbey in the afternoon.

oOo

On Monday afternoon, they met up with Mathilde and Claudette in Hyde Park and Henri walked separately with Claudette and asked her opinion of Mathilde and Le Comte marrying. He realised she was in a difficult position as she had loyalty to her brother, as well as her friendship with Mathilde, to consider. She explained that with two other brothers involved in the business, which was prospering on a global scale and stretching across Europe and the Middle East, the business would miss Ralf's contribution, particularly his contacts in Jerusalem, but it would continue without him and they would operate from London until their Paris office could be re-opened. He asked whether her parents would be amenable to their grandchildren moving to Germany and she said her father would be more likely to raise objections than her mother. She liked Mathilde and would be more open to her finding love with another man and rebuilding her life than her husband would.

When they returned to the hotel to change for dinner, Le Comte dropped his bombshell. 'Henri, I am not going back with you to Versailles. I intend to ask her in-laws for Mathilde's hand in marriage and I need more time to accomplish this task.'

Henri leapt up from his chair. 'Jesus Hans, surely you can take more time to consider before you leap into the fray. You do realise that you could put Mathilde's relationship with them in dire straits, not to mention the fact that you will be the enemy that killed their son in the first place and they may refuse on that ground alone.'

'I'm well aware of that Henri, but short of kidnapping Mathilde and her children, which would be even more despicable, what other option do I have? We will be returning to Germany as soon as the treaty is signed, and the money handed over, which realistically will be within the next two months. Germany is too far away to negotiate with

464

the Courvoisiers in London and besides, I want to marry her now. If I leave her they could force her into another marriage to keep her tied to them.'

Suddenly, Henri realised the task he faced in returning to Versailles without Le Comte. 'Shit Hans, do you seriously expect me to go back to your king and Bismarck and tell them you are too busy to return for duty because you are pursuing a bride in London? Bismarck will have me clamped in irons for allowing you to get into this mess in the first place, not to mention what Anya will do to me as well. You may well be a count and a distant nephew of your king, but you have more courage than I would to take this risk with your military career.'

'Oh Henri, spoken like a true Frenchman whose devotion to duty is exemplary.'

'It has to be, as it is my only source of income. But this could go badly wrong for you and you could end up with no wife and no military career; are you prepared for that?'

'Yes, Henri. I am. Now I have difficulty comprehending how I would go back to the frontline fighting and getting my head blown off, when I could remain at home with Mathilde who blows my mind every time she touches me.'

'Oh, God – you really are smitten, aren't you? I see the same look in your eyes as I saw in Charles's when he fell for Marie. Let's hope it is true love and not just desire. She may be the best woman you have ever bedded, but will it last?'

'I have to take the risk. Rest assured I will write to the King and explain my erratic behaviour and beg his forgiveness – and will absolve you of any blame.'

'Can you just pen a note to Anya as well, to save me having my balls ripped off?'

Le Comte smiled, 'I was going to write and ask her if she would arrange a wedding at Versailles for me as soon as we return.'

'Jesus, you intend to marry in France, not Germany? You really do have some balls, don't you? … and certainly, no concerns that you will fail to procure your bride.'

'I can hardly have her unmarried at Versailles; the King would never permit that and besides, the children need to accept me as their new father. I hope you will be my best man too, and I will ask the King to give my bride away. Perhaps you would ask your sister if Marie-Ann would be a bridesmaid.'

'You really have fallen hook, line and sinker for Mathilde. My concern in leaving you alone is that if her family object they may consider disposing of you and you could end up with a bullet in your back.'

'I know, but that's another risk I will have to take.'

42

Henri had made it from Calais to Paris courtesy of an overnight lift from an empty wine merchant's wagon, which was returning from London. He was dropped off near the Tuileries Palace and looked round to see if he could see any German troop activity but saw no sign. He then found a hansom cab to take him on to Versailles. Once there, he was stopped at the gate, removed by armed guards and taken to Anya's office. She wasn't in her office yet, so he was held outside in the corridor, by the armed guard. Thankfully, Anya appeared around the corner and was shocked to find Henri standing there. She dismissed the guard, ushered him into her office and firmly closed the door.

'Henri, where is Le Comte? What are you doing here alone?'

'Le Comte has declined to return as he has some business to deal with in London, but he will be back as soon as he can.'

'For God's sake, Henri. Will you tell me what on earth is going on?'

'I can't Anya, until I have given a letter to Wilhelm from Le Comte, which explains his absence. Can you get me an interview with him quickly?'

'What in God's name have you two been up to in London? Come with me. The King was at breakfast ten minutes ago.'

Henri followed her to the dining room and as they walked in, Marie and Charles were just leaving. 'I just need a word with the King and then I will catch up with you later,' he said to them.

Anya approached the King and asked if he would speak to Henri in private, urgently. He nodded and left his table, motioning for Henri to follow him to his suite. He went over to the large oak desk and pulled a chair up in front of it for Henri to sit on.

'Henri, you were commissioned to release Napoleon into exile in London, along with Le Comte. Did you succeed in your mission?'

'Yes, sire but Le Comte declined to return yet as he has a mission of his own to pursue. He asked me to give you this letter to explain.' He pulled the letter from his bag and handed it to the King. His dog Fritz came over to give Henri a lick of welcome.

Your Majesty and my beloved Uncle Wilhelm (three times removed),

I beg your indulgence to allow me to remain in London a while longer to pursue the hand in marriage of a 22-year-old German widow, with two French daughters. I have fallen madly in love with her but need some time to negotiate with her French family to allow me to marry her and take her and her daughters to Bavaria. The situation is further complicated by her French husband having been killed by German troops at the Battle of Beaumont. As you will appreciate, this is going to prove a difficult task and I would welcome your prayers to help me reach a successful conclusion, and one which allows me to return alive.

If you need an advisor for the peace treaty in my absence, may I recommend Henri Croizette, who has mastered the art of always looking on the dark side and would be able to predict any disadvantages long before they became a reality? I admit he has done his best to counsel me on taking a wife so quickly and suggested I wait six months, but I regret sire, I cannot wait.

I would be honoured if you would consider walking my future wife down the aisle at our wedding, which I hope we can arrange on my return to Versailles. Please would you ask Anya to arrange the paperwork for me to take Mathilde, Countess von Brixenhof (formerly Courvoisier) and her two daughters, Brigitte (4) and Veronique (2) Courvoisier, back to Germany? Could she also arrange export and import papers for Perseus, a Barbary stallion aged eight, formerly owned by Napoleon III? Perhaps if she is struggling for a category she could list him under "spoils of war" and pursue his paperwork at the French stud.

I hope to be back with you soon.

Your devoted nephew,
Comte Hans von Brixenhof.

Henri watched the King's expression change from incredulity to anger as he read through the letter. He scowled at Henri after he had read the content.

'And you did nothing to stop the idiot? Has he gone stark raving mad?'

'Your Majesty, I did my best to try and dissuade him from such an impetuous decision, but I failed miserably.'

'He seriously wants to marry the ex-wife of a Frenchman killed in battle by our troops and take her and her two daughters back to Bavaria as Countess von Brixenhof?'

'I am afraid so sire, but she is herself German and was raised in London at the English court and is a model of decorum.'

'But her husband only died three months ago, so why is she so desperate to marry Le Comte?'

'I did pose that very same question to the lady myself and it appears she has fallen for him as quickly as he has fallen for her and just wants a quiet life to rear her children and recoup some happiness in her life.'

'You mean she saw an opportunity and grabbed it with both hands. Hans is normally a sensible fellow with his head screwed on and least likely to be conned, particularly by a woman. There is something else going on here Henri, which you are not telling me. I can assure you I will not sanction this marriage until I know exactly what is going on, so you had better sing like a French canary or I will get Bismarck to have Le Comte and Madame Courvoisier and her children thrown into prison as soon as they set foot in France.'

'Your Majesty, there is nothing untoward going on, other than two people falling in love. They are both aware that the timing is inappropriate and that Le Comte is going to have a hard task to convince her in-laws to let her marry him, which is why he wanted to stay on and fight for her hand.'

'Why has he fallen hook, line and sinker in love with an unsuitable woman in less than two weeks?'

'I cannot say Your Majesty, other than that I saw it happen in the same way with my sister and Charles. I have never been in love myself, so I cannot dispute their claims.'

'Rubbish, there is something untoward going on here. Jesus, she hasn't been one of the Prince of Wales' mistresses, has she?'

'No sire, I made enquiries on that score and she has an honourable reputation at court and was nowhere near the prince as she left to marry when just eighteen. Her husband Ralf oversaw their family's merchant business in Jerusalem and she moved there straight after the wedding. Both children were born over there.'

'So, Hans has lost his brain and is thinking with his balls.'

'A comment I made to him personally and he admitted to being smitten.'

'So, he has sampled the goods already and can't remove himself from her charms? What is your appraisal of the situation then, Henri?'

'Provided it is true love, not lust, then I wish them all the best and think he is a very lucky man.'

'I can't see her family allowing this match as they would lose control over their grandchildren.'

'But sire, these are girls not boys and would not have had an influence in the family business. Had they been boys then there would likely have been considerable objection from the family. Hans has no desire to deny them their French heritage or family; he intends them to have contact with their grandparents.'

'Well we will have to wait and see how good his negotiating skills are, but it appears to me that he will be paying a very high price to wed his Jezebel. I dread to think what his mother will have to say when he arrives back in Bavaria with a complete family.'

Henri was summarily dismissed and as he left the room, he considered he had done well not to be consigned to a gaol cell and was grateful he had not had to face Bismarck's anger over Le Comte, which was bound to follow soon.

He went back down to Anya's office but was advised that she had gone into Paris with Bismarck, for meetings. He saw Charles painting in the Hall of Mirrors, so he went over to chat to him. He told him what Le Comte had done, and he roared with laughter when he explained Mathilde's link with Jerusalem. Charles assured him that the delights of Middle Eastern women were well renowned. He had enjoyed the hospitality of Moorish women when he had been in Spain, at an impressionable age. Henri admitted he was intrigued and decided that if ever he got the chance, he would investigate Jerusalem himself.

oOo

Later that evening, Henri had just switched his light off in his bedroom when he heard the door open, and someone entered. He had deliberately left his door unlocked as Anya had arrived late for dinner with Bismarck and he had hoped she would join him later.

Anya came into the darkened room and said, 'Are you awake, my little musketeer D'Artagnan?'

'Of course, I am, Anya – ready and waiting for your presence. Would you like help undressing?'

'Yes, I will need help with my gown.'

Henri pulled the covers back and leapt naked from the bed to assist her undressing. This was complemented by many kisses from him as each new area of her body was exposed.

'I will postpone my questions about Le Comte until after you have made passionate love to me.'

Henri laughed, swept her into his arms and deposited her on the bed and swung himself on top of her. Their passion inflamed, they celebrated their reunion. Afterwards, Anya lay next to him, running her fingers through his hair. 'So, what did you find intriguing about London?'

'Probably the reaction of women to me speaking

English with a French accent. It certainly had more impact than Le Comte speaking English with a German accent.'

'No doubt, D'Artagnan, it opened many doors for you!'

'Yes, it got me into Buckingham Palace as well as several ladies' bedrooms. It is not true that the English are shy and reserved; I found they welcomed me with open arms and legs!'

'Henri, you are incorrigible. Is that why you took your eye off Le Comte and allowed him to get into this mess in the first place?'

'No, I could not have prevented him from falling for Mathilde. He crumbled into a lovesick fool and chased her around Hyde Park like a stag in rut.'

'Ah, Henri you do have a wonderful command of language as well as mastery of the art of sex. Those English girls have me to thank for your prowess as a lover.'

'Well, you were the one who took it on yourself to be my tutor and told me countless times not to fall in love with you.'

'You know you have a special place in my heart, D'Artagnan and always will do. Now tell me about Mathilde; is she intent on snaring herself a German count for the money and position? And why so soon after losing her French husband?'

Henri went to get a bottle of cognac and two glasses, brought them back to the bed and proceeded to tell her exactly what Le Comte had got up to in

London.

She put her arm round his neck and drew his face down to kiss her and they explored each other's mouths for several minutes. Before he could move further down her body, Anya asked, 'What time did you get back to Paris, Henri?'

'I took the overnight ferry from Dover on Tuesday night and then blagged a lift up to Paris with a wine merchant from Calais, who had an empty cart and a team of four horses. He dropped me at the Tuileries Palace at 8 a.m. this morning and I took a hansom cab back here.'

'Really, D'Artagnan? That does surprise me!'

'But why?'

'Well, when Bismarck and I got into Paris at 10 a.m. this morning we were hailed with the news that one of our colonels had been shot heading out on patrol at 7 a.m. this morning, from the Paris barracks where you were stationed before the invasion.'

'Well, what has that got to do with me?'

'He was killed by a sniper using a chassepot French rifle, hitting him directly in the left eye as he trotted away from the barracks. Members of his troop reported that they heard no shot and the only cover was from trees 100 yards away on the opposite side of the road… and nobody else was targeted.' She sat up and switched the bedside light on, observing Henri's face very carefully.

'What possible connection can this incident have with me?'

'The officer was Colonel Dittmar.'

'I don't know anyone by that name!'

'But your brother-in-law will remember him well, considering he was the man who inflicted the whip marks on his body.'

'Are you seriously suggesting Charles murdered him? He was here at Versailles at the time of his death.'

'No, he didn't kill him, but both you and I know who did. There is only one person capable of carrying out such a daring assassination and I am lying right next to him.'

'Anya, I wasn't even in Paris by 7 a.m. and even I would baulk at taking on a troop of Germans.'

'But you didn't target anyone else, did you? Only Dittmar was killed.'

'Judging by his infamy and history of downright cruelty there would have been several Frenchmen whom he tortured besides Charles. In fact, I believe he was responsible for the blow to Courbet's head with a rifle butt. Perhaps you should be looking at *his* whereabouts yesterday morning. Or, perhaps you don't need to because you were in his bed last night anyway.'

Henri parried her hand as she attempted to slap his face. He pushed her back onto the pillow and sat astride her, pinning her arms behind her back.

'Bastard, arrogant lying Frenchmen, you are all the same. Lies pour out of your mouth like a river in full flow. Courbet is the same. Half of Paris saw him blow up the Vendôme Fountain and he still denies he had anything to do with it and suddenly, all the witnesses seem to have disappeared.'

'That's because Courbet was striking a blow for the French Republicans and they consider him a hero now.'

'What's your excuse then D'Artagnan, do you consider yourself a hero too? You promised us that you would not cause any trouble and you have murdered one of our officers.'

'He wasn't worthy of being an officer. He was a cruel and evil bastard and you should not have allowed him the freedom to do what he did. He should never have overseen prisoners and surely, this proves that. Charles cannot have been the only man he abused. He also attacked the young lad in Charles's troop who subsequently died from his wounds at Lille. Perhaps Bismarck should take more care parading around Paris as he does.'

'For God's sake, Henri. Are you threatening Bismarck now?'

'No, of course not, just warning you that there is obviously an assassin out there who has killed once and could kill again.'

'God forbid Henri, you have the cheek of the devil himself!'

'But I'm someone you find difficult to resist Anya, because we both court danger and intrigue.'

He bent down and kissed her passionately on her lips as she twisted to try and get her arms out of his grip. However, he soon found that her resistance faded.

43

Whilst Henri had been in London, Charles and Marie had been to their home with a working party of servants, to clean it ready for their return. Anya had organised this as Bismarck agreed that they could be released in the next few weeks. Charles had also taken Marie into Paris and showed her the devastation the war had caused. They visited the fountain in the Luxembourg Gardens where he had presented her with the engagement ring on bended knee. Although the fountain was still standing, it had been damaged by flying shrapnel during the bombing. Marie was visibly shocked by what she saw. When they went to where the Hôtel De Ville had once stood, Marie dissolved into tears and wept openly in Charles's arms. Charles knew that she would need time to take in the devastation the war had brought to Paris, particularly as she had not been there when it happened. Thankfully, his studio was unaffected, but some areas nearby had been hit. Food was at last getting through and food shops were beginning to re-open, but it would be a long time before the city was open for business as usual. Some areas would have to be demolished and redesigned and built from scratch.

Charles had doubts about whether Marie was mentally strong enough yet to take on the challenge of going back to a normal lifestyle. Ideally, he would have loved to have taken her and Marie-Ann to Rome for a long holiday to give her more time to recover, but he needed to get back to work and re-establish his teaching. She would not want to go alone to Rome unless her parents were there – then, that might be an option. However, after nearly losing them in the war he was in no rush to be parted from either of them again.

They had found letters at the house from potential students and Antonio had written from Rome three months ago to advise that he and Jacques were safe and well and would return to Paris whenever Charles needed them. He was grateful that he had buried a small chest containing cash at the farm soon after the siege started as he knew cash would be desperately required should they survive the war. He had money in the bank but knew that reclaiming it after the war might not be an easy task. He had some cash and Marie's sapphire jewellery and the Napoleon emeralds in the safe at his studio. He had no idea whether the owner of the house was still alive and where they stood legally regarding the rent, so this would require sorting out quickly.

He was sure that when word got around that they were back in occupation of the house he would be able to hire a groom and cook, but he would have to go to Marie's parents' chateau to trace Jeanette who had been a nursemaid/maid for Marie. He intended to go there soon as it was only twenty minutes' ride from Versailles.

oOo

The next day, Le Comte returned to Versailles with Mathilde and the children. Henri was relieved that he had arrived as Bismarck had given him some tasks to do which Le Comte would normally have carried out, which had put him under pressure. He had been included in some of the peace treaty talks and his opinion had been sought on issues to do with administration.

Anya was the first to meet them after the long journey. The children were tired and hungry, so they had some lunch and retired to their room for a sleep. Formal introductions were to be made at dinner.

Le Comte sent a soldier to find Henri down at the stables and after he had settled Mathilde and the children in their room, he met with Henri and Anya.

Henri said, 'Well, how did it go? How on earth did you persuade the Courvoisier family to consider you as a father for their grandchildren, never mind removing them to live in Germany?'

'Well it wasn't easy but once they realised that I did not intend to cut all ties with their blood family, we came to an agreement. I think it would have been harder if they had been boys as they would have expected them to have a share in the family business.

Madame Courvoisier was the peacemaker as she is fond of Mathilde and wanted her to find happiness again. Ralf's two brothers were in favour as well, as it gave them an opportunity to have their own current and future children considered as heirs to the business as they were unlikely to want the girls to feature in the succession of the business. Basically, I agreed to keep in contact with the family and bring the girls back to Paris or London to visit them and when they reach a suitable age, they will stay with them. They agreed to provide dowries for them on marriage and I agreed to educate and provide for them.'

Anya said, 'Oh Hans, are you really sure this is going to work? Your family is not going to be overjoyed at this marriage. They could make it very difficult for Mathilde, especially if you continue your military service. She will have nobody to protect her when you are not there.'

Le Comte sighed. 'I know. We have discussed this problem, but Mathilde is brave enough to deal with it as, when and if it arises. She knows whatever she does, she will be considered a thief and interloper.'

Anya says, 'But does she realise how difficult it can be to overcome family prejudice? I suffered a huge backlash from my in-laws when I announced I was leaving my children to go to war. They wanted me committed to an asylum as an unfit mother but thankfully, my husband stood by me.'

Le Comte asked Henri, 'How did the King take the news?'

'Well, he was not best pleased, to put it bluntly and you will have to use all your charm and negotiating skills to win him over to the idea of you marrying her so soon.'

Anya said, 'He wants to see you alone, so I suggest you do it sooner rather than later. Bismarck has agreed the Durans can be released to their home in the next few weeks as they are close enough to observe from Versailles. This will make it more difficult for you as Marie-Ann will be going and she would have acted as a playmate for Mathilde's children and Marie would have been a staunch ally for Mathilde and would understand her plight.'

'Oh God, I had better go and see the King and make my peace with him. Although, God knows why I should be apologising for falling in love. Surely, it is my business – no one else's. Mathilde is German after all, not French, so why should the King object?'

Anya replied, 'We are all concerned that you do the right thing, Hans. We would hate it to go wrong as the repercussions are for life. You may not be a prince and heir to the throne, but you are a count and the last thing the King needs is scandal in his own court when he returns home.'

Henri left as Anya took Le Comte to see the King and went in search of his sister. He found her and Charles playing the piano in the music room while Marie-Ann was having her afternoon nap.

Charles said, 'Henri, we could just do with your good tenor voice to sing a duet with Marie. However, you look like a man on a mission. So how can we help you?'

Henri replied, 'Le Comte has returned with Mathilde and her children and I was hoping you two would befriend her as she is going to have opposition from the German side as they see her as an interloper and a threat.'

Charles chuckled, 'She needs to speak to me. I am the expert at living with that role, as it was surely how I was depicted by your family when I asked for Marie's hand in marriage?'

'Not by me Charles, I have never doubted your love for my sister or hers for you. I just hope Mathilde is as genuine as you.'

Marie said, 'Have no fear, Henri. I can appreciate what all the fuss is about, but I am delighted she is coming with two children as it will be good for Marie-Ann to have other children around.'

oOo

They assembled for dinner in the salon where the introductions were to be made. Marie-Ann had come with them to meet the family before her nursemaid took her back to bed. A receiving line formed with the King and Bismarck at the top, followed by the Duran family. Le Comte and Mathilde appeared, with Brigitte holding her mother's hand and Le Comte carrying Veronique.

Charles watched with interest as Le Comte introduced Mathilde to the King and she swept into a dutiful curtsey. Brigitte, clinging tightly to her hand, then followed her example. The King gave her his hand to rise and as she stood up, their eyes met for the first time. Charles saw the King smile at her and then bend down to Brigitte and chat to her. He turned to Le Comte and touched Veronique on her cheek; she shyly hid her face in Le Comte's shoulder. As Le Comte introduced Mathilde to him he took her hand and kissed it, giving her a broad smile and said, 'Enchanté madame, your children are so beautiful.'

Marie, determined to make her welcome, kissed Mathilde on both cheeks and then Marie-Ann was introduced to Brigitte who promptly asked her in French if she wanted to meet Fritz and took her by the hand to the rug, where he was having a nap. Charles excused himself and went with her to ensure the dog did not take exception to being awoken from his nap. However, Fritz had developed a close relationship with Marie-Ann and as she stroked his head, he licked her hand and allowed Brigitte to stoke his ear. The two nursemaids allowed the children to play as the diners moved into the dining room. Veronique was handed over to the nursemaid but was interested in what her sister was doing with this big dog and Marie-Ann.

Le Comte and Mathilde joined the Durans' table with Henri, rather than joining the King's table, just to make it easier for Mathilde to get to know them. Marie soon took control of the situation and chatted away to Mathilde as if they were already lifelong friends. Le Comte sighed with relief and gave Henri a smile.

While the ladies were chatting, Charles managed to quietly enquire about how Le Comte's meeting with the King had gone. Apparently, he had been told in no uncertain terms that he was not to contemplate sharing a bed with his fiancée until the wedding had taken place.

Charles smiled and said, 'And do you intend to comply with the King's orders?'

Le Comte replied, 'I certainly do. I need him on my side as much as possible to smooth the path when we return to Germany… and my military future lies in his hands.'

oOo

After the meal, Charles and Marie retired to their room, where Marie-Ann was soundly asleep. As they settled into bed, Charles asked Marie what her first impression of Mathilde had been.

'I don't think she is the wolf in sheep's clothing that people expected her to be. She is understandably nervous of her reception here, but she is enamoured of Le Comte and he of her. He was squeezing her hand under the table and doing his utmost to encourage her to relax. As a mother, she will want to do the best for her children's future, but I don't think she is just grasping after the money and lifestyle. She could have stayed in England and found a new husband as she has connections at the English court and there would have been plenty of men pleased to have her as a wife and future mother to their offspring. She is fluent in all three languages and although tutored at the English court it wasn't in history, politics or economics – it was in languages, music, art, court etiquette and overseeing a household. Traditionally, Queen Victoria educated her sons differently to her daughters as she only expected them to become wives. Maybe I should have followed that path?'

'I doubt you would have taken to some of the subjects dear, but I am convinced you would have taught yourself history and politics anyway.'

'I should have studied medicine in more detail as it would have helped my nursing skills in Lille. I like Mathilde, and her daughters are adorable, especially Brigitte. She will be such a companion for Marie-Ann whilst we are here at Versailles.'

After dinner, Le Comte escorted Mathilde back to her room and kissed the sleeping girls goodnight. He gave Mathilde a cuddle and praised her handling of her first day and she admitted she was thankful for Marie's kindness. He kissed her passionately and then reluctantly, left her room and went to join Anya and Henri in his room.

When he arrived, Anya gave him a big hug and said, 'Oh, Hans you really don't mess around, do you? It was Henri I told to marry a widow, not you! Are you sure about taking this path? Do you both really love each other enough to cope with the challenges ahead?'

'Yes, I love her to bits and I don't think she is after me for my money. Please Anya, I need you to believe me and help get the wedding organised. I do not want to wait until we are back in Germany as it would put us both under intense pressure from my family. The King will meet both of us tomorrow to discuss our wedding, so I need you on my side.'

Anya hugged him again. 'Of course, I will do everything I can to help but I care about you so much and I just don't want to see you hurt.'

Le Comte turned to Henri, 'Your sister was lovely with Mathilde and the children, Henri. Do let her know how grateful I am.'

Henri replied, 'Sure I will, and Charles has offered to speak to her about living under a cloud of family suspicion as he has had experience of it, particularly where my mother was concerned. I never doubted his motives and I knew Marie was smitten with him on the day they first met; she was determined to marry him, and he never stood a chance of escape. It is impossible to change Marie's mind once she has made it up.'

Anya said, 'Your sister is a very lucky woman to have Charles Duran as a husband, but I think she knows that now. He has treated her with such love and compassion and nursed her back to health, both physically and mentally.'

Le Comte said, 'Well, I will leave you in peace as I am shattered after travelling from London with my new family. I am experiencing a very fast learning curve in how to cope with tired and hungry children.'

oOo

The next morning, Charles took advantage of Marie being pre-occupied with Mathilde and the children and joined Courbet painting outside by the fountain. They had a wonderful time chatting as they worked, recalling their time on the barricades. Courbet told him that Anya had prevented him being handed over to the French authorities but knew that once the Germans had withdrawn, the new government might still pursue him.

Marie showed Mathilde to the music room and they amused the children, playing songs on the piano and reciting nursery rhymes. Marie looked after both children when Mathilde went with Le Comte for an audience with the King. She was gone for over an hour and when she returned, stress clearly showed on her face. Le Comte had to report to Bismarck, so she revealed some of what was discussed. The good news was that the King had agreed to support their marriage, but Anya had been tasked with dealing with the clergy and the German administrative paperwork. Thankfully, Mathilde had not taken French nationality on marriage – she had retained her German nationality. However, it would take at least a fortnight to arrange the wedding as the French would have to agree to the marriage taking place at Versailles.

They chatted about what Mathilde intended to wear and they agreed that a full wedding dress would be out of the question as she was a widow, but Marie assured her that they would find a suitable dress for her in Paris and matching dresses for the three girls as bridesmaids. Mathilde assumed Le Comte would wear his dress uniform. Marie promised to speak to Anya to see if she could arrange a trip into Paris and see if Charles Worth had reopened.

44

Five days later, Anya arranged a trip into Paris by carriage for Mathilde, Marie and Charles with Le Comte, Henri and two German cavalry escorts. Charles was going to his studio to prepare for his return to work, with the help of Henri, and the ladies were going to Charles Worth's salon.

The day before, Mathilde had measured all three girls, so they could find some dresses that would fit them. Mathilde had discussed her dress with Le Comte and they had decided she would wear an evening dress, which could then be worn after the wedding at the Prussian court. She would have to wear a veil to comply with church etiquette but could probably get away with a waist-length, pure silk veil. Anya had arranged for two nursemaids to care for and amuse the children whilst they were away for the day.

Mathilde was excited to be going into Paris but was mortified at the destruction she witnessed when they drove into the centre. Marie was hopeful that Charles Worth would be there and open for business but was determined to find something suitable for the occasion, regardless. Henri and Le Comte led the carriage from the front, with the two escort soldiers at the rear.

When they arrived at Worth's, the shop appeared still closed but Henri spotted some movement within and hammered on the door. A seamstress came to open the door and Henri was relieved to hear that Charles Worth was at the shop. He was hastily summoned, and Charles accompanied the ladies into the salon. They briefly discussed what they wanted, and Worth said he would try to accommodate them but had limited stock available. Once certain that the task could be achieved, Henri and Charles departed to the studio. Charles was delighted to be given Perseus to ride as he had not had the pleasure of riding him yet. They left an anxious Le Comte with the two ladies, concerned about how much this jaunt was going to cost him.

Thankfully, Mathilde was tall and slim so would have no problem fitting into any sample sizes he had in stock. Mathilde had agreed with Le Comte that she wanted him to approve her dress to ensure she was not making any faux pas in front of the King. There were no models in residence, but he suggested that after they had selected any suitable gowns, Marie should model them and when they had a shortlist then Mathilde should try them on. One of his seamstresses prepared coffee and Le Comte, Mathilde and Worth awaited Marie's modelling of five or six possible gowns, on the elegant Louis XIV settee. They discussed each gown individually and discovered they all had the same favourite. It was a mint green, silk ball gown with a feathered neckline, puff sleeves and a crinoline skirt and train. Marie looked good in it as it was finely cut on the waist and bodice and accentuated her slim waist.

Mathilde tried it on and with her fair skin and long, blonde hair the mint green looked stunning and accentuated her matching green eyes. It was also perfect in length and fit and would need no alteration. The neckline was not too low, and Worth suggested a cream, silk-trimmed chemise showing above the neckline, which would give extra modesty if required. Mathilde loved the dress and so did not even bother trying on any more dresses. Le Comte was content with how it looked but was worried about the price. Worth left them in search of a suitable silk veil to cover her shoulders, and a tiara. Marie reassured Le Comte she would do the bargaining on price if he wanted; he gratefully accepted. Worth returned, beaming with delight as he had located a pale tourmaline and opal tiara with a matching necklace, earrings and a bracelet. Marie seized the tiara in excitement and delight and gave it to the seamstress to pin the veil to it. Marie quickly twisted Mathilde's hair into a full chignon and then put the tiara in place. A seamstress appeared with some plain, cream silk shoes in Mathilde's size. Mathilde then put the remaining jewellery and shoes on and the effect was stunning. As she looked at herself in the mirror, she was overcome with emotion. Le Comte approached her on the catwalk, lifted her down into his arms and kissed her.

'Mathilde, you look so beautiful. I want to carry you off and marry you now.' The rest of the onlookers smiled and laughed to see such emotion from Le Comte.

Marie asked Worth for a sketchpad. They went to the desk and Marie sketched an outline for the bridesmaids' dresses in cream silk, with a mint green sash and feathers on the neckline, with princess skirts to the knee for Veronique and Marie-Ann and a full-length hooped skirt for Brigitte.

Mathilde said, 'Oh Marie, they are delightful. What an eye for style and elegance you have.'

Worth replied, 'I can get these made up by next week and know a shop where I can obtain the children's shoes as well.'

Marie dealt with the price negotiations for the dresses and accessories and secured a substantial discount. When they got back into the carriage to go to Charles's studio, Le Comte thanked her profusely for all her help. When they arrived, Marie suggested Le Comte take Mathilde for a walk in the Luxembourg Gardens for an hour while she supervised Charles and Henri cleaning up the studio. Le Comte hesitated but she shooed them away.

'Off you go together; you need time with each other to discuss your wedding day.'

That night, when Marie and Charles retired to bed, Charles noted that Marie was very attentive and in the mood for love and he was delighted to let her set the pace and achieve her desire.

Afterwards, as they lay together in each other's arms, Marie said, 'Charles, I have a suggestion to make about going home.' Charles, instantly alert, knew that her compliant behaviour had been leading to something and waited silently for her to continue. 'I was wondering whether, when we move back home, Mathilde and the children could join us as it doesn't appear they will be returning to Germany immediately. Marie-Ann is coming on verbally in leaps and bounds since she has had other children to socialise with, and with Mathilde available to look after her I would be able to spend more time at the studio.'

Charles laughed, 'You little vixen, Marie. How long have you been planning this with Mathilde? Don't try lying either; even though we are in the dark, I know you too well and you can't get away with lying to me. I can see the advantages of having them stay with us, both for you and Marie-Ann and because I am delighted to see you getting back to your old calculating self, how could I deny you?'

'Oh, Charles that would be wonderful and I am sure Le Comte would contribute towards the cost as well.'

'No doubt you have already discussed it with him; I know what women on a mission are capable of. I am just delighted you are ready to go home and if their presence will help, then all the better.'

Marie snuggled up to him, kissed him passionately and said, 'Yes, I think it's time we had another baby as I am desperate to give you the son you crave.'

Charles ran his hand through her hair. 'All in good time, precious one; I need to ensure we have some income first.'

'But it takes time to have a baby. I'm not eighteen anymore, you know. Just let's start trying and see how long it takes?'

Charles kissed her nose and mouth and said, 'Oh Marie, how can I ever deny you anything, my love? May I remind you that you probably conceived within three days of our wedding and at twenty-two, you are hardly likely to be barren yet. However, I can't deny I would dearly love a son, but there's no guarantee of getting one.'

'Oh, yes there is. Le Comte knows how to influence the sex of breeding foals; we just need to carry out the same technique and we will be blessed.'

Charles roared with laughter. 'Oh sweetheart, I do love you so. Don't let me ever hear you complaining of being a brood mare again then!'

'He told Henri how it worked when he pointed out that Mathilde had only produced girls and may not give him an heir.'

'Oh, Marie then tell me what delights I am in for in pursuit of siring an heir?'

'Well actually, it's more about abstention as opposed to frequent coupling. We are to only cohabit prior to ovulation so I will have to keep a careful track of my cycle, which has at least settled into a monthly rhythm now.'

Charles leant over her, shaking his finger and said, 'I don't think I can comply with those restrictions. I like sex as and when the mood takes me, not just when it's right for your breeding cycle.'

Marie hit back with, 'Well, there are other ways of dealing with your desire, which I am more than willing to carry out.'

Charles grinned and said, 'Perhaps I should seek another partner when the desire takes me, and it is not convenient for your breeding cycle?'

Marie turned on him angrily. 'Don't you even think about that option or you will find you haven't the tools to perform at all.'

He gathered her into his arms. 'Sweetheart, I was joking, but I'm pleased you retaliated with such anger. Of course, I will do as you wish. You know I love you and will do anything to make you happy. I never sought another woman while we were apart and now I have you home, why would I stray from my Goddess Diana, especially when she wants to provide me with a son?'

oOo

After two weeks of frantic preparation, Le Comte and Mathilde's wedding day dawned. Anya had performed miracles and persuaded the local priest to officiate at the wedding, accompanied by his choir and an organist. Marie had worked with Mathilde and Le Comte in selecting some of their favourite pieces of music and enlisted Anya's help in finding a small chamber orchestra from Paris. She had then cajoled people into submission to sing the various pieces. Charles had been granted his wish to play the organ and had been rehearsing 'Pachelbel's Canon'. Marie had rehearsed 'Where'er you walk' from Handel's oratorio *Semele;* this was Le Comte's favourite. She had finally persuaded a reluctant but very competent Henri to sing along with Charles to 'The Pearl Fishers' Duet' from Bizet's opera. Marie and Mathilde were working together on the flowers and church decorations. Marie had also been teaching the girls the hymn 'All Things Bright and Beautiful' in English, for them to sing with her and Charles as a surprise. Thankfully, Veronique and Brigitte had so far kept it a secret from their mother. The music room at Versailles had come alive over the last two weeks with practising and had raised Marie's spirits as she enjoyed singing and coaching her pupils. She was delighted with Henri and Charles's duet as both had superb voices, with Charles's rich, warm baritone blending with Henri's higher tenor voice. The children had been instructed in their bridesmaid's duties, with Veronique and Marie-Ann sprinkling lavender as they came down the aisle and Brigitte following, carrying the wedding rings tied to a cushion.

The King had been passing the chapel during one of the secret rehearsals and observed the children being coached down the aisle by Marie. He slipped in at the back to observe. He was enchanted when he heard their sweet young voices singing 'All Things Bright and Beautiful,' unaccompanied but executed in perfect pitch. His admiration for Marie Duran increased tenfold.

Marie and Mathilde decorated the church the day before, so they could concentrate on making the girl's posies of lilies of the valley and cream roses on the wedding morning. Mathilde had chosen to have a hand tied bouquet of cream calla lilies entwined with lilies of the valley. The men were having similar buttonholes.

The ceremony was timed for midday that day, followed by a wedding reception lunch. Marie had insisted that the couple should go to their chateau for their wedding night, so they would be completely alone; the nursemaids would look after the children overnight. As the King had commented to Le Comte that he had already had the honeymoon before the wedding, Marie was determined that they should be left alone without the children for at least one night.

They would be moving back home later in the week, along with Mathilde and the children, and Le Comte would join them at weekends and during the week whenever it was possible.

Marie had chosen to wear the black and white dress she wore at Notre Dame when she had performed at the Christmas concert before Napoleon. She had brought it back from her chateau on a cleaning visit.

The children were bursting with excitement and bouncing around on the morning of the wedding; Marie was grateful for the nursemaids' help so that she could concentrate on dressing Mathilde. Worth had copied Marie's design for the dresses to the letter and they looked adorable in their cream silk dresses edged with mint green feathers and a long bow at the waist.

Mathilde was feeling nervous and just let Marie dress her as she was all fingers and thumbs. Marie had expertly put her long blonde hair into a tight bun and carefully put the dress over her head and smoothed the silk down over the crinoline.

As Marie fastened the back of the dress, Brigitte ran over, put her arms round Mathilde and said, 'Mama, you look beautiful; the dress matches your eyes.'

Not to be outdone, Veronique ran over. 'No, she looks like a princess.'

Marie responded quickly, 'When Mama marries today she will become a countess.'

Veronique said, 'Will Papa be at the wedding?'

Marie saw the shocked look on Mathilde's face and quickly scooped Veronique up into her arms. 'No sweetheart, Papa is up in heaven with God now, but he will be looking down and smiling to see his beautiful girls help Mama marry Le Comte and is pleased you have a new Papa to care for you.'

She took Brigitte over to the nursemaids and Marie-Ann and left them, returning quickly to

Mathilde who was desperately trying to control her tears. She flung her arms around her and said, 'Don't worry, Mathilde. She can't be expected to understand that her daddy is dead – she wasn't trying to hurt you.' Marie passed her a handkerchief and picked the tiara up to pin it in her hair.

Downstairs, the few guests were arriving, mainly consisting of German officers and staff. Charles and Henri, dressed in their French dress uniforms, looked very smart and Le Comte was pacing up and down in his German dress uniform like a caged lion. They had ten minutes to go before they had to take their places in the chapel, so Henri made Le Comte stand still and attempted to distract him and Charles with some news.

'Yesterday, I had a long meeting with Marshal McMahon and my cavalry commander and I hammered out a deal for my future job. We have agreed that I am to be in overall charge of the horses at the barracks in Paris and they insisted on elevating my rank to Capitan, but I am not to have my own troop as they want the flexibility to send me on covert missions for the government. Thanks to you, Le Comte, persuading your side to leave us with your horses stabled at the barracks, we will at least have some horses to ride. The cavalry troops held in the Paris prison camp will be released next week and allowed to return to the barracks and then eventually, we will be joined by other troops imprisoned elsewhere, so I will be leaving Versailles then too.'

Le Comte said, 'Good, I am pleased you have been able to negotiate a hands-on job as you would not take kindly to an enclosed office job and with your talents, you should be out pursuing them.'

45

The clergy procession was gathering so Le Comte and Henri set off down the long aisle to take their seats. A flurry of noise announced the bridal party descending the elaborate staircase and Charles looked up and saw the bride for the first time. She looked magnificent; her skin and hair were highlighted by the delicate mint tones of the dress. Marie followed, in charge of the excited bridesmaids and Charles' heart skipped a beat when he saw Marie-Ann. The realisation that he could have lost both in the ravages of war, struck him hard. Brigitte with her dark hair and olive skin tone looked more like Marie-Ann and echoed her French heritage, whereas Veronique was the image of her mother.

The King came to his side and whispered, 'Please God that this marriage will work as it will be impossible to untangle it if it doesn't.'

Charles replied quietly, 'I don't think you need worry, Your Majesty. They are bringing different skills to the union and they are both in love.'

Marie was reminding the children of their duties and gave them the lavender baskets and Brigitte, the ring cushion. She then came in front of Mathilde and pulled the top layer of the veil over her face and arranged the folds over her shoulders and waist.

Charles stepped forward and took Mathilde's hand and kissed it saying, 'You look divine, my dear, and every ounce a countess.'

Mathilde gasped, 'Thank you so much Charles, that compliment has given me the courage to go down the aisle.'

Marie gave one final set of instructions to her charges, then she and Charles swept down the aisle, hand in hand.

The King approached Mathilde and she swept into a deep curtsey. He bent and took her hand. 'You look beautiful, my dear and may I be the first to welcome you into my family.'

The strains of Wagner's 'Bridal Chorus,' sung by the choir, drifted through the chapel. Mathilde took three deep breaths, looked round and said to the children, 'Are you ready, girls?'

The King took her hand and they entered the chapel at a very sedate walk. She saw Le Comte and Henri turn around to watch her approaching and Le Comte gave her a huge, welcoming smile. As she halted at his elbow, Marie left her pew and ushered the bridesmaids into it, next to Charles. She then stepped in front of Mathilde and pulled back her veil and rearranged it to fall in a single fold like a Spanish mantilla, straight down her back. She then took her bouquet, retrieved the ring cushion from Brigitte, passed it to Henri and returned to her seat.

Le Comte leant over to Mathilde and whispered, 'You look so beautiful, my precious angel.' He brushed her shoulder with his lips, which resulted in a stern look from the King.

The marriage ceremony began, and Charles observed the sheer magnificence and opulence of this ethereal royal chapel. The amount of gold and jewels encrusted in the altar was priceless and the frescoes, murals, marble pillars and mosaics rivalled the Sistine Chapel. The small congregation only occupied the first ten pews on each side of the aisle and consisted of Le Comte's cavalry troop and officers. Charles could see that some of them were as impressed with the chapel as he was, and it had brought home to them how much they were missing their families. At the sight of the bridesmaids, one or two rubbed their eyes, thinking about their own families back home.

He revelled in the warmth that enveloped him, and his eye was caught by Courbet across the aisle. He was sitting with Anya and looked extremely uncomfortable. He kept glancing up to the royal gallery where the King used to sit, and he remembered their conversation when they had been in the chapel together and Courbet confessed he could both see and feel spirits when he entered holy places, which was why he did not attend church. He had no religious belief but had been brought up a Catholic as a child. However, the visions he saw as a young boy and the power of the spirits that he had encountered had terrified him and prevented him going into churches. Courbet had flatly refused to paint in the Versailles Chapel as he was genuinely terrified of what he could see and feel. He thought perhaps God was punishing Courbet for the damage to the Vendôme fountain.

Marie-Ann was sitting next to him and her attention had been diverted by the new dolls Marie had given each girl to play with during the service. He could sense she was about to speak so he picked up the doll and put its hands together in prayer and gave it back to her and whispered, 'Be quiet my little one, we are in church and you must be silent whilst the wedding ceremony takes place.'

The ceremony had now reached the vows stage and the blessing of the rings and Henri had just laid them on the priest's prayer book. Le Comte spoke his vows confidently, looking straight into Mathilde's eyes. She was struggling with her emotions and her voice cracked occasionally, but she completed them. After the blessing, the couple went through to the vestry to sign the register. Le Comte had insisted that as Mathilde had no family in attendance she should be represented by Marie, and the King would represent Le Comte. Marie had joked about how unbelievable it was to have her signature on the same page as a Prussian king at a wedding, held in the Palace of Versailles, for a German count. Only Marie and the King were going into the vestry, so the King bowed to her and then led her up to the altar, where they both knelt and were blessed by the priest.

Charles suddenly realised that he was left in charge of the children and thankfully, they were behaving. However, he had to make his way up to the organ as 'Pachelbel's Canon' was the first piece in the concert. He enlisted the assistance of Anya, left her in charge of the children and made his escape. He had no nerves or fear in playing this piece as he was so honoured to be playing it on the chapel's organ. He played it faultlessly and was amazed to receive applause as he made his way back and took a bow. He smiled encouragingly as Marie passed him to take up her position to sing Wagner's 'Where'er You Walk'. He watched, transfixed, as she sang it pitch perfectly, accompanied by the small orchestra. At last he could see signs of the confident young woman he married, whose spirit had nearly been crushed by a violent war. At last, her eyes sparkled, and he could hear the joy reflected in her voice at the realisation that she had broken out of the shell that had encased her spirit. As she finished, there was a moment's silence and then loud applause and as she stepped down from the altar steps to take her bow, Le Comte jumped up and hugged and kissed her and she blushed bright red. This made the German troops whoop with joy but ceased instantly when Bismarck turned and glared at them. As Marie came to the pew, Charles was ready to take his position with Henri, and Marie-Ann stood up and shouted, 'Tres belle, Mama.'

He could feel Henri's fear. He leant towards him and said, 'Henri, just treat this as if you are going into battle and you will triumph.'

The Pearl Fishers' Duet' was no simple piece to master; Henri was faced with an Italian tenor piece that would have challenged an experienced professional singer. However, he executed the duet as if he had been singing it all his life. As Charles realised Henri was coping, it lifted his performance and they finished to tumultuous applause and many a 'Bravo!' from the German troopers. They were delighted to have performed the French composer's song with such aplomb, to their German audience, in the heart of the French court.

Next, it was the bridesmaids' turn to shine. Mathilde and Le Comte watched transfixed as the three girls, with Marie and Charles for support, sang 'All Things Bright and Beautiful.' Charles was holding Marie-Ann's hand and having seen her parents perform, she had no qualms about joining in with them. Brigitte sang her heart out too. Veronique was a little nervous at first but, encouraged by Marie kneeling beside her, she sang with gusto. When they had finished there was uproar as the applause started and Mathilde and Le Comte came running up the steps and picked their daughters up and covered them in kisses. Charles picked Marie-Ann up, swung her round and gave her a kiss and then grabbed Marie in a bear hug. After several bows and more continuous applause, the wedding party formed a processional line. As the witnesses, the King and Marie led the procession, followed by the bride and groom and then the bridesmaids who were cheered by the troopers as they passed their pews.

They went into the Hall of Mirrors for a photo session and Charles pulled Marie to him and held her face in both his hands and said, 'You were sensational with your singing today. If music can heal the soul, then tell me you are now free from the horrors of war you have experienced.'

She looked deep into his eyes and said, 'Yes, Charles; at last I feel I want to move on and make the best life I can as a survivor, in honour of the memory of so many who lost their lives.' Tears ran down his cheeks as he hugged her and patted Marie-Ann on her shoulder. He felt so protective of his precious family and vowed to himself that they would never go hungry again.

Henri joined them and picked Marie-Ann up and tossed her in the air, catching her as she whooped with joy.

Charles said, 'Can I just say that your father would be so proud of you two today and it is such a shame he wasn't here to witness the exceptional performances you gave.'

Henri laughed, 'So the hours spent learning to play instruments and sing at a very young age have finally borne fruit, have they?'

'Yes, and what a time and place for you both to do it. We may have lost this war but both of you have covered yourself in glory and honour as far as France is concerned.'

After the photos were over, the King took Marie to one side and said, 'Marie Duran, you are an exceptionally talented woman. Napoleon said you were the star of Paris and now I can understand why he held you and your brother in such high esteem. To be so talented in so many different areas is outstanding. You directed the music and drilled the performers to perfection and delivered a wedding ceremony that I will never forget, never mind Hans and Mathilde. Thank you for making their day so enjoyable and special.'

Henri had been watching the photo shoot, leaning on one of the marble pillars and he suddenly sensed someone behind him and recognised the scent worn by Anya. She slipped her hand round the pillar, touched his hand and whispered.

'Now, my little musketeer with the voice of an angel, I will expect you to sing to me tonight when you make love to me.'

Henri laughed, 'Ah, but I don't think I can do both at the same time as there are too many senses involved.'

'Rubbish, Capitan Croizette – if you can ride into battle and kill with a single blow of an axe, you can surely sing and have sex at the same time.'

'But killing inflicts pain whereas making love requires maximum pleasure for both parties. I use all my senses: sight, hearing, touch, smell and taste when making love and these would be impaired if I had to sing as well. You wouldn't want to be short changed, would you?'

'Definitely not, D'Artagnan. See you later!'

oOo

The day before the Durans were to go home, at breakfast, Le Comte asked them to join him at the stables in riding attire as he wanted to show them a new horse. Charles and Marie assumed it was a new foal that had been born as he insisted Marie-Ann, Mathilde, Brigitte and Veronique were to join them too. They all changed into their riding gear and walked down to the stables and headed to the main yard. To their surprise Le Comte, Anya and Henri were there talking to the King. Several grooms were milling around and there was an air of excitement.

The King called them over and said, 'We thought you might like to see one of the rare breed mares from Napoleon's stud.' He signalled to a groom who ran to one of the stables and led out a beautiful, metallic cream coloured mare of around sixteen hands with a flaxen mane and tail, four white socks and two startling blue eyes, already tacked up carrying a side saddle.

Marie gasped in delight at the unusual colour and elegance of the mare, who whinnied and threw her head up as the groom trotted her past the assembled group and floated past in an extended trot.

'Oh, she is stunning. What breed is she? What an

unusual colour; it shimmers in the sunlight.'

Le Comte said, 'She is an Akhal-Teke mare aged eight years, a breed originating from Turkmenistan, lying between Uzbekistan and Afghanistan on the shores of the Caspian Sea. Their rare colour and thin skin was believed to have been selectively bred to make them invisible in the desert and they are descended from Arabs, crossed with one of the original Thoroughbred stallions, the Byerley Turk. She has bred four pure bred foals but last year, she failed to breed. We thought you would do us the honour of riding her before you go home.'

Marie was beaming with excitement. 'Oh, just try and stop me. Give me a leg up, quickly.'

Le Comte legged her up into the saddle while Henri held the mare and said, 'She lacks schooling, but she is an unbelievably smooth ride.' He then led her to the schooling arena and informed Marie that her name was Soraya. The group followed; Charles had to restrain Marie-Ann from getting too close as she wanted to ride her as well.

Marie carefully rode the mare at walk and trot around the school and then tried canter. Soraya had a long, elegant trot but also had a rounded, collected canter, which was very comfortable. Marie tried for some half pass or high school movements, but the mare had not been trained to that level. She brought her back to the gate and asked the King, 'Is there any particular reason why she failed to conceive last year?'

The King smiled, 'Not one the veterinarians can detect, but Napoleon instructed me that when you returned home, Soraya was to be his personal gift to you.'

'For me?' Marie shouted.

'Yes, he told me that your mare Favorit, the two horses Henri gave you as a wedding present and your Borzoi hounds had perished in the war and insisted that Soraya was to be given to you from the royal stud. He also gifted a Barbary stallion to your husband and a little Welsh Mountain pony gelding for Marie-Ann.'

They all turned as two grooms led out a striking bay stallion and a grey pony to the paddock.

Marie-Ann was jumping up and down shouting, 'Is that pony for me, Papa?'

As the groom led in the pony, Henri picked Marie-Ann up and swung her into the tiny saddle. 'Now, you have to sit still and listen carefully to me if you are going to own this precious pony called Snowy.' He then told the groom to walk Marie-Ann around the arena while he gave her instruction.

Charles mounted the stallion and the King said, 'He is an eight-year-old dark bay stallion called Mercury, a direct descendant of Napoleon I's horse Marengo. Napoleon III rode him on the battlefield when he wanted to remain inconspicuous to the enemy and fight alongside his men. He used Perseus to command his troops from the sidelines and to be seen by the enemy, but Mercury was battle trained and very quiet to handle in volatile situations.'

Charles rode Mercury round the paddock, quietly, to get to know him. After a few minutes' schooling he then joined Marie in the centre and stood close to her. Mercury showed no stallion tendencies as he surveyed the exquisite mare in front of him and apart from Soraya laying back her ears and pawing with her front leg in acknowledgement of his presence, they behaved perfectly.

Mathilde shouted, 'Oh, you two look so beautiful together; the contrast of the colours is startling.'

Henri called Marie-Ann and Snowy into the centre and stood her next to her father and Mercury. He handed the lead rein to Charles and said, 'I have checked, and he will lead the pony with no problem, so you can ride out together. Soraya will need a bit more experience as she is more highly strung.'

The King opened the gate and a groom entered, carrying a wriggling bundle of fur in his arms. He walked over to them and went to Marie-Ann, who shouted, 'A puppy!' She leant across the pony to stroke the puppy's head and the King said, 'And finally, Napoleon remembered Marie telling him about the St. Bernard dog you both fell in love with at your father's farm and insisted Marie-Ann have a Leonberger puppy to grow up with.'

As the groom put the puppy down, Marie-Ann jumped down from her pony and ran to the puppy, flung her arms around it and he gave her a sloppy kiss on her face.

The King said, 'His name is Bruno and he is ten weeks old. He will be a perfect nanny for the children when he grows up. I have also arranged for two cavalry horses to go with you to the chateau, so you will be able to get into Paris by carriage and work on the land.'

Marie dismounted from Soraya and handed her to the groom, came over to the King and curtseyed. 'Your Majesty, thank you so much for these magnificent horses. I can't thank you enough.'

The King replied, 'These were Napoleon's gifts and I am sure you can write to him in England to thank him. He wanted to keep in touch with you; he was very fond of you and he thought the Akhal-Teke mare would be a perfect partner for you, with its Russian origins. I also see how fond Marie-Ann is of dogs and a giant Leonberger will be the perfect playmate for her when Brigitte and Veronique leave for Germany.'

46

They were up bright and early, ready for their move back home. Le Comte had organised two hay wagons to transport food, luggage and Bruno for them – as well as feed for the horses. Two grooms were escorting the two German troop horses given by the King, and Jester's groom was riding and leading Marie-Ann on Snowy. Henri and Le Comte were on Jester and Perseus. Marie rode Soraya and Charles, Mercury. Mathilde and her children travelled up front with the driver of one of the hay carts.

Charles had employed a young, local farmhand as a full-time groom now they had a stable of five horses and re-employed their original cook. Jeanette was returning as Marie's housekeeper and Marie was searching for a suitable nursemaid, but Mathilde was happy to help in the interim.

The King bid them a tearful goodbye and was genuinely sad to see them leave. Marie and Anya had a few minutes together and Anya told her how lucky she was to have such a devoted husband as Charles. Marie assured her that she was well aware of how fortunate she was to have him. Both women avoided mentioning Henri, as Anya knew Marie did not approve of their relationship. However, Anya did assure her that she had only ever meant to be a friend to Henri, but she did not regret her emotions taking over.

Anya found a quiet moment to say goodbye to Charles and apologised for his treatment in Colonel Dittmar's hands. She watched his face carefully when she told him of his recent demise and saw a slight flicker in his eyes when she described how he had been assassinated. Charles changed the subject immediately to discuss Courbet; she informed him that she had negotiated his release home but warned that she did not think the French government would leave it at that and had suggested Courbet make plans to leave Paris, should they seek reparation.

oOo

Marie and Mathilde were letting the girls have a ride on Snowy in the fenced schooling area. Marie had been leading Marie-Ann round, instructing her on keeping her legs still and insisting she sit up straight. Mathilde was keeping Brigitte out of the way as she was desperate to have her turn, so she took her and Veronique out of the paddock to sit on a bench and watch Marie teach Marie-Ann. Thankfully, Bruno soon joined them after his nap and distracted Brigitte – she found a ball and was throwing it for him and they both chased after it. Charles was in the stable, grooming Mercury. The groom was brushing Soraya as Marie was intending to ride her after she had finished with the children.

Mathilde heard hoofbeats and looked down the drive to see a man approaching at a brisk trot. She could tell straight away, from quite a distance that it wasn't Le Comte or Henri. Snowy had also heard the approaching horse and gave a high-pitched whinny in welcome. Marie stopped the pony and concentrated on the rider and Mathilde was astonished when she shouted for her to come and hold Marie-Ann and started running towards the gate. Mathilde ran over and grabbed Snowy's lead rein as the horse trotted into the yard.

Marie ran like lightning, shouting, 'Oh, Manet, how happy I am to see you!'

He jumped down from his horse and Marie ran into his arms. He picked her up and twirled her round, planting a kiss on her cheek.

'My beautiful Goddess Diana; you will never know how many times I have dreamt about you and worried for your safety.'

Mathilde observed this with astonishment as she held Snowy, and then Charles appeared from the stables and came over to Manet and hugged him whilst Manet was still holding Marie's hand.

'Manet, how good to see you. Such a lot has happened since I last saw you in Paris.'

Manet replied, 'Jesus, Charles. When I heard you had been marched to Lille I feared you would not survive as you were in such a perilous state of health. Henri informed me of what happened to both of you and I am so sorry I wasn't there to protect you.'

Marie said, 'Yes, my Sir Galahad; where were you when I needed you?'

Manet hugged her to him and said, 'Marie, you don't know how guilty I feel about failing to take Charles back to Le Havre with me; it has haunted me ever since.'

Charles patted him on the shoulder. 'I was a stubborn fool not to go but I wasn't thinking straight either. Still, we all have regrets from our experiences of the war and if we let it overwhelm us then we won't move on. We must be thankful we survived and make sure we put the rest of our lives into our work and family.' Charles suddenly became aware of Mathilde and the children. 'Forgive my lack of manners, Mathilde. May I introduce you to Edouard Manet, and this is Countess Mathilde von Brixenhof and her daughters, Brigitte and Veronique.'

Manet moved into the paddock and took her hand and kissed it. 'Countess, I am delighted to meet you.' His eyes fell on Marie-Ann, sitting patiently in the saddle and observing. 'And this must be my beautiful god-daughter learning to ride.' He kissed her cheek.

Charles said, 'Marie, why don't you take Manet up to the house and put some coffee on? I will supervise the children riding with Mathilde and then come up to join you. You two have a lot of catching up to do.' The groom took Manet's horse to a stable and Manet and Marie walked hand in hand towards the kitchen.

Charles saw Mathilde's questioning look and said, 'They have a very special friendship, but it goes no further than that.'

Marie put the kettle on and Manet watched her closely. 'You look physically very well Marie, but I suspect the mental strain has had far reaching effects on you, as it did on Charles. He never got over leaving you in Lille when you could have gone to London with Whistler. He blames himself entirely for making the wrong decision.'

'It wasn't his fault; if I had been sensible I should have gone with his brother Gustave and Freya to Sweden, but I didn't. I left it too late and got caught stealing a horse and risking our lives when I was captured and surrounded by 2000 men!'

Manet laughed, 'Yes dear, you do have a knack of getting into trouble where men are concerned but it's not your fault you are so beautiful. Henri told me that Reissman fell for you and wanted to make you his mistress. How you managed to fend him off, I will never know.'

'I do feel guilty that in some ways I encouraged him, but I would never have forgiven myself if I had been unfaithful to Charles. You see, I knew Charles would forgive me even if I had been carrying Reissman's child because he is such a wonderful person; he would not have victimised the child. But I would, because I do not have the same strength of character. I would have resented the "cuckoo in the nest" far more than he would, and as I am such a ruthless bitch I would have made the child's life miserable.' She broke down in tears.

Manet hugged her to him and let her cry. 'Marie, you must have been terrified in this horrendous situation, but you used your head and bargained with him. Now explain to me who the delectable countess is and what she is doing here?'

'Oh Manet, you never give up, do you? Mathilde is out of bounds; she has recently married Le Comte after her French husband died in the war. So, please refrain from flirting with her during her husband's absence and giving cause for any rumours. He is besotted with her and would slit your throat if you even looked at her. She is staying here rather than in Versailles until they return to Germany, so that her children can play with Marie-Ann and she can keep me company. She is German but was reared in London at court as she is closely related to Prince Albert.'

The kitchen door opened and Charles, Mathilde and the children came streaming in with Bruno chasing after Marie-Ann. Manet said he had to get back to his studio and so Charles said he would ride back with him to Montmartre and spend some time at his studio.

oOo

Three days later, they were joined at breakfast by Henri, who had decided to devote his final day before moving back into the barracks to helping

Marie teach Soraya some high school movements. Ultimately, Marie wanted to achieve these while riding side saddle, but Henri had suggested she teach the movements astride first so that she was familiar with the aids before she switched to side saddle. He had volunteered to help her from the ground – to teach the movements in hand and then repeat with her on horseback. They had gone down to the stables and Charles said he would follow with Marie-Ann later.

Marie-Ann and Brigitte were playing with Bruno and chasing him around the kitchen because he was confined to the kitchen until he was fully house-trained. Mathilde was upstairs with Veronique and Charles had started reading the newspaper. However, this was soon interrupted by the two girls chasing Bruno round the table and knocking a chair over and he saw the angry look cook cast in their direction, so he decided he had better take them outside before something got broken.

'Right, you two you are going down to the yard to brush Snowy and you can't ride until Mama has finished schooling on the paddock with Uncle Henri.'

Marie-Ann threw herself at him. 'Dada, will you show me how to stop Snowy nipping me when I comb his mane?'

He plonked her on his knee and said, 'Of course, sweetheart; you just have to show him you are the boss, even though you are smaller than him.'

The two girls went running down the yard, with Bruno in hot pursuit. Charles was overjoyed to see Marie-Ann so excited and happy and her speech was coming on in leaps and bounds since the girls had arrived. He picked up Snowy's head collar and grooming kit and opened the stable door. The girls charged in and ran to stroke Snowy.

He heard whinnying from outside and saw Mercury leering over his door, excitedly. He looked towards the drive and saw a coach and four horses approaching. He untied Snowy and ushered the children and Bruno out and set off to greet the coach. Marie and Henri carried on with their schooling session, with Marie now in the saddle, and Henri stood beside Soraya, controlling her hindquarters with a long whip. He shouted to them to carry on as he would deal with the visitors.

Charles recognised it as a hired coach from Paris but had no idea whom it may be. The coach halted in the yard and to his astonishment, the door opened and Pierre leapt down.

Marie screamed, 'Papa!' She jumped off Soraya and ran full tilt from the paddock to the carriage, closely followed by Henri, who threw the reins to the groom who was by the gate. Marie flung herself into her father's arms, sobbing. 'Papa, I thought I might never see you again!' Pierre crushed her to him and sobbed himself, hugging her tightly.

Pierre then slapped him on the shoulder. 'Charles how delighted I am to see you looking so well. After

I had Marie's letter and she told me of your injuries, I did not expect to see you as well as this.' He bent down and picked Marie-Ann up and said, 'You are as pretty as a picture, Marie-Ann. You have your mother's eyes and nose but your father's serious expression.'

Charles replied, 'Pierre, I do apologise that I failed miserably to keep them safe and very nearly lost them both in this horrendous war. I promised you I would protect them, but I exposed them to more danger by moving them to Lille. I bitterly regret not sending them to safety in England.'

'Charles, stop it; you did the best you could at the time and you know as well as I do that Marie would not have left France while you were still there.'

Louise came over and gave Marie-Ann a peck on her cheek and said, 'I see my granddaughter is dressed like a groom. Do you not possess any dresses for her?'

There was shocked silence from everybody at this, until Henri muttered, 'Mother, she is learning to ride.'

Louise interrupted and, looking straight at Brigitte, turned to Marie and said, 'And who is this child – not your husband's lovechild, I hope?'

Marie rounded on her mother, her face full of anger. 'How dare you insult Charles. He would never be unfaithful to me and coming from someone who does not understand the meaning of the word "fidelity," is priceless!' She marched up the steps of the main entrance.

Henri and Pierre stared at Louise in horror. Finally, Henri spoke. 'That was unforgivable, Mother. I insist you apologise to Charles immediately. Brigitte is the daughter of Comte von Brixenhof and his wife Mathilde, who are guests in the household, currently.'

Louise, flustered, muttered, 'Well, how was I to know? I just assumed she was one of your family. God only knows what has transpired over the last two years. I admit I should not have jumped to such conclusions and I apologise to you, Charles.'

He replied, 'I accept your apology madame, but I doubt Marie will accept it. You have no idea of the mental and physical trauma suffered by her and whilst I can cope with your comments, your daughter has not yet recovered sufficiently to laugh them off as I do.' He then bent down, swept Brigitte into his arms and set off up the steps and through the front door.

Pierre grabbed Louise's arm and said, 'Don't you dare make another comment like that. Just because you are angry to be returning to Paris, don't take it out on them!'

Mathilde had seen the coach arriving and from a distance, had seen Marie's altercation with her mother and knew something was wrong. She had chivvied cook and Jeanette into preparing tea, sandwiches and cake and had served it herself to their guests in the drawing room.

Charles managed to corner Marie in the hallway and threw his arms around her and kissed her, reverently. 'Sweetheart don't worry about what your mother said. I have big strong shoulders and can shrug her sarcastic comments off immediately. She was the one who looked the fool, not me. I remained a gentleman and she became the harlot, thanks to your quick wit.'

Charles watched the interaction of the group whilst chatting to Pierre, who was obviously overwrought at his wife's comment. Louise had been left isolated whilst her children chattered in a group further away. Mathilde, sensing the disquiet, joined her on the sofa and engaged her in conversation as befitted an educated lady of the court.

The family left at 3 p.m. and as they went down to the carriage to see them off, Bruno bounded across from the stables to greet his beloved Marie-Ann and in his excitement, produced a big puddle, which Louise inadvertently stepped in. Charles and Henri spotted the faux pas and had to avert their eyes to stop them laughing.

That night, in the privacy of their room, he hugged Marie close to him and told her how proud he was of her and that now she had the three men she loved most back in her life, the two of them could look to the future and resume their lives together.

Printed in Poland
by Amazon Fulfillment
Poland Sp. z o.o., Wrocław

59430491R00312